FIC   Ellis, David.
ELLIS
             Life sentence.

$24.95

DATE			

LIFE

SENTENCE

ALSO BY DAVID ELLIS

Line of Vision

LIFE
SENTENCE

DAVID ELLIS

G. P. PUTNAM'S SONS   NEW YORK

This is a work of fiction. Names, characters, places, and incidents are either the product of the author's imagination or are used fictitiously, and any resemblance to actual persons, living or dead, business establishments, events, or locales is entirely coincidental.

G. P. Putnam's Sons
Publishers Since 1838
a member of
Penguin Putnam Inc.
375 Hudson Street
New York, NY 10014

Library of Congress Cataloging-in-Publication Data

Ellis, David, date.
Life sentence / David Ellis.
p.   cm.
ISBN 0-399-14979-1
1. Legislators—Fiction.   2. Illinois—Fiction.   I. Title.

PS3555.L59485L48   2003   2002068137
813'.6—dc21

Printed in the United States of America
1   3   5   7   9   10   8   6   4   2

This book is printed on acid-free paper. ∞

Book design by Victoria Kuskowski

FOR MY MOTHER, JUDY ELLIS, WITH ALL MY LOVE

PROLOGUE

The demons always come at night. When the last remnants of color leave the inside of his eyelids. When the security of daylight evaporates, replaced with shadows and blackening moods. When the accumulation of anxiety approaches panic, creates such an echoing, silent chime that he almost doesn't hear the sound of the shattering glass on the first floor of his house.

It is muted but high-pitched. First, a single blow, probably to the lower of the two diamond-shaped windows on his door, the one closer to the knob. Then a scraping noise, the instrument of choice clearing out the jagged edges of glass. Four short scrapes for each side of the diamond, performed efficiently to maximize speed and minimize noise.

A momentary pause, no doubt while a hand reaches through the opening into the house, for the deadbolt. The *click* of the lock turning comes quickly. The door opens with a slight creak and a release in pressure that sends a groan through the house.

Bennett Carey opens his eyes and stares into the pitch blackness of his bedroom on the third floor. His eyes move to the clock on his nightstand. It reads "1:58" in square red numbers.

Bennett looks next at the security alarm pad near the bedroom door. A red light signals a breach of security in Zone 1, the front door. But the alarm is not activated, so no shrilling sound accompanies the invasion, no message will reach the monitoring service or the police department.

Footsteps on the tile of the first floor, rapid and loud. But just one set of feet. One intruder. He is not concerned with making noise, it seems. Makes some sense. The only real commotion is the smashing of the glass, which came from the outside. Once inside, there would be little need to mute one's movements. Especially if you think no one is home.

Bennett calculates it quickly. It is early Sunday morning. He has spent all of Saturday in bed, save for one trip downstairs to the second-floor kitchen for some soup. Anyone scouting the place knows that Bennett lives alone and travels a lot. Anyone watching the house today would peek through the garage window and see the car is missing, because it's in the shop. With no entry or exit from the house, no movement within, no car, a work schedule that generally sends him out of town a couple days a week, the most plausible conclusion must be that Bennett is not home.

The footsteps from the carpeted staircase are replaced with the flop of shoes on the hardwood floor of the second level. There is plenty to take there. The DVD player alone would fetch close to a thousand, even from a fence. The laptop computer in the office is brand new and small enough for quick transport. The VCR, of course, also easy to snatch and run. He could go to the kitchen and take the microwave, for God's sake.

Bennett lies perfectly still, save for an arm that drifts to the nightstand. He slowly opens the drawer, careful not to make noise. Why lose his sole advantage?

Shuffling of feet on the second-floor hardwood. Indecision. Turn left for the living room. Right for the office and kitchen.

Or straight ahead, for the last set of stairs to the top floor.

The final staircase aches from the weight of the intruder. His breathing is audible, his movements no less delicate than on the previous staircase. Bennett hears the intruder brush against the wall and stumble back, probably unaware in the dark that the final leg of his path is a winding staircase. A poor attempt at European architecture, Bennett had thought when he bought the place, but it serves to frustrate the intruder's momentum now.

Bennett sits up in bed, relying on his abdominal muscles rather than a push off the box spring, again to minimize his presence. He wipes the sweat from his eyes, eyes that he will need now. A soft light from the street lamp down the road provides the only illumination in the darkness. A light that misses Bennett, actually obscures him even better with the contrast.

Arms outstretched, Bennett poises his weapon. A .38 special, a Smith & Wesson Model 337PD revolver, 5-round capacity. Bennett locks the hammer and aims the weapon at the doorway. He will not see the intruder until he hits the top of the stairs, until he reaches the third floor.

A beam of light hits the wall on the staircase, a small circle that flies about haphazardly. A flashlight, struggling for context. The footsteps return, more furiously than ever, once the intruder has his bearings.

Bennett tries to count the steps but fails. Through the darkness he sees the outline of the burglar, smells the combined odors of tobacco and outdoors and sweat.

The flashlight swings left—the intruder's right—into the bedroom, sweeping the floor, hitting the legs of the bed but missing Bennett. A hand pats the frame of the doorway. The intruder takes two steps and stops in a panic. The flashlight swings in Bennett's direction, shines into his face.

Bennett pulls the trigger a single time. A burst of red light, powder, the sickening sound of flesh penetration. The intruder sails back against the doorway and cries out. Bennett fires again as the man stumbles. The bullet splinters the wood of the door frame. The intruder is already in the midst of headlong flight, staggering and flailing down the stairs to the second floor.

Bennett's feet draw up from under the sheets. He sits on the bed in an awkward crouch, his ears ringing from the gunshots, his pulse vibrating his entire body, sweat dripping into his eyes again. The gun is still pointed aimlessly toward the doorway as the clumsy sounds of the intruder reach the second floor once again.

Bennett allows one foot after the other to slowly plant on the bedroom carpet. He holds the gun away from his body with both hands. Then he moves toward the staircase.

Noise from the second floor. A slam against a wall. A groan. Awkward footsteps, echoing off the hardwood.

Bennett steps over the intruder's flashlight, lying helplessly at the top of the stairs. He descends the dark staircase, his left arm flat against the wall, his right holding the gun facing up, only the balls of his feet touching the carpet of the stairs. His head is cocked, listening for the intruder, who has not yet taken the stairs to the first floor. Bennett hears his breathing, his coughing. No way to know where the bullet had hit.

Shuffling of feet on the hardwood, a body once again in motion. One step on the carpet of the stairs, then a thud, a wounded mass stumbling and sliding down the staircase to the tile of the bottom floor.

His eyes slightly adjusted to the dark, Bennett swiftly follows the curve on the winding staircase and reaches the second floor. He peeks around the corner of the staircase, spots the figure of the intruder on the bottom floor, getting to his feet. Bennett tries to think through his options. Then he decides not to think at all.

Bennett takes the final staircase in leaps, two stairs at a time. He tumbles off the final stair at the bottom, crashing against the wall of the hallway on the ground floor. As he turns, the darkness illuminates with three bursts of light. The deafening pop of one, two, three bullets echoes through the hallway.

AUGUST
2000

1

When my eyes pop open just past four, I reach instinctively to the right side of the bed. My hand hits a cold pillow, a split second before I realize that it was supposed to. My movement causes stirring from the two dogs sleeping on the bed, my pugs. The overhead light is on, and one of them—Jake, the older, ink-black pug—gets to his haunches and looks at me expectantly.

"No," I say, disabusing him of the possibility of a walk or food this early.

This causes the puppy, Maggie, to leap to attention. She's a fawn—brown, the color of coffee with cream. She moves to Jake, in the process walking over a document resting on my bed. I watch her through the fog of sleep, the bright light in the room and the words of the television commentator standing in contrast to the still darkness outside my window.

"No," I repeat, reaching for the paper. It's the memorandum I've read over a dozen times since its arrival on my desk two weeks ago. The document is flipped to the final page, the conclusion of the legal analysis, which confirmed what I'd been saying.

In summary, I concur with the conclusions of Jon Soliday. Under state law as I interpret it, Attorney General Langdon Trotter's nominating papers are invalid. He is therefore disqualified from running for the office of Governor. A proper legal challenge could be filed to remove him from the ballot.

I exhale slowly. Our opponent in the gubernatorial election is not qualified to run.

God, I still remember the call I got a few weeks back from the State Board of Elections, the branch up here in the city. I had called to make arrangements to take a look at Trotter's petitions, which contained the more than ten thousand signatures he was required to obtain to run in the Republican primary for governor. All we wanted to do was look through the petitions for bogus signatures, dead people or people who would be willing to swear that they never signed it. All we were looking for was some negative publicity on Trotter. Hell, the guy ran unopposed in the Republican primary, at least *somebody* had to look at his petitions.

"You better come over yourself," the guy at the elections board said to me. He was one of our guys, a Democrat.

"I just need a copy," I said.

"You should look at it yourself," he repeated.

So I went over, more annoyed than anything. The board staffer dropped the first volume of the petitions on the desk and smiled. I flipped over to the first page, expecting to go on, and stopped. "This is a copy," I said. "Can I see the original?"

"That is the original," he said.

"No, it isn't." I waved him over and pointed to the first page of Trotter's nominating papers, the statement of candidacy. That's the document where the candidate officially "accepts" the invitation of the petition signers to run for office. It's a legal fiction in reality—Trotter was the one who had the petitions prepared, nobody had to "invite" him. But the theory is that all of these people are begging him to run and he says, Well, okay. He does that by signing the statement of candidacy.

"Look," I said. "This isn't the original ink on the statement. This is a photocopy."

"Yes," said the staffer, breaking into a full smile. "It sure is."

I flipped past that page to the petitions, the people who signed to put Lang Trotter on the ballot. They contained the original ink. They were the original petitions. I returned to the first page, ran my hand over it.

I put two and two together and jumped from my chair.

Lang Trotter did not file the original of his statement of candidacy. He filed a photocopy. The filing of the statement of candidacy is a requirement, an absolute prerequisite to running for governor or any other office. And though there is no reported court decision on the issue—and I would know better than anyone—there is no doubt in my mind that a copy of the statement of candidacy is insufficient. I know it and the memorandum on my lap confirms it.

> Attorney General Langdon Trotter's nominating papers are invalid. He
> is therefore disqualified from running for the office of Governor.

The way I'm holding this memo, you'd think it was the original of the Declaration of Independence. I've even kept it in the thick manila envelope in which it was sent, by messenger, to my office a couple weeks ago. The package rests at my feet, the side torn open, the mailing sticker "Dale Garrison & Associates" in the corner. Dale Garrison is the lawyer in town to whom we turned to confirm my original conclusion—that with this mistake in his nominating papers, the prohibitive favorite for governor, Langdon Henry Trotter, is history.

Jake, on the verge of resuming sleep, casts hooded eyes in my direction. I reach for him to pat his mashed-up face, but he leaps to his feet as the phone rings. I jump myself. We stare at each other a moment, the three of us wondering who in the hell is calling at four in the morning.

My voice isn't ready for human conversation. I manage a "hello" in a gravelly voice.

Bennett Carey speaks deliberately, starting with an apology for the call. I almost cut him off with a sarcastic comment, but then his words register. I make him repeat them, in his even style. Then I hang up and head for the closet.

I dress for the occasion, which is to say I take a stab at formality for the middle of the night. A dress shirt with the collar open, suit trousers. I run some water over my hair, then head for the door.

The wet city wind slaps me when I leave the house. I feel like someone has pushed me into a warm shower against my will. I find a cab quickly enough and direct the driver to head across town. Like me, the cabbie doesn't know exactly where Vine Street is. I tell him to head east on Allegheny and look for red flashing sirens.

We find it. The police squad cars have pulled up in stereotypical form, parked haphazardly in diagonals along the street, their red and blue lights flashing long after the emergency has subsided.

I recognize Bennett's place. A brick townhouse built in the '80s, a good 1800 square feet stacked three floors high to maximize lateral real estate space during the yuppie invasion.

An officer stops me at the door. I show him what credentials I possess, a business card from my law firm and the wallet-sized certification the state supreme court gives to every lawyer who passes the bar. The officer accepts my presentation but steers me away from the threshold of the front door. We have to take the other route in, he says, through the sliding glass door. As he moves me back onto the patio, I look over his shoulder at the corpse on the black-and-white tile floor.

I get a better look once we come in the other door. The bottom floor of Bennett's apartment has a large room that some would call a den, but which Bennett apparently considers a workout room. With a thin cream carpet and plain white walls, the room is filled with iron dumbbells, a weight bench holding an imposing stack of plates on each side of a metal bar, and some contraption that seems to allow for pull-ups and other feats of gymnastic agility. Across the tiled hallway is a door to the garage and a door to a laundry room. Otherwise, the only thing to do is take the stairs up to the second floor.

But first, I want another look at the body. I tiptoe with authority, a lawyer officially checking the crime scene. The officer grabs at me; someone taking photos of the corpse glares at me. I move no further but insist that I need to take a look. I tell them I am entitled to see the body in its original pose. That could be true, that could not be true. I don't have any experience in this arena. The plain fact is, more than anything, I simply have never seen a dead body at a crime scene before.

The body is stomach-down, face turned to one side. He is a white guy. Late thirties to an untrained eye. His beard has a day's worth of growth. His face is bent in contortion, something between a grimace and a cry. His arms are away from his body and bent up at ninety-degree angles like goalposts in a football stadium, palms down. His right leg is drawn up, bent slightly. Again, to the untrained eye, giving the impression he was in the midst of flight—an impression I stifle. He is wearing a wool cap and a black leather jacket with three sizable holes in the back, bordered by dried blood. Blood is everywhere, in fact, as I look around. Splatters on the walls and a healthy pool beneath the body.

A middle-aged man comes bouncing down the stairs in a stained over-coat and a shield clipped to the collar. He looks at me and then at the of-ficer behind me. "Who the hell is *this?*" he asks, nodding at me.

I flash the credentials again.

"No, *huh*-uh. Outside." He waves at me with his index finger. I catch a whiff of his aftershave.

"It's his house," I say.

"It's *our* house," says the man. "Crime scene."

Scary thought, but he has a point. We settle on the garage, given the intermittent rain outside. The officer opens the door and I step in. No car in sight, though I recall Bennett drives something silver and foreign. The only sign of it is an oil stain on the concrete floor. The orange pull, used to disconnect the overhead garage remote, dangles lifelessly in the center of the ceiling, next to a single light bulb. A thick strip of pinewood has been nailed horizontally along the two side walls and contains hooks to hold various tools for yardwork and snow shoveling. Even with all the tools and the old window screens propped up against the wall along with the paint cans, the garage seems utterly vacant without an automobile.

There is a small square window on the garage door. Through it I see a small gathering of neighbors huddled outside. I feel a pang of remorse for Bennett.

The door opens. A man comes through wearing shirtsleeves, no tie. "Detective Eric Paley," he says.

I shake his hand. "Jon Soliday," I say.

Detective Paley has a long, comforting face, well-lined, with expressive eyes. He looks like somebody's father. "I'm a little curious why Mr. Carey called a lawyer."

"He called a friend," I say. "We work together."

Paley raises a hand, allows a smirk. "Okay, a friend. But a friend doesn't have the right to talk to him just at this second."

"Then I'm his attorney. And I'd like to see him right away."

The detective purses his lips and nods absently at the ceiling. "You can talk to him," he says, as if he's being generous. He leaves the garage with no outpouring of gratitude from me.

Bennett walks into the garage a moment later. He is naked save for his boxers and a blanket thrown over his shoulders. Bennett is a sizeable man, well over six feet with a thick neck, broad shoulders and an athletic presence. First time I've seen him with no shirt. He has a physique any middle-aged man would envy, a rippled stomach, hard and well-toned muscles that look like they're going to pop out of his skin, the only blemish a two-inch jagged scar on his upper chest, just below his shoulder, that peeps out of the blanket draped over him.

His eyes are understandably dark, his posture slightly altered. His jet-black hair has fallen into his face, veering off from the stark middle part down below his eyes in the shape of a ram's horns, falling to his cheeks. I guess I never noticed how long his hair is because he combs it back at work. In its current state, Ben could pass for a grunge-rocker, though at twenty-nine years of age he might be pushing the limit. Bennett doesn't seem to socialize much, but he certainly has the looks for quite an active extracurricular life. Regardless, his size and physique seem incompatible with the wounded-victim profile.

Someone is standing behind him. I nod to the man, presumably another detective. With no other response, the man closes the door behind himself.

Bennett looks at me sheepishly, almost with embarrassment. "Hey,

Jon," he says. His voice lacks the normal deep resonance; it is soft and trembling.

I put a hand on his shoulder. "You all right, Ben? Jesus Christ."

"I guess so," he says. His Adam's apple bobs violently. "I killed somebody."

"You defended yourself." I search his eyes until they make contact with mine. "Big difference there. He broke into your house, and you defended yourself."

Bennett considers the comment, or maybe he is lost in his own thoughts. He wipes a hand over his mouth, blows out a sigh.

My eyes return to the scar below his shoulder. I nod at it. "That happen tonight? This guy do that to you?"

Bennett looks down, then draws the blanket tighter. "God," he says, "I'm practically naked here." He shivers. "No, that scar's twenty years old. Why?"

"Just wondering."

"Already planning my defense?" says Ben. "Self-defense works better if he cut me first, right?"

My face colors. "Don't start talking crazy."

"I killed a guy, Jon."

"Hey, Ben—what are you supposed to do? He broke into your *house*."

"Yeah." Bennett's eyes wander to the ceiling and hold there. He is thinking of something else at that moment. "What do you think our boss will say?"

"Don't worry about our boss."

"Not the best timing, huh?"

"You had nothing to do with the timing."

"Yeah, but still. Three months from the election?"

"Bennett, listen to me. Don't worry about Tully. You think he'd rather this asshole killed *you?*"

Bennett's mouth parts. His tongue rolls against his cheek. He allows the slightest chuckle, a nervous laugh. "On that, I'll take the Fifth," he says.

2

The police settle on Bennett's kitchen, on the second floor, as a spot where he can sit and wait while the cops do their job and await the chance to speak to him. I leave Bennett with a warning that he himself has probably given to some of his own clients—don't say a word to anyone, not even a hello—and wander back downstairs. The cops should probably be doing a better job of keeping an eye on me, but it's all they can do not to mess up the crime scene on their own. At best, the myriad of uniformed and plainclothes cops and technicians is organized chaos.

I step out onto the sidewalk and punch my cell phone. Middle of the night, Don Grier is not expecting a call from me, and he's certainly not expecting good news when he hears my voice. Don Grier is the press secretary to State Senator Grant Tully, my boss. The senator is the Democratic nominee for governor and uses Don for his political work. But Grant Tully is also the Senate Majority Leader, so Don is a state employee as well. It's hard to divorce the two, because everything the senator does is political, when you cut to it.

"You need to hear this right now," I tell him. The story seems to lay out like this. Bennett was aroused from sleep by the noise of an intruder breaking into his home. He reached for his gun as he heard the intruder come up the stairs. The intruder came into his bedroom and Bennett fired twice, hitting the intruder once, apparently in the shoulder. Then Bennett followed as the intruder headed back down the stairs. He kept his distance and just listened, and ultimately he followed the intruder down the final staircase to the bottom floor. There, he saw the shape of the intruder in the darkness, and he fired off three more rounds and killed him.

It turns out he shot the intruder in the back. That is the obvious problem, if there is a problem. It rings of a vengeance killing, shooting the unsuccessful burglar while he fled the scene. The other catch is that the intruder didn't have a gun. He had a crowbar, which he used to break the door window to get in. A gun versus a piece of iron.

"Christ almighty," Don murmurs. "Is he okay?"

"Seems okay. Feels bad about it."

"He shot him in the *back?*"

"He didn't know the guy was turned away from him," I say. "It was dark."

"Right, you said that." I hear a voice—more of a groan—from his end.

"Got some company there, Don?" I ask. He's single, like I am, now. "Male or female?"

Don manages a chuckle.

"So listen," I say. "Who do we know in the department?"

"The police? I don't know. Top brass?"

"Fuck, *I* don't know." I make a noise. I'm not accustomed to being without answers. As the chief counsel to Senator Tully, I've managed to meet almost everyone with some oomph in the city. But cops? Can't place the name of the top guy, the police superintendent, and don't know him, anyway.

"We'd have to be careful," says Don. "That's a phone call that could come back to bite us."

The rain is starting up again. I shift my feet. "I suppose. I just want to know that he's treated right. That's all."

"Probably better that it's not you making that call," says Don. "I'll talk to the senator, we'll figure something out. Just go take care of your boy."

I click off the cell phone and head back upstairs. A cop hassles me as I re-enter, but I'm too agitated to even acknowledge him, so he follows me up the stairs, hollering after me, until that detective, Paley, waves him off. The whole time, I don't even look at the annoying cop, which gets a rise out of him. Small pleasures.

Bennett is still in his boxers with the blanket over his shoulders. I take the other chair at the tiny kitchen table. "Let's not talk to them tonight," I say. "Tomorrow, we'll put you together with the right lawyer. Paul Riley. Maybe Dale Garrison. Sit tight until then."

Detective Paley approaches us again. He has brought a chair from the dining room in with him. My second good look at the detective leaves me with the same conclusion. He looks paternal, concerned, patient. His shirtsleeves are rolled up now. His eyes are heavy and bloodshot. He was probably a couple of hours from a shift change when he caught this. Now he won't sleep until this afternoon.

"Rough night," he says to both of us. Bennett is still unresponsive.

I start to give my speech to the detective—no interview tonight, we'll be in touch—but I opt to wait it out, see what comes. If the detective isn't looking to hurt Ben, I could just make it worse by ordering him to clam up.

"I think my client's in shock," I say.

"Sure." His voice is surprisingly soft, a higher pitch. Probably works well for the job—not the rough stuff but the interviews. He's the good cop in the routine.

"What do you figure here, Detective?" I ask. "What was this guy doing in here?"

Paley frowns. His forehead is thick and well lined. "Common burglar, my guess."

"A burglar takes things," I offer. "This guy had plenty of stuff to steal but he went all the way to Ben's bedroom."

"That's where the good stuff is, Counsel. Valuables." The detective has a strong city accent, pronouncing *counsel* as if there's no "u." "If he was looking to kill your client, he'd probably bring more than a crowbar."

"You can kill with a crowbar."

"I want my gun back." Bennett has spoken for the first time. This grabs the attention of both the detective and me. I reach out a hand and grab his forearm on the table. He pulls it away.

Paley shrugs. "We'll see about that."

Bennett's eyes narrow. He has returned to present time. "You'll see about what?"

"We might need to hang on to it awhile," Paley says.

"Why?"

Paley opens his hands. "C'mon, Mr. Carey. You're a lawyer."

Neither of us responds. It is evidence, he's saying.

"Do you fear for your life, Mr. Carey?"

Bennett considers the question, blinking slowly. Most of his movements have slowed, in fact. His eyes are deeply set from stress and sleep deprivation. His face is pale save for the brush of redness on his cheeks. "I don't know what I fear," he says.

"I think we're going to stop there," I say. "Detective, we'll be happy to give you a statement, but I think my client needs a few hours of sleep first."

"Now's fine," says Ben, staring into the kitchen table.

"No," I say to the detective. "We'll give you a call, say about noon—"

"No." Bennett exhales, draws himself up. "Whatever else you want to know is fine."

"No," I insist. "We'll talk later to—"

"I just want to go back over a couple points."

I look at my client, then at Paley. "Have you already talked?"

Paley seems to enjoy breaking the news to me. "We went over the whole thing an hour ago."

I stare at Bennett, waiting for him to look at me so I can give him a scolding glare. He just blinks and resumes his foggy stare. "If he asked for a lawyer," I begin, "you can't—"

"He hadn't requested counsel, Mr. Soliday." The detective seems to enjoy the fact that the lawyer didn't get a chance to silence his client.

"He's right, Jon," says Ben. He waves a hand. "I volunteered. I told him the same thing I told you."

I fall back in my chair. "I'd like to see any notes you made," I tell Paley.

"I'm sure you would, Counsel. Only you don't get to." He nods at Ben. "Really, just a couple follow-ups."

"No," I say.

"Jon, it's okay," says Ben. He gathers the blanket over him.

"About the shouting," says Paley. "You don't remember saying anything to this guy?"

Ben shakes his head, no.

"Or he to you?"

I clear my throat. "At least fill me in here, Detective."

Paley regards me a moment. I suppose he could tell me to go screw myself. But all things considered, he seems to be going pretty easy. "Neighbor heard shouting," he tells me.

Bennett frames his hands on the table. "It's what I said before. If you tell me he was yelling, I accept that. But I didn't hear it. I suppose my ears were ringing from firing the shots. I know my heart was pounding like crazy. Everything was happening so fast—"

"The point being," I say, "Ben didn't hear anything."

The detective considers Bennett for a moment, then gives a definitive nod of the head. "It was probably shock," he says. "He obviously didn't expect you to shoot him." Paley rises from his chair and moves to Bennett. He grips his shoulder. "I'd a done the same thing as you," he says. He shakes Ben a little. "Only I'd a dropped him in the bedroom."

"Where do we stand, Detective?" I ask.

He makes a face. "From your end? This is clean. Justifiable. Guy can't shoot a home intruder, who can he shoot?"

I say a silent prayer. I look at Ben, who acts as if he didn't hear Paley. "What do you mean 'our end'?"

"Well." Paley looks over my head. "If I thought someone was coming after Mr. Carey, I'd want to know the whos and whys. But this guy just wanted to steal. He must've seen the car missing from the garage, figured Mr. Carey was out of town. It's a nice neighborhood, nice house—plenty of nice stuff to take. The guy had a crowbar and a bag, to throw valuables in. He wasn't looking for violence."

I sigh. "So we're done."

"We'll get an ID on this guy. We'll investigate what we see fit." He leans into me. "But let's say, other than the ID, you shouldn't expect to be hearing from me again."

I stand up and offer a hand. "Thanks."

Bennett is shaking his head slowly. We are alone in the kitchen now. The din throughout the house has subsided. Anything they wanted to see, they've seen. Cops are filing out.

"You gotta try to put this behind you, Ben," I say quietly. "A bad dream."

"He was gonna kill me." Ben is staring out the kitchen window, though he couldn't see more than his own reflection. He probably needs to believe that. He doesn't want to think that he killed someone who just wanted a Rolex or a diamond to fence. I turn to see Paley waving a silent adios, telling me he's the last of them. Then I turn back to Bennett, whose expression has deteriorated to pure agony.

3

I'm in my car, headed for the west side. I stayed with Ben at his house after the cops left. He didn't even try to sleep, just stared aimlessly over the steam from the coffee clutched in his hands. Once dawn broke, Bennett and I took a cab uptown to my place, where I grabbed my car and drove Ben to his gym. I don't know if Bennett would want or need to work out, but at a minimum he could shower there and throw on a change of clothes.

State Senator Grant Tully is giving a speech today at a union hall on the west side. He is addressing an African-American audience that is probably the most politically powerful coalition of minorities in the state.

Grant Tully is the son of former State Senator Simon Tully, who held office seemingly forever, handing the reins to his son ten years ago. Grant was elected to his first term as state senator at the ripe age of twenty-nine. He was re-elected twice, at ages thirty-three and thirty-seven, and now he's in the middle of his third four-year term. The district he represents basically consists of the city—or its southern half, I should say—which is overwhelmingly Democratic. This means the senator could hold this office the rest of his life, with no fear of a primary challenge and no credible risk of defeat by a Republican.

But the senator is running for governor. He won a contested primary with almost seventy percent of the vote. His opponent in the general election—the Republican nominee—is the state Attorney General, Langdon Trotter. Trotter had no challenge whatsoever, keeping with the Republicans' discipline in ferreting out challengers and avoiding bickering within the party.

Grant Tully currently is the Majority Leader of the state senate. That means he basically runs the senate. The Democrats hold eighteen of the twenty-seven seats. That means if you want a bill to pass in the senate, you have to get Senator Tully's approval.

My title is Chief Counsel to the Majority Leader, which is a fancy way of saying I'm Senator Tully's lawyer. I advise the senator on pending legislation—let him know what a bill does, whom it affects—and guide him through the legal hurdles that come with the office. Bennett Carey is my deputy counsel, the only other full-time lawyer on the staff.

Those are our roles as state employees. In addition, Grant Tully is the chairman of the state Democratic Party. He controls the purse strings, decides where to spend how much on whom when it comes to campaigns. So I'm also the counsel to the state Democratic Party. In this role, I steer the senator, as well as other elected Democratic officials, through the maze of laws governing ballot access, elections, campaign finance disclosures, and the like. In this political job, as well, Bennett Carey is my deputy.

The long and short of it is, Grant Tully is the most powerful Democrat in the state. He runs the senate—the state house of representatives is Republican—and he runs the state Democratic Party. No Democrat with half a brain makes a move without Tully's say-so, and everyone gets out of the way if he wants to run for governor.

At this point on the calendar, the senate is not in session, so I'm working almost full time on the elections. And by far the most important one is the race for governor. It is the highest priority, not only because my boss is the one running, but because the governor gets to appoint thousands of people to paid positions. That's really the key to politics—jobs. The people you employ become your off-the-clock workers as well, your army to sell fund-raising tickets and canvass the neighborhoods and make phone calls when they're not working on state time. These people work hard, too, because in a very real way, their jobs depend on your re-election. The bigger your army, the better you can campaign, and the more easily you can lend out your workers to other campaigns and then call in the favor when you need it.

The Republicans have controlled the governor's office for sixteen years. That means a whole generation of GOP staffers have settled into the state capital. It becomes circular, an obvious advantage to Republicans in terms of manpower. But the current governor is stepping down, and Senator Grant Tully is hoping to break the Republican stranglehold.

The timing of this incident with Bennett—in the heat of the general election season—is less than optimal. Senator Tully likes to hear bad news quickly. So I'm making a personal visit.

I make it to the union hall at about the time the senator should be closing up his remarks. I can hear applause as I wander down the hallway.

Senator Grant Tully stands at a podium on a stage, behind three African-American leaders seated in chairs; they are sitting along with the senator's chief of staff, Jason Tower, also an African-American. The banner over the curtain reads "Tully 2000" in red and blue lettering.

The audience is the Coalition for Racial Progress, a politically active group that has become increasingly powerful over the last decade. They have increased voter registration in the African-American community by almost twenty percent and, more importantly, they have increased voter turnout by almost thirty.

"I *will* appoint minorities to my staff," says the senator, pounding the podium to much applause. "I *will* appoint minorities to the highest posts in this state."

I walk into the back of the auditorium, where I will stay. By my head-count, there are over three hundred people.

"On this very special day, ladies and gentleman, I pledge to you: I will increase African-American involvement in this political system to heights never before seen!"

The senator can get away with rhetoric like this in a way that no other white guy in this city could. The reason is that he means what he says.

The city's west side is part of the senator's district and contains the poorest neighborhoods in the state. The old line is, on the south side, they'll kill you for a twenty-dollar bill. On the west side, they've never *seen* a twenty-dollar bill. But Senator Tully has made it a point to promote tax incentives for businesses out here and take a personal interest in the improvement of the schools. He's rolled up his sleeves for the west side, and they know it.

"Let's bring back free health testing for our children," he says. "Free eye testing. Free hearing testing." The crowd erupts—this is a topic that's been covered before. "Because a child who cannot see will become a child who cannot read. And a child who cannot read"—the senator's voice continues to elevate with the rise in applause, to the point he's almost shouting—"is a child who cannot compete. Let's not turn our backs on innocent children!"

Senator Tully casts a confident look over his audience. He recognizes plenty of faces. He spends a lot of time in these neighborhoods. His big thing is to play piano at the churches, a different one each Sunday. I think he made two stops at churches before the speech today. That's his personal thing. In terms of legislation, he's been a good leader, too. He never misses an opportunity to remind them of that fact.

"I call on the leaders of the house of representatives to pass my legislation to stop predatory lending! Let's help the poorest and the weakest in our society from falling under the burden of outrageous interest rates! It's not about black or white—it's about wrong and right!"

The senator sure has found his audience's sweet spot. This last term, he sponsored legislation to regulate the practice of finance companies who convince elderly and poor people—and far more often than not, minorities—to take out ill-advised, high-interest home equity mortgages on their homes, locking them into long-term deals with huge prepayment penalties and, typically, ending up in foreclosure. The coalition to whom the senator is speaking played a major role in the effort, so they know they can count on Grant Tully.

"Let us not turn back the clock! Let us not roll back affirmative action! Let us not cut subsidies to neighborhood programs and schools! Let's not turn back what we've started! Let's take it to the next level!" The senator pounds the podium with the last point.

The crowd rises to its feet. The speech is done. I move down the aisle and find the senator's spokesman, Donald Grier, standing in the front row applauding. He looks at me like I just accosted him in the shower. He leans toward me. "How's that thing?"

I cock my head. "In the car," I say.

It's another twenty minutes before the senator has finished shaking hands and receiving hugs. In the meantime, I have tossed my keys to one of the two aides accompanying the senator and Don Grier. He'll drive my car back. I need to speak with the senator.

"Okay, Jon." The senator's voice, when he's offstage, is soft, almost boyish. The senator is sitting in the back of the luxury sedan with Don and me. One of the perks of being the Senate Majority Leader is a car and driver. Jason Tower has stayed back to talk with the coalition members before moving on to yet another meeting today.

Grant Tully looks like a senator. He is just under six feet, sandy hair, a baby face at age thirty-eight. The beginning slashes of gray at his sideburns and the newly formed crow's-feet at his eyes do just enough to offset what otherwise might be perhaps too youthful an appearance. He looks young and handsome and dignified.

"Tell me about Bennett," says the senator.

"I just dropped him off at his gym to let off some steam and get a shower," I answer. "He's doing okay."

"What are they saying? The police?"

"They're calling it a justified shooting. Justifiable, I think they say. Ben's in the clear."

"Good, good." The senator, sitting by the door, rattles his fingers off the window.

"Ben thinks the guy was trying to kill him," I add. "Cops think it was a straight burglary."

"Mmm-hmm." The senator nods absently. He's less concerned with the details. He's thinking ahead. News stories, reflection on the campaign.

Don Grier, stuck in the middle seat, turns to me. "What do you think?"

I sigh. "Don't know. The guy had this iron bar to break in and a bag to collect stuff. Doesn't sound like an attempt on his life to me."

"Either way," says Don, "it's someone breaking into his house."

"There is an issue with appearances," I say. "Shooting a guy in the back."

"Tell me about the guy who broke in," says the senator, seeming to ignore my comment.

I shake my head. "No identification yet."

Silence. Conversations with Grant can be awkward at times. He never feels the need to fill in the spaces, and he's rarely in a hurry to speak.

"White or black?" asks Don Grier.

"White."

The senator doesn't respond. Don Grier chews on his lip.

"Good timing, though," I say. "By the time they're writing the print edition tomorrow, it's not news."

"It's not the *same* news," says Grant.

True. There will be a spin by tomorrow's news cycle, no longer just the alarming facts, more likely a reaction of some kind. Will there *be* a reaction?

"The *Watch* is probably covering it on-line," says Don. "We need to find the reporter."

"You talk to him, Jon," the senator says. "This doesn't come from Don."

"Well, I *am* his attorney."

Senator Tully looks at me. "Ben doesn't need an attorney if they're not looking at him. You're a friend who was there, so you're able to comment."

"Right. I think Bennett wants to talk to you, Senator." I always call Grant "Senator" in front of others.

"Sure. That's fine."

We sit in silence. I look out the window. We're driving past a school, empty on a Sunday. A couple of black kids in leather jackets and bandannas wrapped around their heads sit on the steps of the school, eyeing our car suspiciously.

"This isn't the best timing," I say.

"It is what it is," says the senator. "We deal with it."

4

Back in my office after lunch, Sunday. I am a partner at the law firm of Seaton, Hirsch and Sharpe. Seaton, Hirsch is two hundred lawyers located across from the state courthouse in the center of the commercial district. We have a good fifteen different departments—corporate, bankruptcy, health care, wealth management. You name it, the firm has formed a department for it. I do a little work in the litigation department, along with Bennett Carey, but Ben and I are basically a two-man department on election law. We do the political work for the Democratic Party and bill it through the firm. Aside from his state work as senator, Grant Tully takes in some big commercial clients who want to be associated with him and then palms off the work on other lawyers. He brings in some decent revenue, but more than anything the firm likes having the two Tullys on their letterhead. I say the "two Tullys" because Grant's father, former State Senator Simon Tully, still wanders in the door every now and then.

I work at Seaton, Hirsch because Grant wants me close, whether it's work for him or other Democrats. In my role as counsel to the state Democratic Party, I essentially represent every Democratic state representative or senator, at least in their official capacities. All in all, this means that I spend the vast majority of my time steering the senator and the party through the minefield that is our state's election and campaign laws. There are rules governing political advertising, financial disclosures, ballot access, and so on, and I have become an expert. The rules are very complicated, which is exactly how the political establishment wants it. The elected officials have people like me to tell them what's what. The outsiders, seeking entry without the backing of the Republicans or Democrats, typically play catch-up.

It's more than a two-man job, but essentially Bennett Carey and I handle all the work. I have been with the senator since he launched his political career ten years ago, so by now I know most of the rules by heart—hell, I've written half of them for the Senate to pass. What this means is that my knowledge is a rare and valuable commodity. It also means that a vast majority of the Democrats in this city and the rest of the state owe me. Some more than others.

That's me, in a nutshell. I know elections, and I know people.

I go on-line on my computer to check the news stories. The senator's spokesman, Don Grier, was right—our local paper, the *Daily Watch,* is covering the story on the internet edition. It's not the top story, which is heartening. Maybe in a city where people are murdered every day, the story won't play up so much. It's the third story down, below a news event about a U.S. submarine that inadvertently crossed into Chinese waters and a story about a tax-cut debate in Washington.

But third story or not, the headline is enough to increase the adrenaline. It was reported as of 9:15 a.m. LOCAL MAN KILLS HOME INTRUDER. The article says that police are investigating the circumstances surrounding the death late last night of a burglar who broke into a home on North Vine Street. The home intruder was named Brian Denning O'Shea, age thirty-seven, lives on the southeast side. William Bennett Carey, twenty-nine, a local attorney, apparently shot O'Shea in the back as he was exiting the house.

I find my hand cupped over my mouth. Nice spin they put on it. Forget about the fact it was pitch dark in the house. Forget about the fact that a man was standing in his bedroom when he woke up. Forget about the fact that the police have cleared him.

I swivel my chair. Bennett Carey is standing in the doorway.

"How are you, Ben?"

Bennett shrugs. He is wearing a white dress shirt with no tie, navy trousers. His hair is still wet. No socks with his loafers, you can excuse him for forgetting.

"Feeling any better?" I ask.

He's still standing by the doorway, looking awkward and antsy. That sort of fits him. First glance, you make Bennett Carey for a lady-killer, a charming, well-manicured, well-dressed corporate attorney ready to set the world on fire. You expect the deep voice, the confident presence, the playful charm. What you get instead is a very soft-spoken, shy man with rather limited social skills. He has almost no sense of humor, first of all, which means my ever-present sarcasm often leads to blank stares. He doesn't partake in office banter, almost overtly ignores flirtatious advances from the women in the firm. His clothes are very neat—crisply ironed white shirts, subdued ties perfectly knotted—but anything but flashy. The only hint of creativity he ever shows is in his work, when he needs to craft a legal argument. Even then, his personality shows through—his words are simple, his argument concise and to the point.

"Don't really know what to do with myself," Ben says. "Don't want to be here, don't want to be home."

"You can stay at my place," I say. "As long as you want."

"Oh—well, thanks, Jon. I'll be fine." He shuffles his feet, still standing in the doorway. "Talk to the senator?"

"Yeah."

"He's here today?"

"Sure. In between appearances."

Bennett scratches his face. "Did you tell him?"

"I told him."

"How'd he react?"

I open my hand to a chair across from my desk. "Hey, you know Tully. 'It is what it is, we'll deal with it.'" I do my best impression of our boss. "Nobody's blaming you, Ben. For Christ's sake, how could they?"

"Yeah, I guess." Bennett takes a chair, collapses in it. He has splashed on some cologne, a hint of medicine in the scent. He missed a spot shaving below his chin. "I keep seeing that guy's face. When I turned on the light and saw him lying there on the floor."

"The detective was right," I say. "That guy didn't give you a choice."

Bennett's eyes run past me to the face of the computer behind me. "What's *that?*"

"Front page of the internet edition," I say with a half-smile to lighten the impact.

"Great." Bennett shakes his head.

"Do not worry about this, Ben. This is a nonissue. A news cycle or two, tops."

Bennett waves a hand. I have not convinced him. "Paper say anything interesting?"

"They got the perp's name."

Bennett sits up. "What's his name?"

"Brian Denning O'Shea."

Bennett's eyes drift. His face turns sober, loses some color. "Jesus Christ," he whispers.

"You know him?" I ask.

Bennett inhales deeply, then shakes his head. "Brian O'Shea," he says to himself.

"Tell me," I say.

"Brian O'Shea." He grimaces. "Back when I was prosecuting at the county attorney's office. One of my last cases, maybe five years ago. I put away O'Shea's brother for possession with intent. Sean O'Shea, his name was. We were cleaning up the southeast side, hitting a lot of dealers. Found over twenty grams in Sean's place."

"So you put away his brother."

"Goes beyond that," Ben says. "I was at the scene, y'know? They were having the assistants go with. We'd come in after the cops secured it, but they wanted the lawyers there to ensure everything was handled properly. Search warrants were carried out only to their limits, evidence was handled appropriately—that kind of thing."

I remember back then. That was at the height of the call throughout the city for an independent body to take over the collection and evaluation of evidence obtained at crime scenes. Defense lawyers and civil-rights activists were complaining that the cops were tampering with evidence. This problem is what led to the county attorney's office creating a technical unit—the CAT unit—which today has authority over such things, instead of the city police.

"Sean O'Shea's lawyers claimed that there wasn't any coke in his place until we showed up," Ben continues.

"He said it was planted?"

"Oh, yeah." Ben smiles weakly. "The prosecutors planted twenty grams of coke, *and* a scale, *and* a pager, *and* a wad of cash." He waves a hand. "Defense attorneys say stuff like that all the time. You've tried as many of these cases as I have, you start hearing the claims of planting and tampering in your dreams." He blows out a sigh. "So we nail Sean O'Shea on possession with intent. He has a sheet already, so he goes away for—what—I think twenty-five to forty."

"Ouch," I manage.

"Yeah, they don't fuck around with that stuff." Bennett takes a moment with that. I always wondered if prosecutors felt bad sometimes about the stuff they do. "Anyway, Sean's brother gets a lawyer, and they file a civil-rights case against me. A Section 1983 action in federal court. They say I violated Sean O'Shea's civil rights and planted evidence in his place." Ben makes a small circle with his index finger. "He filed the case about three years ago. The case was ultimately thrown out in the district court. The ruling was upheld on appeal. The Supreme Court just denied cert—so the case is over."

"Okay." I lean back in my chair. "So Brian's ticked off about his brother going away for most of his adult life and the fact that you beat him in court."

"I guess so."

"You didn't recognize him at your house?"

"Brian O'Shea?" Bennett shrugs. "If I've *ever* laid eyes on him, I didn't know it. He might have been at his brother's trial, but I didn't notice.

That case he filed against me in federal court, it never went to trial or anything. It's not like I appeared in court. The county attorney's civil division handled it."

To say nothing of the fact that the guy broke into Ben's house in the middle of the night, in the pitch darkness. It's not as if he and Ben had a pleasant conversation over tea. "Well, okay." I come forward and lay my hands on the desk. "So you feel better now? This guy was trying to hurt you. You didn't have a choice."

Ben plays with his hair a moment, brushing at some stray locks that have fallen into his eyes. "I suppose it helps to know."

"Good," I say. "I'll give a call to that detective. Paley. He'll figure it out soon enough, but might as well save him the investigating."

"Okay."

I come around the desk and grab Ben's shoulder. "Hopefully, you can put this behind you now."

"Yeah."

"I'll get word to the big man, too," I say. Ben rolls his eyes and makes his way out.

5

Walking into Senator Grant Tully's office is like walking into a museum. Plenty to admire, nothing to touch. The office is rectangular; oak cabinets on the long wall below the windows feature framed photographs of the senator with various political figures of the last ten years. Two large black leather chairs sit by a desk more notable for its size than anything else. It is a large, ancient piece of hickory, with iron handles on the drawers, that dwarfs the senator in his high-backed chair.

Senator Tully spins around, raises a hand and nods to me. "Keep them where they are for now and run another poll. If she's above forty percent we'll pull them from Isaac." He grimaces as he listens to his caller. "Yes, all three, but forty percent, right? Not thirty-nine." The senator hangs up the phone and looks at me.

"Good news," I tell him.

The senator raises his chin.

"The guy who broke into Ben's house," I say. "It was the brother of someone he put away for drug dealing. It was a revenge thing. So we're okay."

"You call the press?"

"I talked to the police. I'll call the guy at the *Watch* next."

"Good. That's good." Grant Tully grabs a pencil and twirls it in his hand as he leans back in his chair. "Raycroft could play with this."

"He could but he won't," I answer. The senator is referring to Elliot Raycroft, the county attorney—the top prosecutor in the city. Elliot Raycroft is a Republican, of all things, the first Republican to be elected countywide in the last seventy years. There was a special runoff election four years ago when the incumbent county attorney died. The Democrats were feuding back then with the African-Americans, who formed their own party for the runoff and split the Democratic vote. So the unthinkable happened. A Republican won a race in the city. Raycroft managed not to screw up the job and won re-election to a full term two years ago, owing to the power of incumbency.

If you had to pick one office that the local Dems would *not* want to be held by the opposition party, it's the office of county attorney. There are plenty of behind-the-scenes shenanigans in city politics, and the last thing they want is for a prosecutor with the power to issue subpoenas and convene grand juries to start shoving his nose into the pigsty. This is especially true because Raycroft knows he'll lose re-election one of these times, so he needs to make a name for himself so he can move elsewhere, maybe statewide.

It's bad enough that Raycroft is in the wrong party. To add to that, the county attorney's political patron is none other than Attorney General Langdon Trotter. That's what the senator is talking about when he says Raycroft could use this situation for political gain.

"Raycroft's not dumb enough to take the side of a drug dealer's criminal brother over a former prosecutor who put the guy away." I open my hand. "It wouldn't sell. Trotter would never sign off on it."

"All right," says the senator. "You're right. So tell me about our other thing."

"The Ace," I say.

The senator stifles a smile. He's not one for nicknames or informality. Ever since I discovered that flaw with Lang Trotter's nominating papers—and ran back to tell the senator—I have referred to the whole thing as our "Ace."

I could understand how the mistake with Trotter's papers happened. He probably signed in black ink, and it was hard to tell the original from the photocopy. People do it all the time. You're supposed to file originals of all court documents, too, but sometimes only the photocopies get filed. Nobody ever balks. No judge would ever throw out a court filing because the original wasn't filed. It would be elevating form over substance. A lawyer would look foolish arguing the point in court.

But we aren't talking about court. We're talking about election law. The law says the statement of candidacy has to be "signed," and that means the original. A photocopy is not a signed document—it's a photograph of a signed document. I explain it this way—a photocopy of a document is no more the document itself than a photograph of a tree is the tree itself.

Form over substance? Absolutely. But I argued the point several years ago in a race for county sheriff downstate—it was a particularly nasty election and the senator wanted to help out the Democrat. And I won the argument. Some poor Republican got knocked off the ballot because he handed in a photocopy of a statement of candidacy. That guy and his lawyer walked out of the election board hearing looking like they'd had their pockets picked.

It's a very subtle, obscure point in election law, but like I say, that's my specialty. If we put this argument before the board of elections, they will have no choice. The long and short: Langdon Trotter's statement of candidacy is invalid. Thus, he is not entitled to run for governor.

When I found out about the mistake, I raced back to the city. The senator was nowhere to be found, so I ran into Bennett's office and gave him the news. I was damn sure of my position, but we opened up the election statutes anyway, read a couple of court decisions. There was a palpable sense of urgency the moment we looked at each other and realized we had Langdon Trotter's number.

"What does Dale say?" Grant asks.

I let my frown show. He's talking about Dale Garrison, the guy who wrote the memorandum that agreed with my conclusion that Lang Trotter was disqualified from running for office. Dale is a lawyer in town, one of the old horses in the legal community, a guy who's been around so long you'd think he passed the bar during Prohibition. He's a longtime friend of the Tully family, their personal lawyer for some things. He does some lobbying work, if reluctantly, in the state capital. He's one of a handful of people who has the senator's ear.

I don't have a problem with him. He's too chummy with me, but I have to give him his due. The thing is, I'm not too thrilled with the senator seeking a second opinion on my legal judgment.

"Don't give me that look," says Grant, reading my mind. The intercom buzzes. The senator's secretary tells him it's one of his guys, one of our state senators. Grant rolls his eyes but takes the call. I get out of my chair and pace, find myself peeking at a stack of greeting cards on the credenza behind the senator's desk.

Damn. I completely forgot. Yesterday was Grant's birthday. Just turned thirty-nine; he has a few months on me. Typically of Grant Tully, he pooh-poohs the thing, never allows a party in his honor. But here's a group of people who remembered, a good twenty cards at least. I stand at the credenza and leaf through them. A card from the governor, a U.S. senator, various other state legislators, a television news anchor, various attorneys in the community, including Dale Garrison. Garrison's card is brief—"Enjoy your day"—in his handwriting and just "Dale" for a signature. Like anyone else with the slightest political sense, Dale has obviously kept up with the senator, recorded his birthday as well as his wife's and children's. The rest of the cards are pretty standard—"Best wishes," "Good luck on the race," "Anything I can do to help." One of them even refers to him as "Governor Tully."

Grant hangs up the phone and makes a noise. "Fucking D'Angelo," he says. "First challenger he's had in sixteen years. He'll get seventy percent, minimum, you'd think he's in the race of his life." He looks at me as I return to my seat. "So where were we?"

"You were telling me that you want Dale to tell you I'm right."

He cocks his head. "Come on now, Mr. Soliday. It's not like that. Dale"—he waves a hand in the air—"Dale knows the courts. Half the judges used to work for him. I don't need a second opinion on the election laws. I need to know what a judge would do."

"Fine. Well, Dale thinks I'm right, by the way. You saw his memo."

"Did I?"

"He sent it to me. But Bennett was supposed to get you a copy."

The senator looks over his desk. "I probably have it here somewhere," he says.

"Bennett was supposed to make you a copy."

Grant Tully grimaces. "Bennett," he repeats. "I thought we were keeping this just between us."

I open my hands. "Ben's my guy. I ran the idea past him."

"Well, let's keep this under the radar, Jon. Okay?" His voice carries a hint of rebuke.

"What's the damn secret? When we file a complaint with the board of elections, everyone in the state's going to know about it."

Grant purses his lips but doesn't respond.

"You had something else in mind?" I ask.

Grant chews his bottom lip a moment. After a lifetime of political up-bringing, Grant Tully is pretty good at getting ahead of the curve. Sometimes I don't even see where he's headed. "Maybe," he says.

"What in the hell else could there be? We privately ask Lang Trotter, pretty please, to drop out of the race he's been preparing for his entire life?"

My remark brings a hint of a smile to Grant's lips. "You're getting warmer."

"Tell me, Grant."

"You were right about the private part." He waves at me. "Give me a nutshell of the argument."

"You know the argument."

But he waves at me again.

"Everyone has to have a statement of candidacy to run for office," I say. "You fill out the form and sign it, turn it in with all your voter petitions and everything else. Trotter's people screwed up. They made photocopies of everything, of course, but when they turned in the papers, they put the photocopy of the statement of candidacy in with the original petitions. A photocopy is not the original document. It's like he never turned in a statement of candidacy at all."

"Great," says the senator. "Now explain it to a voter."

I sigh. "That's why we have Don—"

"Senator Tully knocked off the Republican candidate on a technicality," says Grant. "Everyone knows he signed a statement of candidacy, everyone knows he wants to run, but because of a paper shuffle, now the voters don't get him as a choice." Grant shakes his head. "Sounds great."

"Well—"

"And what do I get for that? For the voters knowing I used some legal bullshit to knock off my opponent? For editorials across the state lambasting me? I'll tell you what I get. The Republicans get to nominate someone else in Trotter's absence. Am I right?"

"Well, sure." Under state election law, if a nominated candidate withdraws or is removed from the race, that political party is permitted to nominate someone else. The relevant political committee—in this case, the directors of the state Republican Party—simply takes a vote, and whoever wins is the Republican nominee. "You're going to have to run against *someone,* Grant."

He makes a face. In my experience, I find that state senators and representatives find it imminently distasteful when they actually have to put up a fight to win re-election. No one has tried to run against Senator Tully. This is his first contested race.

"They won't appoint someone like Trotter," says the senator. "They'll put a moderate in there. Pro-choice, to offset us. Someone who never could have won their primary but is a good candidate for the general election."

"Jody Thayer," I say. Jody Thayer is the lieutenant governor currently. She wanted to run in the Republican primary, but the party elders deemed Langdon Trotter the better candidate. So she's running for Trotter's job, attorney general. She is pro-choice, pro–gun control, had a very moderate voting record during her time in the state senate. She would be the best candidate against a pro-life, socially conservative guy like Grant Tully.

"Yeah," says the senator. "I'd bet on Jody."

"She'd be tough."

"She'd be better than Trotter." The senator shakes his head absently. "She'll never win a primary but she'd be the better candidate in the general. I wouldn't gain a thing. I knock off Trotter and get an even tougher opponent."

I open my hands, helpless. "That may be."

"To say nothing of the fact," the senator continues, "that now I'm the guy who used a highly technical legal argument to knock off my challenger. How gracious do I look then?"

"Okay, also true."

The senator is contemplative. But he shows no hint of frustration or conflict. He has laid out for me all the reasons that we can't use the Ace to disqualify Langdon Trotter. Yet the conversation is not over. His explanation is not a denouement. It's a segue. "There's another option." He leans back in his chair and stares at the ceiling. "We go to Trotter and show him what we have. We do it privately. A one-on-one meeting."

"Our point being?"

The senator's fingers rise slowly off his table. "The point being, we explain the state of affairs and give him some options. Maybe a trade-off."

"Trading what for what?" I ask.

"I always heard Trotter wanted to be a judge," he says. He considers the thought, then nods. "It would make some sense. A former attorney general appointed to the state supreme court. Or the federal bench, if we keep the White House."

"What are we talking about, Grant?"

"Monte's retiring," he continues. He means the current U.S. senator, Raymond Monte, who has broadly hinted that he will not seek re-election in two years.

I work my jaw a moment, then lean forward, like I'm trying to get a closer look. "Are you suggesting that we show Trotter our Ace, and tell him to drop out voluntarily?"

The senator eyeballs me, a hint of amusement in his eyes. "Trotter dropping out is no different than us knocking him off." He laces his hands together. "No, Jon, that's not what I meant, and I think you know that."

I inhale. "We show this to Trotter and tell him to lose?"

A smile from Senator Grant Tully.

"Throw the election?" I ask, suddenly aware of the volume of my voice. I lower it an octave. "Are you kidding me?"

"Keep an open mind there, Jonny." Grant allows his head to tip backward slightly. His eyes move off me to the ceiling again. "Trotter would sooner lose than be knocked off on a technicality. He wouldn't be able to show his face in public if we disqualified him because his people accidentally filed a photocopy of a critical document. He looks like an amateur."

"Maybe," I offer.

"So—" The senator opens his hands.

"So what?"

"So he'll do anything not to let that come out."

"You're *that* sure he'll lie down."

"It's not a question of lying down. We've got him, Jon. He's done with this race, one way or another." Grant wags a finger with authority. "He's done."

We sit in silence. I can only imagine the reaction of the Attorney General when the news is dropped at his door.

"He still runs for governor," says the senator. "But he runs to lose."

"How's he do that, incidentally?" I do not hide the exasperation in my voice. "Really, Grant. Tell me how a politician loses an election without anyone noticing."

The senator looks away with distaste. "Come on, Jon." He clears his throat. "He refuses to debate. He can justify that to his people. He's a state official, I'm more a local face. He can say he doesn't want to give us the publicity. But we'll crucify him for refusing to debate. So will the papers."

"Okay."

"We can control his ads. We go negative and he doesn't respond. He says he wants to take the high road. That's a loser course, but it lets him lose with dignity. We pound him on television, he says nothing in response, the papers say what a guy, but we beat his ass November seventh."

"I suppose so."

"Christ, he can get sick," says the senator. "He claims he has some virus or something, limits his campaigning. He's got the bad back."

"All of this may be possible," I say. "Until September twenty-third. That's the last day we can file a complaint for a problem with his papers. After that, doesn't matter whether there's a problem or not, you can't touch him."

"September twenty-third. Okay."

"At which point Trotter is free to renege. You lose your leverage."

"Yeah, that may be," Grant concedes. "I think if Lang cut a deal with me, he'd stick to it. But if not, at least I've kept him quiet the next six weeks. I've got a lot of ground to gain between now and September twenty-third."

I steady a stare on Grant. He is probably expecting me to go with him on this. I mean, probably my biggest contribution to the Democratic Party over these last several years has been knocking challengers from the ballot. That's the big thing everyone misses in politics—ballot access. Getting on the ballot in this state is slightly easier than solving a Rubik's Cube or finishing a heptathlon. In general, it sounds easy enough—fill out some forms and get citizens to sign your petition. But in practice, it takes a mountain of work and considerable knowledge of the intricacies of our election laws. First, there are the forms. Statements of candidacy, statements of economic interest, the petition sheets. There are about thirty mistakes you can make just on these forms alone, many of which are fatal to a candidacy right there—Trotter is the perfect example. There are requirements for the people who circulate the petition sheets to get signatures. They must be registered voters of this state; they may only circulate for candidates of one political party per election cycle. The signatures on the petitions can only come from citizens who are registered voters in the district, and they have to live at the address they put down, and they must sign, not print, their name. The list goes on; if you need three hundred signatures to get on the primary ballot, you better get at least nine hundred, because more than half of the signatures will be bounced for one reason or another. All told, with form requirements and signature and circulator restrictions, there are dozens of things you have to do right. So when some upstart, outside reformer tries to get on the ballot against one of our Democratic incumbents, it's even money I will find a way to knock him or her off in a ballot challenge.

Democracy in action. Or maybe anti-democracy. Hey, I'm just the lawyer. I don't make the rules, I just make sure opponents follow them. If they don't, I stick it to them, like any lawyer would do for any client.

But I *do* make the rules. There is not a single piece of legislation in this state pertaining to elections that doesn't cross my desk for approval. So the big parties set the complex rules and use their lawyers to make sure they are followed, and the little guys have to pore over an election code that makes the Internal Revenue Service regulations look like a coloring book.

My point being, I probably don't have the right to get on my high horse here. But it's one thing to challenge Langdon Trotter's ballot access based on the requirements of the law. It's quite another to use the threat of a challenge to essentially force the Attorney General to surrender the election.

"Don't do this," I say.

The senator appraises me a moment before nodding curtly. "You don't want to be part of it—I understand."

"I don't want *anyone* to be part of it. I mean, this is—" I catch myself, freeze in my seat.

"This is what, Jon?" Senator Tully delivers the question with no sense of irony. "Unethical? Immoral?"

"All of those, yes. But I was thinking of illegal."

A subdued burst of amusement from the senator. He rises from his seat, walks to his window. His jacket is draped over his chair; he is in shirtsleeves and navy braces strapped over his narrow shoulders. He looks out the window, allows for a deep inhale. "Jon, do you think I'll be a good governor?"

"Of course I do. I wouldn't be with you if I didn't."

"Yes, you would." He is speaking to the window. "Because you're a friend first. But tell me honestly—do you think I'm the right man for the job?"

"Absolutely."

"Why? Why do you think that, Jon?" He turns to me now. "And don't—don't tell me what you tell other people. Don't give me campaign-speak. Tell me what you tell yourself."

"Because you stand for what you believe in," I say. "You are a pro-life Democrat. You know that's the wrong stance for your party—your own caucus has ripped you a new one for it—but it's what you believe. You oppose the death penalty. You've known your whole life that you'd be running for statewide office, and you read the polls. About seventy percent of our state favors capital punishment. Every Democrat who has run for governor who opposed the death penalty was crucified for it. But you don't care. It's what you believe. You've opposed tax cuts for the last six years because you don't think they're fiscally responsible. That's not a popular position. Some of our own members have pleaded for you to change your tune. But you're looking out for the state." I smile. "You're political, no question—frankly, if you *weren't,* I'd be a little worried. But you're the guy to lead the state."

The senator accepts this monologue with no expression. "Now tell me your honest opinion of Langdon Trotter."

"I think Langdon Trotter would support the death penalty for shop-lifters if it would give him one more vote. I think his only belief is that he should be the governor. It's pure power lust."

"Okay." The senator moves to his desk and sits on the edge. "If I were able to dredge up some ugly secret on Trotter and make it public, what would you think?"

"Part of the game."

"In some sense immoral, though. Right?"

"Sure. But you go in knowing the rules."

"That makes it okay?"

"That makes it acceptable, I suppose," I say.

"This isn't different." The senator drops a fist softly on his thigh, dangling from the desk. "Not in any meaningful way."

"It's different to me, Grant. I'm a lawyer. I have to uphold the rules of ethics. I can't be party to—I can't be a part of this."

"So like I said," says Grant, "you won't be." He opens his hands. "You've advised me on the state of the law. I accept that. You've counseled me not to do it. Your job is finished."

I sigh. "Well—"

"But do me this favor," he says. "Talk to Dale Garrison about this. About all of this. All of our options. I want to make the right decision."

"Okay."

"Just ask him—don't—" He's struggling for words here. "Leave it wide open for him. Tell him we'll do whatever he wants. Don't show your hand. Tell him we'll do whatever he wants."

"Okay."

"Tell him that, Jon. Tell him I said I'll do whatever he wants."

"I heard you the first three times."

"That way, he feels free to give an objective opinion."

"You'll do whatever he wants."

"Good." The senator inhales deeply. "And we'll take it a step at a time."

"Sounds good." I get to my feet. "Maybe I'll still have a chance to talk you out of this." But as I say these words, I sense that it's already a done deal in Grant's mind. I've got the map. He wants me to feel out Dale Garrison because Dale is going to be the messenger. Dale is going to be the one who meets with Lang Trotter and drops the bomb. Dale's a sensible choice, to the extent that there is anything sensible about this scheme. So I'll have to make it my job to guide Dale toward my side. Or I may see my lifelong friend, Senator Grant Tully, make the biggest mistake of his life.

"Say, Jon." Grant is calling to me.

"Yep." I stop at his doorway.

"How's things?"

"Fine. Busy but—"

"You're still hanging your head a little."

I close my eyes. "I'm fine."

"You talk to her lately?"

"Um, no. Not recently." He's referring to my ex-wife, who moved out of the house and out of town about ten months ago. Tracy and I were together for almost five years, until she informed me in the middle of last year that it was time for her to go.

"Come by for dinner this weekend," he says. "The kids are going for pizza with Audrey's folks. We'll have an adult dinner."

Grant's wife, Audrey, is a sensational cook, along with being a hell of a lady. Grant met her when he was first elected to the senate and married her seven years ago. They have a five-year-old, Amy—my goddaughter— and Christopher is three.

"I told you, no pity."

"Oh, c'mon." He raises his hands. "Audrey was just asking about you."

"'How's Jon doing?'" I mimic a female voice. "'Has he gotten over his wife dumping him?'"

Like most jokes, I'm only half-kidding. Grant doesn't like the humor. He doesn't like the self-deprecation and he doesn't like the ring of truth to it. The guy thinks he's my big brother.

"She didn't dump you," he says, informing me how my marriage fell apart. His expression lightens. "Besides, it's not pity. You know Audrey's always had a thing for you."

"Well, sure, I know that." I play along.

Grant smiles. "So give her some hope. She's stuck with a homely Irishman like me."

"I'll think on it."

"Or let's us go out and throw a few back Saturday night."

"Maybe." I pat the doorway. "In the meantime, don't come up with any more stupid ideas about this race."

6

When you work for Senator Grant Tully, you skip the headline of the *Daily Watch*—typically devoted to some national or international incident—and head straight to the article above the fold, then the Metro section. The *Watch* likes to consider itself a national paper and fills pages and pages on Washington and the rest of the world, but the only interesting information to the senator is the state and local stuff. He couldn't care less who is president, or even who gets elected to the U.S. Senate from our state.

Today I approach the paper with reticence, fearing the top-fold story will cover my favorite deputy attorney's brush with an intruder in the middle of the night. But it doesn't. I turn inside, pages 2–3, 4–5, but still nothing.

Then I go to the Metro section, the purely local stuff. It's on the fourth page, which is the last real page, in a thin column on the left side. HOME-OWNER KILLS BURGLAR. The reporter got my information on the intruder, noting his "long criminal record" as well as his brother's arrest and the civil lawsuit against Bennett. Cops called it a justifiable shooting. Favorable story.

Good. I drop the paper and take a sip of coffee, look out over the breakfast crowd. The place is Langley's, nothing more than a greasy-spoon diner that happens to be on the bottom floor of the County Building. The cuisine is average at best; I have half of a feta cheese omelette on my plate that I don't plan to finish. The crowd is a veritable who's who of the legal community. You can't wave your arms in the place without hitting half a dozen judges or elected officials.

I wave to the waitress for my check and I catch the eye of none other than the Republican candidate for governor, Langdon Trotter. He saw me and I saw him. Now I have to say hello to this asshole.

Lang Trotter is carving his eggs into bite-sized pieces, elbows out, working the knife like its object was the political future of Grant Tully. "Jon," he sings as I walk up, before making eye contact with me. He drops his utensils and offers a hand.

"Mr. Attorney General," I say. "Nice to see you."

Trotter is a guy's guy, silver-haired and burly, an outdoorsman, a strong, lined face. He has a commanding voice and a direct manner that, combined with his physique, dominate a room. One of the only guys I know who makes me feel small. The women on staff in the capital tell me that they find him attractive not so much on classical criteria but on his persona. That's women for you. Guys see tits and ass, women see confidence and power.

Trotter opens his hand to his guest. "Judge Dixon, Jon Soliday." We shake hands.

"Jon here is Tully's chief counsel," says the Attorney General. "You won't find a guy in this state more knowledgeable about the legalities of elections and campaign finance. If he weren't such a believer, I'd try to woo him to my side."

"I'm blushing over here," I say, feeling awkward as usual around this guy. Even when you're standing and he's sitting, he towers over you. This guy was born with a cigar in one hand and a rifle in the other.

His eyebrows rise as his fork plunges into some breakfast meat. He will not allow a brief hello with me to interrupt his breakfast. A subtle way of establishing our respective statures. "How is the senator?"

"Working hard," I answer. "Like you, no doubt."

"He's a fine opponent, I'll say it to anyone."

"The feeling is mutual."

"How are we going to play?" Trotter's eyes fix on me now.

"What's that?"

"It's always more fun when we play nice," he says. "The senator and I, we both have plenty of years left."

"True, true."

"He more than I." The Attorney General winks at his breakfast companion. He offers his hand. "I always wish my opponent the best of luck."

I shake his hand for the second time. "Same to you, Mr. Attorney General. Nice meeting you, Judge." I head to my seat wishing like hell I had eyes in the back of my head.

7

Not ten minutes after I arrive to work Wednesday morning, Bennett Carey walks into my office holding some forms. "Take a look at these," he says. "The D-7s." These are financial disclosure forms that our candidates have to fill out every three months. They have to tell the world what money they received and from whom, and how much they spent and on what. Because Ben and I are the lawyers for the Democratic Party, we have to approve every one of these, not only for Senator Tully but for every Democratic candidate for every race for state representative, state senator, and the constitutional offices.

"Ben, I was planning on handling these myself."

He looks at me with a blank stare. His face is drawn somewhat, sleep-deprived eyes and a sag in his overall appearance. "I said I'd do them." That is sort of the beginning and end of it for Bennett Carey. He said he'd do it, he'll do it, even if he just went through a harrowing experience.

"Go home," I say, although home might not be the best place for him.

"What am I gonna do, hide?"

"Maybe give yourself a break. Go visit your—go do something." I almost told him to visit his parents. Ben is an orphan, doesn't even remember his folks after their death in a head-on car accident when he was barely two years old. Ben told me this onetime after a night of drinking. It's the only time we've discussed it.

Ben ignores me, heads out. "I've got a few more. They'll be done by lunch."

"Ben—wait." He stops and turns back. "How're you doing?"

He shrugs. "Fine."

"Do you want to talk to me?"

"I'm fine," he says, before reconsidering. Bennett Carey is not exactly an open book. But jeez, this is no minor event that just occurred. "I thought about his mother hearing the news. Answering a knock at the door and seeing a policeman standing there. Feeling a rush of fear. Feeling her legs give out when she hears the words. Or maybe it's his wife."

"Keep in mind who created the situation."

"Oh, I know." He nods, then casts a glance into the hallway. He takes a couple of steps back into my office and closes the door behind himself. He braces himself a moment, then holds out his hands like he's shaping pottery. "I know this guy broke into my house. I know he started it. Okay? But did I have to finish it that way? I mean, what the hell did I think this guy was doing? Of course he was leaving."

"Dammit, Ben. You couldn't know that."

"Maybe not for a hundred percent, but this guy didn't seem too interested in engaging me any further." Bennett deflates. "He was running away from me, Jon."

I rise from my chair and move to him. "Ben, this is you thinking about it after-the-fact. Big difference from experiencing it on the spot. The longer you think about this, the more obvious it's going to seem to you what this guy was doing. But we're talking about this whole thing unfolding in about, what, thirty seconds? Don't put knowledge into your head that wasn't there at the time. He was gonna hurt you bad, and if he'd have gotten away, he would've come back."

"Even if you're right—" Ben's voice breaks off.

"I am right."

"Someone's still dead."

Not much of a response for that one. Ben isn't being unreasonable here. He understands the circumstances. I think, more than anything, he's just a little spooked by the whole thing.

"So how's the Ace?" he asks.

"Oh—fine," I say. Ben seems glad to move on to a different topic. I'm happy to oblige him, though I'm cognizant of the senator's instructions. Only Grant and I are aware of any possible negotiation with Langdon Trotter about his screwed-up nominating papers. For Bennett's own sake, I will not share the information. "The legal argument seems to be shaping up."

"Garrison's memo looked good," he says.

"Yeah, it did. I'm going to meet with him tomorrow over lunch."

"Lunch tomorrow," says Bennett. "You want some company?"

"Ordinarily, yeah, but it's probably better just the two of us. The senator is really concerned about keeping this quiet."

"Okay, no problem. I'll finish up the D-7s and get them to you."

"Well, if you're sure—"

"I'm sure, Jon. Adios."

I watch Bennett leave my office and go through yesterday's mail in my In box. At the same time I scroll on my computer to the internet, go online to check the *Watch* poll that came out today. I already heard the buzz, but I haven't read it yet.

If the election were held today, Attorney General Langdon Trotter would receive fifty-four percent of the vote. Senate Majority Leader Grant Tully would receive thirty-nine percent. A third-party candidate, a staunch conservative named Oliver Jenson running under the Conservative Family Party, would get two percent.

Not terribly surprising. Our own numbers aren't far off. Trotter has held statewide office for almost eight years. His name is all over the place. As much as Grant Tully dominates the political scene, no matter how you slice it, he's still just a state senator. Everyone knows him in the city, and most people around the state would recognize the name, but his face isn't ingrained in anyone's mind yet. Langdon Trotter is the cowboy who sued the tobacco companies and went after the health-care monopoly downstate. We knew he'd be out to an early lead. Senator Tully is going to have to *live* in the downstate counties between now and November 7, because that's where the election will be decided, and he's not a household name.

Four letters in the mail. First one is a thank-you note from a local alderman whom I assisted on a campaign-finance problem, a correction he needed to file with the city election board. A letter from the symphony house, asking me to re-up for another year's subscription. I don't know why I bother; I have to miss most of the shows anyway. Some ad from an electronic legal research outfit that I don't even open.

The last one is addressed to me but with no return address, no letterhead. When I open it, a single piece of plain white paper falls out. It's one paragraph, looks like it was done on a typewriter, not addressed to anyone:

> I guess I'm the only one left who knows the secret that nobody knows. I think $250,000 should cover it. A month should be enough time. I wouldn't presume your income source, but I imagine if anyone could find a way to tap into the campaign fund without anyone noticing, you would. Or I suppose I could always just talk to the senator. Is that what you want? One month. Don't attempt to contact me about this. I will initiate all communications.

Instinctively, I look up, out my doorway. Then again at the letter. What the hell is this?

My phone buzzes, the intercom from my secretary. I punch the speakerphone button. "Yeah," I say to my secretary, Cathy.

"Jon, Dale Garrison's office called to confirm Friday night at seven o'clock for your meeting."

The secret that nobody knows.

I shake my head. "What now, Cath?"

"Dale Garrison's—"

"What time?"

"Seven o'clock, Friday night?"

"What happened to lunch Thursday?" I ask. But Cathy wouldn't know.

"I had the impression you were the one who changed the meeting," she says.

"Okay—well—whatever. That's fine. Still his office?"

"Right."

"Okay. Thanks, Cath."

Who the hell sent me this? I read the letter two, three times. Then another lawyer down the hall stops in, and I hurriedly toss the note inside my top desk drawer.

8

Friday night, close to five. Even at a sweatshop like Seaton, Hirsch, there is considerable fallout by the last hour of the workweek. I'm near the end, too. Finish up this brief I'm writing, stop by Dale Garrison's office, then head home. Senator Tully is leaving in a couple of hours to spend the weekend down in the southern counties, working his thing. There's a big blue-collar sector down there—union workers—that is the key to the whole election. With the senator out of town, hopefully I can get some relaxation. The closer we get to the general election, the less I'm going to sleep.

I promised the senator I would get back to him as soon as I get the word from Dale Garrison on our legal argument. I admit, I'm a little put out by having to get the counsel of this attorney. Dale Garrison is sort of an elder statesman, and I know he goes way back with the Tullys, so he's owed some deference. But he couldn't possibly know election law like I do. Yet here I am, about to go telling some other attorney that we'll do "whatever he wants"—Grant's words—regarding our attack on Langdon Trotter's nomination papers.

Bennett Carey strides by my office and stops short. His overcoat is thrown over his shoulder, his briefcase in hand. "Staying long?" he asks.

"I'm here till seven."

Ben jabs a thumb behind himself. "Some of us are going for some beers. Flanagan's."

"You?" I ask. "A socialite?"

"Pity on their part." He shrugs.

"Well, Bennett, it's nice to see you go out for any reason."

"Come with," he says.

I shake my head. "I'm meeting with Garrison this evening."

"Garrison? I thought that was lunch, yesterday."

"Nope. He changed it. I get to spend the dinner hour with him. Think he'll pop for pasta?"

Bennett smiles. That's about as much as you'll get out of him in terms of a sense of humor. At least he's lightening up a little. I consider asking him for the umpteenth time how he's holding up, but why bring up the topic? Let him throw a few beers back and put it behind him.

Bennett leaves. I finish up my work—a draft of our legal argument on the Ace—by six-thirty. I want to have my thoughts coherent before meeting with Dale Garrison. Just in case he's thinking that he's going to show me how smart he is. Yeah, maybe I have a bug up my ass.

I stop by Senator Tully's office. He's on the phone, so I wave. He covers the receiver and says, "Let me know." I nod and head out.

I stop a few feet from his doorway and almost turn back. There's another conversation that we need to have. That anonymous letter in the mail. The "secret that nobody knows." But I catch the tone of Grant's voice on the phone—agitated, talking to Don Grier—and decide to bring it up later. It's bullshit, anyway. It must be.

I catch a cab for the ride across town to Dale Garrison's office. I don't know Dale socially but we have had plenty of opportunities to interact over the years. For people who know people, there are plenty of opportunities in this state to supplement one's income. The state has numerous commissions and task forces set up for various projects, and the legislators' pets get on them. Not all of them pay, but the ones that do are plum assignments. Typically, they involve one meeting a month, maybe a biannual report or something.

Dale Garrison has a couple of these deals. He is the chair of COPA—the Commission on Political Appointments—which recommends appointments to the governor for anything from vacant judicial positions to heads of administrative agencies. The job doesn't pay but gives plenty of people plenty of reasons to be plenty nice to Dale. Until about five years ago, Garrison was counsel to the Health Care Planning Board, which regulates health care facilities in the state. Since leaving the job, of course, he took on several hospitals and cancer clinics as clients and regularly represents their interests before all of his former colleagues on the board. You see him down in the state capital lobbying for them.

But that's behind-the-scenes stuff. You ask fifty lawyers in town to describe Dale Garrison's practice, forty-nine will tell you it's criminal law. He does plenty of the bloody stuff, but he's known more for high-end clients, white-collar types charged with financial crimes. A few years back, he represented an alderman in a federal bribery sting. It swept up four or five members of the city council, but Garrison got an acquittal for his guy based on entrapment.

I nod at the security guy in the lobby of Garrison's building. Dale Garrison works near the river in the Merchant's Building. Fifteen floors of offices filled primarily with guys like Garrison, big-time solo practitioners and personal injury lawyers. The building is a turn-of-the-century vintage, square-shaped, overlooking River Street. Garrison's space is on the street side of the building, L-shaped with eleven offices in total—five on each side with Dale's office in the middle, the corner office. If memory serves, a few of the offices are filled by associates in Dale's direct employ and the others by other solo practitioners who work with Dale on occasion.

I don't want the senator to have anything to do with blackmailing Langdon Trotter. That's what it is—blackmail. No need to dance around it. The senator has far too promising a future, whether he wins or loses this race, to throw it away on something so risky. The tough job will be convincing the senator. And Garrison.

Garrison's office is down the hall from the elevator on eight. The front door is a piece of frosted glass that bears his name. I open the door into a lobby, a small waiting room. The reception desk is empty at this hour, so I walk past it to the suite of offices.

I can hear the hum of the music from his office, big-band, Glenn

Miller or something. No one else here this time of the week, after hours on a Friday. The associates who work with Dale aren't getting the big bucks—making connections and getting good trial experience, but not making the salaries to warrant late Friday nights. So it's just me and Dale, probably just as well.

Dale's on the phone when I walk in. First sensation is a hint of odor—mint, more like menthol-rub than candy. I rap lightly on the door but he already sees me. His stooped posture is evident even from his chair. He has only wisps of hair around the ears, age spots on his weathered scalp, very deep-set eyes, and a crooked nose. He is in shirtsleeves, revealing his bony shoulders. His fingers stroke his forehead as he speaks into the receiver.

The office is a shrine to someone who's practiced in state and federal court for over forty years. Framed photographs of Dale at various stages of his career with politicians, judges, and celebrities wallpaper the wood paneling in the room. Picture windows on each side of the corner show the state courthouse and the heart of the commercial district, the banks and options exchange.

Dale hangs up the phone like he does everything else, slowly. He looks up at me with no discernible expression. "Hello, Jon," he says, as he pushes his glasses up the bridge of his nose.

"Dale." I take a chair across from him. "Guy your age shouldn't be working so late." I'm kidding but it immediately hits me, the rumors of his cancer, and the joke seems inappropriate.

Dale laughs in his way, a grunt and a tremble in the shoulders, a hint of amusement in his watery blue eyes. He wags a crooked finger at me. He turns in his swivel chair to the radio behind him—a beat-up brown rectangle that looks older than me—and turns off the trumpet solo in the song. Then he turns back to face me. He rests his elbows on an oversized desk with stacks of papers, a dictaphone resting in the center of the desk. He has a computer, too, probably state-of-the-art, though I doubt he uses it.

"Well," he says. "Quite a . . . thing we have here."

"It's a bombshell, all right."

"I agreed with your take on it." A nice touch by Dale. Answers to no one, but still doesn't hurt to stroke Senator Tully's top lawyer.

"I think we can agree that we're right on the law," I say. "Trotter's papers are invalid. But the senator wants your take on how this will play before a judge." The senator, not me.

Dale wets his lips and stares at me a moment. "Throwing out the leading candidate for governor . . . on a technicality."

"Judge won't have a choice," I start.

Dale raises a hand and smiles at me. "Never tell a judge he doesn't have a choice." He stares at me a moment, perhaps awaiting a response that is not forthcoming. "I'm not saying you're wrong, not saying you're wrong. . . ." His voice trails off. He peers over my head, eyes squinted. "Be the judge a minute. You're knocking someone . . . off the top spot on the ballot."

"Almost every judge in the election division's with us."

"Doesn't matter what they do in the circuit court," says Dale. "This is going to the supremes."

"Sure." No doubt Dale is correct, any ruling on Trotter's candidacy will be appealed to the state supreme court.

"The Republicans will stay with Trotter," Dale continues. "Four Democrats on the court rule against the senator's opponent . . . the press rips them apart." Dale laces his fingers together. "So the question is . . . do we want to ask them to make this decision right now?"

"Hmm." Dale makes a decent point here. Next year, we will go through our legislative redistricting that comes along every ten years after the census—based on the new population figures, new districts are drawn from which elected officials run. It's the big issue for next session. Both political parties try to manipulate boundaries to make their districts safe for their incumbents and add new districts to their total. Whoever wins has a strong chance of ruling the legislature for the next decade. The Democratic Senate and the Republican House will never agree on a map, and no bill will make it to the governor's desk.

Which means the state supreme court will draw the map, which raises Dale's point. Right now, four of the seven supreme court justices are Democrats, a one-vote majority. And we will ask the 4–3 Democratic majority to see things our way. These things usually split down party lines, but all things considered, you still don't want to be asking the Dems on the court for too many favors as the redistricting battle nears. If one of them feels the heat for knocking off Trotter, he might be reluctant to rule for us on the map.

Well, score one for Dale. Hadn't occurred to me. The question is, does Grant Tully care more about the governor's race or the map? We both know the answer.

"Okay," I say. "Maybe—maybe we decide not to file a challenge. You know the other option. Going to Trotter with this."

Dale waves his hands in the air, slow-moving theatrics. "Trotter waits ten years to run for governor . . . he can't even put his nomination papers together without a mistake."

Sometimes you have to try more than once with Dale. "Do you think it's smart to show Trotter what we have? Talk to him about his options?"

A smile creeps onto Dale's face. "Lang Trotter'd cut his dick off . . . before he'd lose on a technicality." Dale brings a fist to his mouth and lets out a hideous cough.

"But he'd never throw an election," I counter.

Dale, still recovering from the coughing attack, waves me off.

"He'd never go for it," I say. "Trotter would never agree to lie down."

Dale frames his hands. He has the floor, and he takes his time. "A man without options," he says.

"He has the option of telling us to stick it up our asses," I say. "He could report us."

This brings a chuckle from Dale, a bobbing of his bony shoulders, before he begins to cough again. I thought he'd be on my side here. He's saying he likes Grant's idea. We should blackmail Trotter.

"Jon, Jon," he says. His smile is humorless. His hands slowly rise. "What does he . . . report? That his papers are bad?"

"He reports that—"

"Then any nut . . . can file a challenge. Someone would. He gains nothing."

"Just because it might work doesn't mean we should do it, Dale."

Now he's showing me his palms. "A political question. For Grant to decide." He drops his hands flat on the table. "You ask me, will it work? I say it will."

"I say it won't."

"You say it won't." The first sign of any agitation from Dale. "You're a very smart lawyer. So tell Grant."

"I'll do that." I rise from my chair and thank him for his time. He nods slowly and solemnly. "I'll see my way out."

I do just that, moving through his hallway quickly, slamming through his front door and smashing my hand against the elevator button.

"Goddammit," I say to no one. I do a slow decompression in the elevator. Dale is copping out. He's saying Trotter would never call Grant's bluff, and he might be right about that. But he's not taking a position on what's right and wrong. He should be telling Grant that blackmailing his opponent is unethical. And more importantly, stupid. Maybe disastrous.

I make it into the lobby, such as it is, of Dale's building and nod to security. I step into the mild air outside and say a silent prayer that I can convince my friend not to do this. I make it to the corner when my cell phone buzzes in my coat pocket. I reach in, almost drop the phone, and punch it on. As I do so, a car honks and narrowly misses me at the curb side.

"Hello?"

"Dale Garrison." That's how Garrison always introduces himself on the phone, never mind that we just parted ways less than five minutes ago.

The connection is bad, so I keep my voice up. "Dale?"

A pause. "Run up for a minute?"

"You want me to stop back—"

"Let's talk about it."

Okay. A second chance. He's reconsidering. I start to answer but the phone goes dead. Sounds like Dale. He hangs up the phone when he's done saying what he has to say.

I stop back into the building and wave at the security guy. Maybe I was a bit too bullheaded in there. I need to work him, gently push him to my position. I'll let him do what someone his age probably is entitled to do—condescend, laugh in my face. But I'll work him.

I silently work over my plan as I leave the elevator and open the frosted-glass door into his suite of offices. Start with an apology. Then an appeal: Grant's my best friend, as a friend I don't want him going down this road. Grant respects you, he listens to you.

I walk into Dale's office, ready to backpedal. But Dale is not ready for an apology. He is lying on his desk, his head resting on his folded arms.

The guy's asleep. What the hell.

I step back out and pretend to be speaking on the cell phone, talking very loudly, so he'll hear and wake up. But when I walk back in, he's still prone. The top of his head is spotted, with wisps of wiry hair. I stand there in the middle of the room, hands on my hips, not sure how to handle it.

"Dale."

Noise from outside. "Hello!"

Don't know if I should reply to that or not. I turn and look into the hallway. A guy steps through reception and looks at me. He's wearing a lime-green top with black pants.

"*Dale,*" I repeat. This could be embarrassing for him.

"Security," says the man. He's a weightlifter, a thick neck, broad chest, the swagger. He walks into the office.

I jab a finger at Dale and speak softly. "He's an older guy," I apologize. "Must have been a long week."

The guard peers at Dale, takes a step closer. "Sir," he says in an authoritative voice.

"Dale!" I call out.

"Holy shit." The man approaches Dale and stops a moment, thinks it over, and puts a hand on his shoulder.

"Oh, fuck." I rush to Dale, the other side of the desk from the guard, and grab hold of Dale by the other shoulder. "Dale? Dale!" I place a finger at his neck for a pulse, but I'm not sure I'd know where to check so I lift him off the desk, place him against the back of the leather chair. Dale's eyes are vacant, his mouth turned downward in an ugly frown. His glasses fall from his face.

"Holy shit, he's dead!" the guard says. He looks at me a moment, like I'm to blame.

I lift Dale from his chair and place him on the floor. "Do you know CPR?" I shout to the guy, but I don't wait for an answer. I don't know what I'm doing but I have to try. I prop up Dale's neck with one hand, squeeze his nose closed with the other, and breathe into his mouth, three short but violent breaths. Then I place my palm over his heart and push down with my other hand three times in succession.

"Zeke!" the guard shouts, presumably into his radio. "We need an ambulance and police up on eight. Suite Eight-twenty. And send everyone up here!"

I lower my ear to Dale's mouth and nose. Nothing.

Static from the radio. "*You want police?*"

"Yeah, police and an ambulance. And get your ass up here. Suite Eight-twenty. Garrison's place!"

"Come on, Dale." I blow air into Dale's mouth again. I stare into his blank eyes a moment before returning to his heart. I repeat the cycle a third time, ending with me once again listening for any breath from his nose or mouth. Nothing. I keep working in vain, my compressions becoming more urgent, blowing violently into his mouth. Sweat falls from my forehead onto Dale's lifeless face. I fight through the soreness in my forearms, the dizzy ringing in my head, the rising panic within me. Finally, I'm breathless myself, after what must be five minutes of working on Dale. Nothing.

Dale Garrison is dead.

I rock back into a sitting position on the floor. "Goddammit," I mumble. I look over at the guard, who seems threatened by my stare.

"You're gonna have to stay right there." His hands move away from his sides, his weight shifts from one side to the other, like he's defending me in a game of one-on-one. "Don't touch a thing. Don't move."

"Take it easy," I say. "And you were a lot of help, by the way."

Noise out in reception, then two guys running down the hallway in matching fluorescent green shirts. Suddenly three guys surround me, all dressed like popsicles.

"Stay right there," the original guard says again. He turns to the other guys, who seem uncertain as to their role and mine. "This guy watched him die, then told me he was just sleeping."

"Relax," I say. I reach for Dale, unsure of the etiquette, and place a hand on his arm. "Jesus Christ, Dale," I say to him.

9

"He lied to me. He said the guy was asleep. He lied—"

"Okay now, hold on a minute." The detective, still in his trenchcoat, raises his hands to calm the security guard, who is anxiously bobbing on his toes.

Dale Garrison has been dead thirty minutes. By the time the paramedics and cops arrived, five members of building security, all decked out in their lime-colored tops, descended on Suite 820. They all stood awkwardly, each with one hand on their weapon, eyeballing me, the guy sitting in a chair.

Paramedics arrived about fifteen minutes later. They handled the affair without comment, examining Dale's body on the carpet and then soberly placing him on a gurney and removing him from the scene. The cops arrived about a minute ago and conferred with the paramedics. The cop in charge seemed irked that the paramedics had removed the body from its "death position." Once he got a preliminary look at the body, he spent the next several minutes trying to shut up this security guard.

"I didn't lie," I say from my spot on the chair.

"One at a time," says the detective. He decides to start with me and, with a firm handshake, introduces himself as Brad Gillis. Gillis looks like a city cop, I guess. His face is heavily lined, pale, rough-complected. His hair is dishwater, thick and straight, cut in a choppy way that makes him look like a scarecrow. His eyes are clear and intense. His mannerisms and posture give the impression of education. His voice does, too—strong but contained, careful enunciation.

I have settled down from the initial shock of seeing a dead person—second one in a week, now that I think about it—and now I'm becoming annoyed. I'm standing now, and I begin to pace. Gillis places a hand on me to stop me. "Let's step out here," he says. He leads me into the hallway. So far he has not brought out a notepad or anything else. He waves at the guards to keep a further distance, to the point that these guys decide just to head into the reception area.

"So tell me what happened," says Gillis.

"I was here to meet with Dale," I say. "Dale Garrison. The—deceased. We talked awhile, then I left. I wasn't two blocks away, and he called me on my cell phone to come back up. So I did. When I came back in, Dale was lying facedown on the desk." I throw up my hands. "Then this guy with the security uniform comes in and after a moment we figure out Dale's not asleep, he's dead."

Gillis is following me with his eyes, nothing in writing at this point. His hands are clasped behind his back. "This security guy says you were lying?"

I shake my head and grimace. "Dale's almost seventy years old," I say. "I figured he'd fallen asleep in his chair. That's what I told the guy. Turns out, I was wrong."

"Okay." Gillis looks back down the hallway, where the guards were before heading into reception. Then back at me: "Why were you meeting with this guy?"

"We're lawyers," I say. "Discussing a client situation."

He looks at me a moment like he doesn't understand. Maybe he figures if he stares at me, I'll keep talking, elaborate. He's wrong. Finally, he raises his eyebrows. "Who's the client?"

"I'm afraid that's privileged," I answer.

"The *name* of the client is privileged." His mouth works into a smirk. "Can't even tell me the *name*."

"Sorry. It's the rules." I don't think that's the case, but why advertise Senator Tully's name if I don't have to?

Now Gillis chews on his lips, his face still expressionless. "He called you on your cell?"

"Right."

Gillis does a half-nod. "Gimme that number?"

"Sure." I hand him my phone, with the number written on the back. He removes a pad of paper from his jacket pocket, grabs a pen from his pants pocket, and jots it down.

"You left, walked down the street, got the call, and came back."

"Yeah."

"So you couldn't have been gone more than five minutes," says Gillis.

"That's about right. Probably a little more than that."

"Okay." The detective works his jaw, ruminating.

"I walked back into the office and saw Dale lying there. I called to him a couple of times to wake him. Then that joker comes prancing down the hall."

Gillis smiles and nods absently, looking around, and hands my phone to me. He pokes his head back into the office for a moment. "Okay," he says, his back to me. He turns back around, his hand wiping at his mouth.

"Can I go?"

"You gave your information to the officer?"

"Yeah." For good measure, I hand him one of my business cards.

The detective stands motionless a moment, his hands on his hips. Finally, he blows out a sigh. "Yeah, take off," he says.

10

I leave the building and wander up to River Street. I go to the corner of Fourth and River and stand by a fire hydrant. For the moment the intersection is empty of people, just a handful of cabs passing by. I let five minutes pass, trying to come down from the creepy feeling of what I've just witnessed, before I walk back toward my office.

I punch my cell phone and dial the senator's number at the office. He isn't there so I leave a message. Then I try him on the car phone.

"Grant Tully."

"I'm glad you're sitting down," I say. I give him the two-minute capsule. The senator doesn't comment during my summary, nor does he immediately respond.

"Dale's dead?"

"Just dropped right at his desk. Creepiest thing I ever saw."

"Oh, Jesus." I hear a horn honking in the background. "They said he was pretty sick."

"I guess so."

Silence. Faint sounds of driving in the street in the background, some soft music on the senator's car stereo.

I imagine Grant wants to ask me what Dale thought about using the Ace. Decorum prevents it, to say nothing of the fact that the "elevator rule"—never talk in a crowded elevator—applies these days to cell phones as well. Never know who might be listening.

"Yeah, well, Christ," says Grant. "Dale's dead."

This will be a big deal. Dale Garrison's death will be seen as more than the passing of a man. He's the old school of trial lawyers in the city, the guys who spent their early years prosecuting, trying cases to juries, instead of joining up with silk-stocking firms and pushing paper. If I could have a dime for every old war story that will come to the lips of attorneys in this city over the next week or so, I could retire to Bermuda.

"You have a history with him," I say.

"Well—of course." A pause. "Damn."

"Okay, I'm heading out."

"All right. Say, Jon?"

"Yep."

"What's with you and dead people all of a sudden?"

I punch out the phone and place it in my pocket. I decide against returning to the office. I hail a cab and make it to my place just after nine in the evening. My pugs, Jake and Maggie, literally mug me when I walk in the door. They want to be fed and let out in the backyard. I take care of their needs, in that order, and open my briefcase. Plenty of work for me this weekend—checking out campaign finance disclosure statements, reviewing campaign ads circulated by Lang Trotter, meeting tomorrow morning with lower members of the senator's campaign staff. Should fill the entire Saturday and Sunday, and I should get started tonight. But instead I let out a shudder and drop my head on the couch cushion, close my eyes to keep out the image of a dead lawyer staring me in the face.

11

Dale Garrison's passing received better treatment from the *Daily Watch* than the death of that guy who broke into Bennett Carey's home. Still, it wasn't headline news, because Dale Garrison was not a recognizable name to those outside the circle of lawyers in this city and state. He was part of a select group of behind-the-scenes shot-callers, often more powerful than the politicians themselves. The tail wags the dog more often than people think. And that's a good gig. Plenty of prestige within their circle, much more money than the elected officials, and virtual anonymity in the public eye.

Within the legal community, where Dale loomed large, his passing was akin to the death of the mayor twelve years ago. The daily legal periodical that circulates in the city ran a special edition devoted to Dale today, Tuesday. A picture of Dale from about, I'd guess, fifteen years ago graced the entire front page. Inside were articles from a state supreme court justice, Grant Tully, Langdon Trotter (who never resided for one day in the city), and the mayor. The edition highlighted Dale's considerable achievements. He filed class actions against asbestos manufacturers, against the grocery store chain that sold milk with traces of salmonella. He successfully defended businessmen in insider-trading prosecutions, that alderman in the government corruption sting, a former congressman in a sex scandal (that one not so successfully).

Dale Garrison's memorial service is today. There's a private ceremony for the family but this is for everyone else—and I mean everyone else. They're using the spacious downtown cathedral for it. The police are managing traffic and the press is covering it. It's the same thing every time a politician or someone with money dies. The proceedings themselves, the funeral and visitation, take on an unintended life of their own. People come to pay their respects for someone recently departed, but their concerns quickly turn to the living. They spend far less time mourning the deceased than they do peering around at the other people in the room.

I sit next to Grant Tully and his wife, Audrey, in the second row, behind the family. Audrey takes my hand in hers and dotes on me before the proceedings begin—have I lost weight, how are the dogs, so sorry I had to be there when Dale died. About the only topic she does not raise is the source of her attentiveness—my divorce. Everyone feels sorry for you when your marriage ends.

In the second row on the opposite side of the aisle from us sits the county attorney, Elliot Raycroft, a serious man with coarse salt-and-pepper hair and steel-rimmed glasses. He was acquainted with Dale, of course, but anything but a close friend. Next to him is Lang Trotter—appropriately subdued but ready with a wink to those who catch his eye—who falls in the same category. A good lobbyist like Dale can reach both sides of the aisle when he needs to, but no one mistook Dale Garrison for a friend of the Republicans. Why these guys are sitting up front is beyond me. There shouldn't be a hierarchy for these things. I suppose I don't belong up front, either, but the Tullys do, and I'm with them.

Grant's father, former Senator Simon Tully, delivers a eulogy. He is dressed in black, genuinely grim, delivering one of his least favorite public speeches. He talks of Dale's more publicized cases but emphasizes the ones that didn't make the headlines. "Most people don't realize how much pro bono work Dale did," says Simon. "It wasn't money or prestige. It was about making sure that the protections of the law—"

My pager blares out. Forgot to kill it. I quickly reach my belt and disable it.

"—applied to those who couldn't afford the likes of Dale Garrison. It was about the law, in its purest form. Equal justice for all."

Simon Tully was never the best public speaker. He grew up in a time when cameras were not omnipresent, when backdoor dealing was even more prominent than it is now. He finishes up and takes a seat next to his son, Grant, while the clergyman continues the ceremony.

We file out. The press stops Grant Tully. His father is overtaken by people offering their favorable comments on the eulogy. I reach a cab and head back to the office.

I get off the elevator at my floor of Seaton, Hirsch, and a passing secretary looks at me like she's seen a ghost. I smile to her but her eyes drop. I head down the hallway toward my office. All the lawyers, everyone, are standing in the hall. My secretary, Cathy, is standing down the way, near my office. When she sees me she rushes toward me. She's heavyset, so it seems unusual to see her moving so fast.

"Jon, I tried to page you. I tried to stop them but they have a warrant. Bennett looked at it."

"It's okay," I say absently and move to my office. Three people are inside, two men and a woman, going through my stuff. Two of them are in police uniforms. The third is Brad Gillis, the detective. He flashes a paper at me. "A warrant to search the premises," he says.

"What the hell are you doing?" My disdain is sincere but also appropriate considering the number of people from my office surrounding me. Bennett Carey walks over and stands next to me.

"We're gonna need to look at your home as well," says Gillis. He is not the least bit intimidated by the crowd. He probably likes it, turning people's lives inside out in full public view.

"You showed up when you knew I was at the funeral," I say.

"We're pretty much done here," the detective replies. Not a reply at all, which is the detective's point. He's in charge, even within my law firm.

I look over the warrant—first time I've seen one—while the detective continues.

"We need to talk to you again, Mr. Soliday. If you'll come with me."

"We'll drive separately," Bennett says to Gillis. "We'll follow you."

"This is outrageous," I say. "This is Elliot Raycroft trying to make me and the senator look bad. Right, Detective?"

The detective smiles. "I wouldn't know about that," he says. "No, Mr. Soliday, it's not about making anyone look bad. It's about the fact that Dale Garrison was murdered. He didn't have a heart attack like you told everyone. He was strangled in his office, while you were the only one there."

I feel the blood rush to my face. "Ridiculous," I say, before Bennett takes my arm to shut me up.

12

"This is ridiculous," I say to the guy who enters the room. I'm at some police station on the near north side, sitting in a plain-looking room with Bennett Carey sitting next to me. We've been sitting here for a good forty-five minutes. Ben and I have gone back and forth about my saying anything in this interview, but I insist on my position. I have nothing to hide, I'm not clamming up. I remind him that he took the same position with me almost a week ago.

"Assistant County Attorney Daniel Morphew," the man says, extending a hand across the table. He has a square jaw, a rough, splotchy Irish face, the standard mustache, thick wavy gray hair. He seems perfectly calm, completely in control, and rather happy about that.

"Jon Soliday." I shake his hand. Bennett introduces himself as well, as my attorney, but it seems they already know each other, presumably from when Ben worked for the prosecutor's office.

"You work for Raycroft," I say.

Morphew considers me a second. "That's right."

"Tell Elliot something for me." Bennett places a hand on my arm but I yank it away. "Tell him if he thinks he can cast a public cloud on me, then release me quietly when there's no evidence to support the allegation, he's in a for a rude surprise. I'll make this whole thing about a county prosecutor who's doing Lang Trotter's dirty work."

"Jon," says Ben. "That's enough."

Daniel Morphew seems not the least bit affected by my outburst. He has with him a thin manila folder, which he fondles. "Are you willing to talk to me, Mr. Soliday?"

I exhale and try to calm my nerves. "Of course I am."

"Okay." Morphew reaches for the tape recorder resting in the center of the table. "I have to record this interview, that okay with you?"

"Whatever."

Morphew turns on the Record button on the tape player and states his name, my name, the date and time. "Also present is Mr. Soliday's counsel"—Morphew looks at Ben's card, just handed to him—"William Bennett Carey."

"I don't need a lawyer," I say. "This whole thing is ridiculous." Best to start the conversation on the proper note.

Morphew casts a look at Ben. "Are you asking Mr. Carey to leave?"

"No, he can stay." I take another deep breath. I need to keep my wits about me. "First of all, are we sure Dale didn't just have a heart attack or a stroke or something? I mean, he had to be in his late sixties and he had cancer."

Morphew purses his lips. He's considering what to reveal to me. His eyes narrow. "He was sixty-eight. He did have cancer. And he was strangled."

"Autopsy?" Ben asks.

"Yep. Cause of death"—Morphew reaches into his folder and holds out a paper—"asphyxiation by manual strangulation."

"Impossible," I say.

The prosecutor tilts his head. "How's that impossible?"

"Because I was the—" I stop myself.

"Because you were the only one in the entire suite of offices with the victim." He measures me a moment. "Right, Mr. Soliday?"

Ben reaches for me, but I respond anyway. "As far as I knew."

"You were at his office to discuss legal matters," says Morphew.

"Right."

"Involving?"

"Involving a mutual client," I say.

"Senator Grant Tully," says Morphew.

"That's privileged."

"Oh." The prosecutor smiles. "I must not have read that case. Mr. Soliday, since we're all lawyers here, let me tell you that it's not privileged. It was Senator Tully, right?"

"Next topic," says Bennett. "He's not discussing it."

Morphew doesn't have much leverage here. Attorney–client privilege or not, I have a Fifth Amendment right to silence. I could stop talking altogether, right now. "So he just dropped right in front of you?"

I clear my throat. Morphew knows what I told Detective Gillis at the time—that I left the office and came back after Dale called me on my cell phone. Seen through the prosecutor's eyes, it's a weak story. I was at the office, I stepped out, someone slipped in to strangle Dale, then I returned. My stomach calls out to me. I start to reconsider Bennett's advice. Morphew has me either way here. If I change my story, he's got me lying, one of the times. If I say the same story, he has me on tape, telling the tale that, the more I think about it, sounds pretty weak.

"You know that's not what happened," I say. "I was in his office and then I left. Dale called me on my cell phone and then I returned. I walked in and found him dead."

Morphew says nothing. The point is to keep me talking.

"Look, just match it up," I say. "You can confirm the phone call, the security guard downstairs saw me leave and return. So figure how I would have had time to kill him in that small window of time."

"I'm sure Mr. Morphew has checked the phone records for Dale Garrison's office," says Bennett, ostensibly to me but for Morphew's benefit. "I'm sure he has checked the phone records relating to your cell phone, too, Jon." Ben turns to the prosecutor. "So?"

Morphew has some years on Bennett; he was probably far higher up the chain at the prosecutor's office than Ben, who was assigned to a felony courtroom when he was there. I imagine Morphew is sufficiently experienced to know what he can give now and what he can withhold. His eyes move from Bennett's to mine. "Tell me what Garrison said to you."

"No." Bennett slices his hand on the table. "Your turn."

Morphew's eyebrows rise, as if the turning of the tables is nothing but an inconvenience. "I want to hear what Garrison said to you when he called you."

"He told me to come back up to his office," I answer, pulling my arm from Ben's grasp. "That's it."

"That's funny." Morphew draws up, as if he's ready for the main course. "Because the phone records show that Mr. Garrison never called you. There are no phone calls coming from that office during that period of time, or even close to it."

I look at Bennett, who manages a poker face. I hold my breath a moment, before the adrenaline rush. This isn't right. This doesn't make sense. I swallow hard.

"Who *did* call Jon's cell phone?" Ben asks.

"Good question, Counsel. One I was hoping Mr. Soliday could answer."

"It was Dale," I say.

"Jon." Bennett grabs my arm tightly. "Be quiet a moment." Then to Morphew: "What do the phone records say?"

Morphew's eye twitches. He waits a beat before answering. "It was a cell phone that belonged to a woman by the name of Joanne Souter. Anyone you know, Mr. Soliday?"

"No," I say.

"Right. Because Joanne Souter's cell phone was stolen from her purse earlier that day."

I raise my hands. "You got me."

"You figure Dale Garrison stole this woman's phone and used it to call you?" he asks. "Does that make sense?"

No. Of course that doesn't make sense. I raise a trembling hand to my face.

"It's clear to me that you didn't act alone," says the prosecutor. His hands are laid out on the table, a gesture of amicability. "Whoever was on the other end of that phone call was a part of this. That's who I want. So why don't we work this out here? Tell me who called you, and your attorney and I can work out a deal. Something that keeps you out of the electric chair."

I pop out of my chair. "There's nothing to tell. I didn't kill Dale. Somebody is setting me up. Can't you see that?"

Morphew points his index finger into the table. "Sit."

I look at Bennett, who nods solemnly. I take my seat again, still fuming, bordering on panic.

"Mr. Soliday is Senator Tully's chief counsel," says Bennett, "and a colleague of Dale Garrison's. Your story doesn't wash, Dan. He's not a murderer. And no one would believe he is."

Morphew looks at Ben a moment. Then his eyes move to me. There is a predatory look in his expression, an animal in the midst of the hunt. "Was someone blackmailing you, Mr. Soliday?"

I close my eyes. That letter. That goddamn letter.

"We're done here," Ben repeats.

Morphew slides a copy of the letter in front of me. "Was this in the top drawer of your desk, Mr. Soliday?"

I guess I'm the only one left who knows the secret that nobody knows. I think $250,000 should cover it. A month should be enough time. I wouldn't presume your income source, but I imagine if anyone could find a way to tap into the campaign fund without anyone noticing, you would. Or I suppose I could always just talk to the senator. Is that what you want? One month. Don't attempt to contact me about this. I will initiate all communications.

"You're the deputy treasurer for Citizens for Grant Tully," says Morphew. "With access to the campaign funds." The prosecutor waits for a response. "Was it Dale Garrison? Was he blackmailing you?"

I look at Bennett, who requires no prompting. "We are stopping this interview."

"Because if it wasn't Garrison," Morphew continues, "it would sure help you if you told me that right now."

Ben has hold of my arm. I am suddenly deflated.

"I was in Dale's office," I say. "And he just up and died while I was gone. I came back in right about the time the security guard was doing his nightly rounds and—"

"He wasn't doing a nightly round," says Morphew. "He was called up to the eighth floor. Someone said there was a disturbance in Dale's offices."

I feel a burning down my throat, into my stomach.

"What was the secret, Mr. Soliday?" the prosecutor asks. "The 'secret that nobody knows,' Mr. Soliday."

Bennett rises and forces me up with him. "We're leaving. Any future contact—"

"Mr. Carey, tell your client that if he can explain how this note didn't come from Dale Garrison, maybe he can avoid being arrested."

"We'll consider that, Counselor," Ben answers. "Now if we can go?"

Morphew stands as well. "*You* can go, Mr. Carey, if you'd like." The door opens, and Brad Gillis walks into the room, handcuffs dangling from his belt.

Panic spreads across Ben's face. "You don't speak to him," he says to Morphew and Gillis. Then to me: "Keep your mouth closed, Jon. We'll get you out as soon as possible."

I stand mute as Detective Gillis reads me my rights and places me in handcuffs.

"What's the 'secret that nobody knows'?" asks Morphew.

I ignore the question and move in to Ben's ear. "You better call the senator," I say.

JUNE
1979

13

Grant Tully's sporty new hatchback sails down the interstate. He drums the steering wheel along with the song on the radio, singing fearlessly as the wind of a midsummer night licks his hair. It makes me think of Shakespeare, and the fact that I will never have to read it again.

"Easy, Tru," I say. "They'll ticket you like anyone else." I say this because Grant Truman Tully—Tru to everyone who knows him—is the son of State Senator Simon Tully, a political heavyweight, a giant in our community. Tru has played on his family connection more than once, but out on the interstate it's state troopers, not local cops, and he's fair game to them. That never stopped Tru; I dare say nothing has ever stopped him. A typically fearless teenager with all of the answers but none of the questions.

"Tell me again where the hell we're going," I say.

Tru and I just graduated high school. We have these three months before we head to college—Ivy League for Truman, state university for me. The primary responsibility for a high school grad is to attend every party possible. There's a big blow-out tonight in the city, but Tru has talked me into leaving the state, driving forty-five minutes across the state line to a party in Summit County. Land of the smokestacks, an industrial town you can see from the towers in the city but which I've never visited.

The thought, I assume, is to get me away from my worries. My girlfriend of two years, Vivian, just ended things between us. She was headed west for school, what was the point, etc. So Tru, who has wanted me to unleash the "shackles" anyway, is taking it upon himself to find some fun for me this summer. I'm up for it, I guess.

Tru belches after a deep guzzle of his beer, which he places back between his legs. He is wearing a plaid oxford and shorts with loafers, no socks. "Rick's party," he says. "Well, it's not his party but he'll be there."

"Rick who?" I ask. "Do I know him?"

"Rick is all I know," he says. "They call him Ricochet. It's like a joke name."

I look at Tru. "Good friend of yours, I see."

"Rick's a good guy," says Tru. "I don't know his life history, okay? Chill out, Jonathan."

"There gonna be talent?" I ask. I'm speaking Tru's language. He's notoriously single, not a lady-killer but he has his way, the confidence and strut. Most of his relationships last shorter than a shower.

He flashes a smile. "Affirmative on the talent. The nice trailer-trash variety."

Tru takes an exit off the interstate. We're on the streets of Summit County now. Tru guns the accelerator. We cruise along what appears to be a tiny downtown. Nothing but dilapidated stores, a dry cleaners, a couple restaurants and bars, a grimy carry-out with the obligatory rusted-out sign, and potholes the size of craters.

Tru makes a wicked right-turn, throwing me in my seat. We drive down a residential street. All of the houses are ranches, nothing even two stories high until we see an apartment building on the end of the block. On the next one, cars are lined along the curbs. We are here.

Tru parks the car haphazardly and stops abruptly. He grabs a couple more beers from under the seat; he must have taken a six-pack and lined it up down there.

The house is third from the corner. This one is two stories, aluminum siding, black shutters on the windows. Four cars parked in the driveway. The noise of the stereo and a raucous crowd greets us from the street.

Tru walks up to the door confidently. He does everything confidently.

I'm a good sidekick for him. I hold my own but have none of his charisma. I get the good grades, play the right sports, and associate with him. That's enough.

Grant Truman Tully doesn't ring the doorbell, he just walks in. The room is filled with people mingling and talking and laughing. The stereo is at full tilt, blasting angry guitar-driven music. A haze of smoke lingers above their heads. Some are celebrating their release from the school year. That is the pretense for the party, at least. But from the look of the age of these people—mostly late teens and early twenties—I imagine that the majority of these people are no longer concerned with school. It's not exactly a diverse crowd in the conventional sense. An all-white party. Wardrobe is mostly T-shirts and blue jeans. These people live in a middle-class community not entirely different from my own, except that I live in the city and they live in a town of industry whose best days are behind it.

We draw our share of attention. We are certainly the first representatives of the preppy-city-boys club, and I have a good feeling we will be the only ones. Typically, Tru is unfazed. I follow him through the crowd, past a group passing a joint on a dingy couch, a couple of guys who appear to be squaring off in one corner, into the kitchen. We raid the fridge for some beers but find nothing better than the lukewarm imports we carried in, again separating ourselves from the pack. As Tru is taking his first swig, he makes a noise and brings the bottle from his lips. "There he is," he says.

His friend Rick, I presume. The guy looks our age, seventeen or eighteen. A mess of dirty blond hair, thick, dark eyebrows, narrow rounded shoulders covered with a black heavy-metal T-shirt. A cigarette dangles from his lips. He gives a sour smile and holds out a hand for Tru.

"Hello, Truman," he says. "Let's make some trouble."

Rick navigates us through the party; I find myself squinting through the thick air that reeks of tobacco and marijuana. We reach a couple hanging in the corner. A girl with her boyfriend. He is completely bald, an egg-shaped head with a thick neck, a cigarette tucked above his ear. He is wearing a beer T-shirt with the sleeves cut off, exposing freckled arms that are sizeable and well defined. One of his hands is parked in the back pocket of the girl's cutoff denim jeans, the other propped against the wall as he hovers over her. They are laughing about something.

"Lyle," says Rick.

Lyle and Rick. I'm more interested in the girl's name.

"This is Gina."

They turn to us. Lyle eyes us suspiciously.

"This is my guy Tru," Rick tells them.

"This is Jon," Tru says, nodding in my direction.

We salute each other with tips of the head. I pay particular attention to Gina. She is the best-looking girl in the room, though that probably isn't saying much. She has bleached-blond hair that falls to her shoulders, perfectly round eyes with long lashes but too much dark mascara. Full lips. Long, lean, tan legs and a tight white undershirt that highlights an impressive chest. Two beers already in me, my hormones are in overdrive.

She brings a cigarette to her lips and blows the smoke upward. "Nice to meet you guys," she says. She appraises us as Rick and Lyle talk.

"So let's go up," says Rick.

"Grab some cold ones first," Lyle says.

I follow the crew back to the kitchen for beers, then to the stairs. Tru grabs Rick by the arm and whispers into his ear. Rick turns back and says, "Nah, man, later." Tru holds out his arms and says, "What the hell am I doing here?" Rick pushes him gently and heads up the stairs. I don't inquire; I'm still a little off-balance from meeting Gina.

We go to a bedroom that belongs, I assume, to whoever is throwing the party. A stereo rests in the corner, albums scattered haphazardly about. The walls are plastered with posters of either rock bands or women in bikinis. The closet is overflowing with dirty clothes.

Lyle goes over to the stereo to fish for a record. Rick walks into the bedroom last, carrying a couple of chairs from some other room upstairs. Tru and I take the chairs, Rick sits next to Gina on the bed. The room smells like mine, like dirty laundry, a faint odor of mildew. The lighting is poor, a three-pronged light fixture in the center of the ceiling with only one bulb operating, covered by a dingy globe.

Rick fishes in his pocket and pulls out a lighter. Then he goes back into his pocket and removes a joint. He sticks it between his lips and nods to Lyle by the stereo. "Nothing mellow," he instructs, the joint bobbing in his teeth as he speaks.

Gina pops open the bottle of beer and takes a drink. Her eyes watch me as she takes the pull. I feel a stirring inside me.

Rick lights the marijuana cigarette and inhales, gripping the joint in his fingers as he holds his breath. He blows out and hands the joint to Tru. Tru follows suit and, holding his breath, hands the joint to me.

Not the first time I've smoked pot, but it's up there. I'm not much for smoke of any kind, have never in my life tried a normal cigarette. But Gina is watching me, and what the hell, I'm on vacation.

I inhale deeply as the lighter burns the marijuana cigarette. The smoke is bitter and hot in the back of my throat. I grimace but hold it in as long as I can. My exhale is more like a cough. My throat burns, my eyes water.

Tru hands me an open bottle. "Chaser, my friend."

I hand the joint to Gina, who smiles and says "Thank you" in a way that probably would be described as courteous and nothing more, but which holds a more provocative inflection for me. I somehow enjoy the fact that her lips are touching the cigarette after mine.

"Breathe it in," she says to me. "Then swallow, like there's nothing in your mouth at all." She lights the joint and inhales. Slowly, she blows out smoke over my head. She hands it back to me. "*Then* blow out."

I'm not exactly ready for the second try, but there's no way I'm passing this up. I light the joint, inhale and swallow, like she said, and hold the smoke in my mouth.

"Easy, right?" she says. Her eyes are slightly bloodshot from the alcohol. She smiles lightly.

I smile back as I blow out the smoke. My gaze falls on her crossed legs. Her cutoff denim shorts leave little to the imagination, but plenty enough for me. "Easy," I say.

Lyle has settled on heavy-metal music I don't recognize. He has it turned up too loud, but lowers it after protest from the group. He pushes himself off the carpet with his muscular arms and sits next to Gina. His presence is like a cold shower, but a guy can fantasize, can't he?

"So what brings a couple city boys out here?" Gina asks me.

"Getting *away* from the city," says Tru. That's close enough. Tru is a pretty heavy partier, but he likes to keep a low profile in the city when it comes to using drugs. People can talk, and he worries about that sort of thing. It makes me think that Tru, separated from the gossip out here in Summit County, is ready for a big night. It also occurs to me that there is twenty miles of driving ahead of us when the night ends. But Tru is right when he always tells me that I worry too much. I do worry. I have little to complain about with my life, but still, I don't seem to travel on the same road as Tru. He is as carefree as they come, doesn't sweat the details, and manages to attract the popular crowd. Hell, he *is* the popular crowd. He doesn't have spectacular looks, little athletic ability, but he is blessed with this confidence, a certain recklessness that draws people. Me, I have above-average grades and a decent sense, but I'm not destined for greatness. I'm not one of those guys who gets out front. I can walk into a room without anyone noticing. I can't tell a story. I don't turn heads. I am in the middle in every sense of the word, and it isn't any easier watching Tru glide through life.

But Tru is right. I won't worry. I watch Gina grab Lyle's bicep, whisper something to him but shoot a glance in my direction. I have caught her eye. It won't mean anything at the end of the day, but she noticed me, not Tru. I accept the joint and take my third toke. For once in my life, I won't worry.

14

All five of us are on the bed. Rick is leaning against the wall, sitting Indian style, singing with some angry song. Punk music, I think. I'm in the middle, between Rick on one side and Tru on the other. Lyle and Gina are lying horizontally on the bed. Their feet are dangling off. Lyle looks over at us and says something like, "The preppy boys are getting stoned." I laugh surprisingly hard. Tru calls Lyle "egghead" and all of us laugh. Gina asks me if I'm ticklish and I lie, I say no. She tickles my foot and it doesn't tickle. So I guess I wasn't lying. Rick pronounces the third joint "dead" and flicks the stub over Gina and Lyle to the floor. I try to follow its flight pattern but I lost it. I lost it. Maybe that was the fourth joint. Lyle says he has to take a piss and he gets up. Rick tells him to get more beers. I don't know if Lyle answered. He may have but I didn't hear it. Gina is looking at me again. Her eyes are really round. Her body is unbelievable. I realize that I have an erection but I'm not embarrassed. I kind of laugh. Gina laughs, too, and her white T-shirt creeps up a little. I can almost see her navel. I really want to see it but I can't. Gina gets up and walks over by the stereo. There is a beer there. I didn't know that. But she gets up and I watch her butt move in those jeans-shorts, and I think she knows I'm watching. We all are watching. Tru leans into me and whispers, "We gotta get rid of Lyle," which makes me laugh. Tru says, "She wants you, Jonathan." I guess he means Gina. I say, "True, that's true."

Then I point at Tru and say, "*That's* Tru." I laugh, and Tru laughs. I think he's laughing at me. Rick asks Tru, "What's your major?" and he laughs. I'm pretty sure Rick isn't going to college. Tru says, "English." I say, "You haven't learned English yet?" and everyone laughs. So I keep going. I say, "What do you speak now? Russian?" Rick says, "German?" Then Rick says, "How's it going, Adolf?" Gina is laughing so hard that beer spills out of her mouth. She is still standing by the bed, and she puts her hand over her mouth, but some of the beer spills onto her shirt. Rick lights up another joint. I'm laughing pretty hard but I still manage to take a drag on the joint. It's easy. Just suck in and swallow, like there's no smoke at all. Then just sit there awhile and then blow out. I do it and bow my head to Gina, because she's the one who showed me how. But when my head comes back up it's kind of woozy, and I can't see Gina too well.

What time is it? Gina is sitting next to me. One leg is tucked under her. It's just the two of us. I ask, "Where did everyone go?" She laughs, kind of gently. She says, "They went for a score." I say, "What's a score?" She laughs again and nudges me. She says, "They went to get some blow." I say, "Oh." She says, "So what's your full name?" I say, "Jon Soliday." She says, "Nice to meet you, Jon Soliday. I'm Gina Mason." I say, "Tell me about yourself." She shrugs her shoulders and the bottom of her T-shirt raises up. She says, "I'm a waitress. Live with my little brother and mom." I say, "What does your mom do?" She says, "She drinks." I laugh but Gina doesn't. She says, "She's a waitress like me. She works the midnight shifts. She drinks during the day." I say, "How old's your brother?" She says, "Eight." I say, "Is he home by himself?" She says, "No, he has a babysitter until I get home." I say, "You're not leaving, are you?" She says, "No, the sitter will spend the night if I'm late." I say, "Oh," because I can't think of anything better. She says, "Why, do you want me to leave?" I say, "No, I want you to stay." She smiles. Then she says, "Tell me about *your*self." I say, "Nothing to tell. Going to the state university this fall." She says, "What's your major?" I tell her, "Poli sci." She says, "What's that?" I say, "Fuck if I know." We both laugh. Then I say, "It's about politics." And she says, "Are you gonna be a politician?"

And I say, "Sure, why not?" She moves a little closer to me. Why the hell can't I be a politician or some big shot? Tru isn't the only one who's smart. I can figure it out, too. Gina says, "I'd vote for you." She puts her hand on my foot. My mouth is really dry. I try to swallow but there is no saliva. I say, "I'd vote for you, too." She makes a face. She says, "What the heck am *I* ever gonna run for?" I say, "You could run for anything you want. It's a free country." She says, "Yeah, right," and she takes a hit from the joint. "So Lyle's your boyfriend, huh?" I say. She eyes me. Smoke drifts from her mouth. She makes a perfectly round "o" with her mouth and blows the smoke out. After the smoke evaporates, she asks me, "Why?" I say, "I don't know. If he wasn't, I might ask you out some time." She smiles and says, "It's a free country." She holds her stare on me. Then she jumps off the bed and goes to the stereo. She says, "I hate this music." She pulls the album off the record player. I think about getting up but I can't, not very easily. Then the three guys all walk back into the room. Lyle, Rick, and Truman. Lyle tosses me a beer and I take a long drink because my throat is dry and hot. Lyle is talking to Gina. Political science is a good major for starters, my dad said. He said a liberal arts program is a good solid background. Maybe he was just being nice, because I didn't get into the business program at the university anyway, so I went for liberal arts. Poli sci seemed as good as anything else. Tru says, "The snowman cometh." I laugh for no reason. Rick drops a mirror on the floor and then I understand. That's why Tru wanted to come all the way out here, to do some coke. Rick is his supplier. He doesn't want to do it back in the city, where people might whisper. Then Tru and Rick and Lyle and Gina sit down on the floor around the mirror. Rick says, "C'mon, Jonny." Tru says, "Only if he wants to." Then he says to me, "You don't have to, Jon." I look over at Gina. She pats the floor next to her. So I get up and sit down next to her. She looks over at her boyfriend, Lyle, who is busy opening up the cocaine from a little packet. Gina puts her hand on my leg a second. It seems like she's running it up my leg. But then she moves it, just as Lyle turns around.

What time is it? Lyle says the "eight-ball's finished." That's the second one done. Lyle asks if there's any more. Tru says, "No way, man." I'm more awake now. It's weird, way weird. I'm all foggy but I'm wide awake. Tru's on the bed, talking to Lyle. They're whispering. I can't hear what they're saying. Gina left a minute ago. Or I think it was a minute, it could have been half an hour. She smiled at me when she walked out. I'm on my feet now. Rick is holding up Tru, helping him walk out of the room. Lyle leaves ahead of us and goes down the stairs. Rick says, "The night's young, Jonathan," and he grabs my shoulder and shakes it. I don't really care what we do because I'm wide awake. It's weird because I'm wide awake but I'm confused. But I hope whatever we do includes Gina. We're walking down the stairs now. I have to hold on to the railing. The stairs are shifting on me, coming in and out of focus. My legs feel like they aren't attached to my body. When I get downstairs, Gina is not there. There aren't that many people down here at all. Maybe ten. Maybe twenty. I don't know. The floor is sticky and smells of alcohol. It reminds me of the night Tru and I spent at his brother's college fraternity before his brother died. The room is not fully lit, it's sort of a hazy lighting. I turn behind me and keep turning until I've gone in a full circle. Rick puts a hand on me and laughs. He slaps me on the back. Tru says, "Let's go!"

We're walking to the car. We're splitting up. Tru is going to a different car; he's being held up. I yell to him, what's going on, Tru? He says he's going home but to have fun. I tell him to come along but he just waves me off. Somebody grabs my shirt from behind and I almost fall over but I keep my balance, and I get into a car. It's not Tru's car.

Where the hell are we? I get out of the car and start to walk up the lawn. But it's not my house. "No, Jonny, go around. What the fuck did I tell you?" That's right. I'm supposed to go to the window on the side. I knock on the window like it's the door. I start to walk away and then I'm walking in a circle and then I walk back up to the window and look in. It's Gina. She's sleeping in her bed. I knock on the window again and her head rises off the pillow and she looks out at me. I wave at her. She looks at me for a while and then she walks over to the window. She pulls up the window and says, "Jon?" I say, "Yeah." She helps me climb into her room. It's not easy, I almost fall backward into her yard, then I almost fall forward onto her bedroom floor. It's dark in here but light enough that I can make out that face. She says, "You sure know how to make a girl feel wanted." I try to say something to her, to tell her that I want her very much, but I can't find the words so I just bring my hand to her face, then her hair, and show her.

15

The sunlight can be your worst enemy when you're working on a roof, slapping black tar. By noon, I'm over halfway through a workday that began at five bells. The sun is at its peak, raining heat down on a beaten body.

I spent all of yesterday in bed, following the all-night binge in Summit County. Most of that night was a fog. I spent Sunday vomiting and trying unsuccessfully to convince my parents that I wasn't hitting the sauce the night before. Christ, I don't even remember how we got home. Literally. The last thing I recall vividly is climbing out of Gina Mason's window after staying for more than a few minutes and falling back into the car. I woke up in the morning with the scent of Gina's perfume on my shirt, which I slept in. However glorious the smell, it was drowned out by the smoke and alcoholic odors that infested my clothing. First thing I did, however painful, was strip my clothes and hit the shower. The shower water struck me like acid, especially on my knee, where I had a pretty ugly scrape, source unknown.

Lunch break. I need liquids badly. First time it's taken more than twenty-four hours to recover from a party. I take the ladder down to the ground and find two men. One of them is coming out of the elementary school where I'm working. The other one is standing there, awaiting me. They are in police uniforms, brown ones, not the blue ones local cops wear.

"Jonathan Soliday?" The taller of the two men is talking. He's bulging from his uniform, thick biceps, arms on his belt, reflective sunglasses. The other guy is black, shorter, a bit of a stomach, arms folded.

"Yeah," I say. I look at the car in the parking lot. An all-white sedan with gold lettering.

"We're sheriff's deputies, Mr. Soliday," he says. "Some people in Summit County want to talk to you."

"What about?" I'm squinting in the sunlight, acting clueless.

"How old are you, son?"

"Seventeen."

The deputy grimaces. He is disappointed. He waves a finger at me. "Turn around, son. We're taking you into custody. We're transporting you to Summit County."

"Why?" I plead, not moving. "What's the charge?"

"Turn around right now, Mr. Soliday, and hold out your hands behind you."

I comply. The deputy grips my hand and places a handcuff over my wrist. "The charge is murder, son," he says.

16

"Mis-ter Soliday." Tru sings the words over the phone.

"Grant—"

"I don't know how you managed, my brother—"

"Listen."

"—but I hope it was worth it."

"Grant, shut up and listen to me. Just listen. I've been arrested."

"What now?"

"Just listen—" I lower my voice an octave. I'm using the pay phone in a holding cell in the County Sheriff's Department. "Gina Mason—that girl?"

Silence, at first. Grant can't like a connection between law enforcement and Gina. "The girl from the other night," he says cautiously.

"Right. She died. She's dead."

"She's dead and they think *you* had something to do—"

"They think I *killed* her."

A short burst of laughter from Grant. Then a pause. "Are you putting me on?"

"No, I swear—"

"Where are you, Jon?"

"I'm at the sheriff's office, Grant. They're sending me to Summit County for questioning."

"Holy *fucking*—" A heavy exhale from Tru's end. "This is for real, isn't it?"

"It's pretty damn real, all right."

"Did you make it to Gina's that night?"

"Yeah. I was there. I went—"

"Wait, Jon. Don't say anything else. Hang on. Just—just hang on a second, okay? Let me think."

I turn back and look at one of the officers, who is probably listening to what I'm saying.

"Okay. Here's what we're gonna do. We're gonna get you a lawyer. Right now. A lawyer."

"But I don't know any—"

"Dammit, Jon, shut up a second. My dad knows a hundred of 'em. We'll get one down there right now."

I groan. "My parents are gonna die over this."

"Your parents don't need to be involved. If you have a lawyer, I don't think you need your parents."

"You sure about that?"

"I'm not sure of much of anything right now, Jon. We'll have a lawyer down there right away."

17

I sit as idly as possible for two hours, awaiting the lawyer the Tullys are sending. I struggle to put the puzzle together, the whispers of memories from two nights ago.

You probably shouldn't be here, Gina said.

You want me to leave?

You can stay awhile.

What's your boyfriend going to think?

He's not really my boyfriend. And he doesn't own me.

The rest is bits and pieces. Our clothes off, first on the bed, then falling to the floor. Time is, was indecipherable, but I think in my intoxication I held out pretty long. It wasn't like other times, awkward and uncertain. It was full throttle, passionate, hair-grabbing, nails on the back. When I was done, I collapsed on top of her. I think we fell asleep there, on the floor. That's the last thing I remember, save falling back through the window at some point, onto the grass outside her bedroom.

But she wasn't asleep. She was dead.

I shudder at the thought, but only as I might if I were watching a grotesque scene in a movie. I am numb. I didn't know she was dead. I don't feel connected to it. That doesn't stop the tears—it hasn't stopped them for the last hour or so. But I think the tears are for myself, not Gina.

Footsteps. An officer approaches my cell. "You're getting out," he says with little animation.

My jaw drops, but I keep silent as the deputy unlocks the door and leads me to a different room. A man is standing there.

"Jon Soliday?" he asks. "Jeremiah Erwin. I'm your attorney." Mr. Erwin is a tall, grave man, a heavily lined face, salt-and-pepper hair. He is wearing a black pinstriped suit, white shirt, bright red tie.

I take his hand. "The Tullys called you?"

"They did, yes. I'm taking you home."

I take a step back, momentarily taking in a surge of elation. "I'm free to go? I thought I was under arrest."

Mr. Erwin shakes his head. "No, they just took you into custody to deliver you to Summit County. No one's charging you with anything at this point. You're just wanted for questioning."

"So I have to go there?"

"Let's get out of here first." Mr. Erwin places a hand on my back and escorts me from the station. I take a look back at the officers, my captors, but no one is watching me leave.

"I've spoken with the authorities there," he says as we walk outside, the sun beaming in my face. "I've informed them that you won't be providing any testimony today. We'll agree to a meeting down the road, perhaps."

"What are they saying?" I ask.

Mr. Erwin doesn't look at me, just keeps his eyes focused on his path. "A young woman named Gina Mason was found dead in her home. They say you visited her the night before she was found dead. They think you raped and killed her." He turns to me. "Just because they say it doesn't make it true."

I fight through the nausea and try to pull anything else out of that night. The rest of our short trip to the car is in silence. Mr. Erwin drives a Chevrolet, a luxury model, and the leather seats are quite a relief from the hard cement in the holding cell.

"Where are we going?" I ask, once we're on the road.

"To the Tullys. We need to have a conversation." He looks over at me. "You and Grant need to have one, too."

Grant is waiting for me at his home, at the threshold of the door. He's dressed more formally than usual, his Sunday best—a starched cream shirt open at the collar, nice trousers. His eyes are horribly bloodshot, his hair out of place, his face stained from the same tears that licked my face. He steps out of his house and greets me with an arm around my shoulder and a tremble to his lip. I stifle any overflowing emotion and maintain a solemn expression.

The Tully residence is not necessarily what you'd expect to be the home of a powerful family like that of Senator Simon Tully. It's a nonde-script, two-story house, half an acre of surrounding lawn, simple land-scaping in the front with shrubs tucked in a bed of wood chips. That says a lot about the Tully family, or at least about Senator Simon Tully. He is neither flashy nor loud, but rather a quiet man, deadly serious, a man who elevates loyalty to the level of familial love.

I walk in with Grant but don't see the senator or Grant's mother. "I'll be in here," says Jeremiah Erwin to Grant, nodding toward the den near the front door.

Grant pats my back. "Let's relax a minute and talk about this," he says.

The living room is empty. I sit on the couch. Grant brings in a glass of soda and sits next to me.

Grant clears his throat and keeps his eyes cast on the floor. His hands rub together. "Mr. Erwin wants to hear your story," he says. "So we need to get it clear."

"I don't really *have* a story," I say. "There's not much to tell when your memory is a black hole."

Grant sighs. He struggles a moment, finally opens his hands. "Tell me what you *do* remember, Jon."

I close my eyes. "I went there. I went with one of those guys. Lyle or Rick."

"Lyle," says Grant. "Must have been. Rick took me home."

"Okay, Lyle then. So I went into her house. Her window, actually."

"She let you in?"

"Yeah. And we—you know." I wave my finger in a circle.

Grant grimaces. "Yeah? All the way?"

"Well—yeah."

Grant grabs a pillow from the couch, like he wants to throw it.

"I left behind evidence," I say. "That's what bothers you."

"They'll be able to prove it was you." He returns the pillow to the couch.

"Well, the sex part, yeah, it *was* me."

"Where was Lyle?"

"In the car," I answer. This seems confusing to Grant. "I mean, I assume he was in the car. But now that I think about it, why was Lyle dropping me off so I could have sex with his girlfriend?"

Grant allows for the contradiction with a nod of the head. "I think 'girlfriend' is a little strong. Anyway, that's my fault, Jon. I bought the—the stuff that night—and Lyle owed me one. I asked him what he thought of Gina, he didn't seem to think too much of her, so I said would it be okay if you hooked up with her at some point." He smiles apologetically. "I didn't mean *that night*."

"So Lyle drives me to Gina's house as a payback for free coke. Jesus."

"So then what, Jon? After you two got it on?"

"I don't know. We were done, I fell on top of her. I think I passed out. Then I woke up and got out of there, I guess."

"But you don't remember."

"No," I concede.

"What about her? Gina?"

"I don't know. I don't!" I chew on my lip. "I—you know, when I left, she was out. Asleep. I didn't wake her up or anything. I just left."

I burst into tears again, my throat choking. Again, I can't pinpoint the source. Am I scared or remorseful?

Grant studies me. My collapse has emboldened him. "Okay." His voice is surprisingly strong. "What did you say to Lyle?"

"I have no idea, Grant. I barely remember leaving out her window. I think probably Lyle helped me."

"Lyle," Grant mumbles to himself. "Lyle, Lyle, Lyle." He runs a hand over his face. "Wonder what *he's* saying about all this."

I ask Grant if Lyle's been arrested or questioned. He shrugs. He couldn't know any more than me at this point. "But we need to find out what Lyle's saying," he adds.

"Well." I roll my neck. My shoulders are as tight as they've ever felt. "I don't suppose we can just call him."

"*You* can't, Jon. You have to keep your mouth shut."

Grant's right about that. I am probably the last person who should reach out to that guy. But Grant shouldn't, either. Besides, it's not like we even know this guy.

"A guy like Lyle," says Grant, "he'll probably say anything to keep himself clean."

"I don't know." I drop my head. "I don't know what to do."

I feel a hand on my shoulder. "Let me take care of Lyle," says Grant. "You've got other things to think about. Or I should say, remember."

"What does that mean?"

Grant brings one leg under another, propping himself up on the couch. His hands are together in prayer. "It means, Jon, that you can't tell the police that you have no memory of anything happening. If the cops are saying you raped her and killed her, you can't say, 'We had sex but I don't remember the details.' And you can't say, 'I don't know if she was alive or dead when I left.'" Grant reaches for my arm. "You have to say you had sex but it was with her consent. And she was definitely alive when you left."

"Jesus Christ." The words, even stated in my favor, bring a crisis to my bowels. I'm suddenly claustrophobic, my eyes darting about the room. "Did I force myself on her? Did I—did I rape—"

"No." Grant's voice is calm but firm. "That's not you, drunk or not. This girl was digging your act. She let you in, didn't she?"

"Yeah. That part I remember."

"All right, then." He waves a hand. "No way you raped her."

"Then how did she die?"

He shrugs. "We don't know. Did the cops say anything to you?"

"Nope."

"Then we'll have to find that out, too."

"They—" My eyes drift to the ceiling. "They're saying I forced myself on her, she struggled, and I killed her. That must be what they're saying."

"A lot of things will happen before they say that," says Grant. "They'll have to do an autopsy, right? They'll have to have a witness."

"Lyle," I mumble.

"I'll handle Lyle." Grant exhales slowly. "And we'll see about the autopsy."

"What does that mean?" I ask. "How will we—" I freeze. Grant doesn't respond or look at me. This is something, I suddenly realize, that will never be fully explained to me.

"Your dad," I say.

Grant nods solemnly.

"Your dad knows people out there? In Summit County?"

"My dad knows *everybody*." Grant does not say this with affection.

"I don't know about this." I sigh. "I don't want to get sent to some juvenile hall or anything, but why don't I just tell them what happened and see what comes? I'll tell them that I would never have forced myself on Gina. I liked her. And there's no way I killed her."

Grant's look could freeze the sun. His face reddens. He wets his lips before starting. "First of all," he says slowly, his voice trembling, "they'll try you as an adult if it's murder. You could get who-knows-*how*-many years in a penitentiary. *Second* of all, my friend, if you tell them you don't remember things, then you can't rule out the possibility that you *did* rape her, and that you *did* kill her. Telling them 'it wouldn't be like me' is not a defense. Especially when you were drunker than I've ever seen you."

He pats his chest harshly. His eyes have filled, not from rage but regret. "This is my fault, Jon." His face contorts, and more tears follow. But he continues through the pain. "I got you mixed up with these people. I got you doing drugs you've never done in your life. And then I left you. This is my fault, and I'm going to clear this up. I'm not going to let anything happen to you. I'm not going to lose you, too—" He catches himself. "I'm not going to let that happen."

Grant's talking about his older brother, Clayton Tully. Clay died in a head-on car accident three years ago. He was in the middle of an Ivy

League education, an intelligent, clean-cut, ambitious twenty-year-old with classic good looks. Grant absolutely idolized him. In many senses, Clay completely overshadowed Grant. Far superior grades, a better athlete, much more involved in the political circles.

Clay did a lot for his little brother. Some of it was the obvious stuff, counsel and encouragement. But it was more than that. Clay sheltered Grant from the weight of his father's expectations. Grant told me once that his father planned on handing his senatorial seat to Clay when the right time came. It was something Clay wanted. It is not something Grant wants. Grant is more of a free spirit, a rebel, someone who has taken advantage of the golden path he's been given but who doesn't want to cash in. I don't know what Grant plans for his future, but a few years ago, I'd have pegged him for someone who would be, in any real sense, nothing more than the brother of Senator Clayton Tully and the son of the former senator, Simon Tully. That would probably be enough for a good living. Grant would con his way through school, get a law degree, join a prestigious law firm, and have a boatful of clients looking to get on Clayton's good side. He would have an easy life.

But since Clay died, Grant seems to have been elevated to his brother's spot. His dad has never said the words to him, but Grant thinks his father now wants *him* to succeed him in the senate. And Grant has never said the words, but I know it terrifies him. He lost more than an older brother in that car accident. He lost the life he wanted.

I remember that year, after Clay died. Grant hit the party scene even harder, started in on cocaine for the first time. He'd deny it to me, his more clean-cut buddy, but he seemed to be bordering on an addiction. His grades went downhill—they weren't too spectacular to begin with—and he dropped high school baseball, where he'd had some talent. It's only in the last year, really, that Grant has truly rebounded. I think the thought of leaving home for college has energized him, the unconscious feeling that when he's away from his father, his life is his own.

The look on Grant's face at this moment reminds me of his expression after Clay's funeral. A combination of pain and disbelief and despondence.

"But you have to do your part, too," says Grant. "You have to tell them that Gina wanted to have sex with you, and you have to tell them that when you left, she waved goodbye to you with a smile on her face." He gathers himself, leaving aside the emotion and focusing on the task at hand. "And let me take care of the rest."

18

The office of the Summit County Prosecuting Attorney is located in a three-story, shiny new building that stands out on an avenue otherwise full of downtrodden structures. The symbol of justice in a humble community.

I take the dozen marble steps almost arm-in-arm with Grant. On either side of us are Grant's dad, the senator, and Mr. Erwin, our lawyer. The pitched, pillared entranceway, the large state and county flags, the tiled hallways are quite successful in intimidating me.

Now we sit in the waiting room of a large office. Grown-ups in work shirts and ties hustle in and out with briefcases and files. They are holding more than papers. They are holding people's lives in their hands. I try to steady my heartbeat by playing with my tie. Grant and I are in shirts and ties with slacks, on order of Mr. Erwin. Our attorney is in full lawyer gear, a dark pinstriped suit and a bright red tie. Senator Tully wears an oxford and khakis.

Grant is sitting formally, attentively. There is no contact between his father and him. Simon Tully has a leg crossed and hands resting comfortably in his lap. I have no idea what conversations have taken place between father and son over this incident. I imagine that Senator Tully has many thoughts in his head, including adverse publicity for himself and for the son who one day will take his place in the state legislature. I do not envision many warm feelings toward me dancing in his head.

A man walks out and looks at the four of us. "Mr. Erwin?" he asks.

Our lawyer stands. "Jeremiah Erwin," he says. "Counsel for Mr. Tully and Mr. Soliday."

The prosecutor is tall and wiry, dark hair with shots of gray, a thick chin with tired eyes. "Gary Degnan," he says. He looks casually dressed by comparison, a cotton shirt with a tie pulled down and collar open. It brings me a measure of relief.

"Mr. Tully first," he says.

Grant briefly grabs my arm before rising. Jeremiah Erwin holds out an arm and follows Grant and the prosecutor out of the room. Grant is a witness because he was with me at the party. He can't tell them anything about the rape and murder, but he can tell them about the events before we parted company. What this means, essentially, is that he'll tell them that Gina Mason was highly intoxicated and quite affectionate toward me.

Now it's just Senator Simon Tully and me, each staring ahead. We haven't spoken one-on-one since the incident. His silence, his complete lack of acknowledgment of my presence, is a fitting rebuke from him. He is not the type to berate. He is not quick to anger, and when it comes, it does not take the form of raised voices and flailing arms, but of that patented glare. Even when he slows down, when he's out of the spotlight, he is understated. His sense of humor is dry, a cutting remark with a straight face, rarely a smile. He always seems to be calculating, plotting one step ahead. It's a life where everyone genuflects, where everyone calls him "Senator." Even Grant calls him "sir" more often than "Dad."

Watching Grant and his father together has always been a little strange, more so since Grant's older brother died in the car accident. Grant is no longer the rebellious younger brother who would come around eventually, following in his elder brother's footsteps. He is now heir to the throne, and after a grace period to mourn the death of Clayton, Senator Tully became more demanding of Grant. Grant has become more involved in politics, working on campaigns—anything from handing out fliers door-to-door to organizing groups of workers to making phone calls. Doesn't matter what the person stands for or where they come from, only that they're Democrats. Now, Grant can throw out names of the precinct captain here or the county commissioner there faster than I can name the starting lineup for our pro basketball team.

I check the clock in the room, confirm with a glance at my own watch. Twenty-eight minutes since Grant left.

"Your parents are good people, Jon." I turn to Simon Tully, who has broken the silence. He is still looking forward, one leg swung over the other. "They deserve better than this."

"Yes, sir." I broke down last night and told my parents the whole thing. I couldn't evade them with more lies. I sat in our living room while my parents sat expectantly, after I'd announced that I had something to tell them. My plan had been to hold back some, limit the story to intoxication on liquor only. No parent is surprised that a child experiments with booze. But I told them everything, except that I left Grant out of the part about cocaine. I told the story chronologically; it was not until I was in full swing that I had the courage to ride the avalanche down to the bottom—that I am a suspect in Gina Mason's death.

There is no proper reaction to such things. My parents responded initially with anger, until they saw my tears, and then they listened with a desperate anticipation as they wondered why I was confessing this to them. My father collapsed at the finale; my mother rushed to me and held me tight. We talked for another hour before my father called Grant's father. His voice was initially heated—he was no doubt put off by Senator Tully's complicity in hiding this from my parents—but his tone eased as Senator Tully laid out the whats and hows of what would come next. In the end, I'm sure, my father was grateful that we had such a powerful ally.

"You had a good talk with Jeremy?" the senator asks me. He means Mr. Erwin, I assume. We went over my story for hours. Well, kind of. We spoke in generalities once we got to the part about the events at Gina's house. I think Mr. Erwin was tipped off that I had a memory deficiency at that stage, and this seemed to trouble him. So we danced around it, speaking in hypotheticals. He said we could "fill in the details" later.

"Yes, sir," I say to the senator.

Grant's father breathes in slowly. "Did you understand everything?"

"Yes, sir."

"He's a good lawyer. He's going to take care of you."

"Thank you, sir."

"I promised your father I would take care of this, and I will."

"I can't tell you how much I appreciate this."

Senator Tully gives an emphatic nod. End of discussion.

"Senator?"

"Yes, Jon."

"I'm very sorry."

He considers what I've said. He wets his lips and pauses a beat. "Don't apologize to me, Jon. You should be apologizing to your mother and father. And it should be in more than just words." He turns to me for the first time. "Make your parents proud. Work as hard as you can in college and don't get caught up in this kind of thing ever again. Do you understand?"

My eyes fill. I look away to the dilute the emotion. "Yes, sir."

I can feel his eyes still on me. But he says nothing more.

Grant returns with Mr. Erwin. His face is ashen, but he walks with his head up. He avoids my eyes and takes the seat next to me, next to his father.

Jeremiah Erwin waves to me with a cupped hand. "Jon."

We walk through a corridor with white walls and tile, a sterile environment. I am in a dream. One night, I take a chance with some drugs, meet up with a gorgeous woman, and the next thing I know, my life has come to strolling a corridor with a defense attorney. One night, and a young lady is dead.

"No talking today," Mr. Erwin says. "You don't open your mouth."

"Okay." We pass a couple of men in suits walking with a purpose. "Did Grant talk to them?"

"Grant did his part," he says. "But your situation is different. With you, we give a statement later. Just let me do the talking."

We stop at a conference room where the prosecutor, Mr. Degnan, is sitting with a yellow notepad flipped open. He nods to us when we enter. "Have a seat," he says. He extends his hand to me. "My name is Gary Degnan, Mr. Soliday."

I take his hand and say, "Nice to meet you, sir."

"I'm an investigator with the Violent and Sexual Crimes Unit of the Summit County Prosecutor's Office. Do you understand that?"

I look at Mr. Erwin, who nods to me. "Yes, sir," I say.

"We are investigating the rape and murder of a young woman named Gina Mason. Do you understand that?"

"Yes, sir."

Mr. Erwin raises a hand. "My client understands the nature of the investigation. He will not be answering any questions at this time."

Degnan grimaces. His eyes slowly draw off me to my lawyer. "Someone's going to cut and run," he says. "It's going to be you or Mr. Cosgrove."

He means Lyle. I never got his last name at the party.

Mr. Erwin pauses a moment. "I've spoken to Mr. Cosgrove's attorney. I don't see a case here. Against *either* boy."

"I guess you'll take your chances, then."

"I believe you wanted to take some specimen samples," says Mr. Erwin.

Degnan continues with the sour look but deflates. He turns to me. "We are going to take samples of your blood, hair, skin, and urine now. Did your attorney explain that to you?"

"Yes, sir."

"Fine." Degnan closes his file up and rises. "Someone will be right in." He heads for the door but turns back. "Let me give you and your attorney some advice, Mr. Soliday. Don't be the last one to cut a deal. The last one always loses." He waits a moment for a response, but neither of us speaks.

19

My parents and I are silent at dinner. I move the chicken and potatoes from one side of the plate to the other. There is no conversation. We are awaiting the phone call. It comes right on time, at six-thirty.

"I'm going alone," I tell them. We have debated the point. My father wants to accompany me, but for some reason he has allowed me to work directly with the Tullys and Mr. Erwin on this. He surely respects what the senator brings to the table here. But still, he could insist on coming along. His acquiescence has introduced a new facet to our relationship. In some rather twisted reasoning, this ordeal has allowed my father to see me, for the first time, as an adult. That, combined with an abundance of assurance from Senator Tully, has led him to back off. My mother has been a different story. She has been more attentive to me than she has since I was a little boy. She practically follows me around the house, trying to give me space but desperately wanting to throw a protective shield around me.

My family, each of us in different ways, has been doused with a cold splash of reality. I have become an adult not upon starting college, or taking a job or a wife, but upon being accused of murder. I am being treated as an adult because law enforcement will treat me as an adult.

"Mixed bag, all in all good news," Grant says to me when he answers the door. He shakes my arm eagerly and opens a hand to the den. "Go talk," he says.

Jeremiah Erwin rises from the sofa. He's in a suit as always, not even a loosened tie. His suit is grayish and shiny over a blue shirt and bright yellow tie. He certainly gives the impression that I'm in capable hands.

We shake hands. I take a seat in the adjoining chair. We exchange pleasantries in the awkward manner adults and teenagers do.

"We should get to it," he says. He has several files spread out before him on the glass table. "She tested positive for your semen," he says. "Blood match."

"Okay." I try to sound upbeat. This isn't a surprise. But I suppose it's not good news, either.

"The autopsy came back rather inconclusive." He reads from the report. "She died from an internal hemorrhaging." He looks up from his notes. "Easy way of saying it is, she choked on her vomit. That's a common reaction to an overdose."

"An overdose."

"Well—call it whatever. She had high levels of marijuana, cocaine, and alcohol in her blood. She passed out and vomited. She was lying on her back and she choked on it."

"So—" I open my hands. "No murder."

"That's our position. There's another side to it."

"Okay."

"Bruises on the back of her head and her neck. Could be, she was roughed up, and she vomited during the struggle."

I remember falling off the bed with Gina. That definitely sticks out. But I thought I took the brunt of it. I really don't remember. I could hardly feel it, anyway, in my condition.

"That would be a murder," I say.

"Maybe." He sets down the report. "But you'd need a rape first, for the story to fly. And you didn't rape her."

I wish I could have the same level of certainty as the man defending me. I admit to a certain feeling of security in his words.

"The other boy backs you up," he adds.

"Lyle?"

"Right. Lyle Cosgrove. He says he dropped you by her house, waited in the car, and you went in and did whatever you did. He can't say about the sexual part, but he can say that he walked up to the window after a while and you were saying goodbye to Gina. She kissed you goodbye."

"Holy shit," I murmur. I feel an unfamiliar sensation course through me, something close to a sense of salvation. Salvation in the legal sense, at least. There is no evidence against me. I can walk away from this. But there's something inside me dousing the flames of euphoria. I have no idea what strings Grant pulled to get Lyle to say what he said. Maybe Lyle's telling the truth. I want to believe it so much that it hurts. But I can't discount the possibility that he's covering for me, for some unknown quid pro quo from the Tully family.

"Out there in Summit County," says Erwin, "they have what they call an 'inquiry' for juvenile cases that could lead to adult charges. It's like a preliminary hearing in our state, but it's not run by a judge. It's run by the prosecutor's office." He looks at me. "Are you following?"

"Sort of."

"Okay." He adjusts in his seat. "Before charging any juvenile as an adult, the prosecutor holds an inquiry to decide whether to prosecute. He listens to all the evidence and makes his decision."

"They'll try me as an adult?" I know the answer to the question. But asking it returns me to several weeks ago, when I didn't know the answer, when I was innocent. I want to be innocent again.

"Yes," Mr. Erwin answers. "For murder? Absolutely. You're only a year shy of adulthood. That's an easy call." He measures my reaction, the force of his words. "But this is our chance to nip it in the bud. They haven't decided to prosecute. This is our chance to convince them not to. And this hearing is confidential. Sealed. If we convince them not to proceed, this will never come to light."

"Okay," I say with lukewarm optimism. "What are our chances?"

"Good, maybe excellent." He leans forward. "The coroner did his part. The other boy helps. They don't have any witnesses. There's only one witness who can put you away." He directs a stare at me.

Message received.

"Are you ready to talk about your testimony, Jon?"

I wring my hands. "I'm ready," I answer.

20

I expected something like a courtroom but got a conference room. My lawyer and I are sitting at one end of a long table. At the other end, two people are seated and conferring quietly. One of them is that investigator, Gary Degnan. The other is a man named Raymond Vega. He knows my lawyer, Jeremiah Erwin, which was obvious from their exchange when we walked in.

A woman is sitting next to Vega with a small typewriter. She will be typing everything that is said in this hearing. Vega nods at the woman and she begins typing.

"Raymond Vega, Assistant County Prosecutor for the County of Summit, and with me is Gary Degnan, an investigator with the Violent and Sexual Crimes Unit. We are here today on case number 79-JV-1024. The Summit County prosecutor is conducting a juvenile delinquency inquiry pursuant to Section 24B-18 of the Criminal Code. Our purpose today is to determine the sufficiency of the evidence against Jonathan Soliday, a minor, in regard to possible charges of sexual assault and homicide. The juvenile, Mr. Soliday, is present along with counsel, Mr. Jeremiah Erwin."

I remain silent, of course, but the shot of dread flows through me as the prosecutor clears his throat. "Let's begin with the report of the Summit County Coroner, Vincent Cross." He looks at the typist. "Let's call this Exhibit one. Mr. Erwin, you have a copy?"

"I do, yes, thank you, Counsel."

"We have agreed that the coroner need not be called to testify," says Vega. "The cause of death in Exhibit one is asphyxiation caused by internal hemorrhaging. The report concludes that the decedent suffocated after vomiting while lying on her back." The prosecutor's eyes scroll down the page. "The report notes very high levels of alcohol, cannabis, and cocaine in the decedent's system. The report notes that contusions were found on the decedent's neck and at the base of her skull. However, the coroner cannot determine whether these bruises are related in any way to death."

He flips the page and reads from it. "There is evidence of sexual intercourse preceding death. Semen was found in the vaginal canal containing O-negative blood. There was no external or internal evidence of force in connection with the intercourse." He looks up from the paper. "No evidence of rape."

My heart does a flip.

The prosecutor sighs, returning to the report. "In short, the coroner finds it more likely than not that the vomiting, which led to the asphyxiation, was caused by the combination of intoxicants in the decedent's system, as opposed to any violence which may have attended the sexual intercourse."

The prosecutor sets down the report and slides a copy to the typist. "The court reporter will please officially mark this report as Exhibit one."

The investigator, Gary Degnan, eyes me with a cold stare. I break the contact and concentrate on the prosecutor, Raymond Vega.

"On the issue of sexual assault, we have affidavits submitted by counsel for the juvenile, Mr. Erwin. He has submitted five affidavits from various men attesting to their sexual relationships with the decedent. We will call these Group Exhibit two."

Degnan leans into Vega and whispers something to him. "Oh, yes," says Vega. "We all understand that the rules of evidence do not apply here. At trial, if there is one, the people would oppose the admission into evidence of this testimony, certainly by affidavit, but even if by live witnesses. On the other hand, we understand that under current precedent in this state, evidence of the complaining witness' sexual history is relevant to whether she consented to sex on the particular occasion. Because one of the issues we are investigating is rape, this evidence will be considered in this inquiry." He leafs through the affidavits. "For the record, the affiants in Group Exhibit two are: Steven Connor, Henry Cotler, Harold Jackson, Blair Thompson, and Jason Taggert. I will not read these fully into the record because they are part of the record. I will summarize."

Vega clears his throat. "Mr. Connor states that he first had sex with the decedent when she was sixteen years of age. He states that they engaged in intercourse over a dozen occasions during a three-week period. Mr. Cotler states that he engaged in both oral and vaginal sex with the decedent on five separate occasions, while the decedent was 'dating'— that's what it says—while the decedent was 'dating' another person, Mr. Harold Jackson." The prosecutor makes a face and flips the page. "Mr. Jackson confirms this infidelity. Mr. Jackson states that he and the decedent engaged in sexual intercourse over forty times during a four- to-five-month period, and that it was not unusual for them to engage in sex after partaking in marijuana. Mr. Thompson testifies that he and the decedent had sex 'about two dozen times,' both at his home and hers, at her place of work, and in his car." Vega's eyebrows rise. "Oh-kay. And Mr. Taggert states that he engaged in . . . 'sex acts' with the decedent since November last year until the present time on over five occasions." He looks up. "For the record, the decedent was only nineteen years old at the time of her death."

The prosecutor looks at my lawyer. "I guess we'll call Mr. Cosgrove now," he says.

Gary Degnan leaves the room. I look at my lawyer, who says nothing to me but nods curtly. For the most part, I stifle the conflicting emotions. What I have heard so far is good. The autopsy findings don't support a rape or murder charge. Nor does it appear that Gina Mason was someone reluctant to engage in sex. And there's something else. The pace of the proceedings. This prosecutor is running through the evidence so efficiently; it's as if he's in a hurry to conclude.

Lyle is escorted into the conference room. His head is freshly shaved bald. He is in a red polo shirt and jeans. His eyes connect and withdraw from mine quickly. Seeing him for the first time since that night causes a stirring within me, something I can't pinpoint, an itch I can't scratch. He nods to the prosecutor with no enthusiasm, and without intimidation. He is a menacing figure, thick arms and a hard look. A tough, tough kid, even in these surroundings. He is facing across from the prosecutors, while my lawyer and I have his profile.

"The court reporter will swear the witness."

The typist—I guess the court reporter—swears in Lyle Cosgrove.

"State your full name."

"Lyle Alan Cosgrove."

"Residence?"

"Four-oh-eight Benjamin."

"Here in Lansing?"

"Yeah."

"In the County of Summit?"

"Right."

"How old are you?"

"Seventeen."

"Are you a high school student?"

"No. I dropped out. I work in construction."

"Okay. Let's get to the details now."

Cosgrove tells the room that he went to this party with Gina Mason. He says she was not his girlfriend but that he had "messed around with her"—later clarified as sexual intercourse—on several occasions over the last several months. He cracks his knuckles a few times and squirms in his chair, but he is pretty direct in his answers.

He turns to the party-within-the-party upstairs. "We had some weed," he says. "Me and Grant and Jon and Gina were smoking weed." No mention of Rick. The fewer witnesses, the better, I've heard from my lawyer—especially when that witness was a drug dealer. "We drank beers, smoked about four or five joints. Then someone had cocaine. So we did some of that. I mean, the coke part, that was me and Jon and Gina."

Grant has been left out of the cocaine part. A small gift he has thrown in for himself. I'm more than willing to accommodate; it is a small favor to pay considering what Grant has done for me. I could see that. No way he could admit to his father he was snorting cocaine. Marijuana's bad enough, but coke—Grant couldn't do it. That was the whole point of being in Summit County, I now realize, a place where Grant could do what he wanted in anonymity.

It tells me something else, as well, which I struggle to block from my mind, at least for now and maybe forever. Lyle is telling a story here. Already he has lied, which means most or all of this might be fiction. And if he has to lie about the truth, then what *is* that truth?

"How much cocaine?" Vega asks.

He shrugs. "I don't know. Maybe a few grams. We were all pretty messed up."

They work on that topic awhile. Lyle goes through each person in the room—minus Rick and, now, Grant—and estimates how many lines of cocaine they snorted up their noses. The prosecutor covers the same with the beer and marijuana. Then they move to when the party broke up.

"Well, we left," says Lyle. "Gina left first and went home. Grant, he left when we did. He went home. Jon and I drove to Gina's house."

"Why did you do that?"

"Gina said she wanted Jon to stop by later. He didn't know the way there so I took him."

"And why would you take Jon to see the person you brought to the party, Mr. Cosgrove?"

Because he owed Grant one for the coke, and he didn't give a shit about Gina Mason. I don't expect to hear that answer.

He shrugs again. "I don't know."

"You don't know?" Vega presses. "You don't know why you drove Mr. Soliday over to your date's house?" He opens his hands. "She wasn't your girlfriend, you said?"

"Nah. She wasn't. *I* didn't care any."

"Okay." The prosecutor is not especially impressed. "So then what?"

"Well, Jon went to Gina's house and went in. He was in there about a half hour."

"And what were you doing all this time?"

"Well, y'know." He shrugs. "Had a couple cigarettes, drank a beer. Played a new tape I bought on my stereo. I might've fell asleep part of the time, too."

"What happened after this half an hour?"

"I got sick of waiting, so I went over to Gina's window on the side of the house. I was gonna bang on it but Jon was just about to leave. He was saying goodbye to Gina. Kissing her goodbye."

"He was kissing the decedent goodbye."

"Yeah."

"And then what?"

"Then nothing. I took him home. Then I went home."

The prosecutor nods, scribbling some notes on his pad. "Mr. Erwin, any questions?"

"Just a couple, Mr. Vega, if you please."

"By all means."

"Mr. Cosgrove," my lawyer begins, "while you were upstairs at that party, did Gina give any indication that she was fond of Mr. Soliday?"

Lyle stares at Jeremiah Erwin a minute. "She was touching him some. Put her hand on his dick once." He looks at the prosecutor. "Sorry."

"She placed her hand in his crotch?"

"Yeah, right." He points at Erwin.

"When she told you she wanted Jon to come visit her later, can you tell us the exact words?"

"Something like, Tell him to stop by. Tell him I'm waiting for him."

"I have nothing further. Thank you."

"Thanks, Mr. Cosgrove," says Mr. Vega. He looks at my attorney. "We anticipated calling Gina Mason's brother Billy next. Her brother is eight years old and reported her death to the police. That's on the police report, which—let's mark that as Exhibit three, while I'm thinking of it." He slides that document to the court reporter. "And let's mark his police interview as Exhibit four." He raises his hand as my lawyer, Mr. Erwin, begins to speak. "Understanding the hearsay problem."

"Double hearsay, for the record," says Mr. Erwin. The investigator, Mr. Degnan, grimaces.

Mr. Erwin, following the prosecution's case in a three-ring binder he has brought along, flips to the police interview with Billy Mason. It wasn't much of an interview at all. He was an eight-year-old boy. He called the emergency room of a local hospital at 5:22 in the morning, reporting that his sister wasn't breathing. The police attempted to speak with him later that morning at his home. The prosecutor, Mr. Vega, reads the contents of the short report into the record as I follow along:

> Billy was unresponsive, incoherent at best. He was unable to discuss the events of the prior night at all. His mother, Virginia Mason, ceased all questioning after fifteen minutes.

> 6/24/79
> Billy appeared unhealthy. He had lost weight, confirmed by his mother. He was not entirely unresponsive to questioning but he was unable to provide any details of the incident in question. He stated that he found his sister dead on the morning in question but slept through the events themselves in the early hours of that morning. His mother stated that Billy would not be available to testify in any criminal investigation and she asked that he not be questioned further. Billy had several cuts on his body from what appeared to be a nonserrated knife, two on his left arm, one below the collarbone, width of approx. two–three inches, but he could not tell us the source of the cut. The wounds were fresh and likely self-inflicted. Mrs. Mason confirmed that she had found her son inflicting the wounds on himself yesterday. She indicated that Billy was receiving counseling and would not be left alone in the house for the foreseeable future.

"Christ almighty," I mumble, though this is not the first time I saw the report. Was he trying to end his life? Or just punishing himself? Am I part of what's happened to him?

"We have been told by Mrs. Virginia Mason, their mother, that Billy will not be testifying." The prosecutor, Mr. Vega, settles his hands in front of himself. "We have the power to compel testimony here at our discretion. We will elect not to do so in the context of a young boy, over the objection of his mother, particularly under the circumstances. We will take no presumption, favorable or unfavorable, from the refusal to testify. We will not engage in speculation. What we can note for the record is that Billy Mason has been hospitalized for treatment and intensive counseling." Mr. Vega sighs. "Okay. Let's move on."

The prosecutor confers briefly with his investigator, Mr. Degnan. Where the prosecutor, Vega, shows little emotion in these proceedings, Degnan appears quite unhappy with the state of affairs. He is sulking, to use one of my teachers' words.

Mr. Vega turns to my lawyer. "Counsel, are we finished?"

Mr. Erwin clears his throat. "I'd like to call my client, Jonathan Soliday."

"Very well. Mr. Soliday? Please take a seat in the witness chair. Mr. Erwin?" Vega motions to a seat near him. The point is to have us near the court reporter, I imagine.

I stand up on uncertain legs and grimly take my place where Lyle Cosgrove was just sitting. I am relatively calm as I await my lawyer's questions.

The court reporter looks at me. "Do you swear to tell the truth, the whole truth, and nothing but the truth?"

"I do," I answer. And God, please help me.

I could do the examination without the lawyer at this point, we've gone it over so many times. Gina was flirting with me at the party. She grabbed my crotch in full view of the others. She said she'd see me later. So Lyle and I drove to Gina's house. She invited me in and we had sex. At one point, we fell from the bed, she banged her head—accounting for the blow to the head. Later, I said goodbye, we kissed, I saw Lyle outside the window, and Lyle and I left together.

"And did Ms. Mason ever make physical contact with you, at that party?"

"Yes. She ran her hand up my leg."

"Where did she stop?"

"My—crotch."

As I testify to these events, I settle on a view outside the window, behind Mr. Vega and Mr. Degnan. I can't look at my lawyer and I can't look at the prosecutors. Instead, I focus on the park down the street, where a young woman is playing with her child on a swing set. It's a small boy, who appears to be pleading with his mother to push the swing harder, to allow him to swing higher in the air. He is kicking his legs to aid in the momentum.

I keep my voice flat, free of inflection, simply detailing the cold facts to which I can't honestly say I have any memory.

"So there you are, in Ms. Mason's bedroom. Can you tell us who initiated any sexual activity?"

"She did."

"Can you elaborate?"

"She took off her robe. She was naked. She unzipped my pants and took them off."

"And what did she do then?"

"She started doing—she started with her mouth—"

"Did she perform oral sex on you, Jon?"

"Yeah."

I will never know what happened between Gina and me. I will never know what I did. I know that if I did do something—it's hard to even *think* the words—if I did cause her death, it wasn't anything I ever knew was within my capacity. I would have to assume it was purely unintentional, an accident, chalked up to drunken sex or some bit of rage born of absolute intoxication. It's not me. I'm not that person.

"She kissed me goodbye and asked me to stop by again sometime."

"Was she standing up? Or sitting? Or lying down?"

"Standing up. She kissed me goodbye."

"Anything else happen?"

"I asked her if she wanted me to stick around, to talk or something."

"What did she say?"

"She said she needed to sleep. She said she felt nauseous. Like she might need to throw up."

"She felt nauseous? She felt like she might vomit?"

"Yeah."

"And then you left?"

"Right."

The prosecutor's turn to ask questions comes, and he makes no attempt to trip me up. He couldn't, probably, even if he wanted to, but it's clear to me he won't even try. He is confirming my story, covering all the bases for the inevitable conclusion that the Summit County prosecutor will not try Jonathan Soliday for the death of Gina Mason. The criminal investigation will be closed.

There is a very strong part of me that disapproves of what Grant has done, with the help of his father's political power. He got to the prosecutor. He got to the coroner. He got to Lyle Cosgrove. Maybe he got to Gina's brother, Billy. But I can't escape the fact that I'm accepting his help. I don't want to go to jail. I don't want my life ruined. I'm seventeen years old, I may have done something truly awful, but I can't say for sure and I'm willing to give myself the benefit of the doubt.

Jeremiah Erwin escorts me from the building. It is not until we are outside that he pronounces his optimism that we'll prevail. I'm young but not stupid. This was a foregone conclusion from the moment we walked in. Gina Mason is just a young nobody and I have friends in powerful places.

"They'll decide by next week," says my lawyer. "And then, hopefully, you can put this behind you."

I will. Time will bring many things. It will bring a cushion, a gentle ebbing of the fear and pain and guilt. It will also bring a fading of what little memory I possess, and with it the inevitable revisionism. In a year, I'll remember this as a childish mistake that maybe, just maybe resulted in a truly evil thing. Five years, it will be that I was out-of-control stoned and not really responsible for my actions, and anyway who can say what really happened? Twenty years, it will be that one incident after high school with the promiscuous chick who wore tiny shorts and heels and grabbed my dick and got all coked up and OD'd, and I almost got blamed. That's what scares me. I don't want to forget. I don't want to revise. I want to remember this always as I do now. That I was part of something bad. And that, regardless of any legal vindication, evidence or not, I'll never really know whether I am responsible for the death of Gina Mason.

We reach the car in the parking lot across the street from the court building. I take a last look back and see a boy standing on the sidewalk, the massive structure and stone stairs framing him. He is too young to be alone, a small boy dressed in a raggedy T-shirt and oversized shorts. He offers no reaction to my recognition, just stands completely still, arms at his side, watching me with the awkward posture of preadolescence. There is little to discern from his expression. Not hatred, not anger. A curiosity, perhaps. Mr. Erwin follows my line of vision and sees the boy. He looks back at me, but we say nothing. I start to ask the question of Mr. Erwin, but I'm sure he never met Gina Mason's little brother, Billy.

I consider some kind of gesture, a wave or a solemn shake of the head. But what I can I say to this boy? His sister is gone, maybe because somebody did something bad, but no one will be punished. He doesn't know who, he doesn't know why, but he knows it was wrong. I make a silent vow to this boy that I will not forget. I will not allow myself a pass on this event. I will impose my own punishment. I will do the only thing that I can do, live a good life and repent and ask forgiveness from God.

And above all else, remember my debts.

SEPTEMBER

2000

21

I was arrested for the murder of Dale Garrison on that Tuesday in the station house. The press got wind of it immediately and featured it on the evening news. Senator Tully did not comment initially. Bennett Carey, acting as my lawyer for the time being, angrily denounced the arrest as politically motivated. That stirred things up even more, and though Bennett's spin helped my cause, what it did more than anything was pique the media's interest further.

The press didn't—still doesn't—have the full story. All they have are the literal facts of the supposed crime. I was the last one seen with Garrison, I claimed to have stepped out of the office before returning, and the forensic evidence showed death by strangulation. What is not clear from any media stories is the why. They have no idea why Senator Tully's lawyer would want to kill Dale Garrison. The county attorney's office doesn't know, either, but they have a blackmail letter that must count for something. They have not shared the letter with the press yet. I assume they want to know what it means before they disclose it.

I was arraigned the following Thursday. The charge was first-degree murder. Bennett told me that it was possible I'd get bail but not likely. So I went into the proceeding with low expectations. Without my prior knowledge—probably because I wouldn't have approved—State Senator Grant Tully walked into the courtroom and told the judge that he would put up whatever bond was set, that he would personally guarantee my presence in the state, and that I would remain in his employ at all times. The judge, an old guy named Aidan Riordan who wouldn't be on the bench without the help of Senator Tully's father about twenty years ago, seemed rather taken aback by the whole thing but then set my bond at half a million dollars. Grant put up fifty thousand dollars—ten percent as required—and I was sprung that morning.

That certainly made for a news item. Senator Tully held court, so to speak, outside the courthouse with reporters, angrily declaring my innocence and stating, "This is no time to desert a friend, a totally innocent friend." As always, Grant managed to turn a potentially explosive news item into a semi-positive.

I say *semi*-positive, because all is not wine and roses for Grant Tully with regard to this case. Aside from the fact that I am linked with him, the blackmail note refers to him:

> *Or I suppose I could always just talk to the senator. Is that what you want?*

So the police have been trying to get at Senator Tully. They questioned him about why I was at Dale's office and what "secret" I might have been holding from him. Grant hired a lawyer of his own and met with the prosecutors. He told them, essentially, nothing. Grant refused to disclose the subject matter of the discussion between Dale and me on the grounds of attorney–client privilege. And he properly noted that, if I was holding a secret from the senator, then how would *he* know what it is?

The lawyers at Seaton, Hirsch sent me a gigantic card with words of comfort scribbled by all the partners. *We believe in you. We know you'll beat this.* Stuff like that. It meant a lot, more than I could express. Bennett tells me that the attorneys at the firm are outraged, that they're sure this is more a persecution than a prosecution, a phrase Ben has down quite well by now. That's good to hear. I'm on an island of sorts at the firm, basically just Senator Tully's guy, and I'm friendly with others but not very close. It's nice to know they're behind me.

Today's Friday. I got to spend last night in my own bed and with my dogs, so I'm feeling that much better. I haven't really moved off my original mood—pissed off. But over the last day or two, the anger has mellowed and a growing fear has invaded. Not out-and-out terror, not panic, but an ever-present nervousness. I have tried to remove all the distractions, including the effect of this arrest on Grant Tully's campaign for governor and my career, to focus on the who, what, and why of Dale Garrison's death. That's what I'm doing here with Bennett Carey, having lunch downtown at a sparsely populated pizza joint with a terrific chicken parmesan sandwich.

Bennett has his jacket off, the standard crisp white shirt and yellow tie. "We're running a check on any former clients of Garrison," he says. "Ex-cons recently released from the penitentiary who might have a grudge."

"Killing his defense lawyer because he didn't do a good enough job on his trial?"

Bennett bobs his head. "A cliché, yes, but a standard line of inquiry whenever a cop or prosecutor is murdered. No reason it should be any different for a defense attorney."

"Can't hurt. You're using Cal Reedy?"

"Yeah." Cal Reedy does opposition research for the Democratic Party. It's not something discussed at cocktail parties. I know of only a handful of party officials who have Reedy's number, and I've rarely mentioned his name aloud. Nothing illegal, of course. We don't tap phones or anything. But he can examine someone's life inside out in short order.

"Okay. What else?"

"That phone call," says Ben. "We're gonna talk to that woman whose phone was stolen. We'll see if we can't find out who used her phone to call you."

"Right." I shake my head. "That was so weird. It was Dale. I know his voice. Dale called me."

The waitress arrives with our food. Chicken parm for me, a plain breast of chicken in a heart-healthy lemon sauce for Bennett.

Ben fiddles with his napkin. "Someone had a gun to his head? Forced Dale to call you, then killed him to set you up?"

I laugh, not out of humor. "That's so hard to believe."

"That's why it's perfect," says Ben. "Now you have a story that you stepped out of the building for five or ten minutes, then came back in to find Dale strangled. It's ridiculous."

I swallow hard. It does sound ridiculous. I have to concede the point.

"The truth is bizarre sometimes," Ben says, trying to lighten the impact.

"So we're saying I was set up." My eyes move skyward. "Oh, God, that just sounds so pathetic."

"But plausible, Jon. If this was a plan, then he got it set up perfectly. Someone's hiding in Dale's offices somewhere, waits for you to leave, moves in and kills him, then brings you back to the scene with a call from an untraceable cell phone."

"Pathetic," I repeat. "I'd never buy that in a million years."

"I disagree. You have to accept the premise that there was a plan, a setup. Once you do that, the rest makes perfect sense."

"Why don't we move on?" I say. "Try cheering me up."

Ben cuts into his chicken. "Cause of death," he says. "We go after the autopsy findings."

"Do we have an argument?"

"I know a guy," says Ben. "A guy I used a couple times when I prosecuted. A forensic pathologist downstate. If there's anything to argue, he'll find it."

"Will there be anything?"

"Maybe." Ben chews his food and points a fork at me. "I've seen better reports than this one."

I observe Bennett a moment. He is impressive physically, a real presence, and I saw him on the news ridiculing the prosecutors. An animation I'd never seen from him. And I know from what happened when someone broke into his house how Bennett Carey reacts when he's cornered. I clear my throat. "Ben, I'm gonna be blunt with you a minute."

"Shoot."

"Can you handle this case? You're a kid."

He allows a smile. He's twenty-nine to my thirty-eight. "I prosecuted criminal cases for four years, Jon. They moved me to felony after six months, way ahead of schedule. I've tried exactly ten murder cases. All convictions. All cases told, I've had over fifty trials. I lost once."

"Tell me about the one you lost."

"Mail fraud case," he says without hesitation. A good trial lawyer probably remembers the defeats more than the wins. "Should have been a federal prosecution but the U.S. Attorney passed. Some lady with four kids and no husband was running a scam through the mail. Selling nude photos for money, offering to meet the guys but then never showing." He wipes at his mouth. "The defense attorney gets in the evidence of the four kids at home, no father. The jury didn't want to put her kids in foster homes. They nullified." He shrugs.

"How'd they get that evidence in about the kids?" I ask.

Ben opens a hand. "The attorney asked her, and she answered."

"You didn't object?"

"It slipped my mind." Ben returns to his food with a wry smile.

I smile but quickly grow serious. "No fucking around, though. You've been through some shit yourself, Ben. And this is going to be balls-to-the-wall. Are you up for it?"

Bennett scoots his food away and drops his hands on the table. "No fucking around, Jon. I know I'm quiet and I don't get out much, but that's me in private. You haven't seen me in court. You want a guy like Paul Riley—no problem, no offense taken. He'll cost you two hundred grand but any amount of money is worth it. Really. Do it. But if I didn't think I was the best man for the job, I'd say so."

I believe him. I believe that Ben is a terrific trial lawyer because that's all I heard when I checked his credentials before hiring him. I wondered, in fact, why the hell he'd want to join up with me and do legislative and election law. A guy who thrives on being on his feet and showboating, now poring over campaign finance rules and the election statutes?

More to the point, I believe that Ben would tell me if he thought someone else was better suited to the task. The guy doesn't have a trace of ego that I've ever seen.

"Plus I'm free of charge," he adds.

"You're hired," I say, offering a hand. He takes it heartily, and we enjoy a brief moment of optimism. Then Ben grows quiet, staring into his lunch.

"Jon, we have to talk about this blackmail."

"I don't have a damn clue," I say. "I'm not hiding anything. Especially not from the senator."

"Think hard." Ben stares me down. "Because the cops are."

"I know."

"You've known the senator your whole life, right?"

"Yeah."

"Nothing over thirty-eight years? Nothing that the senator wouldn't know about?"

"Something worth two hundred fifty thousand dollars?" I ask. "Hell, no."

"Okay." Ben speaks cautiously. "By the way, did I ever tell you the first rule of criminal defense?"

"No."

"Tell your lawyer everything." Ben places a finger straight down on the table. "Everything."

"Honest to God, Ben. I'll think on it, but nothing comes to mind."

My lawyer lingers a moment before accepting my statement and attending to his food. I try to focus on my sandwich while I battle a memory from long ago.

22

Life has returned, in many ways, to a state of near normalcy despite my arrest. It is astonishing, in a sense, that everyday life continues on just as it did. My bills still beckon me from their pile in the middle of my kitchen counter, an oversized breakfast bar. My dogs still need food and walks and attention. I still shower and shave and read the newspaper and watch the stock market.

And the house is still empty, in any real sense. I thought of moving when Tracy walked out. I probably will at some point. The thought rings somewhat hollow, making the assumption that there will be a point in time down the road that I *can* move. In any event, this is not the time to consider it. Too much to do. Too busy. Always too busy.

Too busy, I suppose, could be a two-word summary of the deterioration of my marriage. The job sends me downstate, to the capital, for most of the week for the six months or so the legislature is in session. Probably a big hole in which to start a marriage. I was too caught up in my work. Not selfish. She never called me selfish. "Self-absorbed," was the word Tracy used. I thought what I was doing was more important than anything she did. More important than us.

I never thought that. I *never* did. But I suppose my actions spoke louder than my thoughts. She resented me, I resented *her* for not accepting me—I did have this job when we met, after all—hell, we resented each other. She became consumed with her job—a PR firm in the city—to the point that she was out of town or working all hours the months that I was up here in the city. That was her right-back-atcha for my time in the capital. That was how I saw it. The way she saw it was, how is it okay for me to let work dominate my time but not okay for her to do the same thing?

She had a point. I wish she could have known how I felt. The things I said to her, not when we were together, with gloves off in our respective corners, but when I was alone in a hotel room in the capital. Those, sadly, were my most intimate moments with Tracy. I told her how much I respected her, how much I admired her, how scared I was to lose her.

The chasm became too wide. I knew that about two years ago or so. That was the low point. Everyone thinks the hardest part of a divorce is the moment the unspoken words are spoken, when the decision is made. That's wrong. The lowest point is when you realize, in the depths of your soul, in a brutal moment of honesty with yourself, that neither of you will ever be happy in your marriage. Then you're just sleepwalking, waiting for the other shoe to drop, anticipating the moment that one of you will have the courage to make the call.

This is not to say the particulars of the breakup are a walk in the park. You don't split apart physically right away, at least we didn't. You co-exist. You make plans, discuss them delicately, and almost go out of your way to avoid each other. There is an immediate distance—maybe the same distance that was already there, but now it's more palpable. I brought up the subject of the house, who should move, or should both of us move? That's when she told me—this, the day after we had decided to split—that she had taken a job on the East Coast. A real step up, she told me, a promotion, a very exciting opportunity for her, and I'm trying to be supportive while I'm thinking the whole time, She took the job while we were still together.

In the end, we kept it amicable. We looked at each other and decided we would not hate each other. I told her I was excited about her career move, because she seemed pretty pumped about it. I imagine that was only partly true, that she'd taken the job less on its merits and more on its location. It's probably better that we're not in the same town. For Tracy more than me. Senator Tully's name is in the news on a weekly basis, and a public-relations consultant follows the news. It would be a constant reminder to her of my presence, the reason we split, in her mind.

I stop in the center of my kitchen, unsure why I walked in here to begin with. I'm starting to understand how my dogs feel.

I'll say this—there is nothing like a criminal indictment to keep your mind off your ex-wife. In some very bizarre ways, this is easier. There's no guilt, because I didn't do anything. I can get on my white horse. An innocent man accused. Something I can't say about my marriage. There's blame to pass around, life is too complex to nail it down to a single act or moment, but at the end of the day I take the fall for the breakup.

A knock at my door. I look to the window on instinct but I have pulled the curtains shut. Let's say it like this—the media has been less than respectful of my privacy. But I'm not the biggest news story going anymore, owing to a nuclear crisis in the former Soviet Union. Besides, anyone who wants my picture by now has taken it.

"Who is it?"

"Grant."

I open the door. I dutifully look over his shoulder. His car is parked in the driveway, no sign of reporters. Jason Tower, his chief of staff, is talking to another staffer in the backseat of the car.

Grant steps inside, offers a hand, thinks better of it and wraps me in an embrace. Then he holds me at arm's length, sizes me up. "How ya doin', Jonny?" A throwback to our youth, the blunt city-speak so easy to catch and hard to shake, a reminder of our history together. The senator bends over and greets the pugs, Jake and Maggie. He lets Maggie bite his fingers like a puppy does, just a little bit too hard, before rising again.

"You've got better things to be doing," I offer.

"Aw." He makes a face. "Too early to go full bore. Hey, I'm only down eighteen right now." I'd heard about the poll through the grapevine, a private one commissioned by our campaign. The senator's numbers are actually moving backward. It's still too early, the figures are soft, but any way you slice it, he has an uphill road.

I offer him a drink but he declines. He takes the chair, I go for the couch. My living room is what you'd expect, hardwood floors, simple grassy-brown furniture, oversized television, a fireplace. A former married home that's been "bachelorized," according to Grant's wife, Audrey.

"I told you to stay away," I say, trying to scold. "You shouldn't keep coming here."

He ignores me. His eyes drift to the fireplace mantel, the pictures. He's in one of them, he and Audrey, Tracy and I at the pier after a boat ride on the lake about four summers ago. Another picture of Tracy alone, a posed portrait, has the prominent center position on the mantel. Grant's expression registers his disapproval that I'm keeping her around, clinging to the past. He never really liked her anyway.

"Tell me what to do, Jon," he says. "Tell me what you need. You got it."

"My inclination was to get as far away from you as possible," I say. "But you pretty much screwed that up."

Grant laughs. "No way Aidan was gonna look me in the eye and tell me my guarantee was insufficient," he says, referring to the judge who gave me bail. The senator calms a moment, turns serious. "You'll work as much as you want." He nods his head slowly, about as emphatic as he'll get. "You're still the chief counsel. You're still my number one guy on this campaign."

"Listen—I'd say no but it's a condition of my bond." I struggle for words. "I'll keep the lowest profile possible. Won't be seen in public. Not for now. Hopefully, we'll get a quick trial and I'll beat this."

A quick pep talk from Grant. You bet your ass, you'll beat it. The jury won't take five minutes to acquit. Nobody thinks I did this. The county attorney's gonna be running for cover. "And listen," he continues, "you work as much as you want. We'll set up a fax line here. You can play as big a role as you want. I *need* you, pal. This isn't just generosity. Plus, you know"—the senator wags a finger back and forth between us—"we have to look out for each other."

"Seems like you're always doing the looking out, buddy." I manage a weak smile.

"Aw." He waves his hand. To an outside observer, Grant and I have always had a bit of a strange relationship. Politics is one of the few places where friendship and business mix. Politicians keep their friends around. Which means that, in my case, your best friend is your boss. Best friend is the term I use, but in some sense, I always wondered if I became his brother after he lost his older sibling in the car accident. He protected me like his brother protected him. He's kept me near him ever since. I carry my own weight, no doubt. I'm valuable to him. He doesn't make a move without my legal assessment. But that's because he chose me. He made me his chief counsel when his father, Simon, suggested someone else, an older attorney who'd been around the capital for over a decade. Grant insisted on me.

"Anyway." Senator Tully claps his hands together. "Do you have everything you need?"

"I think so, boss."

"Bennett's going to be your lawyer."

"Yeah. I feel good about that. I wish the evidence were a little more helpful."

"Yeah," says Grant. "About that." He opens his hands. "Blackmail? What the hell is that about?"

"No idea," I say.

He looks away from me, toward the floor. "Could this have something to do with Trotter's nominating papers?"

The thought is obviously painful to Grant. He knows I hated using the Ace, at least the way Grant wanted to use it. Now I see why Grant's aides were left to wait in the car outside. This is a very private conversation.

"The Ace?" I ask. "I don't see how."

Grant leans on his knees. "It just seems so odd. The two things happening so close together. That note—" He looks in my direction, though not at me. "You think he figured we wanted to use it privately with Trotter, and he was threatening to go public? Something like that?"

"Blackmailing the blackmailers?" I laugh. "Nah. Not Dale. He was a team player."

"I guess so." Grant chews on that a moment. "Anyway, forget about the Ace. Forget it. We're not touching that thing now."

I'm happy with the conclusion, sorry for the reason. Grant's better off not using the Ace, privately or publicly.

"Okay." Grant pops up. "You'll tell me if you need something."

"I'll tell you. Thanks, pal. Really."

Grant reaches with his left hand and clutches my right, shakes it briefly. I follow him through my front window as he reaches his car, looks up at an increasingly hostile sky and braces for a storm.

23

"Jon?"

I close my eyes and grip the receiver. It's midafternoon and I've been working on my bed, going through the myriad pieces of campaign literature Grant will be sending out for compliance with state and federal law. The first response is dread, a regurgitation of guilt and utter sorrow.

"Is it true? Are you okay?"

"Hey, Trace."

My ex-wife sputters a series of questions in succession, her panic rising as she continues. The lack of an immediate response from me tells her all she needs to know.

Yes, I was charged with murder.

"Talk to me, Jon. Tell me what's happened." Most notable is her tone. She is upset but keeping some semblance of a distance. Time, experience gave her that. She can't unwind the last two, three years that easily.

"I'm innocent," I tell her, with a lame laugh at the end. It sounds so trite even to have to say it. I'm doing the same thing she is, putting up a shield.

"You've been arrested? Charged?"

"All of the above. I'm okay, Trace."

"How could this have happened? How could anyone think you're capable of something like this?"

"It looks political." I keep my calm as the emotions flail about within me. "The prosecutor's a Republican. It's an election year."

"But this? Does it sink *this* low?"

Tracy's not just talking about the politics of the county attorney. She's talking about politics, period. My life. The career I chose.

She senses the unintended rebuke. "Jonny, what are you going to do?"

"Defend myself," I answer. "And win."

"Do you have a lawyer? Do you need money?"

"I'm covered. Really, I'm okay."

"I can't believe this. I . . . can't believe this."

A lapse in the conversation. A struggle, unspoken. The Tracy Stearns I fell in love with was sweet and giving, quick to laughter and respectful of my moods. She changed as we changed. She hardened. She changed her priorities. She even cut her hair, innocuous enough but symbolic to me, because I used to play with her long curls endlessly. I came home from session two years ago and found her with shorter hair than mine. She hadn't even told me. She just gave a steely smile and said, "Sur-prise."

"You didn't call," she says.

I wanted to, Trace. More than I'll ever let on. I didn't trust myself, afraid of what I might unleash with the revelations. When a relationship crumbles, you make your heart turn to stone.

"A hard call to make," I say.

"I know, I know. But *Jon*—" An audible sigh from her end. "Tell me—tell me what I can do. Do you want me—I don't know."

Do I want you to come back home? That's what she was going to ask. The question itself brings a spasm of hope, unreal, cruel hope, that has lain dormant in me these last months. But the fact that she didn't finish the question is itself the answer.

"Just keep in touch with me. Okay, Trace?"

This brings an unintended result. Sniffing, tears from the other end. My dog, the older one, seems to sense some heightened emotion in me and brings his cold nose up to mine.

"Is that Jake?" Through her sobbing, Tracy has a burst of laughter. "That Jakie?"

"Yeah," I say. "He misses you, too."

My former bride, Tracy Stearns Soliday, makes me promise to call her every day or whenever I want, any time, any reason. I keep up my brave front, before realizing that, in that last comment, I added the word "too."

24

The office Bennett Carey and I enter is small by any lawyer's standards. A single walnut bookcase seems to wilt under the strain of countless files and bound notebooks. The desk overflows with more files filled with papers jutting out from all angles. There is an open drawer sitting on top of the desk, a makeshift In box that seems to hold anything that couldn't find a spot elsewhere. The only sign of order is a small space directly in the center which has been carved out for work requiring immediate attention.

"Bring back memories?" I ask Bennett. We are in the offices of the county attorney—specifically, Daniel Morphew's office. The guy who interrogated me at the police station will also serve as lead counsel in my prosecution.

"This floor is for the top brass," Bennett says. "I never made it past first chair in a felony courtroom up on fifteen."

"You probably never wanted to make it past courtroom duty."

Bennett considers that, then smiles. "No, I probably didn't."

"Isn't Morphew a trial lawyer?"

Ben makes a face. "Used to be. He's a supervisor now, third in command, I think. But he'll handle the occasional case."

"The big ones," I say sourly.

Bennett speaks from the side of his mouth. "It won't surprise you to learn that this case holds some public interest."

"Sorry for the wait." Assistant County Attorney Daniel Morphew rushes into the room. This is a real figure, I reluctantly note, a sizeable man brimming with confidence, comfortable with his authority. He skips a beat when he sees me, then offers Bennett his hand. "Nice to see you again, Ben. Mr. Soliday." I shake his hand.

"Jon comes to everything," Ben says, sensing Morphew's surprise. It's not typical for the client to attend every little meeting with prosecutors, particularly one as preliminary as this.

"Your call." Morphew takes the seat behind his desk. "Okay." He looks despairingly over his desk, then reaches into a drawer and removes a notepad. "So—Bridges, huh?" he says to Bennett.

Our judge will be the Honorable Nicole Bridges. She is a former prosecutor herself, an African-American woman on the bench for the past five years. A Democrat. Ben considers her a good draw. He says she's fair-minded, an astute observer, someone unlikely to exalt her own agenda over the proceedings. There were a few judges I had hoped for, guys with ties to the senator. We wondered whether these judges, if selected, would recuse themselves because of their link with Grant Tully. Bennett's best judgment was no. All judges in state court are elected, and if every judge withdrew from every case with some connection to an elected official, there would be no one left. At any rate, this dilemma did not confront us. Judge Bridges was elected from a circuit on the west side, backed by an African-American alderman, Danny Rose—in other words, not with the senator's assistance. I've met Alderman Rose but hardly know him.

"Nicki's a good pick for you," says Morphew. Even from across the desk I smell the coffee on his breath.

"She's good all the way around," says Ben.

"Did you two practice together?"

Ben shakes his head. "She was a supervisor by the time I was at felony. You know her, though."

"I *know* her, sure." Morphew searches for something on his desk, I'm guessing a pen. "Sometimes down here on five, we wonder if she isn't trying to prove her independence *too* hard."

"She won't stand for a shoddy case, if that's what you mean." Bennett allows a brief smile with the jab.

"Yeah, okay." Morphew smirks. He finds a pen and begins scribbling. "Okay. First off, we're not seeking a three-eleven."

Under Supreme Court Rule 311, the prosecution has to give notice to the defense if it is seeking the death penalty. As a conversation starter, Daniel Morphew is casually informing us that he will not ask the jury to put me to death.

"I don't blame you," says Bennett. "With these facts."

Head still down, Morphew's eyes creep up to meet Bennett's. "Down, boy." He finishes his writing and looks up at Ben. "I've got your guy at the scene of the crime, the only one with opportunity, making up a story to a security guard. And I've got some kind of a blackmail thing going on."

Bennett thinks better of a direct response. He rests his hands in his lap. "Was there anything else?"

Morphew sighs. "I know how you guys are playing this," he says. "I can read the papers. A political persecution, lah-de-dah. But for the record—scratch that—*off* the record, I wanted you to know that if it were up to me, I wouldn't pick Mr. Soliday here for a defendant if he were the last guy on earth."

"If I were you," says Bennett, "I wouldn't, either."

"Not on the merits of the case," he says. "I think we've got you. That's not what I'm talking about. I'm just saying, look, this guy's tied to Senator Tully, my boss is tied to his opponent. It gives you room to beat up Raycroft over this. So if you're thinking that we're chomping at the bit here, think again."

"Bullshit," I say.

Ben reaches for me. "Okay," he says to Morphew. "You've said your piece."

"Well—I want you to know, this wasn't my idea." Morphew laces his hands together. His next words are delivered like he's expelling his lunch. "We're willing to deal."

"You expect us to plea out?"

"Murder two, five to eight. A recommendation for minimum security, Kensington."

The offer disarms me. I thought we were coming here to discuss stipulations on evidence, or a joint recommendation for a trial date. I look at Bennett.

"With any luck," says Morphew, "your client serves three years sweeping floors and he's out."

"Well." Bennett bows his head slightly, runs his tongue over his lips. "Of course, I'll discuss it with my client. But I'm confident—"

"No deal," I say.

Morphew considers me a moment before turning to Bennett. "This offer lasts exactly twenty-four hours, then we go forward. The pigeon's out of the cage at that point."

"No deal," I repeat.

"Mr. Soliday, your lawyer will tell you that this is the sweetheart of all deals. With good behavior, no more than three years in a dormitory for a calculated murder."

I look at my lawyer, sure of the coloring of my face and the pounding of my heart. I shake my head slowly.

"No deal," Bennett says.

"Once we figure out how he was blackmailing your client, it's over. And we *will* figure it out." He waits out Bennett a moment. A game of poker, I'd say in other circumstances, but we have completely shown our hand. Finally, the prosecutor nods. "I was hoping you'd say no. Because personally, the political side of this doesn't mean shit to me. All I have to say is I made you the offer."

"And we've turned it down."

"And just so we're clear—the offer's not coming back."

"The pigeon left the cage," says Ben.

Daniel Morphew's considerable frame rises from behind the desk. He places his hands flat. Even in a leaning position, his size is menacing. "We're *going* to solve the riddle," he says to Ben. "This little secret he and Garrison had. And when we do, you're gonna be begging for this deal."

25

When I return from a half-hour morning jog, the pugs greet me like they haven't seen me in a month. They've become spoiled. To call a pug spoiled is redundant, a statement of the obvious. There is no living, breathing mammal on this planet that will take advantage of love and affection and kindness more than a pug. I'm told they are dogs, but most dogs show remorse when you scold them. Pugs stare at you defiantly, sometimes even bark right back at you. They are completely demanding of your time, completely oblivious to any other concerns you might have. They have flat faces, almost no visible nose, which means their grunts and snorts resemble a nonstarting engine. They make more noise standing still than the ruckus I used to hear when I lived by the elevated trains. My pugs, Jake and Maggie, don't just sleep on the bed; they have taken over the pillows. I push them off but then they lie on my chest or head, which is worse, so I've taken to adding a third pillow and hoping I can have that much. It gets worse. Maggie, the pup, has not yet accustomed herself to waiting until she's outside to take care of her "business." Some veterinarian who I swear I'll pay back some day, some way, assured me that the second pug would be easier to house-train because she'd take a lesson from the other one. Well, Jake's fully house-trained, and for that matter I am pretty well, myself, but Maggie is still having what is politely termed "accidents." I prefer to see it as a deliberate, stubborn, even calculated move by Maggie to show me who is boss. I think Jake pulled Maggie aside the first day and told her what a pushover I was, and how I could yell all I wanted but in the end it wouldn't matter, I'd still feed them and walk them and love them.

But the worst part is they bring you in somehow. I love these damn dogs like nobody else on the planet. Their sad, clownish faces, their cocky swagger, their uncompromising demands somehow coalesce into a twisted charm. So I'm stuck. I'm their slave forever. I don't own pugs. They own me.

I'm spending the day reviewing ads, both print and television, both for Senator Tully and his opponent, Langdon Trotter, for compliance with the state and federal election laws. If Grant's stuff has a problem, we fix it before we send it out. If Trotter's stuff is wrong, we file a complaint with the state board of elections or the FEC—the Federal Elections Commission—and get a news article out of it and make them spend more money fixing it.

I have copies of all the literature and a videotape of all the TV spots. One of Trotter's ads doesn't have the attribution—"Paid for by Friends of Langdon Trotter"—in large enough print on the screen. So I'm drafting letters to all the television stations running the ad, demanding that they cease and desist from running this spot in violation of federal law. By week's end, we'll have a complaint on file with the FEC.

Another is a standard leaflet containing the biography of Langdon Trotter. The literature is green with black print, contains color photos of Trotter with his wife and three kids in a yard, Trotter speaking at a podium, Trotter meeting with constituents. It tells the essential story of Lang Trotter, who grew up the son of a judge in Rankin County. Rankin is on the east side of the state about eighty miles south of the city. The county is just south of Interstate 40, which those of us in the city use as the marker between the city and its suburbs on the one hand, and the rest of the state—the boonies—on the other. Trotter was the county attorney in Rankin County for four terms, and in 1992, was elected the state's attorney general. There's nothing in this literature that violates any campaign laws that I can see.

The pugs, Jake and Maggie, are enjoying my constant presence at home more than I am. Maggie, the baby, is snoring on my lap. It's midmorning, they've been up with me since eight, so excuse her if she's a little drowsy. Jake is on the couch as well, his eyes precariously close to shutting completely. He's already grunting and wheezing more than most humans do in full slumber.

Jake's head pops up as the phone rings. He turns to me, wondering if I'm going to get off the couch. If I did, no doubt he'd be right behind me. But I have the portable sitting next to me.

"Jon, it's Ben."

"How's things?"

"Fine. Listen, we got a list of those ex-cons who've been released recently. Guys whom Garrison defended."

"Anything good?"

"Not really. One guy got out two months ago from a federal pen. A white-collar thing, insider trading. He served eleven months. Nonviolent. Copped a plea."

"Not our guy," I say.

"Nope. Another guy was released four months ago for mail fraud. Also a federal pinch. And he moved out of state."

"Not our guy."

"No. This next one, maybe," says Ben. "Served twelve years for armed robbery, just got paroled about a month ago."

"That's violent," I say. "And recent."

"Yeah, we haven't found him yet. But I looked up his appeal—one of his claims was ineffective assistance of counsel."

"Meaning Garrison messed up his trial." A surge of adrenaline. "So he gets out, he's pissed off at his lawyer, he kills him."

"That's the idea. Jon, don't get your hopes up here. It's a long shot at best. You understand that, right?"

"Right. But it might be good for one of your inflammatory accusations."

He laughs. "Like I say, Cal's looking into this guy. We'll check for alibi, look for anything weird. If we find one hint of trouble with Mr. Cosgrove, we'll pounce."

"Cosgrove," I say. "That's his name."

"Yeah. Cosgrove," Ben replies. "Lyle Cosgrove."

I cover the phone a moment and catch my breath, temporarily whisked from my lungs. It only takes me a moment before the name registers.

"Hello?"

What does Lyle Cosgrove have to do with Dale Garrison?

"Jon."

I guess I'm the only one left who knows the secret that nobody knows.

"Do you know Lyle Cosgrove?" Ben asks.

"Sorry," I say. "No. No, of course not."

"You had me worried there a sec. Thought maybe you were old friends."

I laugh a little too receptively.

"The next one," says Ben. "Not so promising. Released almost a year ago. . . . ."

An old friend? Certainly not. I calculate the odds that there are two people with that same name. Quickly dismissing that notion, I do the odds on whether this "secret that nobody knows" in the blackmail letter is not related to politics but to a time long ago, to an event I've tried to bury in my mind. And as Bennett continues, describing the fourth and fifth ex-cons who might have a grudge against Dale Garrison, the words echo in my head like a haunted limerick:

I once knew a man named Lyle.

26

The courtroom of Nicole Bridges is on the fifteenth floor of the County Building, the same floor on which Bennett used to work as a prosecutor. I'm hoping this will bring good luck. Because luck is something a criminal defendant searches for around every corner, especially when he's more likely to find a small gaggle of reporters who want a photograph and a comment.

There are four by my count, someone from the *Watch* and smaller local papers, only one from television. We are setting a trial date today, nothing more, so there's not much for a story. But anything having to do with this prosecution will merit at least a paragraph on page 3 of the Metro section.

We stride right by the media, Bennett politely refusing to comment. I try to smile myself, like I've seen countless public officials do in the midst of scandal. But I'm not cut out for it, never was, and I'm unable to muster any facial movement beyond a frozen glare.

The courtroom is not heavily populated with spectators, only a handful of people sprinkled throughout the seven rows. The walls are walnut, decorated with the state and county seals and the U.S. flag.

A young woman in a light blouse and curly hair approaches us. "Mr. Carey?" she asks. She appraises him, seems favorably impressed. I can't imagine a woman who wouldn't be. "The judge wants the parties in chambers."

We follow the woman behind the bench, through an open door. Daniel Morphew is already seated in the secretary's office. "Gentlemen," he says.

The young woman opens the judge's office door and speaks softly. Then she turns to us. "You can go in."

Morphew rises and extends his arm. We walk in first. My first look at my judge.

Nicole Bridges is not in her robe. She is seated at her desk, wearing a buttoned lavender silk blouse. She has large eyes, thin eyebrows, smooth dark skin. Her hair is long but pulled back in a clip at her neck. A sensation I never would have imagined in meeting the judge grips me. She is undeniably attractive.

"Counsel," she says without looking up from a paper she appears to be signing. She looks at the court reporter, sitting in the corner of her office with hands poised over her transcriber. "Let's go on."

"Good morning, Your Honor," says Ben. "William Bennett Carey appearing with the defendant, Jonathan Soliday."

"Morning, Judge. Daniel Morphew for the People."

"Nice to see you all." Her Honor's voice is appropriately even, no hint of a city accent. She places her hands on the desk and looks at us. "You're here for a first status."

"That's correct, Judge." Bennett speaking.

"Okay." The judge looks at some notes. "This is a first degree?"

"The defendant is charged with murder in the first degree," says Morphew. "He is charged with murdering Dale Garrison in his office on August 18, 2000."

"Let me stop you there, Counsel." She gives the prosecutor something close to a smile. She is not overly sober, I can see, a nice relief from some of the sour old judges in these courtrooms. "Dale Garrison appeared before me on two occasions, two different cases. Looking back over my files, I see that he represented defendants in cases of aggravated kidnapping and an attempted murder. To the extent it's relevant, each of his clients was found guilty by a jury. I don't see anything to show that these convictions were overturned on appeal. I found Mr. Garrison to be highly competent and professional. Other than that, I don't have any personal opinion of the deceased. I don't see even a hint of a conflict here. But I wanted to make everyone aware. I don't take SOJs personally."

A motion for substitution of judge, she means. Every party in every case, criminal or civil, gets a "free one," the right on at least one occasion to ask for a different judge. If we looked around for a judge who never had Dale Garrison in his or her courtroom, we'd either end up with a fresh-faced juvenile court judge or someone out of state.

"We're comfortable," says Morphew.

"We agree with Your Honor's assessment," says Bennett.

"Fine. Why don't we start with a trial date."

"Your Honor," says Ben, "we seek the earliest trial date possible. These charges are outrageous, and my client seeks the earliest possible moment for vindication."

Daniel Morphew gives a quick look at my attorney. He seems surprised. It was something Ben and I discussed, something Grant and I considered as well. Some would say, take as much time as possible, especially when you're trying to find the real killer. But I want to win this case right now, as soon as possible, before the election. I want to win this thing and turn it around on Langdon Trotter and his henchman, Elliot Raycroft.

"Then you will not waive the speedy trial," the judge says to Ben.

"For the record, no, Your Honor."

"Mr. Morphew?"

"Thank you, Judge. Certainly, Your Honor, we understand the need to move expeditiously. The constitution gives us ninety days. We would be happy with sixty."

"Why do you need sixty days, Mr. Morphew?"

"Standard preparation, Judge. As well as schedule conflicts."

"Well, Mr. Morphew." The judge raises her eyebrows. "If you have other trials scheduled, perhaps I would take that into account. I was under the impression that your trial schedule was rather light these days."

Morphew laughs. "It's good to be back in the trenches," he says. "I'm certainly willing to be as flexible as need be. I'm not asking for trial on the ninetieth day."

"But I'm still waiting for a reason why we couldn't try this case in a month."

The prosecutor regards the judge a moment. There must be something between these two; Morphew used to be in charge of her when they worked together at the county attorney's office. Now she's calling the shots. My take on Morphew is he's probably a little gruff, certainly old school. It wouldn't surprise me if there was tension between a career prosecutor who grew up in the office before there were any females and probably few African-Americans, and an intelligent, ambitious black woman.

"A month? Judge, I have witnesses to line up. We're still—we're still putting the case together."

"If I could, Judge." Bennett. "If they haven't put their case together yet, then I have to wonder why my client was arrested at all."

"I think everyone here knows better than that." Morphew adjusts in his seat. "I'm in no way suggesting that we have anything other than a rock-solid case against the defendant. By the defendant's own admission, he was the only person with the victim when he was strangled. I hope opposing counsel will keep that in mind before he vents his indignation."

"We all understand the rigors of formally preparing a case for trial," says Judge Bridges. "But can we be more specific, Mr. Morphew?"

"Judge, I'd like to go off the record, if we could."

The judge considers the request. "If we go off the record, that's fine. But then we will go back on, and I will decide to what extent our off-the-record conversation goes on." She nods to the court reporter, who places her hands in her lap.

"Judge." The prosecutor speaks in a quieter tone. "We found a blackmail note written to the defendant. It was fairly cryptic. We think the victim was blackmailing the defendant. The defendant won't tell us why he was at the victim's office. That's his right. But it means we have to dig around."

"Motive isn't an element of the crime," says Ben. "It's just icing."

Morphew opens a hand. He maintains his composure. "Of course it's not essential, in the technical sense, to our case. But we're trying to put together a puzzle." He pauses a moment. "Am I asking you to extend this trial beyond the constitutional limit? No. Am I seeking the last possible hour of the last possible day? No. I'm just asking for sixty days."

The judge turns, without offering any overt response, to Bennett. "How do you feel about forty days?"

"What's the date you're thinking of, Judge?" Ben opens his calendar.

"Wait," she says. "I can't do that. I have a trial starting at the end of that week that will go at least two weeks."

Both the prosecutor and Bennett hold their breath. That means she'll set the trial closer to sixty or closer to thirty, depending on how she's leaning.

"October . . . October second."

She went our way. Just over thirty days until trial.

Four weeks before the election.

"Fine with us, Judge."

Morphew does not conceal a frown.

The judge places her hands under her chin. "Anything else?" Both sides say no. "Okay, let's go back on." She nods to the court reporter, who poises her hands.

"We've set a trial date of Monday, October second. Let's hear motions *in limine* September twenty-ninth. File them with me two days before." The judge looks up from her calendar and folds her hands on the desk. "Before we continue, I want to address something Mr. Carey raised. There is obviously a volatile aspect of this trial. I've read the papers. I've read the articles linking the defendant to Senator Tully, and I've read the articles where you, Mr. Carey, have accused the prosecution of doing the dirty work of the Attorney General. That's your right, in the media. But I want it clear that I do not look favorably on unsupported accusations in my courtroom."

"Of course, Judge." Bennett nods.

"I will be entertaining any appropriate pretrial motions on that point, and I will expect any opposition to those motions to be supported by facts."

"Of course."

"Now, Mr. Morphew, you had a motion for a protective order, I believe."

"Yes, Your Honor. The People ask that the parties be barred from commenting on the facts of this case to the media. There is a jury pool out there, Your Honor, that is being treated to daily doses of unsupported accusations about the motives of this office." The prosecutor is wisely picking up on the judge's earlier admonishment. "For the next several weeks, potential jurors will be tainted from these unfounded reports."

"As well as information accusing the defendant of the crime," adds the judge. "Information which favors your side, Mr. Morphew."

"All the more reason, then, to shut off the faucet." A nice response from the prosecutor. "Let's not give the jurors any bias for *either* side. We don't want it. We don't need it. Let's get the best jury we can."

The judge seems impressed with the argument. She looks at Bennett.

"Your Honor," he starts, "there are constitutional rights at stake here. A court should only abridge the right to expression where it is necessary for the rights of the accused. Well, Judge, we're the accused, and we don't want the gag order. If anything, the gag order will prejudice us more."

"Could you explain that to me, Mr. Carey?"

"Judge—whether detailed information comes out or not is only part of the problem. The mere fact of the prosecution itself—under these circumstances, when my client is a top adviser to Senator Tully—the mere fact of the prosecution is news. As are the comments of nonparties to this case. Editorial writers, commentators, other politicians. Everyone and his brother have an opinion on this, if not an ax to grind. And none of those people would be covered by your order. So the public will read endless articles about this high-profile trial of Senator Tully's aide, and how any surprises may or may not impact the race for governor. It's out there, Judge, it's all over the place, and there's nothing we can do about it. The prosecution now wants to say that we can't give our side of the story. That's outrageous. That's a complete affront to our rights."

The judge observes Bennett a moment, making sure he's finished. "Mr. Morphew? Anything else?"

The prosecutor shrugs. "On the one hand, Mr. Carey accuses me of wanting to drag this whole thing out. He says we want to stain his client and Senator Tully in the media. But I've filed a motion to keep everything inside this courtroom *out* of the media, and now he accuses me of trying to abridge his rights. Counsel is speaking out of both sides of his mouth." He leans forward, frames his hands in front of himself. "Judge, we've kept this evidence about the blackmail note out of the public eye. We haven't breathed a word of it. We could have. It would have been perfectly within our rights. But we are trying to be responsible. We don't know exactly what the facts of this blackmail note are yet, so rather than run to the media with a lightning rod of an accusation—can you see the headlines, Judge?—we are keeping it quiet. If we really wanted to stain Senator Tully, we'd be yelling 'blackmail' at the top of our lungs." He pauses a moment, then adjusts his tone. "We believe that what happens within the corridors of our office should stay there until trial."

"But you're not suggesting I keep out the media?" The judge has a look of concern. "It's one thing to tell the parties not to grandstand, another to tell the press they can't come in."

"I'm suggesting we hold all pretrial hearings in chambers—no press—and that the parties not speak out at all."

The judge looks down at her desk. "You both make good points. I understand that the defense does not want the gag order, and that's an important concern. But my overriding concern is the integrity of this trial, which includes but is *not limited to* the concern for the defendant. If the defense intends to use its access to the media to stir up a wave of support, I worry for the taint to our jury pool. And I certainly can't issue an order which limits Mr. Carey to only making certain comments and not others. So in the interest of the integrity of this trial, I must grant the People's motion. The parties are hereby barred from making any statements to the media concerning this trial."

We can't talk to the press? I look at Bennett; he returns the stare briefly before considering his next move. We want the idea of a political persecution to play out not only for my defense in this case but for Grant

Tully's sake in the campaign. The senator has been careful not to comment on the matter, and so far his colleagues in the senate have followed suit. It has been Bennett, in his capacity as my defense attorney, who has taken the lead. Now he can't?

"Judge," says Bennett, "we withdraw our jury demand." This catches the attention of judge and prosecutor. "We'll take a bench trial."

My mouth opens briefly before I catch myself. A bench trial. Judge Bridges as the trier of fact. It makes some sense, I suppose. Bennett had mentioned the idea to me. I just didn't know he was going to decide on the spot.

"You are waiving the right to a jury trial?" the judge asks.

"We are," says Ben. "And we would hope that you will reconsider your ruling in light of this fact."

"Well—" The judge looks at Morphew. "Counsel, can you think of any reason to issue a protective order when there's no jury to taint?"

Morphew adjusts his glasses. "Well, Judge. This is a different set of circumstances."

"Mr. Soliday?" The judge is looking at me. I was not prepared to be addressed in this room. "Do you understand that you are waiving your right to a jury trial?"

"I do," I answer without hesitation. For some reason, I sense the need to appear confident, in control.

"Well, in light of the withdrawal of the jury demand, I see absolutely no reason for this order. So I will reconsider my ruling and deny the People's motion for protective order." She looks at Bennett with a wry smile. "Mr. Carey, your First Amendment rights are alive and well."

Bennett thanks the court. The Honorable Nicole Bridges sets a date in a couple of weeks for a status hearing. The three of us leave her chambers, walk in silence out of the courtroom.

We allow Daniel Morphew the first elevator. We won't travel together. When the doors close, I turn to my defense attorney. "Nice switch-up," I say. "But a bench trial?"

"It's what we want anyway, I think," says Ben. "You have a lot more latitude with a bench trial than with a jury. A judge trusts herself to disregard testimony that is irrelevant or inflammatory much more than she trusts a jury. That's the theory, at least."

"And that helps us," I say, more a question than a comment.

"Yeah. We may have to point a few fingers in this trial. Most judges would put a clamp on us before the jury heard too much. Judge Bridges would make us go back in chambers and explain ourselves, and have a solid foundation for our accusations before we got back before the jury. But with a bench trial, judges usually let you go on, assuring both sides that they can separate the relevant from the irrelevant in reaching their verdict."

"And that helps us," I repeat.

"Sure it does. Because no matter how much you say you'll ignore irrelevant testimony, it's not completely true. Judges are human beings. They can't just shut out information in their possession because it's technically irrelevant. The brain doesn't work that way. Especially when it helps the defense. No way she'll convict someone who she believes in her heart is innocent, whether that's based on relevant or irrelevant evidence."

"Bennett." I take his arm. "You still haven't told me how that helps us."

"It helps us because we've got a blackmail note out there that we can't explain. So I might have to get creative."

"Creative," I say, "as in throwing out some inflammatory, possibly irrelevant accusations?"

An elevator opens up for us. "Of course, Jon. If that's what it takes." Bennett steps into the waiting elevator. I watch him pass and regard him a moment before following him in.

27

Used to be, I walked with my head held high when I entered the offices of a Democratic state senator. I'm the guy whom, at a minimum, they treat with respect, because I'm part of the Majority Leader's team. In some of the senators' minds, I'm almost in charge of them, looking out as I do for Grant Tully's interests. More likely, during the course of their political lives, they have relied on me in one way or another. I review and approve every Democratic senator's petitions to get on the ballot, at the very least. For more than half of them, I've knocked off a challenger or two, maybe even spared them a primary race altogether. It's the trade-off Majority Leader Grant Tully makes with his fellow Dems in the senate—hang with me, show your loyalty, and I'll take you through your next election: make sure your nominating papers are clean, help you knock off primary challengers, throw you some cash.

Jimmy Budzinski is one of the senators who takes the senator up on his invitation, which means he has relied on me plenty. Over his three terms as state senator on the southeast side of the city, Jimmy has been challenged in the primary every time. The last time—two years ago—Senator Budzinski faced his toughest race. The demographics of the senator's district had changed considerably over the years, thanks largely to an influx of downtown yuppies looking for an alternative to the pricey near-north side. The socially conservative, blue-collar Polish community was now under siege by liberal, upper-middle-class types. A local activist, a feminist named Anna Robbins, emerged as a progressive alternative to Jimmy in the Democratic primary.

So Jimmy turned to me, like they all do. First thing, I looked into Anna Robbins' nominating papers. It turned out she had brought in volunteers from a pro-choice group to circulate petitions for her candidacy. Six different women circulated petitions and got the candidate upwards of eight hundred signatures, far more than the three hundred necessary for ballot access. But what somebody didn't realize, or didn't *know* to realize, was that three of these women also had circulated petitions for a pro-choice *Republican* in a different race up north. Imagine their alarm when they learned—through a complaint filed by me—of a state law requiring that circulators in a given election cycle may only circulate petitions for one political party. So every signature obtained by those three circulators—just over four hundred of the eight hundred—was automatically thrown out. That left me with the rather simple task of finding something wrong with only one out of every four remaining signatures based on the usual stuff—that the person who signed the petition was not a registered voter within the district, or not a registered voter at all, or that the signature was printed, not signed. By the time we were done, Anna Robbins had just under two hundred and fifty valid signatures, well short of the three hundred requirement. And Senator James Budzinski was the unchallenged Democratic nominee for re-election.

It's my least favorite part of my job, no question, but I don't make excuses for myself. It's part of my job and I do it. And as a result, people like Jimmy Budzinski owe me.

I'm out on the southeast side now, in Jimmy's district office. Like many of them, it's informally run: one or two staffers who do everything from answering phones and tracking poll numbers to ordering drinks for the fridge and paying the heat and electric bills. An overweight woman in a massive cotton sweater is busy trying to close an uncooperative file cabinet when I walk in. "Can I help you?"

"It's Jon," I say without thinking. Funny that I didn't say my last name. Afraid she'll put the name with the recent news and freak out?

"Jon, come in!" The voice comes from the inner office. Jimmy's voice.

He meets me as I enter his office. Jimmy is squat, a little on the heavy side, a cigar-chomping pol whom most everyone likes on a personal level. The odor in his office confirms his tobacco preference.

He pumps my hand. "God, Jon, it's just a crime what they're doing. Come on, have a seat now."

"Appreciate you seeing me, Jimmy."

"You?" He makes a grandiose display, arms waving. "Come on now."

"I half expected Anna Robbins to ambush me on the way here." Might as well remind Jimmy of my most recent favor before I call it in.

He stops short of his chair behind the desk, holds his hands out like he's beseeching the Lord. "That one. She doesn't quit. Already working the neighborhoods. Says she's going to be smarter this time." He points to his brain then casts the finger away.

"She's running again?"

Jimmy takes his seat with a sigh of relief. Back problems, if memory serves. "She's running again. This time, I see her coming." He directs his index finger in the air. "Listen to this. I have three of them lined up. Two years away, they're already lined up. Diane *Robinson*. Rosa Sanchez. And this one's the best—she's the daughter of one of my precinct captains—*Ann* Haley." He cups his hand. "I was at her baptism. Known this girl her whole life." He claps his hands with delight.

A classic move for an incumbent facing a real challenger. Flood the primary with other challengers to split the anti-incumbent vote, hold your base, and squeak by on a plurality. Looks like Jimmy's gone one better—he's found someone with a similar last name, and another one with an almost identical first name, to his principal challenger. Anna Robbins will probably finish second, but it will be a hard climb to overtake Jimmy.

"So," he says. "You were so—what's the word—" He waves a hand.

"Cryptic?"

"Cryptic, yes—you were so cryptic on the phone."

"I thought the conversation might be better in person."

"All right." Jimmy's mood settles. "Tell me what I can do."

"Jimmy—" I lean forward in my seat, lending a more intimate tone, perhaps a more *pleading* tone. "You know I don't want what you can't do."

"Ask first," he says. "I'll tell you what I can't do."

"Okay." I rub my hands together. "You still tight with the folks over the border?"

"What, Summit County?" His face reads a combination of confusion and relief. The topic seems to be outside his expectations. What, I wonder, did he think I wanted from him? "Sure, of course. They're not ten minutes from this office. I raise money for Aldridge, the mayor. I threw a golf outing for him. You gotta see this one on the course."

I try to manage a smile. He appraises me.

"You had someone in particular in mind."

"The chief prosecutor," I say. "You know him?"

"Do I know him." It's not a question; he's mimicking. He waves at me, like he's telling me to go away. "Maples," he says. "Frankie Maples. I play with this guy, what, four, five times a summer."

Golf, I assume. Normally, Jimmy would spend another ten minutes with a story or two. But he's read enough so far. This isn't time for idle chitchat. "You need something."

"Just some information," I say. "I'd like to get a look at a file."

"A file—a case?" He raises his hands. "They're not public information?"

"Well, some might be." Actually, I'm not sure about that. I don't know what the public is allowed to see with regard to criminal files. But the one I have in mind, I'm quite sure is confidential. "It's a juvenile file," I say.

"You want access," he says.

"Just access. Just to take a look. We won't remove anything. I just need to see something."

"We," Jimmy says. "Who's we?"

"It won't be me. Not under the circumstances." I don't come out and say that, as a condition of my bond, I'm not allowed to leave the state. "An investigator. I'll give you his name if you want."

"Do I want?"

"Probably not. Listen, Jimmy—technically, juvenile files are sealed. So in that regard, this request is—it's a real favor. But other than that, we won't do anything that would cause any worry. Someone can watch my guy the whole time. He won't destroy anything or take anything. He'll just take a look at what's there and then leave. And I absolutely promise"—I adjust in my seat—"you have my word, no one will ever know we were there. This information will never come to light in any way that would suggest that we had a peek. It's completely untraceable."

Jimmy allows his head to lean back. He brings his hands to his expansive stomach. "I take it this relates to your case."

I give him a look. "Do you want me to answer that?"

"Do I?"

"I'd say no."

"Fine." A grand nod. "A friend is asking for a harmless favor. Just a peek."

"Just a peek."

"I'll mention it to Frankie," he says. "If he says yes, how do we do this?"

"I'm flexible," I say. "It might take some searching. It's an old case, and I don't know the particulars. I'm not sure I even know all of the names—"

"Jon." The senator raises a hand. "More information I don't need to know?"

I manage a smile. "Right."

Jimmy leans forward again, his elbows resting on his desk. He waves a hand at me. "A crime, what they're doing to you," he says. "I'll make the call."

28

The state Democratic Party headquarters is located in a building two down from Seaton, Hirsch. We rent half a floor from a personal-injury lawyer who owes us because we have blocked tort reform proposed by the Republicans for over ten years. The pro-business Republicans want to put caps on recoveries for pain and suffering—the most recent legislation they proposed limited pain-and-suffering awards to three times the costs of medical expenses incurred as a result of the injury. That means people who get hurt because they thought it was okay to take a piss on the third rail of a railroad can't recover ten million dollars from the transit authority for failing to "protect" them. This would seriously thwart the business of personal-injury litigation, especially in this city, where the juries love to sock it to big business.

So the Democrats in the senate kill the legislation every time the house sends it to us. And for this, we have the deep appreciation of every plaintiff's lawyer in the city, who annually throw close to three million dollars in our coffers. We also get these pretty nice digs.

Sitting around the table in the main conference room are the senator; his chief of staff, Jason Tower; his press guy, Don Grier; and me. This is a perfect situation for my appearance because it's off-camera, completely behind the scenes, and the senator respects my opinion probably more than anyone else's.

It's a strategy rap. We've just gone over a number of campaign stops the senator is poised to make over the next six weeks, the number of hands he must shake, the money people he needs to visit.

"Issues," says Jason Tower. Jason has been with the senator's staff for three years now. He lived the early life of the stereotypically poor, inner-city African-American. A life in public housing, strong mother, a brother he lost to the gangs. Jason got a scholarship to the state university, turned it into a graduate degree in public policy at Harvard, and worked as a congressional aide in the U.S. Senate until deciding to return to his roots. His skin is coffee-colored and smooth, a long youthful face, very short kinky hair, small wire-framed glasses. He's a relatively handsome guy save for rather crooked teeth, which he is treating with those state-of-the-art clear braces. He didn't have health care as a child, he's told me more than once, nor dental care. I was surprised he's correcting the problem; he always wore it as a badge.

The senator blows out a sigh, pinches the bridge of his nose. I don't know if this is from the weariness of an already long campaign about to get longer, or the fact that he's going to have to listen to us beat him up again on some of his campaign positions.

"We ran the tax plan through focus groups," says Jason.

"Let me guess," says the senator. "They hated it."

Don Grier laughs. He's been with the senator since the beginning, since before then, really, with Grant's father, Simon Tully. So he can laugh where others can't.

"They weren't real happy about it, no," says Jason.

"Well," the senator responds, "did you package it with the fact that we'll improve the schools?"

Jason shrugs, starts to answer.

"It doesn't matter," says Don. He's wearing a light cotton sweater, reddish-orange, which matches the shade on his cheeks. "You can name twenty different benefits about a tax increase, but in the end most people only care that you're raising their taxes."

"And lowering some of them," says Senator Tully. He looks at Jason. "Did you tell them *that?*"

"He told them that," I answer for Jason. "I saw the videos. One guy, I think, hit it right on the head. He said, 'Liberals always say that something good comes out of a tax increase, but in the end the only thing I see is a higher tax bill.'"

The senator shakes his head dismissively but doesn't speak. The senator's idea is to change the way the state funds education. Currently, we pay for most of our schools locally, through property taxes. So wealthier areas, with higher property values and higher property taxes, have more money for their schools than poor ones. Senator Grant Tully wants to fund education through the state income tax, so that all schools are funded equally student-for-student. The senator would have to raise the income tax to do this, of course, but he would then cut the property tax to the extent it previously funded education.

"When it's all said and done," says Don Grier, "almost everyone will have a higher tax bill, and the only gain is one that most people can't see or appreciate—better schools in the future."

"People might thank you down the road," Jason joins in, "but they might not elect you in the first place."

"The problem is what Don said." The senator rolls his neck. "A tax bill is something you can hold in your hand, something you notice feels heavier. Gradually improving schools is not."

Jason watches the senator, making sure he's completed his thought. "The bottom line is, it doesn't sell. This isn't a point to pursue."

Senator Tully brings his hands together in prayer, drops his chin on his fists. "This is a unanimous feeling? The three of you?"

"I'll speak for myself," Jason says.

"A loser," says Don.

The senator looks at me.

"A great idea that's not ready for prime time," I say. "Something to propose midterm."

"Midterm," says Senator Tully. "I tell the voters I'll do one thing, then halfway in, I give them something new."

"You *propose* something new," I add. "You wouldn't be making history with that move."

"I see. And if we scrap my idea, then what is my education plan? My tax plan?"

"Fund education first," says Jason. He's referring to legislation that has been proposed by the senate Democrats, a law stating that fifty-one percent of every new dollar of revenue must be spent on education. "And no tax increases."

Senator Tully wags a finger at his chief of staff without looking at him. "That sounds like a prudent course, Jason. A very safe course." He nods at Don. "Is that what you want, too?"

"You've got many good ideas about education you've already outlined." Don scratches at his beard. "But this one adds a tax increase. I like Jason's idea."

"Jon," says the senator. "Don and Jason like their idea. What do you think?"

"I'm just the lawyer," I say. "But I agree with them."

The senator sweeps an open hand around the table. "That's three-for-three. My great minds. Don't get me wrong—I've had about ten members of the caucus give me the same basic advice." He's referring to the senate Democrats, many of whom, for various reasons—a dislike of the young senator, a desire to take over his job as majority leader, some patronage jobs to fill—very much want to see him elected governor.

"What do you think?" I ask Grant.

The senator drops his hands on the table with bravado and rises from his chair. "I think you're all full of shit." He leaves the table and walks toward the window and a view of the downtown, the courthouse, and the civic center. The three of us look at each other with poker faces, each disappointed. Jason could even be described as alarmed.

"Why don't we take five minutes," I suggest. Jason and Don head out the door, Don patting Jason on the back and uttering one of his reassuring offerings I've heard time and time again. I sit up on the table and look at Grant, his back turned to me as he peers out the window.

"Don't start with me," he says.

"I'm not starting. Let me ask you a question."

Grant turns his head so I'm looking at his profile.

"Do you want to win this race or not?"

"What the fuck is that supposed to mean?"

"You should have fired me," I say. "But you didn't, and I can't resign because it's a condition of my bond that I remain with you. So we're stuck with that decision. Let's not make another bad move."

"We're not."

"Pull your head out of your ass for a second, Grant. The plan's a good idea, but the ten-second sound bite is that you want to raise taxes."

The senator turns and leans against the bookcase along the window. "I'm not in the mood."

"*Get* in the mood," I say. "You're not being smart about this, buddy. It's not like you. This plan—if you were consulting someone else who wanted to be governor, you'd tell him this is a dog. You'd counsel him up and down not to do it."

Grant's expression softens. He's beyond a smile at this point, or a joke, but the ease in his face seems to indicate he sees my point. "It's the right plan," he says.

"Maybe. Probably. But you won't win on it. You'll just be another Democrat who wants to raise taxes."

"And what will I be if I take your advice?"

"With a little luck, governor."

"Pussyfooting my way to get there?"

I shake my head with exaggeration. "Am I talking to the guy who ran the senate the last ten years? Is this your first day in politics?"

"Same person," he says. "But now I'm not running for the senate. I'm not trying to keep a majority. I'm running for the chief executive office. I'm supposed to lead, not follow. I'm just—" The senator pauses, considers his words.

"Tell me," I say.

The senator's hands freeze in midair, forming a frame. "This is mine. This is something that nobody else can tell me how to do."

I nod along with Grant Tully. I get it. He's talking about his father. His father the former senate majority leader, who handed his son Grant a senate seat with a bow wrapped around it, who cleared the path so that

Grant could be the majority leader without ever really earning it, who has leaned over Grant's shoulder more times than Grant would care to remember, telling him to work with this guy and stand up to that guy and bury this legislation and send money to this campaign but not that one, not until their numbers come up.

But Simon Tully never ran for governor. *Never had the balls,* was how one politico once said in my company, not realizing for whom I worked at the time. Grant is reaching beyond what his father did, and he's saying he wants to do it on his terms. It's not how I would have expected Grant to rebel against his father. I always figured Grant would just say no to politics, or maybe perform some act of self-destruction to ruin his career. But he took a different approach. He's taking the path cleared for him by his father but one-upping Simon, accomplishing something his father never did. This is how politicians think, measuring their success by elections, by steps taken, by offices held. This is how a politician shows his politician father that he's better.

"It's the right plan," Grant says. "I wouldn't be doing it otherwise."

"I know that."

"Poor kids get better schools. Most people hardly feel a tax raise."

"Then that's what we do," I say. "We spin the hell out of it, but that's what we do."

Senator Grant Tully returns to the table, takes his seat, and pats my leg. "That's what we do," he says.

29

"Hello, Cal." I open my door to my private investigator. He steps in and does a once-over of my house. Cal is a heavyset guy, fleshy in the chin, vague scars on his cheeks from a childhood of acne. His nose is thick and reddish. A good Irish drinker, I know that firsthand. Kind of guy who sweats in the winter. He's wearing a short-sleeve golf shirt in this air-conditioning and there's a sheen on his forehead.

We sit for a minute. Cal drops his briefcase and declines my offer of a beverage, including one of the alcoholic variety, which tells me he's not looking to stay long.

"Sorry to make you come here," I say. "The phones—I don't like them."

"Understood." Cal wipes at his mouth. "I don't know who you guys know out there, but those boys in Summit County sure were cooperative. Turned the warehouse upside down. There aren't a lot of cases that old lying around."

"I was afraid that might be the case."

"This one was kept around," says Cal. "On orders."

"Whose orders?"

"Don't know. Some prosecutor. Scribbled a 'hold' order on the top of the box."

"Not just recently," I say, drawing up. God help me if Daniel Morphew and his cronies at the county attorney already know about this.

"Relax," says Cal. "It was a while ago, I think—they told me they hold cases for fifteen years. So before they tossed it, someone decided to hang on to it. It doesn't always happen, but it's not that unusual, either. I saw a couple boxes from the sixties."

"I guess I'm a little paranoid."

"Under the circumstances." Cal nods grimly. "By the way," he says. "This is just you and me, right?"

"Right. This doesn't go through the firm or Bennett. I'll pay you myself."

"Not necessary." Cal waves a hand. "I'm happy to help a friend."

I seem to be getting by with a lot of help from my friends. "I appreciate that." I drum my fingers on my knees. "So—what did you see?"

"The box was pretty empty," he says. "There was part of a transcript inside. Looked like it had fallen out of the binding." Cal removes a letter-sized envelope from his briefcase. "Just a handful of papers, was all."

I stare at the envelope. What little remains of 1979. I manage a smile for my investigator. "Didn't even peek, huh?"

"Officially? No." He leans forward. "Off the record, y'know, while I'm throwing pages on a Xerox, a few words catch my eye. A name or two I recognized." He fixes on me, eyes enlarged. "But Jonathan, my friend, hear me when I say this." His look is as intense as they come. "I'll deny I ever saw a thing."

I thank Cal again as he shows himself out. I'm left with the transcript staring at me. I let the pugs out the back door and return to the couch and battle the nerves a moment. I open the envelope and pull out the paper, three sheets in total from the transcript. These are Xerox copies, the originals presumably placed back in their box. A part of Cal's finger is copied onto one of the pages. The font is an old-fashioned Courier, the spacing and indentations awkward in a word-processing age.

I recognize the first two pages immediately. The words, even without context, pop into my memory.

    entered the room?
  A: She, um, she touched me.
  Q: She touched you where, Jon?

A: My, uh, private parts.

Q: Your penis?

A: Yeah.

Q: What else, Jon? Anything else happen?

A: She did the same thing with, with her, uh, mouth.

Q: Jon, are you telling us she performed oral sex?

A: Yeah.

Q: Did she disrobe you?

   [Witness nods.]

Q: Please give a verbal answer, Jon. You have to answer out loud.

A: She kind of, yeah, I guess. She pulled down my pants.

Q: Did you ejaculate, Jon? At that time?

A: No.

Q: Then what?

A: Then we had sex, you know.

Q: Can you tell us the position, Jon? I mean, who was on top?

A: She was.

Q: She was on top. Was that the case the whole time?

A: Um. No. We turned over.

Q: And what happened when you turned over?

A: We fell off the bed. She hit her head.

Q: Okay. Was she okay?

A: Yeah. She said it hurt.

Q: Her head hurt.

A: Yeah.

Q: Did she ask to stop?

A: No.

Q: What did she say?

A: She said, you know, don't stop.

Q: Were those the words, Jon? Her exact words?

A: Um. No.

Q: Jon? What were her exact words?

   [Witness answer inaudible.]

Q: Jon, I realize this is difficult. But please speak up. What were Gina's exact words to you, after you fell to the floor together?

A: Fuck me harder.

I close my eyes, swallow hard. I remember the coaching from my lawyer as well as—better than—my words at the hearing. Gina pulled down my shorts and dropped to her knees. She was on top. All of that makes it seem more consensual, not rape.

I fling the papers into the air without purpose. I didn't remember a goddamn thing that I said under oath. I just danced to the song written by my lawyer. Willingly.

The next paper catches my eye. It doesn't register on the first look. Not a document I recognize. But it's been a while—

No. Never seen this thing before. It's handwritten.

I have grave reservations about the conclusions being reached in this investigation. I believe that the autopsy results have been interpreted in an overly generous fashion. I further believe that the deceased could not have consented to sex under any circumstances given her intoxication, even if I were to accept the version of events advanced by Mr. Soliday, which I do not. I believe that Mr. Soliday and Mr. Cosgrove have rehearsed their stories and relied on the absence of any further witnesses to escape a criminal charge. I believe that Jon Soliday should be arrested and charged with criminal sexual assault, at a minimum.

This statement should have been made part of the record. I am inserting this into the file, despite the prosecutor's refusal to include it.

The note is signed in a scrawl, but I can make out the name. Gary Degnan. I remember him well. The guy saw through the whole thing.

And he put it in writing.

I get up from the couch, my legs shaky. I pace the room before returning to the couch and grabbing the portable phone. I punch Cal Reedy's cell phone number.

"Half hour, you already miss me," he says.

"I need something else," I say. "I'm sorry." I await a reaction from him. As much as Cal Reedy doesn't want to know what he doesn't want to know, he's crystal clear on the fact that what he just did in Summit County was against the rules. He was trying to retrieve a sealed juvenile case. So I'd excuse him if he were reluctant to hear my request. But he just waits me out.

"I need to find someone. Two people."

A pause. "Okay?"

"Just find them. That's all."

"Give me the names. I'll find them."

"First one is Gary Degnan," I answer. "D-E-G—"

"That guy's dead," says Cal.

"Dead?"

"Yeah. I saw his name on one of the papers, and the guy helping out down there knew him. He was some kind of investigator, right?"

"Right."

"Yeah, he retired about five years ago and died of cancer, the guy told me. He said about two years ago."

"Okay." I exhale. Never good news to hear someone has passed. And I would have liked to have had a good heart-to-heart with this guy. But I'm not unaware of the trouble this investigator could have brought me.

"The other one?" Cal asks.

"Lyle Cosgrove," I say. I spell the last name.

"Yeah, saw that name, too. Tell me what you can."

I give him what I know. Grew up in Summit County. Ex-con. Recently released.

"Bennett can't know I'm asking," I say. "He knows about this guy. He may have you looking for him right now."

"Nope."

I open the backdoor and allow the dogs back into the house. "Sorry for the cloak-and-dagger, Cal. The time may come, I tell Bennett about this."

"Hey." Cal lives in a very black-and-white world of morality. There is an invisible line between us, on one side my business, on the other side his.

"I know, I know. I appreciate it," I say. He shrugs off the thanks and hangs up.

It seems so obvious now, this need I have. The need to know the truth. I turned my head in 1979, willing to let Grant Tully and his father pave a trail to my exoneration. It didn't feel right and never has. I hope that truth prevailed, that Lyle Cosgrove told the truth about me. But I never tried to reach Cosgrove for confirmation. I kept my head in the sand. It's time to pull it out. And once I discover the truth, I'll be left with only one question.

What then?

30

"Welcome to another edition of *City Watch*. I'm Jackie Norris."

City Watch is a local show, one of the few shows on public television that competes with the mainstream offerings.

"Tonight, the race for governor." A graphic emerges on the screen, poll numbers. "Attorney General Langdon Trotter continues to hold a commanding, fourteen-point edge on his Democratic challenger, State Senator Grant Tully." The poll shows Trotter with forty-nine percent, Grant with thirty-five, the third-party candidate, Oliver Jenson, with three percent. "The numbers show literally no movement for Senator Tully since the March fifteenth primaries." The screen now compares the two polls, taken then and now. Grant was down sixteen back then.

"I'm joined tonight by the Democratic nominee for governor, State Senator Grant Tully. Senator, thanks for joining us."

The senator is seated on the opposite curve of the semicircular table, a faux landscape of the city behind him. He's dressed conservatively as always, a blue suit, blue shirt, red tie. He is smiling broadly. "Thank you for that warm introduction," he says with sarcasm.

Jackie Norris allows for a soft laugh before turning serious. "Senator, why no movement in these polls?"

Senator Tully nods, as if understanding her confusion. "The election is still two months away, Jackie. The numbers are soft, not to mention a significant margin of undecided voters. The voters of this state are saying, We don't know Grant Tully well enough yet. This campaign gives me the chance to introduce myself and let them know what I've accomplished."

Jackie Norris takes little time going to the tough issues. The worst is abortion, which is supposed to be the best for a Democrat. Grant opposes abortion, like several Democrats in the state, except that he will say this in the open while others will not. A pro-life Democrat, Senator Tully is, which is a little like being a pro-Jew Nazi. This is one of the key issues that Dems typically use in general elections to beat Republicans over the head in the fight for swing voters, but Grant has refused to back off his personal convictions. He reminds the television host that the U.S. Supreme Court has validated abortion and he would, of course, govern under that ruling, but when pressed he concedes his opposition to abortion.

It is not a good two or three minutes. Grant has the same position as Trotter, but many of the leading members of the GOP in this state are pro-life. Grant's views have alienated many Democratic voters, who feel betrayed that one of their own is on the wrong side of this issue. So pro-choice women might actually vote for the "consistent" candidate—Trotter—over the turncoat.

My relief at the change of topics is short-lived. Jackie Norris wants to discuss capital punishment. Another loser for us.

"Senator, some would say your views are out of touch. Almost two thirds of this state favors the death penalty in some form."

"Ask those people," Grant says, "whether they favor putting to death someone whose guilt is not clear. We've seen too many examples over the last few years of innocent people coming dangerously close to execution. No system is perfect, Jackie. But we have to know we're doing everything we can to convict only the guilty, before we impose the ultimate punishment. We *also* have to be sure that the penalty is not used disproportionately against minorities. Current studies show that African-Americans face a far greater chance of being executed for the same crimes committed by whites."

Not bad. A quick nod to the base. Move on, now. The less said, the better. I can picture Trotter's Tully-is-soft-on-crime ads right now. A picture of a lovely child, next to it a menacing criminal who murdered her, then a voice-over telling us that Senator Tully would not favor the death penalty for this brutal murderer.

"Are you saying, Senator, that if the system were improved to your satisfaction, you would favor the death penalty?"

"What I'm saying is, it's the law right now. So at the very least, we should do everything to make sure it is being used appropriately."

"But Senator." The anchor lightly pounds the table. "If the legislature sent you a bill to outlaw the death penalty completely, would you sign it? Would you abolish the death penalty if it were up to you?"

Shit. Here we go now, Grant. Tell them how the Republican-controlled house would never pass such a bill, we have to respect the law as it is, you feel the most effective thing to do is to push these reforms you spoke of—

"I would abolish it," he says, "because I don't believe the taking of a life is proper. I don't think a civilized society should sanction the official killing of people."

Oh, Grant. I hurl a pillow at the television. Maggie looks up from her perch on the couch and cocks her head.

The man is principled. It's why I admire him. But he should be dancing around this stuff more. You can't be a good governor until you're governor.

"Let's move on to another topic. Senator, your top aide, Jonathan Soliday, has been charged with murder."

I close my eyes. From the television, I hear the senator answer simply, "Yes." For the most part, he has deferred comment on the issue and nothing more. I hope he keeps to that plan.

"Is Mr. Soliday still on your campaign?"

"In some capacity, yes." The senator nods, showing no outward signs of apology. "Jon's first priority right now has to be to prepare to defend himself against these outrageous charges. To show everyone he is innocent. But he's always been a valuable part of this campaign as our chief attorney, and to the extent that he is able to still contribute, he will."

"You call the charges outrageous," says Norris. "His attorney claims that the prosecution is the result of influence from Attorney General Trotter's office, that the Attorney General has influenced our county attorney to press these charges to embarrass your campaign. What do you say to this?"

The senator's eyes narrow ever so slightly, his way of showing sobriety. "I say that Jon is innocent of these charges. Regardless of why he is being prosecuted, he is innocent. I'm completely confident that the facts will bear that out. Whatever *else* they may bear out down the road, let's leave for down the road."

Jackie Norris nods. "Senator—"

"Jackie, if I could. I'd like to say something else." The senator directs a finger onto the desk. "My friend is no different from any other citizen of this state—he is presumed innocent. If the people of this state are looking for someone who will turn his back on a friend the moment the going gets rough, they should vote for someone else. If the people of this state want someone who won't stand up for what he believes in, who will govern simply by testing the wind and reading the polls, then they should vote for someone else. But *I* believe a governor should have principles, and should act in accordance with his beliefs. *That* is what I can promise as governor."

"All right, Senator, but Mr. Soliday remains on the state payroll, doesn't he? He's still on your staff?"

"He is, yes."

"Do you think the taxpayers should be required to pay the salary of Mr. Soliday simply because you believe he's innocent?"

"I think a man wrongly accused should not have his job taken away from him until the prosecution has proven he's guilty. Which they won't do."

Jackie Norris turns to the camera. "We'll be back with more from the Democratic candidate for governor, Senator Grant Tully."

"Dammit." I knock my head against the pillow, the one I haven't already tossed at the screen. He should put me on leave. Or fire me. The senator can't maintain a tough-on-crime posture—essential to this election—while opposing capital punishment *and* having an accused murderer in his inner circle.

For all practical purposes, I'm a murderer. I'm innocent and I'll prove it. But that's window dressing. I've been irreparably tarnished. I will always be the guy who was charged with murder. Murder suspects who are acquitted are almost always viewed with some taint, at a minimum. This will follow me forever.

He stood up for me. He didn't apologize or rationalize or even hide behind something as technically accurate but practically unsatisfying as the presumption of innocence. "He's innocent," he said. It's the proper thing to do politically—as long as he keeps me around, what else can he say? But the point is, he *does* believe it, and he's keeping me around at considerable political cost. He's even promised me the spot as chief counsel if he's elected, a job that, a month ago, I would have taken for granted.

What the hell am I doing? This guy has stuck his neck out for me not once, but twice. The first time almost involuntarily as a teenager, reacting to my plight swiftly and without hesitation. And this time, inescapably after consideration to his political future, he has once again taken my side.

I look over at Jake, who has taken up residence on the couch next to Maggie. "Think we can make it on a grocery clerk's wages?" Both of them are at attention now, heads cocked, wondering if I've invited them for a walk or an early dinner.

It's not like I have a wife or a family to support. Or that I'm without resources. The senator could do something for me, under the radar. A nice in-house position maybe, a governmental affairs post at a corporation. I won't lobby; my face won't be too welcomed. But I could steer anyone through the myriad of hurdles awaiting them on their way to legislative success in our capital.

I blow out a sigh, try to shake off the tremble in my limbs. I never thought it would come to this. But in public life, when it comes, it comes fast.

So that's that. I will continue to stay on leave with the firm and serve as some kind of consultant to the senator—after all, it was more or less a condition of my bond. But when this case is over, my career with my best friend is finished.

31

The coffee shop down the street from my law firm is filled with college-age kids with laptops and mugs of expensive java on little tables with fancy art designs. The place is humongous—the shop took over some empty neighboring space and converted the place from a quaint little coffee hut to an internet java warehouse.

I'm a little early, so I take a seat in the corner and jealously guard my space. I sit in a plush velvet high-backed chair and ask myself, for the three hundredth time, the question.

Isn't it possible that Gina Mason *did* overdose? She passed out after I left, vomited, and choked herself. That's possible. Right?

Sure it is. Of course. We had consensual sex and then she passed out, maybe before I left, maybe after.

But then how does Lyle Cosgrove come in? Is it merely a coincidence that the man who provided me an alibi in 1979 happened to have been released from prison just before Dale Garrison was murdered, and just around the time I received a cryptic blackmail note?

Bennett Carey catches my eye and waves. I shake out of my trance. Time to leave my former problem and visit my current one. Ben points to the bar, I mouth "Black" and he buys us some coffee. He comes to the table with the coffee and his briefcase slung over his shoulder by the strap. In the side pocket, a single manila file is jutting out with the words "Lyle Cosgrove" peering at me.

Ben places two steaming mugs on the table and takes his seat. I bravely take a quick sip, unsurprised to find that the liquid is about as hot as molten lava.

"Lot to discuss," he says. He draws a legal pad from his briefcase and sets it on the table.

"Hi, Ben."

He smiles. "Cause of death, Jon."

"We have something."

"Something. Not everything. But something." He nods his head. "My guy downstate has a theory."

"Dale choked himself?" I ask.

"Natural causes, smart guy." He taps his pad. "More or less, he could have suffered a blood clot in his neck."

"Your guy will say that?"

"Well . . ." Ben winces. "If you put a Bible under his hand, he'd say best bet is strangulation. But we can argue a theory. It's a hell of a lot better than nothing. And maybe I can get the county coroner to agree with me."

"That would be something."

"Stranger things," says Ben.

"Okay. What else?"

"We have subpoenas out," he says. "Dale's phone records, bank accounts. The records should come back next week."

Bennett reaches back into his briefcase and removes a small case. "Computer diskettes," he says, dropping them with an echo onto the wooden table. "Everything from Dale's hard drive."

"My assignment?" I ask.

"Thought it would be a good use of your time. Pull up the documents and take a look at them. See if anything comes up."

"Prosecution's looked at them?"

"Who knows?" Ben shrugs. "Yeah, if they have half a brain. They're looking for evidence of blackmail."

"They haven't found it on his computer. The blackmail letter."

Ben shakes his head. "They'd have to tell us, anything they plan on using. I'm thinking more about other people Dale was working with. Cases he was working on. Anything we can come up with, Jon. We may have to throw up a screen."

"Who would want to kill a dying old lawyer?" I ask absently.

"And set you up in the process."

"God, I hate the sound of that. I was framed, and Oswald didn't act alone."

"Let's keep going," says Ben. No time for self-pity, he's saying. "Suspects. I've had Cal look at some people. This one"—he removes the "Lyle Cosgrove" folder from his bag—"is the most promising."

"Who's that?" I ask, innocently enough.

"Lyle Cosgrove. I was telling you before, he's got a violent record. Served twelve years for armed robbery, got out not long before Dale's death. Appealed his conviction claiming Dale screwed up. So he's violent and he's pissed off at Dale."

"Anything else in his past?"

"Oh yeah." Ben is enthusiastic. "Punched a cop when he was in his twenties. Copped a plea and only got a year and a half because he flipped on the other guy. And a rape charge."

I draw up. "Rape," I repeat.

"When he was nineteen," says Ben.

I close my eyes. The company I kept.

"He copped to a lesser charge," Ben continues. "Assault. Spent a little over a year for it."

My adrenaline surges. "Anything as a juvenile?"

Ben shrugs. "That stuff is sealed. Inadmissible in any event, so of no use to us."

"Inadmissible." I try to sound nonchalant. "I didn't know that."

"Yeah, you can't use that stuff. Plus, the guy's in his thirties, so it's been a couple decades, even if there were something to find. Irrelevant. Prejudicial. Let's see." He looks through the documents he has. "Only thing as a juvenile is that he lost his driver's license. That's not criminal, that's public info. This guy had three DUIs in the first six months he had his license. He lost it in '78 and never got it back."

"So he's a real solid citizen," I say. I calmly ask to see his file. Ben hands it over to me. I open the file and glance over the two pages. I commit Lyle Cosgrove's address to memory—4210 West Stanton, Apartment 2D—and show optimism in my expression to Ben. So Ben must have asked Cal Reedy to find Lyle Cosgrove, too, after I did. Cal hasn't got back to me yet.

"West Stanton," says Ben. "That's subsidized housing. DOC puts a lot of its ex-cons there."

He's talking about the Department of Corrections. The parole division of DOC helps inmates find housing and a job after they're released.

Ben points to the file. "Looks like Cosgrove was working that night, the late shift at a convenience store/pharmacy. His shift started at six."

"Dale died after seven," I say.

"But Cal got a look at the sign-in sheet at the place. It's just a piece of paper with a pencil. It's not like you punch a clock."

"So he could have lied on it," I say. "Came in late and acted like he was on time."

"That's possible." Ben nods. "Cal talked to a couple of the other workers. They said he was there on time. They asked Cal if he was Lyle's parole officer."

"So they could have been covering for him."

"Right. That has to be our story."

I open the file on Lyle Cosgrove and take another look. My eyes don't focus on anything in particular. I'm buying time, thinking this through.

"This guy's a career felon," says Ben. "He's our empty chair."

"Say again?"

"Oh. Just an expression. Always easy to point the finger at the empty chair. Someone who can't defend himself."

"But they could haul Cosgrove into court. Then he *could* defend himself."

"Sure, maybe," Ben agrees. "We'll hold off on disclosing him as long as

possible. We'll wait until it's deep into the case and throw out his name."
He rubs his hands together violently. "I'd like to turn him upside down."

"You'd *like* to," I query. "But you won't?"

"Can't," he says. "Not yet. Not like we can search his house or anything."

I cock my head. An idea that hadn't occurred to me. "Because if we asked for a search warrant, we'd be showing our hand."

"Pretty much, yeah." He smiles. "I wouldn't put it past Cal, if we unleashed him. But we're not doing that."

"No," I promptly agree. "We're not breaking into anyone's house." Ben nods absently. I clear my throat and ask, "But out of curiosity, how would he do that?"

"Do what?" Ben looks at me. "Break into his place?"

"Just out of curiosity," I say. "I mean, short of an obvious break-in."

Ben's eyebrows rise. He sighs. "I suppose you'd use some kind of ruse. Some of these guys I used to prosecute—" He laughs.

"What'd they do?"

"Well, the point being, they always say it's easier to just walk in the front door and act natural. Flash some phony credentials or something."

"Yeah, I suppose."

"Actually, I've been to some of these housing developments," says Ben. "Back when I prosecuted, these landlords would open a door for you the minute you said 'DOC' or 'County Attorney.' These ex-cons get visits all the time from the G."

Information I'll store away. "That must be fun."

"But the point here," says Ben, "is we have to stay on the fringes for now. We can't get too up-close-and-personal with Mr. Lyle Cosgrove until the state's resting its case. Then we issue subpoenas, ask to search the premises, go through his records, go after him like all bloody hell."

I look up at Bennett Carey. "And if this guy's innocent?"

"Then at worst, he endures an unpleasant afternoon with me questioning him."

I close up the file and slide it to Ben. "I know how it feels to be wrongly accused," I say. "I'm not sure I want anyone else to feel that way. The guy's no saint, I know that. But he drinks and drives when he's sixteen and he holds up a convenience store twelve years ago—that doesn't make him a murderer."

"For now," Ben answers, "all we're doing is looking around. We don't have to decide this now."

"I know, Ben, but—"

"The only thing we have to decide right now is whether you want to win this case." Ben does not attempt to lighten the impact. His eyes are directly on me.

"Hell, yeah, I want to win the case," I say. I wave at him. "Do it. Look into it." I grab the computer diskettes and raise my hand to toss them somewhere, but I think better of it. I place the case back on the table.

"Sorry," I say. "Sometimes—sometimes the walls close in a little."

"I understand that. You have to trust me."

"I need to go for a run or something. What—what do you do, Ben? When things don't seem to make sense?"

Ben considers me a moment. What's he supposed to say? How does he help a client who's going out of his mind with grief and anxiety? He reaches for his wallet. He pulls out some photos in a plastic seal and tosses them across to me. "I think of them," he says.

These are his parents, I assume, the ones Bennett lost to a car crash when he was an infant. The father looks like Ben, only not as bulky. His mother is quite attractive in the black-and-white photo, an angular nose and prominent eyes, flowing hair. I shouldn't be surprised, looking at the man sitting across from me.

"My parents are deceased, too," I say.

Ben nods solemnly. "Do you think about them much?"

"Every day. Sometimes I talk to them."

"Sure." Ben grips his coffee mug but doesn't lift it. Men aren't good at such conversations.

"Do you remember your parents?" I ask.

"Not really." His eyes narrow, peering into his memory. "I have one fleeting vision of them. I'm in the backseat of the car. I can't see all of their faces. They're talking about something." He shrugs. "It's not much." He snaps out of his trance and looks at me. "Reason I bring it up is, when I'm nervous about something I think of them. I think of how their lives were cut short. I think of how crazy life can be, but then you die. It just ends."

"That brings you comfort?"

"Yeah, for some reason. It makes me think that we take some of the details too seriously. We don't see the bigger picture. That calms me."

Okay. I see the point, I guess. Bennett Carey and I do not lead the same lives, that much is for sure. "You mind me asking, Ben? What did you do? When they passed."

"Bounced around foster families a little while," he says. "Then I had an aunt who took me in. I hardly even remember those other people. My aunt sort of became my mother." He draws a pattern on the countertop with his finger. "She had a pretty tough life, too. But she was always there for me. She used to walk me to school, nag at me to do my homework. The normal stuff. When I was fourteen I brought a girlfriend home and she about ran her out of the house." Ben laughs. "She was pretty protective."

"Well." I don't exactly know what to say. "I guess you just have to put the bad stuff behind you."

"Yeah?" he replies. "I think it's good to remember what was taken from you. Gives you perspective."

"Yeah, huh?" I guess I know what he means. This really sort of explains Bennett Carey. This is a guy with all the tools to have a social, outgoing, full life, who instead retreats. A fear of getting too close again, I imagine.

Ben nods his head behind him. "Get out of here, Mr. Soliday. Go play with your dogs or run along the lake. Go focus on something good for a change."

I take his advice, grabbing his shoulder for an informal thank-you on the way out.

"And I'll focus on the bad guys," he says.

32

Today, the sun has chosen to appear for the first time this gloomy September, and thus I find myself overdressed in a long-sleeved oxford and trousers. I walk to the Maritime Club and brush past a guy in a uniform. The Maritime Club is where the city elite meets for cigars and drinks and a game of squash. It's fourteen stories high, with hotel rooms, workout facilities, libraries, banquet halls, and formal dining rooms. Until about fifteen years ago, it was men only, with a weekly lingerie show that, I'm told, packed the house every Friday for lunch. The gender barrier broke when the first female federal judge was appointed in the city. The club extends automatic memberships to the federal judiciary, and they were caught short when the first woman put on the robe.

It's more liberated now; the Maritime Club has even elected its first woman president. But it still reeks of old-school, traditional male bonding. Actually, it reeks of cigars.

Simon Tully breaks from a conversation with two men and finds me across the lobby floor. The senator has been retired for a decade now. Though his involvement in the political moving and shaking of the city has not ended, on a daily basis he is less active. You can almost see the relief in his manner. He has loosened up considerably, even undid his collar button every now and then. Today, he is freshly showered from a workout, in a blue cotton shirt and trousers. His silver hair offsets his tan nicely.

"Jon." A firm handshake as always. He greets me with a somber expression. We've never really gotten along famously, not since the incident in 1979. It's telling that I can recall his single moment of warmth toward me since then—ten years ago, when his son Grant won his first primary for Simon's senate seat, and he wrapped me in an embrace at the victory celebration.

"Thanks for seeing me, Senator."

"Not at all, not at all. Are you a member?"

"No," I answer. I've been here dozens of times as a guest but I can do without the considerable monthly fee.

"We'll have to see about getting you a membership." It strikes me as quite the gesture on the elder senator's part—not the offer, of course, but the assumption that I'll be thinking of things as frivolous as a club membership in the near future. Simon places a hand on my back and directs me to an elevator. We get off on the seventh floor and head for a dining room. On Fridays, he tells me, the absence of coat and tie is excused.

"Well, Jon." Simon shakes his glass of water as if it were a glass of fine wine. "I was very sorry to hear about this turn of events."

"Thank you, Senator. I was, too."

The senator's steel eyes shine against his browned skin. Simon Tully has aged gracefully, but even he cannot avoid the extra folds of flesh near his mouth and under his chin. "We all know that you're completely innocent, of course. No one has a doubt."

"I appreciate that."

"Now what can I do to help?"

I struggle for a moment, actually start and stop once, all to the senator's interest. "I just wanted to ask you something," I say. "Not related to my case. Another—another topic."

"Okay." Simon's brow knits but he says nothing more.

"It's something we've never really discussed. Not since it happened."

Simon raises his chin, like he's about to nod in realization, though I suspect he's not sure.

"The summer before Grant and I went to college," I say.

"Nineteen-seventy-nine." The former senator raises a hand to the approaching waiter, asking for a moment of privacy. "What of it?"

"Obviously," I say, "you and your son were very generous in the support you lent me during that ordeal. I hope I've made that clear to both you and Grant."

"Grant helps his friends," says Simon, leaving himself out of it.

"I guess there's some information I'm looking for."

"If I can answer, I will."

"Okay." I find myself surprisingly nervous. "I guess I was wondering what your and Grant's point of view was on the whole thing."

"I can't speak for Grant," he says.

"Sure, of course," I say. "But anything he may have said to you."

Simon Tully adjusts in his chair. "What exactly is the question you want answered, Jon?"

I pause a moment; I was hoping to ease into the conversation before cutting to the chase. "Okay. Here's my question. Did you and Grant think—" My eyes dart around. I lower my voice. "Did you think I—that I was guilty?"

Simon draws up. For a moment, he appears on the verge of answering. Then he brings a finger to his mouth, which one might read as a signal for quiet but which, if memory serves, was a signature gesture of Simon Tully's when he was Majority Leader. He looks to his side and nods; a waiter appears almost out of the blue, recalling an old Mafia movie. The analogy is more apt than anyone would care to admit. "Tim, club soda for me." He turns to me.

"Water's fine."

"And we'll have a couple shark sandwiches."

The thought pops into my mind, I've never eaten a shark in my life, but it drifts in and out while Simon Tully avoids the question.

"Well, Jon." Simon taps the table. "That's a loaded question. And I'll give you an answer. Do you mind me asking first, why you're interested?"

"Mistakes always come back to bite," I say. "I'm trying to keep this from biting anyone." I assume Simon reads me here, my reference to his son as well as me.

Whether he catches my meaning, he doesn't let on, but that's not unusual for a Tully. "To answer your question," he says, "I was told you did not hurt that girl. Grant was absolutely convinced of it. So I accepted it as the truth. And we proceeded from there."

"And you may have saved my life," I say. "I owe both of you so much. But I wonder if I could pursue the point."

Simon allows a faint smile as another waiter places his drink in front of him and addresses him by his former title. He looks at me, awaiting the question.

I ask, "Did we ever have any understanding of what the other boy's version of the events was?"

He peers into my eyes, trying for a better look, it would seem. "Did he not provide his version of the events? At that hearing?"

"He did. He did."

Simon nods knowingly. "You suspect it wasn't the whole truth."

"Something like that."

"Ah." The senator draws with his finger on the tablecloth. "And have you considered the notion that some questions are better left unanswered?"

"I've more than considered it," I answer. "I've lived it. For twenty years."

"These questions could haunt a fellow." He raises a hand. "But why now?"

Simon Tully, like the rest of the public, is unaware of the theory that I was being blackmailed. The prosecution has not breathed a word of it.

"I'm wondering whom it may haunt."

We are dancing around the fact that I have no memory of the events that night. Well, I'm dancing, anyway. It's possible that Simon doesn't even know—Grant may have buried my confession of a memory loss even from his father. I could see that. Grant would have a better chance of enlisting his father's help if his father truly believed I was innocent.

"This holds some relevance, I take it, to the present proceedings."

"To that, yes," I say. "As well as to the governor's race." I shrug.

"Guilt by association. 'Grant Tully can't even pick the right friends.' Something like that."

Simon grimaces. "Well, the answer is I don't know. I never asked. Whatever may have transpired with this other boy, I have no idea. I suspect you're giving me far too much credit."

He's telling me he had nothing to do with any coordination of my defense. He didn't get to the other guy, Lyle. He didn't talk to the coroner or the prosecutors.

I wish I could buy it. I don't, not for a nanosecond. But there's no point in pursuing the matter further.

"Look." The former senator brings a hand to his face, scratching the corners of his mouth. He is weighing his words. "I've never judged you, Jon. I'd like to think the better of people, which means I've always been happy to accept Grant's judgment that you did nothing to that girl—even though Grant couldn't possibly know that for a fact. But whether you did or not is a separate matter, at least as far as I'm concerned. What is far more relevant to me is that regardless of the circumstances, my son was dragged into a rather sordid situation. He stepped up for you at considerable risk to himself. Then and now."

"I understand that, Senator. I always have."

Simon Tully scans the surroundings before fixing on me. "My son has a soft spot for you, Jonathan. Ever since he lost his brother, you've become his surrogate. Only instead of being his older sibling like Clay was, you became a little brother. That's something I've never said to him or anyone else, for that matter. But it's true. He looked out for you when you got in trouble that summer, and my guess is, he's trying to look out for you now."

"That's true," I concede.

"I don't know if you happened to see him on Jackie Norris this week." I nod, yes. "So you understand, Grant would sooner lose this race than see you smeared, much less convicted."

"Yes, I do understand that."

Simon Tully measures me a moment. "Listen, Jon," he continues. "Grant has never asked you for anything. He probably never will. For that matter, I never would, either. But you asked me to lunch and brought up the topic, so let me make this request of you."

"Sure."

He leans forward and speaks in a slow, deliberate manner. "Protect my son," he says. He draws back and nods at our waiter, who delivers our sandwiches as if on cue.

33

Another world, less than ten miles from where I live. On the south side of West Stanton Avenue is a brick wall, the boundary of a cemetery that runs the entire block, complete with barbed wire along the top of the masonry and tree branches overhanging. Leaves have fallen onto the sidewalk and street, but most have been blown against the curb due to the daily car traffic, or are stamped by the evening drizzle onto the broken pavement of the thoroughfare. To the north is a hulking pile of faded brick, an apartment complex in theory, more like a fortress after the battle. The single working streetlight casts a reflection off the sheen on the wet road. There is a sickening decay about this forgotten neighborhood, a smell of garbage, an emptiness. An industrial block after the industry left.

I've parallel-parked between two cars that might have one undented door between them. I button my trench coat, grab my briefcase, and move with my head up—always with the head up in a neighborhood like this—but eyes straight forward. I pass a young man on a bench, asleep, sitting up, chin buried in his jacket, two days of growth on his face and matted hair that peeks from his ski cap. A couple of middle-age men are huddled outside the entry way of 4210 West Stanton Avenue. They disperse when they see me. No accident I'm wearing a trench coat. A long coat and a suit means government, either a cop or a welfare worker. I keep my hands in my pockets to maintain another false impression—that I have a weapon. I give the two men a hard look, nothing threatening but to show I'm in charge. No clue what these guys are up to, if anything, but doesn't hurt to make an impression.

I pass through the doorway and find a guy at a small counter. He's an old African-American man with glasses at the bridge of his nose, a button-down sweater vest over a rust long-sleeved shirt. He's reading a paperback and takes his sweet time looking up at me.

"DOC," I say. I open my wallet and let the badge, such as it is, dangle. Every year the Department of Corrections puts on a tour of a penitentiary for the people in the state capitol. I went about four years ago. They gave us temporary badges, which I managed to find in a stack of memorabilia I've accumulated for a scrapbook or something down the road. I whited out the VISITOR logo and taped on a photograph of me for this guy's perusal. Upon close examination, the story won't pass muster, and I'll have to hustle my way out.

But he doesn't even look at my display. "Name," he says, setting down the book and turning back toward the board full of keys.

"Cosgrove," I say. "Two-D."

He hands me the key and I head to the second floor, heartbeat at full flutter. Lyle Cosgrove is at work tonight, at a pharmacy about two miles from here. I called the place earlier today and asked for him; they told me he'd be on at six tonight.

So I'm relatively confident no one's in the place, but my nerves batter about anyway. I've never broken into someone's place before. I'm probably not very good at it, either. At least I brought a pair of gloves to cover prints.

The place is a studio, no interior walls except for the bathroom. An unmade bed sits in one corner of the place, clothes on the floor nearby. A television set on the other side of the room rests on an overturned box, a cord winding its way across the dingy carpet to the outlet. A grand total of one chair—a love seat of black velvet. There's a small kitchen with old, brown appliances and one very large stain on the beat-up tile. So Lyle Cosgrove is not exactly living the life of Riley here.

I do a quick once-over of the place, but I'm not surprised that I don't see what I'm looking for. If it's here—and that's a big if—it wouldn't be out in the open, I assume.

Next to the bed is a dresser, antique oak. I go through the drawers efficiently, putting my hands straight down and shuffling around. I'm looking for paper. Anything related to me, to Gina Mason. I make my way through the five drawers with no success, just a small assortment of clothes and underwear.

A gym bag rests in another corner of the room, near the bathroom. I see a folder with an official emblem on it. It's from the Department of Corrections, entitled "Parolee Guide Book." It has pockets on either side with documents stuffed in. I flip through them. One is the rules for parolees. Rule number one, in bold print, is NEVER MISS AN APPOINTMENT WITH YOUR PAROLE OFFICER! Another sheet contains a list of employment services that are willing to use ex-cons, a hotline number to call, etc. I pass through several more—"Frequently Asked Questions," "What To Do If You're Arrested," a list of rehabilitation counselors and religious services available. Behind all of that is a newspaper article, unevenly cut and weathered, looks like from the *Daily Watch*.

TULLY WAR CHEST REACHES THREE MILLION

It's a story run last year, showing that Grant Tully had already amassed a sizeable amount of cash for a run for governor. A small photo of Grant, not very flattering. The article mentions his announcement for the governor's race the prior week. We were showing off the money to scare off any challengers.

So Lyle Cosgrove was well aware of Grant's money.

I consider for a moment what to do with this article, finally deciding to slide it back into the pocket where I found it. No sense in keeping it. What am I going to do, run to the police with this?

Nerves at full throttle, I move quickly through the papers in the other side pocket. They are court documents, petitioning for parole and the official proclamation of the grant of parole. I jump as the telephone rings, a blaring call from across the room, causing me to spill the documents from the folder.

"Shit." Settle down now, go through them quickly and put them back in order. The first document was the petition for parole, Cosgrove's written plea that he be released from prison. I grip it as my eyes wander to the bottom of the page, the attribution of the lawyer.

Respectfully submitted,
Dale T. Garrison
Counsel for the Petitioner

I drop the paper from my hand, almost falling backward in my crouch. I stand up for no particular reason and look around the room.

Dale Garrison was Lyle Cosgrove's lawyer for his parole hearing. Dale helped Lyle get parole. Hardly a motive for murder. Lyle didn't kill Dale out of revenge for screwing up his trial, not if Dale was kind enough to throw his weight behind a parole application. But maybe he killed him for another reason.

More to the point: they've been talking recently.

I move quickly to the documents I haven't reviewed yet, the bottom of the small pile on the carpet. One is a two-page letter bearing the letterhead of Dale Garrison's law firm, with Dale's stamp on the signature line. The letter is dated August 6, 2000—twelve days before Garrison was murdered.

Mr. Cosgrove:

I enjoyed meeting with you today. Congratulations again on your parole. I write only to make clear something we discussed today, which left me troubled. You asked me a precise legal question—the statute of limitations for murder—and I gave you an answer, that there is no statute of limitations for murder. But other comments you made left me wondering why you asked.

You never openly stated your intentions, or why you requested this knowledge, and it wasn't my place to ask. But our discussions about the long-ago past make me curious about what you plan to do with this information. Let me advise you, very strongly, that you should not attempt to dig up something from over twenty years ago. You stated to me then, and I believed you, that Jon Soliday did not force sex on that young woman and that she was alive when he left her house. I believed you when you told me, and you swore to that fact under oath. The prosecutors accepted your sworn testimony, and other evidence corroborated that testimony.

If you attempt to swear differently now, you may be open to prosecution for any number of crimes, including perjury, obstruction of justice, and tampering with evidence. You should also be advised that juvenile proceedings are confidential, and the disclosure of anything related to them could lead to a criminal charge as well. I have not reviewed the relevant laws on this subject, but I must advise you of the possibility.

Let me say again what I said in my office today: that while our discussions were protected by attorney–client privilege, this privilege does not attach to discussions between attorney and client regarding *future* crimes. If I were to learn that you are attempting any crime related to the events of 1979, I would be required to revisit our conversation and determine that we were discussing a future crime in my office today. In that event, I would be compelled to disclose the substance of our conversation. At this point, however, it does not appear to me that you are planning any future misconduct, so unless something happens to change my mind, I am bound by the attorney-client privilege to keep our discussion confidential.

Please think hard about what I've said to you. You should focus on the future, not the past.

Regards,
DALE GARRISON
Dale Garrison

I place the document on the floor gingerly and struggle to keep my wits about me, to resist the avalanche. I walk across the room, back and forth, a nervous pace, a moment of utter panic, before I force myself down from the ledge. Lyle's not coming home anytime soon. I can sit here a moment and think this through.

Dale Garrison was the lawyer for Lyle Cosgrove in 1979. Hired by the Tullys. He got Lyle on the same page with my story and I walked.

I read back over the letter from its position on the carpet, afraid to touch it. Dale's letter serves two purposes, to warn Lyle off blackmailing me and to cover his own ass. He "believed" Lyle in 1979 when he said I didn't do anything wrong. He "believes" it now. Of course. Otherwise, he suborned perjury. He "wonders" why Lyle Cosgrove wants to know the statute of limitations for murder. It "does not appear" to him that Lyle's planning to commit blackmail. Sure. Because Dale would have to report it, and bring down a tidal wave of an inquiry about Senator Grant Tully's chief counsel.

Lyle had to kill Dale after this letter. And he framed me. If you're going to set someone up for the murder, who better than the one person who can't point the finger back at you?

There is, after all, no statute of limitations for murder.

34

I'm back at my law firm, Seaton, Hirsch, for the first time since my arrest. Walking in at close to midnight is a little strange, but Bennett gave me the assignment to go over the documents from Dale's computer, and I don't feel like having the dogs distracting me at this particular moment.

I open the letter from Dale Garrison to Lyle Cosgrove, which after some deliberation I decided to take. I didn't find anything else in the apartment, and I left as soon as possible.

It's possible that I didn't kill Gina Mason. Still, it's possible. Maybe Cosgrove told Dale he was willing to lie about it—implicate me—for a nice payday from the senator's campaign fund. Cosgrove's not above lying, is he?

It's possible I didn't kill her. Even if I did, I didn't know what I was doing. I never would have done something like that in a right state of mind. It isn't me. That's not me.

The computer hard drive contains a number of documents not worth checking—the guts of the computer, so to speak, that couldn't shed any light on any funny business Dale Garrison might have been up to. So I go to his word-processing system and begin looking at documents. Like me and probably everyone else, Dale's case load is organized by folders. I quickly find the folder marked "Cosgrove, Lyle" and look at the list of documents within it. They seem to relate to his work on the parole hearing. "Petition.Parole." "Brief.Support.Petition.Parole." "Certificate.Service." No mention of a letter, not from the list at least. So I open each document in the folder and read through it. None of them are the letter.

I go back to the list of folders for something like "Correspondence," where Dale might have kept his letters, but it wouldn't make sense to separate letters from the rest of a case file. At any rate, there is no folder for general correspondence.

It hits me, then, to do a full-text word search, to search every single document in Dale's system for a specific phrase or word. It takes me a minute to figure it out. I fell between the generation that never used a computer and the kids who grew up with them. So I'm okay but not great. I find the template that allows me a "text search" and I choose "all files." I look back at Dale's letter, pick out a unique phrase, and type the words for the search:

statute of limitations for murder

The pointer on the computer turns to an hour glass for a moment, then the results come back. "No hits." Nothing on Dale's computer.

Dale erased the letter, or didn't use his computer. That would make some sense, I guess. Not surprising that he'd want to be a bit discreet about this subject.

I open another document I have with me, the blackmail note, and search for a memorable phrase from that letter:

secret that nobody knows

Same result. "No hits."

Dale didn't send the blackmail letter, at least not from his computer. Not surprising but needed to confirm.

Bennett has taken the assignment of looking through the "hard" files—the documents themselves in Dale's case files. I walk to his office and don't see the boxes, then recall the conference room we have set up to review all discovery.

The conference room is well organized, which fits Bennett. Accordion files rest along each wall, all the way around the room. It's just a question of finding which one.

"Cosgrove, Lyle." Easy enough to find. There are about six folders within the accordion file. One of them bears the typewritten word "Parole." I go through the documents. Many of them, I saw on the computer. There are a few letters as well. Otherwise, nothing. I search through the others for anything related to 1979, but there is nothing. Long time ago, probably purged by now.

I return to my office and continue with word-searches on Dale's hard drive:

Soliday

The search brings up three documents:

Memo to Tully

Schedule

Schedule

I pull up the first document and find the memorandum Dale prepared on the Ace, which contains my name at the conclusion:

In summary, I must concur with the conclusions of Jon Soliday.

I wonder if the prosecution has figured out, without either Grant or me telling them, that this memo was the reason I was at Dale's office. No doubt they've found this document. But nothing has come of it. We have not filed a petition with the board of elections to remove Trotter, and we won't. Still—you'd think they would be investigating this point. Maybe Ben was right—maybe they haven't scoured his computer. But that's hard to believe.

The second document is just one sentence:

Lunch with Soliday at Carter's, noon Thursday.

That was the lunch we had planned, which was changed to Friday night. The next and final document is almost as brief:

Soliday rescheduled, meeting at 7 P.M. Friday, my office.

I didn't reschedule that damn meeting. My secretary, Cathy, told me about the change. What was it she said—"Garrison called to confirm," or something like that? Come to think of it, what Cathy said sounded like I was the one doing the rescheduling. That's just a misunderstanding, but I have to run this by Cathy. I look at the words again. Read one way, they give no indication as to who rescheduled. I'm already thinking like a defense lawyer.

I check my watch. Just past one in the morning. I'm tired, and I found what I wanted. Or I should say, I *didn't* find what I didn't *want* to find. If the letter from Garrison to Cosgrove is not in the files, the prosecution doesn't know about it. That puts me in control. At least I have that much. I can decide when and how to use this evidence. Or whether to use it at all.

35

The phone rings at just past nine in the morning. I've overslept. Not like I have any appointments or anything. I battle through the pugs, Jake and Maggie, and reach for the phone.

"It's Ben. I have news." The excitement in his voice cannot be contained. That's saying a lot for Bennett Carey. "Remember the lady whose cell phone was stolen? The phone that was used to call you back to Dale's—"

"Yeah, of course." I clear my throat. "Souter or something?"

"Right. Joanne Souter. Cal Reedy spoke to her last night."

"Okay?"

"Her purse was swiped from a public library on Friday, that Friday Dale died. Late afternoon. She stepped away from the table to go the stacks or something, and some guy waltzed off with it."

"He knew he'd have some time to use it," I say. "Before she called the company to cancel the service."

"Right," Ben agrees. "She cancelled all the other stuff first—credit cards, you know. The stuff that can really run up in a short time. A cell phone was the least of her worries. By the time seven o'clock had rolled around—we're talking like three hours after the theft—she's hardly left the police station filing the report. But here's the good part, Jon."

"Let's hear the good part."

"She thinks she saw the guy who did it. A creepy guy, didn't seem to fit in."

"What'd she say?" I sit up in bed now.

"Medium height, denim jacket." Ben pauses. "Long red hair in a ponytail."

"That's our man?" I ask.

"Matches Lyle Cosgrove to a tee. Right down to the denim jacket, too. Gets even better."

"I'm still listening."

"Cal," he says, "you gotta love him. He brings a spread of photos with him, including Lyle Cosgrove's mug shot. She ID's Cosgrove as the guy who stole the cell phone."

"Holy shit." My dogs, both of them, have nuzzled their way onto my lap.

"Lyle Cosgrove made the call that brought you back to Dale's office," says Ben.

"Or someone else did," I say. "And Lyle did the killing."

"Right. Sure. And get this—a few days later, Joanne Souter gets a package in the mail. She opens it, and it's her purse. Everything in it untouched. Except the phone, which is gone. So I guess Mr. Cosgrove has strange priorities. Murder is okay, robbery is not."

"That just proves our point," I say. "Only reason he stole the purse was to use the phone."

"I know." I can hear Ben tapping his fingers on the desk. "I wonder if we should put a material-witness tag on him."

"What's that?"

"Oh—I'm wondering if we should have him detained as a material witness."

"We can have the police hold him?" I ask.

"Yeah. Otherwise he might run."

"Do we want to do that? I thought we wanted to lay low on him for the time being."

"I know," Ben agrees. "But that was when he seemed like nothing more than a good empty chair. Now, I'm thinking maybe we have our guy."

"Well—but do we need him for any of this? We have the lady to say Lyle stole the phone. We have the records to show that Cosgrove just got out and had a grudge against Dale. If Lyle testifies, he'll just deny the whole thing. Maybe it's better if he's—y'know—the empty chair. If he can't defend himself."

"Hm. Well, that's a thought," says Ben. "Plus, that way, we don't have to show our hand. We wait until we put on a defense, slap a subpoena on Lyle, and go at him. The prosecution doesn't get a head's-up."

"Makes some sense," I say. I'm not entirely sure of my motives here. I'm telling Bennett not to call attention to Lyle Cosgrove right now. Maybe I'm just delaying the inevitable. But an objective observer might say I have another idea in mind.

36

Senator Tully drops behind his desk at Seaton, Hirsch. The weariness is apparent in his eyes and his posture. He's back in town for the first time in over a week. It's Wednesday night, and Grant is ready to spend a long weekend downstate. This was my only chance to meet him.

"How's the case?" he asks.

"Fine, I guess. Bennett's trying to turn everything upside down." I nod my head and kill a moment. This is the time to bring it up. "There's a detail I need to discuss with you."

"Okay." Grant's looking for some aspirin in his desk drawers.

"Bennett doesn't know that Dale Garrison represented Lyle Cosgrove in Summit County way back when." I speak casually, as if I've known all along about Garrison's connection to the 1979 trial.

Grant looks at me like I've dropped my pants. "Why are we talking about *that?*"

"It's true, right?" I push. "Garrison was Lyle's lawyer."

"Lyle," says the senator, a hand cupping his mouth. "God, yeah." He looks at me. "Yeah, Dale represented that kid. You didn't know that?"

"I was in the dark," I answer. I suppose it would never come up, over the years that I worked with Dale Garrison sporadically. Dale would never find the occasion to tell me that he helped me out back then.

"Okay, well, it's true," says Grant. "But I can't imagine it's relevant?"

"Well, that's the thing." I adjust in my seat as the senator awaits elaboration. "It might *be* relevant."

"How's that?"

"Lyle Cosgrove's been in jail for years," I say.

"Probably where he belongs."

"But he just got out, Grant. About a month before Dale was killed."

Grant works on that a moment, showing nothing but a blank stare. "We're looking at this guy for killing Dale?"

"Yeah. I think he did."

"Why?"

"Let's not get too specific," I say. "But I think Lyle decided that now was a good time to call on an old acquaintance to help him with his future financial needs."

"The blackmail," says Grant.

I slide the note across to him.

I guess I'm the only one left who knows the secret that nobody knows. I think $250,000 should cover it. A month should be enough time. I wouldn't presume your income source, but I imagine if anyone could find a way to tap into the campaign fund without anyone noticing, you would. Or I suppose I could always just talk to the senator. Is that what you want? One month. Don't attempt to contact me about this. I will initiate all communications.

I continue as the senator reads the note. "Lyle was blackmailing me. He was threatening to expose my little secret unless I gave him money from your campaign fund. He was well aware that you had a big war chest."

Grant peers over the document with narrow eyes. Finally, he looks up at me. "How is Dale involved?"

"Dale tried to talk him out of it."

"How do you know that?"

"I just know it. Dale helped get Lyle Cosgrove parole. They were talking. He mentioned the idea to Dale, and Dale tried to stop him. So he killed Dale."

"Tell me how you know that, Jon."

"No." I slowly exhale.

He casts me a look of disapproval. "Has this guy—Lyle—has he tried to contact you again? Can you tell me that much?" Grant fingers the blackmail letter. "He says he'll initiate all communications."

I shake my head. "I figure he's spooked off after I was charged with Dale's murder."

"Where is this guy? Lyle?"

"He's in the city," I answer. "Condition of parole."

Grant swallows hard.

"Not a good situation," I say.

He laughs bitterly, angles his head. "No, I'd say not."

"Tell me what happened back then, Grant. Tell me about 1979. The 'secret that nobody knows.'"

Grant takes the question badly. He squirms in his chair and breaks eye contact.

"You and your dad hired Garrison to represent Lyle."

He considers me a moment. That much, surely, he can acknowledge. "True."

"But Lyle wasn't in trouble. He didn't need a lawyer."

"Easy for us to say," Grant answers. "He was being questioned."

"But you hired him a fancy, expensive lawyer to control him. To make sure he and I were singing from the same hymnal. Everyone says Jon Soliday is innocent."

Grant folds his hands together and looks at me. "A boy in that situation will do anything he can," he says. "He'd roll on you in a heartbeat to save himself. You think the police weren't saying that to him? 'Give us the other guy and we'll let you skate'? Jon, just because we got him a lawyer doesn't mean we made him lie. It doesn't mean you did anything wrong."

"What was Lyle saying to the police?" I ask. "Before you hired Garrison for him."

"*I* don't know." He shrugs. "Probably, he kept his mouth shut at first. I'm sure it wasn't his first scrape with the law. He wasn't stupid."

"Tell me what you knew, Grant. Tell me what you knew about my involvement."

"I knew you were innocent." The words come quickly. "That was the only possible outcome."

"Because I was your pal."

"Because you're not capable of it. Drunk or stoned or whatever." He waves his hand. "It's just not a possibility." He leans forward and directs a finger at me. "Listen, Jon, this blackmail—it doesn't mean Lyle lied back then. Don't you see that? The mere *mention* of that case would smear you, and me. He knows that. He probably knows I'm running for governor. He knows neither of us would want that topic brought up." He settles back in his chair. "It doesn't make you a murderer."

"So you didn't know anything back then?" I ask. "Anything that implicated me? You didn't talk to Lyle about it? Or that other guy—Rick?"

"Rick." Grant shakes his head. "What a crew, those guys."

"Anything," I repeat.

The senator stands, removes his tuxedo coat and cuff links and rolls up his sleeves. He looks like he has gained a few pounds during the campaign, which is understandable—the lack of exercise and the omnipresent food at various stops. He is still slight but a hint of a paunch has crept over his belt. "You want to know?" he says. "Okay."

I cross a leg and wag it.

"This Rick—or what did they call him, Ricochet—that guy called me afterward. After I talked to you from the jail. I can't remember the details. It's been, what, over twenty years?"

"Give me a nutshell."

Grant nods. "He was talking crazy. The cops had visited Lyle, and he was freaking out. Rick had supplied the—you know—"

"The cocaine."

"Right." Grant settles on that memory for a moment. He resumes in a calmer voice. "Rick wanted nothing to do with this, because if that girl overdosed and he supplied the stuff, he could be in trouble. And Lyle was quite upset about being questioned himself."

I open my hands. "So you struck a deal."

"You make it sound so sinister." He purses his lips. "Yeah, I guess so. I told him to tell Lyle, we'll get him a lawyer and keep his mouth shut. I told Rick that we'd keep him out of the whole thing, as long as—just so—"

"As long as Lyle behaved himself," I finish. "As long as Lyle Cosgrove exonerates me, everything will be fine. The Tully family machine will take care of the rest. The prosecutors, the medical examiner, all of these people will be surprisingly friendly to Jon Soliday, and as long as Lyle backs the whole thing up, we can all go home in the end."

Grant's jaw tightens, but he doesn't immediately respond.

"It was a fix-up, the whole thing," I continue.

"It doesn't mean you committed a crime," says Grant. "Did we work some connections? Yes. Did Dale steer Lyle to a certain version of events? Maybe, I wasn't there—but maybe. But we were doing this stuff for an innocent person."

"You don't know that."

"I believe that. I always have."

To my surprise, I feel relief in this answer. Although the picture is starting to get clearer on this point, I am somehow heartened by the fact that Grant never actually thought I was guilty.

"Okay." I raise a hand. "Okay."

Grant resumes his seat, runs a hand through his hair. "Jesus Christ. So this guy Lyle is suspect number one now?"

"I'd put even money on it."

He makes a show with his hands. "Wonderful. Great."

"Bennett doesn't know about 1979," I say. "Or my connection to Lyle. But he does know about Lyle in general. He knows he just got out of prison, and apparently, when Lyle was last convicted, he claimed on appeal that his lawyer—Dale—was ineffective. And now we have Lyle tied to the stolen cell phone."

"So Bennett wants to point the finger at Lyle Cosgrove."

"Yeah."

Grant makes a steeple with his hands, his elbows on the desk. "And in doing so, there's no escaping the fact that the events of 1979 will come to the surface."

"No escaping it," I say.

The senator drops his hands flat on the desk and hums—maybe groans—to himself.

"I'm painted into a corner, Grant. I'm being charged with a crime I didn't commit and I need to do whatever I can."

"I know that, I know that." He inhales, freezes a moment. There must be some battle raging within him, his desire to be governor balanced against his wanting to help me. Knowing him, it's not much of a fight. "Does that mean you're going to tell Bennett? You're going to make what happened back then public?"

"It will hurt you," I say. "At a minimum, guilt by association. I'll be even more of an albatross. And if people start digging, they might come up with the idea that you helped me out back then. Maybe cut some legal corners. That could hurt."

He makes a face, like what I've just said is meaningless. "I'm worried about you," he says. "If you bring this up, can't they still say that you murdered her? Can't they revisit that?"

"Yeah, they sure could. I wasn't acquitted. There's no double jeopardy." I look at the ceiling. "That's some line of defense I'm looking at. I beat one murder charge by implicating myself in another one."

"Not true." Grant's response is so quick he almost cut me off. "You didn't do anything back then. They'll never make that case."

"Grant." I adjust in my chair as if I'm talking to a four-year-old. I'm surely not, but when it comes to me, Grant's fraternal, if not paternal side clouds his judgment. "The county attorney is Elliot Raycroft, remember? He sees a chance to revive a murder investigation against Senator Tully's top aide—with all sorts of sensational drama, a rape and murder of a young girl, and with you there on the periphery—you think he'll hesitate one second? Even if it doesn't pan out, he'll ruin us. He'll ruin you."

"We'll figure something out," says Grant.

His calm disarms me. I want to shake him. "You're saying I should do it," I say. "Tell the whole story. Point the finger at Lyle Cosgrove, explain how he and I are connected, argue that I was blackmailed and framed and how I didn't commit either of the two murders." The description deflates me. What a spot I'm in.

Grant Tully leaves his chair and takes the one next to me. "If you have to, of course. You make it sound so dire. Forget about the race a moment, just for a moment. You argue that this Lyle was blackmailing you, Garrison didn't go along, so he killed him, framing you in the process. Tell them you didn't do anything in 1979 but Lyle was threatening to bring it back up, anyway. Just to smear you." He opens his hands. "That works. That makes sense."

"And you lose the race," I say.

"Or you go away for life. For a crime you didn't commit. Which is worse?"

Tough to rebut that one. Grant seems entirely comfortable with this. He's always derived some satisfaction playing the big brother to me.

He smacks my cheek lightly. "And don't assume I'll lose the race."

I let out an enormous sigh. "If I had any other choice—"

"I know."

"—but I don't."

"I know."

I nod, unable to say anything more. I rise and head for the door. I'm near the hallway, patting the door frame, when the senator calls back to me.

"Do we have to reveal *every*thing?" he asks.

I know what he's talking about. The drugs. The cocaine. The fact that Jon Soliday got messed up and potentially implicated in a murder is one thing. The fact that Senator Grant Tully was snorting cocaine beforehand is quite another. The hearing back in 1979 was obviously focused on me, and there's no evidence out there that puts Grant with a straw up his nose.

"No," I answer. "All I remember you doing is having a few beers."

Grant nods with me. "Is that okay?"

"It'll be just like it was back then," I say. "I remember doing drugs with Lyle and Gina. I don't recall you being upstairs with us. You and Rick didn't get mixed up with the drugs."

Grant shudders. He seems to feel guilty about this, as if the monumental favors and risks he's taken for me add up to nothing. The fact is, I pretty much have to stick to what I testified to in 1979, anyway. It's the story that helps me walk.

"I'll have to let Bennett know about this pretty quick," I say.

"I know." The senator is not looking at me. "Go win the case."

I thank him and walk down the hallway. I stop briefly at my secretary Cathy's station, looking for any mail that may have come my way, allowing a moment to let the electricity settle within my body. From Senator Tully's office, I hear a commotion, the sound of several files of paper flying across the room and slapping against the wall.

37

Today is Thursday. My trial begins in a little over a week. Bennett's been working on all of our pretrial motions, so he's up to his ears. I don't know where the time has gone but we are in the final stages now, with not a lot to show for it. Bennett has pursued the notion of an alternative cause of death, but among the various forensic pathologists he's talked to, none of them thinks that his theory is more likely than the easy call—that Dale was strangled.

I still haven't spoken to Bennett about Lyle Cosgrove. It took me a while to accept the fact that all of this fit together like it has, that Lyle was probably blackmailing me about my past and Dale Garrison got in the way. I suppose I was protecting Grant Tully as well as myself in trying to bury this stuff. But now it is clear I don't have a choice, and Grant has even given his blessing.

I'm doing laundry this afternoon—after five weeks of build-up, I've been reduced to wearing underwear with rips and holes—when I hear the pugs going ballistic upstairs. Their nails slip on the hallway tile as they run. Their normally muted barks are at high pitch. Someone's at the door, in other words. I ignore it initially, because most likely the caller is soliciting for something and I'm not interested. But the dogs are still making a racket when I get to the top of the stairs, so I drop a basket full of clean undies and go to the door.

It's Bennett Carey, looking rather worn down.

I push open the door. "Hey."

Ben has been working furiously on my case, following leads, writing the pretrial papers to get certain evidence excluded. For the most part, he tells me, there's nothing critical in any of them. This case comes down to my believability, and to pointing the finger at Lyle Cosgrove. The only key piece of evidence Ben is trying to exclude is the blackmail letter. There's nothing tying Dale Garrison to the letter, so there's no relevance.

"You said to stop by today," he says. "I needed a break."

"Sure, now's fine." I lead him into the living room. He declines my offer of a drink or anything to eat. I let the dogs out so they won't be a distraction.

"So what's up?" he asks, slapping his hands together as I return to the room.

"Lyle Cosgrove." I take the couch opposite his chair. "We need to talk about him."

"Okay . . ." No doubt, Ben can read my facial expression. He is calculating now. He's probably wondered all along if I have a skeleton in my closet, something to which the blackmail letter could be referring.

"And I was going to tell you this earlier," I start. "I should have, I realize that. At first, I wasn't sure, because I knew that once you had the information you'd use it to its maximum extent—and I wasn't sure I wanted that. But that's settled now."

Ben opens his hands. He seems to anticipate that he will not enjoy hearing what I have to say. He delivers his response with a somewhat icy tone. "Tell me now."

I rub my hands together. "I've never talked about this," I say. "I—I have some history with Lyle Cosgrove."

Bennett's lips part but he waits me out. His tongue appears to be working furiously inside his mouth. This is not good news, what I'm about to impart.

I start with the basics of what happened in June 1979—at least to the extent that I'm willing. Grant and I drove to Summit County for a party. We met up with Lyle Cosgrove, some guy named Rick, and Gina Mason.

I omit the fact that the whole reason we went to Summit County was because Grant couldn't use cocaine around his neighborhood, not the son of a senator, so apparently he found a guy across the state line.

"So anyway," I continue, "we're at this party. Lyle, Gina, and I go upstairs. We start with weed. We're getting pretty stoned—at least I am, I don't have much experience with the stuff. Then Lyle shows up with coke. Long story short, next thing I know it's past midnight. Party's over. I'm messed up beyond belief."

"Where's Tully?" Ben asks, eyes narrowed.

"Grant went home."

"Grant went home." Ben considers this. "Without you?"

"Yeah."

"And the other guy—Rick?"

"Went with Grant. Drove him home."

"So where did you go, Jon?"

"Well—I went with Lyle. To Gina's."

Bennett's head inclines slightly. He is fixated, his eyes intense, his hands clutching the chair as he leans forward.

"She was expecting me," I say. "I—I went into her bedroom and we"—I twirl a finger—"we had sex."

"She was expecting you."

"That's what I said, Bennett. She was expecting me." I gather myself a moment, ignoring the sweat on my brow. I steady a hand. "Look. That's it. We had sex, and I went back to the car, and Lyle drove me home."

My lawyer has not lost his intensity. No doubt, my story has not ended.

"So—apparently—well, that night she died."

"She *died?*"

"She died. I think she overdosed. That's what the coroner probably thought happened."

Ben shifts in his chair, his glare severe. "*Probably . . . thought?*"

"There was some thought," I continue, "that she might have been killed. Maybe even raped and murdered."

"By?" Bennett already knows the punchline.

"Well, by me." I exhale. "But the evidence didn't prove it. They investigated the thing and closed it. I wasn't charged. No one was charged."

"So tell me what this means." Bennett is shaking his hands, either in plea or fury, perhaps both.

"Well, I think Lyle Cosgrove was—"

"Blackmailing you." Bennett nods. The color has left his face. He swallows hard. "Threatening to bring all of this up. You don't raid the senator's war chest, he exposes a dirty secret in the middle of a campaign."

"Something like that."

"And how does Garrison fit in?"

I purse my lips. "You want some water or something?"

"I'm fine. How does Garrison fit in?"

"Garrison was Cosgrove's lawyer back then."

Bennett blinks rapidly. The revelations are coming one after the other, and the trial is around the corner. "So—Cosgrove was investigated, too, back then."

"Well, sure. Initially. But they knew I had had sex with her. I was the easy target."

Ben falls back in his chair, staring at the ceiling. "Garrison was handling juvie stuff back then?"

"Dale was hired by the Tullys, Ben."

He makes a face. "So Cosgrove was friends with Grant—"

"It's not so much that," I interrupt. I want to tread carefully here, but my lawyer needs to know what's lurking out there. I lower my voice for some reason. "The Tullys hired him to protect me."

Bennett's eyes, still cast to the ceiling, close. I've told him plenty here. He places his hands on top of his head and sighs. "How formal was this investigation?"

"They had what they called an inquiry."

"So it was formal."

"I guess."

"Transcribed," says Ben. "Evidence presented into the record. And you were arrested."

"All true except the last part," I answer. "I was never arrested."

His eyebrows rise. "That's quite a courtesy. I don't even want to know how *that* was arranged."

"You probably don't. Frankly, I don't know myself."

Bennett finally breaks out of his trance. He looks at me directly. The hint of scolding in his voice has not completely disappeared. "Did Cosgrove testify at this thing?"

"He did."

"What did he say?"

"That things were fine. He dropped me off to go into Gina's house. He came to get me when he was getting impatient, and I was kissing her goodbye."

"Kissing her goodbye?"

"That's what he said."

"But is that true?" Ben persists. "You said you *thought* she was alive when you left. So I assume you weren't kissing her goodbye."

I wave a hand. "The fact of the matter is, I don't remember, Ben. Okay? I don't remember. I remember being with her—you know, I remember the sex, at least kind of. And I remember crawling out the bedroom window—I banged up my knee, I remember that. In between that, afterward, I don't know. I don't recall."

Bennett studies me, trying to read between the lines while, at the same time, absorbing all of this information. "What *do* you recall next?"

"Waking up in the morning."

"No," he says quickly.

"Yeah. That's it."

"You're being totally straight with me, Jon? You don't remember a thing after that?"

"I don't, Ben."

He evens a hand. "You're telling me everything? You're leaving nothing out?"

"Ben, Jesus. I swear."

"You remember crawling out the window and next thing, it's morning in your bed?"

"Right."

Bennett's elbows hit his knees; his hands lace together. A man praying. His tongue rolls along his lips.

"You're worried that I can't effectively rebut what Cosgrove will say."

Ben doesn't answer. He is still sorting out the thoughts. Thoughts of the impact of this information on the trial. Thoughts of his friend, his boss for the last several years. How far I must have fallen in his eyes, in the space of ten minutes. Finally, Ben gets to his feet. He stands awkwardly, unsure of his next move.

"Ben," I say. "I'm sorry I didn't tell you this stuff sooner. But I'm not sure we're done here."

Bennett turns to the window, though he doesn't appear to be looking at anything at all.

"Maybe we continue this later," I offer. "I'll stop by later tonight. At the office."

Bennett nods absently but says nothing. He opens the door with caution, moving slowly to the driveway. My eyes follow him through the window to his car. He gets in but looks up at the house and makes eye contact with me. He is no doubt wondering who the person is looking back at him.

I pick up my portable phone as Ben drives off, and punch the numbers. Cal Reedy answers on the third ring. "Cal, it's me. I've got something else. Find a guy. Sure, Bennett knows about it. This one could be tougher, so I'm paying you, I insist. Your regular rate. I don't know his last name, that's the thing. Not even sure of his first name. He could be dead, for all I know. Or in jail. There are only a few details I can give you."

I hear Cal murmur to himself as he reaches for a pen and paper.

"Summit County," I say. "Nineteen-seventy-nine. First name, Rick. Nickname, Ricochet."

38

Bennett Carey looks better when I find him in his office at seven o'clock that evening. This is not to say that he looks particularly well—fourteen-hour days preparing for your friend's murder trial will do that, to say nothing of the history I laid on him earlier today—but at least he's not shell-shocked.

"I've made some notes," he greets me. "I have some thoughts. And some questions."

I take a seat in his office. "I'm sorry I didn't tell you sooner. I wasn't sure this was connected to 1979, and I was afraid once I told you, you'd use it. I wasn't sure I wanted you to."

"I got that," says Ben. "It was a bad move but I hear you."

"Okay." I pat the arm of my chair. "Do you want to start or me?"

"Me." Ben's holding a pencil over a legal pad. "Explain why Lyle killed Dale Garrison."

"Dale got Lyle parole recently. Dale was the lawyer. So they had contact."

"Huh."

"And Dale knew what happened in 1979. We'll never know exactly what attorney and client discussed, but Dale probably had a pretty good grip on things."

"Right."

"So, when Lyle got out of prison, he broached the topic with Dale."

Ben raises a hand. Stop. "Are you saying Lyle talked to Dale about blackmailing you?"

"Yeah. Not in so many words. But Dale got the drift. And Dale tried to talk him out of it."

"Dale tried to—" Ben fixes on me. "How do you know that, Jon?"

I open my briefcase and remove the letter I found from Dale to Cosgrove. "One of the things I was gonna show you before you wandered out of my house in a trance."

Ben takes the letter and looks at the paper itself before reading it. It's thick stock, creased at each third from when it was mailed. The original. I've made a copy, which I hold.

My attorney looks at me, ready to ask me where I got this, but I say, "Just read it," so he complies.

Mr. Cosgrove:

I enjoyed meeting with you today. Congratulations again on your parole. I write only to make clear something we discussed today, which left me troubled. You asked me a precise legal question—the statute of limitations for murder—and I gave you an answer, that there is no statute of limitations for murder. But other comments you made left me wondering why you asked.

"Cosgrove wanted to know if you could still be prosecuted for murder," says Ben, commenting as he reads along.

"And he learned I could," I add.

You never openly stated your intentions, or why you requested this knowledge, and it wasn't my place to ask. But our discussions about the long-ago past make me curious about what you plan to do with this information. Let me advise you, very strongly, that you should not attempt to dig up something from over twenty years ago. You stated to me then, and I believed you, that Jon Soliday did not force sex on that young woman and that she was alive when he left her house. I believed you when you told me, and you swore to that fact under oath. The prosecutors accepted your sworn testimony, and other evidence corroborated that testimony.

"Christ," Ben mumbles. "He's trying to keep Cosgrove tied to his testimony back then. He's telling Cosgrove that nobody would believe him if he implicated you."

"Right," I agree. "Because he swore otherwise under oath in 1979, and because 'other evidence' backed up that testimony."

If you attempt to swear differently now, you may be open to prosecution for any number of crimes, including perjury, obstruction of justice, and tampering with evidence. You should also be advised that juvenile proceedings are confidential, and the disclosure of anything related to them could lead to a criminal charge as well. I have not reviewed the relevant laws on this subject, but I must advise you of the possibility.

"Threatening Cosgrove," Ben continues.

"With bullshit," I answer. "Cosgrove couldn't be prosecuted for any of those crimes now. The statute of limitations is long gone on perjury and obstruction."

"Yeah, Dale's bluffing, all right. But he's right about the juvenile stuff being sealed. You can get in trouble for messing with that."

Let me say again what I said in my office today: that while our discussions were protected by attorney-client privilege, this privilege does not attach to discussions between attorney and client regarding *future* crimes. If I were to learn that you are attempting any crime related to the events of 1979, I would be required to revisit our conversation and determine that we were discussing a future crime in my office today. In that event, I would be compelled to disclose the substance of our conversation. At this point, however, it does not appear to me that you are planning any future misconduct, so unless something happens to change my mind, I am bound by the attorney-client privilege to keep our discussion confidential.

Ben nods along as he reads. "No one ever accused Dale of being dumb. He's right, too. The privilege doesn't extend to discussion of future crimes. Dale's saying, If you try to blackmail Jon Soliday, I'll tell the police."

"Dale did his best for me. And look what he got for it."

Ben places the letter on his desk. "Now can I ask you where you got this?"

I avoid eye contact. "What if I told you I found it in Dale's files—what the prosecution gave us?"

"Then I'd say you're wrong. There's no number stamp." At the bottom of each page the prosecution turned over to us was a number made with a stamp, so that each page has an identifiable number. A standard practice when parties share documents. "Plus, this is an original, not a copy."

"Right."

"So, Jon. Where'd you get this?"

"What if, in the midst of copying the documents for us, this one slipped through the cracks and they ended up dropping the original in our files?"

"Jon." Bennett shakes his head. "This letter was folded. It came from an envelope. This would never *be* in Dale's office. This was the one he mailed to—" Bennett's head rocks back. A long, quiet moan escapes from his throat.

My expression softens, not to be glib, but to indicate that he's on the right track.

"You got this from Cosgrove," he says.

"Landlord'll let in anyone who mentions 'DOC.'"

"Oh, no. Jon—I wasn't trying to give you *advice* on how to—"

"I know that. I know. I just needed to see where this all adds up."

"So you broke into Cosgrove's house and"—he picks up the letter and waves it—"you stole this from his place?"

I shrug. "I needed to know if he was blackmailing me."

Ben flails his arms, leaves his chair. "I mean—you realize this evidence can't be introduced at trial. Right? We can't admit this."

"Yeah, I sort of figured that," I say. "At the time, it seemed like a good idea. I was a little panicky."

"For good reason."

"Look, Ben. I know it was wrong. But I'm on trial for murder here. All things being equal, I'm not losing sleep over invading Lyle Cosgrove's privacy."

My lawyer studies me for a long moment. All things considered, rebuking me for this is not at the top of his list. He has plenty to occupy himself before the trial starts. "So Cosgrove had to kill Dale to blackmail you. Otherwise, if Dale heard about it, he'd turn Lyle in."

"Right," I say. "I don't think Dale ever would have reported it, because he wouldn't want this made public any more than I would."

"But Cosgrove didn't know that."

"So now you know, Ben. Cosgrove's the bad guy."

"Yeah. Wow."

"So maybe we should get to your questions and comments," I suggest.

Ben nods. There's no time for bemoaning our fate now. "Fair enough." He looks at his notepad. "Let's talk about this hearing they had back then. Lyle Cosgrove testified, you said. He testified that you went to this young lady's house—"

"Gina," I say. "Gina Mason."

"All right, you went to Gina's home and then when he came to get you later, she was kissing you goodbye. Right?"

"Right."

"Did you testify, Jon?" Bennett seems to be holding his breath. His client on record is probably not something he wants. Especially when I confessed to him earlier today that I don't remember a thing.

"Yes, I did. And yes, I testified that I kissed her goodbye, to answer your next question. I testified that she was alive and well and smiling and waving goodbye."

Bennett makes a small "o" with his mouth. Wow. Quite the conundrum, his client has.

"You lied under oath."

"It's perjury if it was a lie. It might have been true." I wince as I make the rationalization. Bennett does not rush to soothe me. His estimation of me continues to deteriorate.

"I need to look at that file," he says.

"You're in luck," I answer. I reach into my briefcase and remove the copies of the three pages, the only three pages left in my file from 1979. I note the look on Bennett's face. "I had Cal dig it up."

"Of course you did." The surprises never end.

"The first two pages aren't much." I hand them to him. "My testimony. Not pretty."

He reads the questions and answers from the juvenile inquiry with an ascending expression of horror. His hand comes to his mouth. "Oral sex," he mumbles. "Gina was on top. You fell." He swallows. "'Fuck me harder'?"

"That's what I said. And you'd be correct that I didn't remember any of that."

"You—made up a whole story about this."

"Yeah."

"You were coached well." He says it without rebuke. Time is short, deal with what you got, which includes an asshole of a client who held back material information until the last minute. Bennett drops the papers.

"Here's the one you're really gonna love," I say, handing the final page to my lawyer. "The investigator on the file wrote this, stuffed it into the record after it had been compiled. Seems he was seeing through the whole thing."

Bennett takes it and reads to himself.

I have grave reservations about the conclusions being reached in this investigation. I believe that the autopsy results have been interpreted in an overly generous fashion. I further believe that the deceased could not have consented to sex under any circumstances given her intoxication, even if I were to accept the version of events advanced by Mr. Soliday, which I do not. I believe that Mr. Soliday and Mr. Cosgrove have rehearsed their stories and relied on the absence of any further witnesses to escape a criminal charge. I believe that Jon Soliday should be arrested and charged with criminal sexual assault, at a minimum. This statement should have been made part of the record. I am inserting this into the file, despite the prosecutor's refusal to include it.

"He's right," says Ben. "Someone heavily intoxicated can't consent to sex."

"That's the law?"

"Yeah."

"Maybe it wasn't back then. Back in the late seventies, a lot of evidence about a rape victim could come in that can't now." I know this from my work in the legislature. We have amended the "rape-shield" law twice since I've been there. Used to be, when someone claimed rape and the accused claimed she consented, the jury was allowed to hear all about the sexual history of the victim. The theory was, someone who was so unchaste as to have premarital sex in the past was more likely to have consented to it with the accused. It reminds me of the juvenile inquiry, when the prosecutor read through several affidavits of people who had slept with Gina Mason. Nowadays, in our updated way of thinking, most of that evidence is inadmissible.

"Well." Bennett stretches his arms, showing me the palms of his hands. "This is not good, Jon."

"I know."

"They'll find this. The prosecutors."

"Yeah."

"Good God." He collapses, brooding a moment, collecting and filing the information. His brow furrows. "Two questions. One, how could a twenty-year-old case that never went to prosecution still be lying around?"

"The way Cal explained it was, they toss stuff over fifteen years old unless someone orders it kept around."

That catches my attorney's attention.

"Someone put a 'hold' order on this box," I add.

"Who? Who?" Bennett is plaintive.

"Someone scribbled a signature. Cal couldn't make it out. But he said it was five years ago. I was thinking it was irrelevant."

"Irrelevant," Bennett repeats with a harrumph.

"You had a second question."

"Yeah." He directs a finger at the document. "Why just these three pages?"

"Well, they fell out of the transcript."

"Okay, fine. But then where's the rest of the transcript?"

"Oh." I play with my earlobe, a nervous habit. "Hadn't thought about that."

"It was pulled. Someone pulled it."

"I think you're being too dramatic here, Ben. Yeah, it's possible. But that thing could be anywhere now. It's probably buried somewhere in a garbage heap."

Ben allows for that with a sweep of the hand.

"So here it is, Bennett. You've got the picture now. And the picture is that I'm pretty much screwed."

"I don't agree with that."

"No? Then let me spell it out for you. There is definitely someone I can point the finger at for Dale's murder. Lyle did it. We've got him stealing the cell phone that was used to bring me back to the office. We've got him holding a grudge against Garrison for screwing up his defense twelve years ago. He complained on appeal that Dale was ineffective, right?"

"Right."

"And now we know that he wanted to blackmail me, but that Dale was threatening to expose him if we did."

"All true," Ben agrees.

"But here's the catch. If I implicate Lyle, what happened in 1979 comes up."

"Yes, it will."

"And I can still be on the hook for the murder," I say. "I beat one murder rap and buy myself another one."

"Not likely, Jon." Bennett runs his hand over the table. "They couldn't prove it then, they won't now."

"Don't be so sure about that. Look, back then—I kept my head in the sand, but I'm pretty sure the Tullys pulled quite a few strings. I think they got to the coroner. I think they got to the prosecutor."

"You think," Ben summarizes, "that if someone were to revisit the evidence, they might think again about prosecuting you."

"Yes, I do. And think about who our county attorney is. Elliot Raycroft? Lang Trotter's boy? He'd love to lend whatever help he could to Summit County. He absolutely ruins me, if I'm not already ruined. And whatever chance Grant had in this election—over, done. Because Grant helped me out. Or at least, he was there."

Bennett settles back in his chair, in professorial mode. "One thing at a time. First, yes, they could re-open the investigation, but they wouldn't convict. Second, I hate to say it, but Grant Tully isn't going to win this election, Jon. You hear the poll he just ran?"

"No," I'm embarrassed to admit. Normally, I'd be the first one to know. What a difference a couple of months make.

"He's down twenty with five weeks left," Ben tells me. "That'll close a little before the end, but he's not gonna beat Lang Trotter. He's done."

"I'm not willing to concede that. And I'm not as confident as you that I won't be convicted of murder from 1979."

"Jon, you have to realize something. The blackmail note, this letter from Garrison to Cosgrove—this only proves that something ugly happened in 1979. Ugly enough for you that you don't want it brought up. That's reason enough for blackmail. It doesn't mean you killed that woman."

He sounds just like Grant. "You give me too much credit." I run a hand through my hair. "I'm not sure you're getting the proper flavor here, Bennett."

"Then help me."

I work my jaw a moment. He's my attorney, I might as well give all of it to him. It spills out quickly, a vomiting of the unthinkable. "Think about this—not as a friend, thinking the best of me, but think about it as a dispassionate attorney. If all Cosgrove wanted to do was blackmail me about the mere fact of this ugly incident, he could have. Hell, he could have gone straight to the *senator* with it. That would have made more sense. He wouldn't focus exclusively on me like he did. And he wouldn't have written the note the way he did."

"How did he write the note?"

"Remember? He says he's the 'only one left' who knows the secret. He says he 'could always just talk to the senator.' He's not threatening to go public with his secret. He's threatening to go to *Grant*. And why is he doing that, Bennett?"

My lawyer opens his hands.

"Because Grant thought I was innocent, that's why. That's what he told his dad, that's what he told me, that's probably what he told Lyle. But Lyle knows the truth, and he's betting that I'll pay him a quarter of a million dollars to make sure Grant *doesn't* learn about it."

"He's threatening to tell the senator that you killed that woman." Ben says it softly.

My lack of response is confirmation.

"And who knows *what* evidence he might have to support that," I add. "Maybe it's my word against his, maybe not. I have no idea. If I point the finger at him, he could bite me in spades. I'm royally fucked, Ben. The only person who I can claim murdered Dale has immunity. Unless I'm just willing to roll the dice. Call his bluff."

My lawyer deflates, conceding the point. "Well—so where does that leave us?"

"This is my question to you, Ben." I settle in a moment. "Is there any way we can point the finger at Lyle without 1979 coming up?"

"I—" Ben waves his hands helplessly. "I don't see how."

"The ex-con-with-a-grudge theory? He had a motive—Dale messed up his trial. He stole the cell phone, which proves his involvement. He's a violent felon. Isn't that enough?"

"Yeah, Jon, maybe, in a vacuum. But when we mention Lyle, they'll dig up his criminal record, and who knows? Maybe they connect him to you. Plus, don't you think Lyle is going to bring it up himself when he's hauled into court—by the prosecution, if not by us? He'll say, Jon Soliday killed that woman in 1979. I lied about it because the lawyer the Tullys hired for me, Dale Garrison, made me. But Garrison and I both knew the truth—that Jon's a killer. So Soliday killed Dale Garrison to cover up the 'secret that nobody knows,' and he framed me. He waited all this time I was in jail, and then when I got out, he killed Dale and set me up."

A moment of silence, as the blood rushes to my face. He's right. I'm trapped, as long as Lyle Cosgrove is around to point the finger right back at me.

Bennett suggests we think on the subject, but he's just learning about it, I've been battling it for some time now. I keep coming to the same conclusion. Wherever I turn, I'm stuck. As long as Lyle Cosgrove is around.

39

Assistant County Attorney Daniel Morphew walks into the courtroom with a woman at his side. The clerk, sitting at her desk next to and below the judge's seat, looks up and asks, "Is everyone here on *Soliday*?"

Bennett and I stand. Morphew walks over and introduces us to his campanion.

"Bennett Carey, Jon Soliday"—he opens a hand to the woman—"Erica Johannsen."

We all shake hands. She seems to treat my handshake no differently than Ben's. She is almost my height—close to six feet—with short dishwater hair, a strong face, and hazel eyes.

"Erica's going to run this thing," says Morphew. "I can't break free, it turns out."

Bennett nods matter-of-factly. Relief flows through me for some reason. Morphew is top brass, and even if he has less experience recently in the courtrooms, it says something that he will no longer handle the case. Not that I know a thing about Erica Johannsen.

Today is Friday, September 29. My trial begins in three days. We are here to discuss the logistics, witness lists, and the like.

"The judge will see you in chambers," says the clerk, a diminutive redhead who peers over the glasses resting at the base of her nose.

We head back to the judge's office. She is waiting for us in her black robe. "Counsel," she says.

Daniel Morphew introduces Ms. Johannsen to the judge. Judge Bridges says, "Nice to see you again, Counsel." So I guess they know each other, perhaps former colleagues at the county attorney's office. Maybe that's why the switch of prosecutors.

"I've read the pretrial briefs," says the judge. "Any changes?"

"Not that we know of," says Johannsen.

The judge reads the papers before her. "You're calling the ME"—the medical examiner, she means—"a security guard, a detective, a Ms. Joanne Souter, and a Ms. Sheila Paul."

Joanne Souter is the woman whose purse was stolen, and whose cell phone was used to call me back to the office. Sheila Paul is Dale Garrison's secretary. Her testimony will largely consist of seeing Garrison alive when she left the office at five, and the fact that it was I, not Dale, who changed the time and place of the meeting.

Judge Bridges looks up at the prosecutor. "Is that all, Ms. Johannsen?"

"Yes, Your Honor."

"This shouldn't take more than a few days, then, for the case-in-chief?"

"That sounds accurate."

"Okay." The judge looks at Bennett. "Counsel." She looks down at her papers. "The defense has listed the defendant himself, as well as Senator Tully, Gabriel Alucino—"

Gabe Alucino is someone who works for the HMO that would have covered Dale Garrison for his lung cancer treatment. I say would have, because Garrison didn't treat his cancer after the initial diagnosis and one unsuccessful surgery.

"—Dr. Roman Thorpe—"

An oncologist who treated Dale for his cancer initially.

"—and Attorney General Langdon Trotter."

"That's right, Your Honor," Ben says.

The judge looks at both attorneys. Both candidates for governor are named on this witness list.

"We'd certainly like to be heard at the appropriate time," says Erica Johannsen. She's referring principally to our listing of Attorney General Trotter. The judge won't hear argument on whether this testimony is admissible at this point, because we haven't called him to testify yet. All we've done is reserved the right to call him by listing him as a witness. In fact, we might not put on a defense at all. As Ben has explained it, most judges don't make the defense justify their witnesses at this early stage because it forces them to show their hand. Judges want to respect the defense's right to keep their cards close to their vest. Among other reasons, it provides an incentive for settlement of cases.

"I understand that," says Judge Bridges. "And I'm going to order that this witness list remain sealed for the time being. Mr. Carey, do you have any problem keeping your prospective witnesses to yourself?"

"No, that's fine," says Ben.

"What else?" the judge asks.

Ben clears his throat. "Judge, can we have Mr. Garrison's computer present in the courtroom?"

The judge looks at the prosecutor.

Erica Johannsen shrugs. "Sure," she says. She shows no outward signs of hysteria. I have no idea how long it's been since she was handed the reins, but I'm willing to bet it hasn't been that much time. That's what I want to believe, of course, fantasizing as I am of utter and total chaos in the prosecutor's office.

"Is that all?"

"Oh, Judge—" The prosecutor looks at her notes. "I almost forgot, I apologize. The defense has moved to exclude the letter we found at the defendant's office."

"The extortion letter."

"That's right."

"Counsel, I'm going to hear argument on the motions on Monday morning."

"It's not that, Judge. We are withdrawing it as evidence for the time being."

"You don't want to use it?"

"Judge, frankly, we haven't been able to tie it together with this murder. Until we do, it's of little use to us."

"Assuming I allowed it to begin with," the judge says.

"Sure. Yes. And we are still investigating. If we can tie it together, we would ask for the opportunity to make an offer of proof. I just don't want anyone accusing me of unfair surprise. If we can tie the letter into this murder, we will argue its relevance at that point. Until then, we don't plan on using it."

The judge looks at Bennett. "Counsel?" A good judge never wants to make a contested ruling if she can get both sides to concur. She can't be reversed by an appellate court if the parties agreed.

"That's fine," Ben says. He then adds, "If the defense will have the same opportunity."

Erica Johannsen looks at Ben with surprise, calculates on the spot. Ben is saying he might want to introduce the blackmail letter, which runs contrary to his pretrial motion to exclude it. "Sure, that's fine," she finally says.

Bennett and I went over this point. We expected to lose the argument on the admissibility of the blackmail letter, anyway. Bennett wanted the letter to come into evidence and then spring it on Lyle Cosgrove when the defense put on its case.

"That's fine, then," says the judge. "The parties agree to argue the admissibility of the extortion letter if and when it comes up. We'll see you on Monday." The mention of the day stirs the contents of my stomach. There was a small part of my brain that wanted the judge to decide, for some reason, to move the trial date, just to keep the possibility of a conviction that much farther away. But the longer the prosecution has to uncover the evidence about 1979, the better their case against me. It's possible that they'll never figure it out. It's not like I was arrested, much less prosecuted. I was simply investigated, and in a case out of this state. And how likely is it that they'll go all the way back to 1979 to find cases Dale worked on?

Cal has not yet found the guy "Rick" from 1979. I think this guy was a serious drug dealer who kept a low profile, maybe even used a fake name. He's probably stashed away in a jail cell or living in South America by now. But he was Lyle Cosgrove's friend back then, so maybe they still keep in contact. Maybe he was in on this somehow.

We all walk out together into the main courtroom. Bennett writes up the judge's order—in state court, attorneys write the orders and present them to the judges for their signature. While we are doing that, Erica Johannsen looks over Ben's shoulder. I say nothing. Daniel Morphew looks like he's late for a meeting, bobbing from one foot to the other.

We head to the elevator together. Johannsen gets off before the rest of us, headed for another court appearance. That leaves us with Morphew. Ben turns to him and extends a hand. "I was looking forward to it," he says.

Morphew looks at Ben's hand a moment, like he's not sure where it's been. He reluctantly takes it. Some prosecutors get that attitude about defense counsel. "From here on, talk to Erica," he says. "I'm washing my hands of this." He turns to me and says, "Good luck to you," as the elevator doors open at the fifth floor.

"That was weird," I say to Ben as the doors close again.

My defense attorney nods solemnly. "This whole thing is," he says.

I find myself walking more quickly than usual to keep up with Bennett Carey as we walk along the plaza outside the courthouse. It's like a circus in the plaza, people enjoying the extended summer. A man is standing on the southeast end juggling baseballs, with a cup in front of him for donations. I have some spare change so I toss it in.

I avoid serious injury by stepping over a skateboard that sails into my path. "What do *you* think is so weird about this?" I ask.

Bennett shakes his head absently. "Like I said, everything. They offer a plea right out of the box. A pretty damn good one."

"They wanted a conviction," I say. "However they get it, whatever the terms. It's better than losing. Especially for Trotter."

"I guess." Ben almost crosses a street where the sign has just turned to a solid "Don't Walk." I grab him and he snaps out of his cloud. "Morphew drops out. And he makes it sound like he's disgusted. 'I'm washing my hands of this.' And they drop the blackmail letter like a hot potato. They've never said word one about it. The whole thing's strange."

"Well, okay, Ben. Strange, maybe. But good, right? They offer a plea, the case must not be so good. The top guy drops off, maybe he's jumping off the *Titanic*." I take his arm for emphasis. "Goddammit, tell me this is good."

Bennett stops on a dime. He raises a hand, which balls into a fist. Frustration. "A trial lawyer doesn't like surprises," he says. "And there could be a hundred lurking around the corner." The light changes, and Bennett steps into the crosswalk, leaving me behind.

40

Darkness. A man sitting upright, Indian-style, silently in his empty, pitch-black house. Meditation would be a good guess, but I've never been spiritual. Never been much for religion, always just figured that if I led a good life I'd be rewarded.

There are shadows in the dark. Never noticed that. Brief but dramatic variations in the blackness. A cooling of the temperature, internally and externally. A freeing of the mind. The emergence of possibilities, turns in the road, never before envisioned. The decision won't come from my mind but from my heart. The logic has been thought through. It's down to instinct, to the urge for survival that grips us at our core.

My phone rings. I don't plan on answering but I peek at the caller-identification and recognize the number.

"Hey, you."

"Hello, Tracy."

"Are you holding up?"

"Yeah. Holding up."

"Good. Bennett's a good lawyer."

"Yes."

"You have to believe you're going to win."

"I do."

"Are you sure you're okay?"

"I'll be fine."

"I wanted to ask you something."

"Sure."

"Would you like it if I came out there to visit?"

"Not necessary." Ask me that a couple days ago, you would have gotten a different answer.

"I know it's not *necessary*. But you—it can't be easy going through this alone."

"You're thinking of me. You're praying for me. That's enough."

"Are you sure you're okay? You sound funny."

"I'm fine."

"I'd love to see a bunch of people. I haven't seen Jen and Krista and those guys for months. I wouldn't be a distraction. I could take a long weekend. We could just have—"

"I don't want you to see me like this."

There is so much in that statement, more, she realizes, than she can possibly discern. I indulge Tracy's protests but move her to a close and place the phone in my lap. That wasn't me. But maybe it's the new me. I stare into the darkness, challenging assumptions, thinking the unthinkable, rationalizing and fantasizing until I drift to sleep.

When I awaken, I put on my shoes and head downstairs.

41

This isn't me. The words are nonsensical and hauntingly familiar, harkening back to a time when I didn't fully appreciate the consequences of my actions. This isn't me.

But we are a sum of our parts. And nobody, no thing is a contradiction. There is no such thing. One of the underlying assumptions must be incorrect.

This *is* me. And maybe it always has been.

The remnants of the evening rain spill off the awning of Avery's Pharmacy. All of the customers have left the store. The lights in the front of the establishment are off, and someone working there has locked the door.

I check my watch. It's two minutes after one in the morning, early Saturday. Lyle Cosgrove started his shift at six and is closing. I only caught a glimpse of him inside the store. The only thing prominent, from my view across the street in my car, was kinky red hair, pulled into a ponytail and reaching the collar of his denim jacket.

He was bald in 1979. And big and muscular, all in all a pretty scary dude. I couldn't get much of a read on him from my distance this evening, but he lacked any kind of a swagger as he made it to the store. Prison can break a man's spirit.

A young woman, Asian, walks out of Avery's Pharmacy alone. She has no business walking on the southeast side by herself this time of night, but it's a quick trip to her car in the parking lot around the corner from the pharmacy.

Lyle Cosgrove walks out of the store and stops, facing but not seeing me. He cups his hands and lights a cigarette, pulls up the collar on his denim jacket, turns east, and continues walking. He favors his right leg, a pronounced hitch in his step.

I wait until he's a block away before starting up my car. I won't lose him. I know where he's going.

I unwrap the memo from Cal Reedy to Bennett, summarizing the criminal background of Lyle Cosgrove.

No juvenile history obtained. Driver's license revoked on 12/18/78, following DUI convictions on 2/24/78, 8/29/78, and third arrest on 11/04/78. Pleaded no contest to final charge. Agreed to surrender license for five years.

Arrested for sexual assault on 6/19/81. Pleaded guilty to simple assault. Served fifteen months in medium-security prison.

Arrested on 4/15/88 for armed robbery. Convicted on 8/28/88. Served twelve years, paroled on 7/22/00.

The logic swims through my mind, much as I try to block it out. The different angles, the repercussions of each, the brutal honesty that must enter the equation. All roads lead to one conclusion. Lyle Cosgrove has my number. He's got my fate wrapped around his finger.

I don't have a choice.

And this asshole killed Dale. That has to count for something.

I grip the steering wheel until my knuckles are white. The turmoil is welling up within me, a combination of rage and frustration and fear that blurs my thought processes, the logical reasoning. There is a certain freedom to it, the elimination of any rational barriers, the readiness to surrender to impulse. Maybe this is how it happens.

I promised that I would spend my life repenting, making good on my silent promise to Gina Mason's little brother, that I would live a good and decent life and not bring harm to another person. Instead, I followed

Grant Tully into the world of scorch-the-earth politics, where moral rewards are there to be taken but only in the murky sea of power lust and envy and insincerity. And now, grasping the mantle of the unjustly accused, of the defender of good and evil—now this.

Where is the guilt? Where is the concern for what really happened to Gina Mason? When did my survival take precedence over all else? But that's an easy one, that last one. The answer is June of 1979. When I knew that Grant Tully was covering for me but didn't want to accept it. When I lied, instead of telling the truth and letting the chips fall where they may.

I drive down the avenue now, accelerating until I pass Lyle Cosgrove, walking alone on the sidewalk. I mumble to myself and slam a fist into the steering wheel. I go down three more blocks and pull into a bank parking lot, screeching the tires in the process. I'm not being discreet, not being careful, and I like it. I drive into the area farthest from the street and sidewalk and kill the engine. I sit in silence, my breathing heavy. The fury washes over me; it's all I can do not to slam the car door as I get out.

I try to control the heaving in my chest as I creep forward in the darkness of the parking lot, as the illumination of the sidewalk ahead of me is broken by the shadow of an oncoming figure. I stifle the question screaming inside me, with such a wicked, piercing voice that I almost can't hear the approaching footsteps of a limping pedestrian.

What is happening to me?

42

Showtime. It's been Monday, October 2, for four hours. I've been awake for every one of them. I've settled on staying in bed for the time being, the covers gathered to my neck, though the temperatures remain mild in the city.

The pugs are sharing the pillow next to mine. They've slept fitfully, periodically raising their heads to wonder what I'm doing sitting up. At the moment, they are grunting and snoring contently.

The portable phone rests in my lap. I've partially dialed the number five, no six times. But I'm not going to wake her in the middle of the night.

I'm sorry, I tell her again in the silent darkness. I'm sorry I wasn't the person you thought I'd be. I'm sorry I made you believe I was someone I was not, that you wasted five years of your life with me. I know nothing's black and white. I know we share the fault. But I'm ready to take the generous portion. I was the one who started the downward slide. I didn't spend the time with you. I made you feel unwanted. You weren't—you never were. But I was too self-absorbed to know what I was doing to you. You tried to tell me and I didn't listen. And so you stopped loving me.

I'm sorry for everything I've done. But I'll make you this promise. I won't be sorry again. From here on out, things are different. I won't lie. If they ask me, I won't lie about anything. I'll let my lawyer do everything he can to get me acquitted. I'm not giving in. But I'm doing it the right way now.

43

"Jonathan Soliday is charged with murder in the first degree," says Erica Johannsen. "He was found with the victim—Dale Garrison—in the victim's office. He was found with Mr. Garrison dead. And when he was found, he did what a murderer in that situation *would* do—he tried to talk his way out of it. He tried to convince an approaching security guard that Dale Garrison had simply fallen asleep. He tried to get the guard out of the office before he could realize the truth—that Dale Garrison had been murdered."

It's the afternoon now. Because this is a bench trial, no jury, the judge didn't mind cleaning up some other matters before the trial began. We finally decided to kick it until after lunch.

Erica Johannsen is standing behind her table in the courtroom, wearing a herringbone jacket and long black skirt. She speaks plainly and matter-of-factly about these events. Perhaps that's because there is no jury at this trial, or perhaps that's just her way. Either way, it plays well for her. It will be all the tougher to claim that this is a political smear job when the prosecutor is speaking so quietly and soberly.

"We will show you that the defendant scheduled an appointment with the victim that was originally set for lunch on Thursday, and that the defendant rescheduled it for after-hours on Friday night, when no one would be there except the victim. We will show you that Dale Garrison was murdered by strangulation. We will show you that a security guard named Leonard Hornowski found the defendant in the offices of Dale Garrison and that the defendant lied to Mr. Hornowski about what had transpired. And we know one final thing. We know that the defendant was the only person in that suite of offices with Mr. Garrison from the time he was last alive until the time he was strangled."

The prosecutor steps away from the table, toward the center of the room. I'm still stuck on something she said near the beginning—I scheduled the meeting for after-hours. That's not true. We were planning to meet for lunch on Thursday and Garrison's office called me and changed it to Friday night at seven. Their story makes sense, that I wanted no one else around so I could commit murder. But that's not what happened.

Erica Johannsen takes her seat after a brief summary, all in all a very simple opening statement. This is a very straightforward case from their perspective. I was the only one there and I told a bullshit story when I was caught.

Before we started today, Bennett informed the judge that he wanted to reserve his opening statement until the defense puts on its case. So the prosecutor turns to her first witness.

"Dr. Mitra Agarwal."

Mitra Agarwal is a tall, angular woman with kinky salt-and-pepper hair with no apparent style in mind, just falling to her shoulders. She looks like a professional in the world of science or academia, unconcerned with physical impressions. She is wearing a yellow blouse with a clasp at the collar. Her skin is light brown and freckled, with deep worry lines on her brow. Her spectacles rest on the middle of her nose.

Erica Johannsen takes the doctor through her credentials. She is the chief deputy medical examiner in the county coroner's office. Practiced over twenty years. Lots of schooling.

Next, Dr. Agarwal testifies to the basics of this case—receiving the body of Dale Garrison in the morgue, performing the autopsy, sending an investigator to the scene and to consult with the police. She describes the precise incision she used, the organs she examined and weighed. The judge, who undoubtedly has put on MEs during her stint as a prosecutor, seems to know that this information can be glossed over. Even I lose interest. Bennett raises no objection to the prosecutor's request to certify the doctor as an expert.

"In the course of your autopsy, Doctor, did you reach an opinion as to cause of death?"

"I did," says the doctor. She has a slight Indian accent, speaks quietly and deliberately. "The cause of death was asphyxiation by manual strangulation."

Erica Johannsen takes a step away from the lectern where her notes rest. "On what do you base this diagnosis?"

The doctor blinks rapidly, pushes her glasses to the top of her nose and examines her notes briefly before looking up. "The presence of external evidence of abrasions and contusions on the skin of the neck. Internal hemorrhage beginning with the sternocleidomastoid, the omohyoid, the sternothyroid, and the thyroglossus." She begins to go on but stops herself. "I'm referring to what we call the 'strap muscles' of the neck."

"So—abrasions on the external neck skin and internal hemorrhaging in the neck?"

"That's correct."

"Go on, Doctor."

"There was petechiae in the eyelids. Hemorrhaging, in other words."

"All of these findings are consistent with your diagnosis?"

"Yes," Dr. Agarwal says. "It's the only logical diagnosis."

The prosecutor approaches the witness with photographs of Dale Garrison at the morgue. Some are full-body shots, others are close-ups that turn the stomach. A shot of his eyes, his neck, his face. Doctor Agarwal confirms the external evidence of hemorrhaging.

"Okay." Erica Johannsen moves back to the lectern. "And did you fix a time of death?"

"I would say the time of death was sometime in the evening of Friday, August eighteenth."

"And what do you base that on?"

The doctor blinks quickly again, narrows her eyes. "Based on the livor mortis, rigor mortis, and algor mortis. In other words, from looking at the settling of the circulating blood, the freezing of the muscles, and the cooling of the blood. One can never precisely determine time of death. In fact, it becomes slightly more difficult with a cancer sufferer such as the decedent."

"The decedent had cancer?"

"He did, yes. He suffered from cancer of the lung and lymphoma. That will affect rigor mortis because patients with cancer do not show rigor well. And algor mortis—the cooling of the blood—is less helpful than usual because the rule of thumb is that a body cools off by 1.5 degrees centigrade an hour, but this presupposes that the original temperature was normal, which is not necessarily true of the cancer patient. So when we—" The doctor stops as she notices Bennett on his feet.

Bennett holds up his hands. "I certainly didn't mean to cut off the doctor," he says. "But in the interest of saving the doctor's and the court's time—we would be happy to stipulate that the range of the time of death included the hour of seven p.m. on the evening of August eighteenth."

This is a fairly minor point all in all. There is no doubt Dale was dead by around seven because the security guard can testify to that. But unless I testify—which is never a guarantee—they need to set an earlier boundary for his death.

The prosecutor turns to the doctor, who nods and says, "Certainly." So Erica Johannsen says, "We will stipulate."

"Just one final question, then," says the prosecutor. "Doctor, to what level of certainty do you—oh, I'll just speak plain English. How sure are you of your diagnosis as to cause of death?"

"I am entirely certain. There is no alternative."

Erica Johannsen thanks the witness and takes her seat. I see the slightest measure of relief on her face.

Bennett is doodling on his notepad, which contains scrawlings from his interview with the forensic pathologist at the downstate university. "There was hemorrhaging in the eyelids," he says without looking up.

"Yes, there was."

"Hemorrhaging internally as well, in the strap muscles of the neck."

"Yes."

"What about the brain, Doctor?" Ben asks. "The brain was swollen significantly, wasn't it?"

"Yes, there was cerebral edema," says Dr. Agarwal.

"Herniation of the brain stem?"

"That as well."

"And therefore asphyxiation."

"Correct."

"Thank you." Bennett writes something on the paper. After a moment's pause, the medical examiner actually begins to leave her chair. Ben looks up with a smile. "Not quite done, Doctor." She settles back in, crosses a leg, an embarrassed smile on her face.

Ben says, "Tell the court, if you would, what the superior vena cava is."

The doctor's eyes narrow slightly. She is confused. "The superior vena cava is the vein leading to the heart from the head."

"It's how blood travels from the head to the heart."

"Correct."

"Okay. Now, wasn't there a cancerous tumor found near the superior vena cava?"

The medical examiner holds her look on Bennett a moment before pushing up her eyeglasses and reviewing her notes. While she reads over her autopsy findings, Ben wags the pen in his hand. The prosecutor is looking through some papers as well.

"There was," Dr. Agarwal says. "A tumor of approximately two and a half inches in diameter arose in the mediastinum—the chest cavity—near the superior vena cava."

"Thank you. And if you would, please describe what's known as superior vena cava syndrome." Bennett drops his pen. "In layman's terms, if you could."

Dr. Agarwal cocks her head. She opens her mouth but stops, considering the question a moment without a hint of defensiveness, more with academic curiosity. "Superior vena cava syndrome involves obstruction of the superior vena cava."

"Obstruction by a cancerous tumor," says Ben.

"That's correct."

"Blood is cut off."

"Or partially obstructed."

"Okay," says Ben. "But *completely* obstructed in fatal cases."

"Yes, typically."

"And SVCS—that's what you call it, right?"

"You can refer to it that way, of course."

"SVCS occurs most commonly in patients suffering from cancer of the lung or lymphoma, isn't that true?"

"That's true." The doctor seems to be glancing at her notes now.

"The very cancers Dale Garrison had."

"That is so, yes."

"To put it simply—a cancerous tumor intrudes on the superior vena cava and obstructs, partially or completely, the flow of blood from the head."

"That's correct."

"And"—Ben raises the notepad, making a point of reading verbatim—"with death caused by SVCS, there is marked vascular congestion of the head and neck, with petechiae."

"That's correct."

"Which were present in Mr. Garrison."

"Yes."

"And the tumor obstructing the superior vena cava can be rather small, can't it?" Ben once again reads deliberately from his notepad. "No bigger than the size of a grape, isn't that so?"

The doctor answers through veiled eyes. "I believe that's correct."

"Okay. So." Bennett claps his hands lightly. "SVCS is accompanied by hemorrhaging in the neck."

"Yes."

"And in the eyelids, too?"

"That could be, from the increased venous pressure, yes."

"And swelling of the brain—cerebral edema."

"Yes."

"Which leads to herniation of the brain stem."

"That's right."

"Which leads to asphyxiation."

"Yes."

"And all of these characteristics I have just named—hemorrhaging in the eyelids and neck, swelling of the brain, herniation of the brain stem, the presence of a cancerous tumor at the superior vena cava—all of these things were part of your autopsy findings in this case."

"Yes, sir. Which is not to say I believe SVCS is the cause of death. But yes, you are correct."

Bennett folds his hands on the table and stares at the doctor for a moment. Certainly, he is not pleased with her qualification. "You can't rule out asphyxiation as a result of superior vena cava syndrome as the cause of death, can you?"

"I find the theory untenable," she says curtly. "The victim died as a result of manual strangulation."

"But surely you're not saying you rule it out completely?" Ben is holding his hands out.

"I would say it is highly unlikely but conceivable."

"You say you find death by superior vena cava syndrome *untenable*." Ben leans back in his chair. "How many times have you diagnosed death by SVCS?"

"I don't believe I ever have." The doctor frowns. "I don't autopsy everyone who dies, sir."

"You autopsy deaths of suspicious, usually violent origin, right?"

"And virtually all children under the age of twelve," the doctor adds.

"So you've never diagnosed SVCS?"

"No, sir, I have not."

"Well, have you ever even *seen* it?"

Dr. Agarwal wets her lips and searches her memory bank. "Once, in an academic setting. Maybe ten years ago."

"Oh." Ben is slightly condescending here. He smiles out of the side of his mouth. "Well, how many times have you diagnosed asphyxiation by manual strangulation?"

"Oh—many times." The doctor's voice rises with authority.

"Dozens, Doctor?"

"I would say over thirty cases, probably closer to fifty."

"Thirty to fifty cases." Bennett nods agreeably, turning to the prosecutor as he does so. "And not one SVCS case in the bunch."

"It's an uncommon process," she says. "Particularly in a fatality. People do not often die of SVCS. It's very treatable."

Bennett straightens. "Doctor, are you aware the decedent was *not* treating his lung cancer?"

"Objection." Erica Johannsen follows Bennett's lead and remains in her chair. "There is no foundation for that testimony."

"I'll try again, Your Honor." Bennett fixes on the witness. "Dr. Agarwal, did you find any evidence that Mr. Garrison had been treated with chemotherapy or radiation?"

"I don't believe I did."

"Or any other medical treatment for cancer?"

"I saw no indication that the victim had treated his cancer."

"And, Doctor, if the decedent had chosen not to treat his cancer for whatever reason, would it surprise you to learn that he had not treated his SVCS, either?"

"Objection," says Johannsen. "Assuming facts not in evidence."

The judge considers the objection, but before she rules, Bennett offers to rephrase. "Doctor, regardless of whether you believe it was the cause of death, aren't you forced to agree with me that the decedent suffered from superior vena cava syndrome?"

The doctor purses her lips and takes her time with the question. "Certainly, there was a tumor around the superior vena cava. Whether it constituted an obstruction of the SVC is another matter."

"Okay, but you can't rule it out, can you?"

"No, I can't rule it out as a condition from which the decedent suffered. I absolutely do not agree it was the cause of death."

"Just as you've never found it in any other strangulation death you diagnosed."

"That's correct."

"And you'd agree with me, wouldn't you, that SVCS is more likely to be fatal when it's never treated?"

"Like any malady, it is more dangerous if not treated."

Bennett pauses a moment, takes his pen, and scans the page. "Thank you, Doctor."

Erica Johannsen rises violently from her chair. I don't think she had any idea that we would be challenging the diagnosis. Bennett did not name a forensic pathologist as a witness for the defense, in part for the sake of surprise during Dr. Agarwal's cross-examination, in part because all of the medical examiners we consulted believed that death by manual strangulation was far more likely.

"Doctor," Johannsen asks, raising the volume of her voice, "do you consider it plausible that the decedent died as a result of superior vena cava syndrome?"

"I do not consider it plausible, no."

"Please tell the court why not."

The doctor inclines her head toward the judge. "Two reasons. First—something that the defense attorney didn't mention. The abrasions and contusions on the neck were of sufficient force that I don't believe they could have been self-inflicted. The second reason is that death by SVCS is sudden, and my findings are not consistent with sudden death. The abrasions on the neck would not have been produced by a single, sudden clutching of the throat. The hands were on the neck for a longer time than that. There was friction that caused the abrasions, which is indicative of movement between the victim and the assailant—a sign of struggle, in other words. Moreover, the decedent's collar and tie were out of place. His collar was unbuttoned." She raises a hand. "There are too many inconsistencies. This man died from asphyxiation by manual strangulation."

"Thank you, Doctor."

The judge and witness turn to Bennett for recross. Bennett brings his hands to his throat. "Wanna see how fast I can open my collar and grab my throat?" he asks.

"Not particularly," says the doctor. The judge smiles. Someone in the courtroom laughs. It's the first time since the beginning of today's proceedings that I'm aware of the spectators.

Ben releases his hands. His smile fades. "Two reasons you gave why my idea doesn't work. One, the force on the neck."

"That's right."

"Aren't you aware of cases where people who are suffocating grab their throats?"

"Of course."

"And you *completely* rule out the possibility that such a grabbing—a quick, violent grab of the neck—could cause abrasions and contusions? You're saying, there's no *way* that could happen?"

Dr. Agarwal sighs audibly. "One might be able to make some mark on one's own neck. Perhaps a very minor contusion. But I would not expect the skin to be abraded. We must also account for the fact that this man was frail from cancer. He was elderly. We are making rather large leaps, sir. A frail, ill, elderly man nearly dropping from sudden death by a SVCS-induced asphyxiation simply could not make those marks on his own neck."

"Again—you *categorically* rule it out? Yes or no?"

"He also wouldn't have the time," she says. "Not to undo his collar, grab his throat with that amount of force. I would have to say that, under these circumstances, the likelihood is so infinitesimal that it's hardly worth discussing."

Bennett can't stop here, so he moves on to the issue of timing. The medical examiner states that SVCS-induced death would be from one to three seconds. Yes, it is conceivable that Dale had time to make some marks on his neck within that time, but it is unlikely that he would do so while seized with a blood clot. Highly unlikely, she adds before Ben can continue. Ben moves to his safest area—that Dr. Agarwal wasn't there, she can't know for certain what Dale did, in what order, for how long. It's window dressing. He just didn't want to end on a bad note. I can see it in the judge's face as well, an ease in her expression, the lack of concentration. She has lost interest. The medical examiner was right. Ben's theory is nice on an academic level, makes for a decent cross-examination, but in the end nobody thinks Dale Garrison died of natural causes, not with the bruising on his neck. The best Bennett can do, in closing, is to get Agarwal to concede that SVCS-induced death is conceivable.

"Thank you, Doctor, that's all." Ben returns to scribbling on his notepad. Dr. Mitra Agarwal gathers her papers and leaves the witness stand. I can't help but feel slight disappointment. I muster a silent pep talk. We had nothing to lose with the ME. Our primary defense is the truth—that even if Garrison were strangled, it wasn't by me.

Bennett looks at me with a poker face but nods shortly. He wouldn't give me a big thumbs-up under any circumstances, even if the judge weren't here, but I imagine his assessment is the same as mine. I lean in and whisper "Well done" to him as the judge recesses for the day.

44

"The security guard's tomorrow," says Ben. "And the secretary. We might even get to the police detective."

I sit up in the chair. I'm in the conference room at Seaton, Hirsch with Ben, working this evening after the first day of trial. Our war room looks more like a warehouse for banker's boxes and manila folders.

"Tomorrow night's the debate," I say, referring to the first of three televised debates between Grant Tully and Langdon Trotter. "I want to go."

"If there's time," says Ben. "The security guard could be big."

"Do you have anything good?"

"Not really, no. I don't know that I need to beat him up, anyway." The phone in the corner of the conference room rings. Ben walks over and answers. "Send him up," he says. Then he turns to me. "It's Cal Reedy."

Ben sits and awaits our private investigator, drumming his fingers on the table.

"Yes or no," I say. "Does the judge buy our cause of death?"

"No," says Ben. "My best bet."

"Mine, too." I deflate for some reason, hearing the official prediction from my lawyer.

We sit in silence a moment. "What's Cal want?" I ask.

"Don't know, Jon."

Cal Reedy speeds into the conference room. He's wearing a yellow T-shirt and dirty jeans, a grungy baseball cap on his crown. "Big news," he says.

Bennett and I await the word.

"Lyle Cosgrove," he says. "Cosgrove didn't show for work the last two shifts. The guy who runs the pharmacy is supposed to tell the parole officer if he misses a single day. But the guy's a bleeding heart, I guess, so he gave him another day. Then he called. So the parole officer calls his apartment, no answer—"

"Cal, for Christ's sake," I say.

"He's dead," Cal says. "They found him dead in his apartment. Dead as disco. Strangled."

The three of us do not move initially. My eyes dart at Bennett Carey, who is staring back at me.

"They think he was killed a few days ago. Late September, sometime."

Ben whispers something I don't catch.

I sit back in my chair and battle the nerves.

"They found some stuff, too," Cal continues. He wipes at some sweat across his forehead, then notes our reaction. "I still have friends on the force."

"But you didn't ask on our behalf," Ben says.

"No, no—come on. Just a curious George, I was."

"Tell me what the hell they found," I say.

Cal turns to me. "They found a sealed envelope containing a pair of women's undies."

My mouth drops open. Cal has done enough work on this case that he probably knows what we're thinking. Gina Mason's underpants, and all the evidence that may come with it. It tells me more, too. It tells me that Lyle was ready to back up his blackmail with more than his word. He had physical proof. DNA, semen, pubic hair, whatever. The thing is, I always admitted I had sex with Gina that night.

"They also found a key to a safe-deposit box," Cal says. He has settled into a chair now, between Ben and me. "They're going to go the bank it's assigned to and search it."

I close my eyes a moment. Ben's voice comes next. "Are they making any connection between Cosgrove and Dale Garrison?"

"No." Cal's voice. "Not so far as I can tell. They figure, it was probably a drug deal gone bad, or maybe some payback for something Cosgrove did before he went in the clink twelve years ago. He's a lifelong jailbird. They won't waste too much time on this."

I open my eyes again. "You'll keep on it, Cal? See what the safe-deposit box shows?"

He taps the table. "You got it, partner."

"Thanks, Cal." The investigator rises and leaves the conference room. I'm left with Bennett Carey, who's wondering if he's looking at a murderer.

"Well," he says, "I guess we have our empty chair, don't we, Jon?"

I divert my eyes and don't bother with a denial. I don't even look at my lawyer.

"Is there anything you want to say to me?" Ben asks.

"Yeah," I answer. "Tell me how this changes our strategy."

"Oh, you want to know how this changes our strategy? Okay." I can hear Bennett, in his anxiousness, move in his seat. "Okay. The county attorney finds the connection between Lyle and Dale. That *will* happen. They'll do a routine cross-check. They'll see Lyle was a preliminary suspect in Garrison's death and put two and two together. Sooner than later, they throw you into that mix. Then they look **hard** at the idea that you killed Cosgrove."

I rub my hands together slowly and absorb that reality.

"I need to know," says Ben.

"All you need to do is get me acquitted," I answer. "Look at that guy Rick from 1979."

"Rick? You think he's involved in this, too?"

"Maybe." I grit my teeth, the darkness rising within me again. "Or maybe Cosgrove's death is unrelated. The guy's an ex-con. He lives among ex-cons. Maybe it was a grudge. Maybe an old prison score was settled."

"I need to know," Ben repeats.

I leave my chair and head for the door, still without looking at my lawyer. "Just win the damn case," I tell him on my way out.

45

When I return to my home, there is a blue sedan parked in my driveway. I don't recognize it and see nothing through the driver's side window to give me any indication.

When I try the door, it's open. I open it slowly and hold my breath. The dogs, Jake and Maggie, come racing to me from the kitchen. I hear the scraping of their nails before I see their chubby little bodies rushing toward me. Then I catch the luggage, the traveling bag I bought three years ago, Christmas, sitting by the staircase in the hallway. Next to it, a pair of heels.

My former bride, Tracy Stearns Soliday, walks out of the kitchen and stops at the threshold. She's in work attire, a cream turtleneck, muted plaid skirt and simple jewelry. Her dark hair, grown out some, is clipped back. She looks thinner than even when we were married. Her cheekbones, her chin, her nose all seem more defined. She's out of her heels and has taken off her earrings.

Her green eyes are defiant. "I have a say in this, too," she says.

"What's that?"

"In whether I come out for a visit. I don't need your permission."

My mouth eases into a smile. "No, I suppose you don't." I wave my hand about the room. "Technically, you're still on the mortgage."

"Darn right I am."

I sniff the air. "Don't tell me you cooked."

"Well, hey, every once in a while."

I reach for my heart, feigning surprise. I'm just buying time. We're still standing across the room from each other and we haven't yet negotiated how we'll greet each other.

She looks different. This woman, whom I saw every day for the last eight years of my life, looks different from any time I've seen her. Better, I guess, though in some ways better is worse.

We gradually make it toward the center of the room. I take the lead and extend my arms. She is relieved I've made the call. Our hug is platonic. Not brief but not intimate, either, ending with pats on the back. When we pull away, she measures me. "We always promised we'd be friends. Didn't we promise that?"

I smile at her. "We are friends."

"Then what's this 'I don't want you to see me like this'? You had me worried."

I pat her arm but do not respond to the statement. "You look good, Tracy. You look great."

She is very pleased by the compliment. She's never been particularly vain. It's not that she's flattered. She's glad I feel sufficiently at ease to say such a thing.

She returns the compliment and I laugh at the thought. "I've got gray hairs on my *feet*." I've dropped about ten pounds since I was arrested, weight I could afford to shed, but I've aged. I've seen it mostly in my eyes, not so much bags or wrinkles but a darkness beneath them.

She tells me she made a stew so I could eat it for a few days; it will be ready in a half hour. She brings in a bottle of red wine and we sit, immediately joined by the dogs. Jake remembers her but he's always been more my dog. Maggie never met Tracy but she throws herself at her, rubbing her face in her lap.

I start by asking Tracy about herself. She gives me the skinny on life on the East Coast. She's already been promoted once in her PR firm, now a vice president. Funny that I didn't even know that. She hadn't called to tell me. She's even done a little bit of work on a political campaign, a mayoral race, which she presents to me as ironic. With a little prodding, she reluctantly informs me she's been dating. A doctor, she tells me, a surgeon, which I accept with a smile on my face and a shot to the gut. She checks on the stew and announces another half hour before it's ready.

She completes her summary and we occupy ourselves a moment by doting on the dogs. I am suddenly nervous, for some reason. There have been so many things about the breakup of my marriage that seem to lack reason. Or maybe it's just that the reasons themselves lack any meaning.

"I was thinking terrible things," she says. "After talking to you on the phone. You sounded spooky."

"Sorry. This thing, y'know. Brings out some weird emotions."

She brings a hand to her forehead. "I can't even imagine."

"We're gonna beat this, Tracy. You should know that."

"I do know that."

"No you don't." I smile at her. "I appreciate the sentiment. But the evidence is pretty weak. They've got me caught in a bad coincidence. But there's not much for proof. Not much for motive."

She waits me out but I don't elaborate. She gives me a hopeful expression and we both pray like hell that I'm right. Her cell phone rings and she rushes to her purse to shut it off.

"Someone expecting you?" I ask.

"Oh—no. No."

"Go have some fun, Trace."

"No, Jon. It's just Krista." She shrugs in apology. "I didn't know when you'd be home. Or if you'd be up for company. I know you're in the middle of trial—"

"Tracy." I touch her hand. "I should probably get some sleep. The trial, like you said. Thank you for making the dinner. I look forward to eating some home cooking. I have some stuff to go over. How long you in town?"

"I don't know. As long as—I don't know."

"You're not here on business," I say. "You took vacation."

"Well, why not?"

I give her the most reassuring smile I can. "I really appreciate that. It was—it was really great seeing you. Maybe before you go, we can get together."

"As much as you want. You have to tell *me*—"

"Okay. Great. I will. I know your cell."

"No, it's a different one."

Oh. She has a different cell phone, too. Funny how minor things can pull at you.

She gives me her new number. "I'm staying with Krista."

"Great. I have her number." I wink at her. "Go see your friends. Have fun." I get up from the couch to move this along.

She does, too, but she's ever stubborn. "I came here to see *you*, Jonathan. I want to help."

"You have. It means a lot." I touch my heart. "Really. I just—I need to focus."

"Sure. Of course. Of course."

I give my former wife another hug. I close my eyes and, as discreetly as possible, breathe in her scent—the perfume, she has not changed. She'll let me take the lead again. I could hold her for an hour, she wouldn't budge. I could ask just about anything of her at this moment, and I truly believe she'd comply.

"I'll call you," I promise her.

"I'll think good thoughts." She brings her hands together in prayer. I see Tracy Soliday to the door and watch her drive away. Then I return to the couch and wait for the drumming of my heart to subside.

46

The prosecution calls Leonard Hornowski to the witness stand. This is the security guard who found me in Dale's office.

Hornowski wears a frown naturally. Maybe it's the downward turn of his handlebar mustache, but it seems to fit his demeanor. He is beyond serious, more like glum. His eyes are set close together, separated by a thin nose and pointy chin. His hair is stiff, chocolate brown. He is trim but appears to be well built; his neck is thick, with prominent veins.

He states his full name with an official authority. His voice is strong, a south-side accent. He comes on a little strong, the physique and the energy, and he appears to be nervous.

Erica Johannsen takes him to the big day. His shift began at five p.m. lasted until the wee hours of the morning. Security works all day, all night, every day of the year.

"Let's go to the hour of seven o'clock that evening," says the prosecutor. Once again, she's standing at the lectern between the prosecution and defense tables. She feels no need for dramatic positioning or gesturing at a trial where the judge is the finder of fact.

"I received a call on my radio of a disturbance on the eighth floor."

"Who was the call from?"

"The lobby."

"What time was this?"

"About seven-thirty."

"Was the call any more specific than the eighth floor?"

"North end," says Hornowski.

"And what suite of offices are on the north end of the building?"

"The law offices of Dale Garrison and a realty company."

"And where were you when you received the call?"

"Sixth floor. I took the elevator to eight. The elevator's on the north end, so I got off and went to the realty company first. I went to the door but it was locked."

"The outside door was locked."

"Right."

"So what did you do?"

"I went to the Garrison offices."

"Was that door locked?"

"No, it was unlocked. So I went in."

"Tell us what happened next."

"I walked into a lobby—a reception room, I guess. There was no one in there so I kept going."

"Did you announce yourself?"

"Oh—yes, I did. When I first walked in. I went into the hallway and saw the defendant standing in the corner office. I walked up to him. I went into the office."

"What did you see when you entered?"

"I saw an older gentleman lying facedown on his desk."

"What was the defendant doing? Oh, wait." The prosecutor stops herself. "Do you see the person you saw standing in that office in court today?"

"He's right there." Hornowski points at me.

"Stipulate to identification," Ben says in a bored voice.

"All right, Mr. Hornowski." Erica Johannsen shuffles her notes on the lectern. "You're in the office. You see a man sitting at the desk with his head down on the desk."

"Right."

"What was the defendant doing?"

"He was standing in the middle of the room. He seemed nervous. Not happy to see me."

"Move to strike," Ben says without standing.

"Don't read his mind, sir," the judge tells the witness. "Sustained."

"Did you have a conversation with the defendant at that time?"

"I did. He told me to be quiet. He said the man was sleeping."

"How did you respond to that, Mr. Hornowski?"

"Well—I looked at the man. He coulda been sleeping, I guess, but he didn't look like it to me."

"What was your impression?"

"Objection."

The prosecutor points at Bennett. "I believe the defense will argue that Mr. Garrison appeared to be asleep. The witness's observations on this point are relevant."

The judge overrules the objection.

"Well, all I had to do was stare at him for a good ten seconds or so, and I could see he wasn't breathing."

"His body wasn't moving?"

"No. He wasn't taking breaths."

"So you went to him."

"Yes, I did."

"And?"

"And he was dead. He was dead."

"What did you do at that time?"

"I told the defendant not to move. To stay right there. And I called down to the lobby to send everyone up."

"Did the defendant say anything else to you?"

"He told me that he had left the office for a short time, but then the— Mr. Garrison called him back into the building. And when he came back into the office, Mr. Garrison was 'asleep.' Or dead."

"Did you move the body from its original position, Mr. Hornowski?"

"No, I did not."

"Did the defendant?"

"Yes, he did. He pulled him out of the chair and laid him on the floor. I think he was pretending to perform CPR. But he was altering the scene."

Oh, right. I turn to Ben but he slowly shakes his head. Show no emotion, he's told me.

The prosecutor asks a few questions about the follow-up with the police. She concludes by asking him five different ways whether anyone else was in that suite of offices besides me and the security guys. Hornowski says no way, no how. He checked every office, covered the exits, and all that. The prosecutor takes her seat.

Ben stands at his chair. "It took you ten seconds to know that Mr. Garrison wasn't sleeping."

"Yeah, about that."

"You had to wait to see if he was breathing, if his chest was expanding and contracting."

"Right."

"There wasn't any blood, was there? Mr. Garrison wasn't bleeding."

"No."

"No gaping wounds."

"No."

"No external signs, from your perspective, that Mr. Garrison had been wounded."

"No."

"Sitting in his chair as Mr. Garrison was—his arms folded, his head down—you couldn't really see his chest at all, could you?"

"No. I guess what I mean is, when someone breathes, they move up and down."

"But you couldn't see his chest, from your perspective."

"No."

"And my client had that same perspective, standing just about exactly where you were."

"Yes."

"And if my client had walked back into the office just a moment before you had, my client would not have had ten seconds to look at Mr. Garrison, true?"

"I don't know how long he was in there."

"But if he had just returned to the office," Ben says. "He sees Mr. Garrison for a moment, then you walk down the hall and he's looking at you, right?"

"Right. He was."

"So when you join him in the office, that's the first time my client would get a full ten seconds to look at Mr. Garrison. Right?"

"If his story is true, yeah."

"And you can't state for a fact that his story is false, can you, Mr. Hornowski?" Ben opens a hand. "You have no idea, do you?"

"I have an opinion."

"But you have no factual knowledge, do you, sir?"

"No, sir, I don't."

Ben drops his palms on the table and looks up at the witness. "You never drew your gun, did you?"

"No."

"So when you told my client not to move—after you discovered Mr. Garrison was dead—he didn't resist you, did he?"

Hornowski considers the question. "I think he knew better."

"The point being, you weren't required to draw a weapon."

"No, I didn't draw my weapon."

"My client didn't run."

"No."

"He didn't try to fight you."

"Fight me?" The witness smiles broadly. The notion seems preposterous to this weight lifter.

"He didn't fight you, did he, sir?"

"No, sir."

"In fact, he tried to save Mr. Garrison's life, didn't he?"

"He pulled him off his chair and put him on the floor," says the witness. "He altered the scene and put his hands all over Garrison so he could explain later—"

"Judge." Ben waves at the witness.

"Let's continue," she says.

"He was trying to perform mouth-to-mouth resuscitation, wasn't he, Mr. Hornowski?"

"He was—making like that."

"*Making like that?*" Ben moves from the table and approaches the witness. "He was pumping air into his mouth, pounding his chest. Right?"

"Yeah."

"More than *you* can say, isn't it, sir?" Ben jabs a finger at the witness. "You just stood there, while my client tried to save his life."

"I was calling on my radio, trying to secure the scene."

"Here was a man dead, and Jon Soliday's trying to revive him, and you're on your radio."

"I was calling for an ambulance, and the police, and additional security." The witness's face has reddened. He braces himself in the witness stand.

Ben takes a seat. "That's all," he says.

47

Bennett insists that I have something to eat, but I don't want to leave the courtroom so he smuggles in a sandwich. The courtroom is relatively empty during the seventy-five minutes the judge gave us for a lunch recess. I am on my feet most of the time, doing a slow pace around the tables and the jury box, even whistling at one point. That's a nervous habit of mine, the whistling, but I'm aware that it gives an impression of casualness, even confidence.

I am neither casual nor confident. I thought once the trial started, the nerves would ease a little, but the truth is, things haven't gone particularly well. Not that there's been anything earth-shattering. No smoking gun. The medical examiner didn't really hurt, I guess. Just because Garrison was strangled doesn't mean I'm the one who strangled him. And the security guard, well, he hurt a little. If the judge believes that I was telling a bullshit story, then I guess I'm cooked. But by itself, it's not unreasonable for me to assume that Dale was simply asleep. It's the who-strangled-him part that hurts me.

God, it was great for her to have come to town. She knew I wouldn't have much time to see her. She looked tremendous. She looked fresh. That's the word. Different, which carries with it a certain distance, but in the end the same Tracy I came to love. She was gentle and kind and loving, even after everything. It's all I can do not to pick up the phone and call her, schedule a lunch or a dinner. I feel like a schoolkid.

But I can't. I won't. I'm not a schoolboy and we don't have a clean slate. She's moved on with her life and I'm glad for that. She needs to know she did what she could to get me through this. But that's all she needs. She doesn't need me anymore. She doesn't want me anymore.

I shake out of my trance and look over at my lawyer, who is sitting at the table reading over some papers. He is mumbling to himself. His steel-blue eyes are narrow, his concentration so intent that he appears not to be reading the paper in front of him but, rather, thinking of something else altogether.

Ben's a pretty strong guy, carries a lot of weight on his shoulders without showing much wear. But this must be pretty intense for him, defending a friend against a first-degree murder rap. To say nothing of the fact that, even with his criminal trial experience, this is still by far the biggest case Ben has ever handled.

I haven't put myself in his shoes. It hasn't really occurred to me how hard this must be for him. Maybe it's something I should have considered more. Maybe, as disciplined as he is, as prepared he is, as talented as he is, Bennett Carey is in over his head.

That thought finds a landing in the pit of my stomach, causing some chaos that makes me glad I ate a little lunch. Is Bennett over his skis on this case? Am I asking too much of him? And more to the point—why am I just thinking about this now?

"Two minutes," says a clerk who pops into the courtroom.

I look over at Bennett again. His mini-prep session has ended. He is sitting with his back erect against the chair, breathing in with his eyes cast to the ceiling. He seems pretty calm. Intense and focused but calm. And really, his cross-examinations have been pretty good.

"You've resorted to prayer," I say to him as I return to the table.

Ben smiles, pats my arm. "Things are going fine, Jonathan."

I start to answer, to engage in a discussion that I continually have with myself on the progress of the trial, when the clerk enters with Judge Bridges. "All rise."

The prosecutor calls to the stand Sheila Paul, the former secretary for Dale Garrison. Bennett spoke with her a few weeks ago and pronounced her testimony relatively harmless. She puts Dale in his office, alive, at five p.m. and recalls that I was the one who changed the date.

Sheila Paul takes the witness stand and looks out with little interest over the courtroom. There is a gloss to her face owing to a summer tan. She looks like someone who has lost a good deal of weight. She is rather petite but there is slackness at the chin and cheeks. Her perfume is strong, something a little sweet for my taste, which lingers from when she passed me on her way to the witness stand.

She fidgets until the prosecutor asks the first question. Then she settles down and speaks with a volume that belies her tiny size. "I worked for Dale for over twenty years," she tells Erica Johannsen.

"Can you describe Mr. Garrison's law practice for us?"

She nods without any affect. "Mostly criminal law, over the years. He lobbied, too. When the legislature was in session, he'd go down to the capital for clients."

"Did he have any associates working with him?"

Sheila Paul shakes her head.

"Ms. Paul, could you give a verbal answer?"

"No," she says. "Not at the time—not at the end. He had a lawyer or two working under him on occasion. There were other lawyers in his office; they'd share stuff sometimes but they weren't partners. And there was a law firm down the way, three or four younger lawyers who started their own firm. Dale would hand stuff off to them if he didn't want to do it. Or maybe he'd have them do some small work on cases he had. He really liked those guys. He said they reminded him of when he was young, just starting out."

"Okay." The prosecutor jumps in to stop the narrative. "So—no associates at the time of his death?"

"No."

"That's fine." Erica Johannsen clasps her hands together and directs them toward the witness. "Did Mr. Garrison do any work for Senator Grant Tully?"

I edge forward in my seat but make a concerted attempt not to react to the sound of my boss's name. Bennett does not react at all, just watches the witness.

"Yeah, sure. He was an adviser, really, more than anything. He didn't get paid. But he gave the senator legal advice on his personal affairs and on some political matters." She shrugs. "The senator pays it back in different ways."

"Explain that, please."

I look at Bennett, who remains motionless. I start to elbow him but the judge speaks next. "Ms. Johannsen, what is the relevance of this?"

My heart does a small leap. The judge, unprompted, is coming to the defense of the senator. She knows, everyone knows how the senator "compensated" Dale Garrison. Dale is a lobbyist, one of the chosen few in the capital who can walk into Senator Tully's office and get things done.

I never knew Garrison's precise connection to the Tully family. I figured it was something going back with Grant's dad, Simon, but I didn't know the specifics. The reason was me. Garrison paid an ultimate favor to the Tullys—he kept some bad guys from pointing the finger at me and, to be fair, at least indirectly at the Tully family, too. That's a cynic's view, at least, but I've never been confused for an idealist.

"I'll withdraw the question," says the prosecutor. It strikes me as quick surrender, especially in a bench trial, where your argument is made to the trier of fact. "Ms. Paul, can you tell us whether Mr. Garrison did any work with the defendant, Jonathan Soliday?"

The witness does not look in my direction, a sign to me of hostility. I suppose that would be normal, except for the small fact that I'm innocent. "I had never met Mr. Soliday," she says. "I know from Dale's correspondence and from phone calls that they worked together."

Erica Johannsen reviews the notes placed on the lectern. "Now—to your knowledge, did the defendant ever have an appointment to meet with Mr. Garrison?"

"Yes, he did. They were supposed to meet on Thursday, August seventeenth, for lunch."

"That would be the day before his death?"

"Right."

"To your knowledge, was that appointment kept?"

"No, it was not." For the first time, Sheila Paul acknowledges my presence. "He called and moved the appointment to Friday night at seven."

"Objection." Bennett gets to his feet. "Lack of foundation."

"Sustained." The judge raises her eyebrows at the prosecutor.

Erica Johannsen moves toward the witness. "Ms. Paul, did there come a time when you received a phone call about that Thursday lunch meeting?"

"Yes."

"When?"

"I believe it was the day before—Wednesday, I think. Yes, Wednesday morning, I think."

"Did the caller identify himself?"

"Yeah. He said he was Jon Soliday."

"Objection, Your Honor." Bennett on his feet again. "Hearsay. Lack of foundation. Move to strike."

"Hearsay?" the prosecutor says. "It's the *defendant's* statement."

"Sustained as to foundation," says Judge Bridges. "You haven't *shown* it was the defendant's statement."

The prosecutor brings a finger to her lips. Maybe she did not foresee the evidentiary problem with this testimony. Or maybe, as with the medical examiner's testimony, she was not expecting a fight. "Ms. Paul, regardless of how the caller identified himself, did you recognize the voice?"

"Not particularly, no."

Try again. The prosecutor grinds her teeth and stares at the witness. Her outward appearance is stoic but I know she's sweating a little. "All right, Ms. Paul. Aside from how the caller identified himself, can you tell us what else he said?"

"Same objection." Bennett stands as an after-the-fact gesture; he blurted out the objection before the witness could answer. "Hearsay."

The judge blinks twice. "I'll hear the answer."

The witness is no longer entirely sure what the question was, only that there seems to be much ado about her response. She answers with trepidation, expecting one lawyer or another to pounce when she's finished. "He asked to change the time of his meeting with Dale from lunch Thursday to Friday evening at seven o'clock."

Well, we can play all the legal games we want, but the judge knows whom the witness is talking about—me. Nobody else would have called to change the time of the meeting from lunch Thursday to Friday evening. The thing is, that call never happened. *They* called *me* to change the meeting.

Ben leans into me. "She's been coached," he whispers. "She wasn't nearly so clear a few weeks ago."

"So what did you do, Ms. Paul?"

"I asked Dale if Friday at seven would be okay."

"And how did he respond?"

"Well, he said okay, but he wasn't happy about it. I mean, who meets at seven o'clock on a Friday night?"

My reaction exactly, at the time. I scribble a note to Bennett, that we need to talk again with my secretary to explain that this is wrong, that it was Garrison who changed the appointment. But that doesn't explain Sheila Paul's testimony here. For her to be wrong, she not only is mixing up which one of us changed the appointment; she's creating in her head an entire conversation with Dale Garrison in which he was upset about the change of plans. Lyle Cosgrove must have made that call.

The prosecutor turns now to the day of Dale Garrison's death. "Do you recall Dale Garrison's day, his work schedule?"

Sheila Paul nods. "He had a court appearance that morning, a meeting with one of the attorneys down the hall—who was doing work on one of his cases—sometime that afternoon. Then he met with Mr. Soliday that evening at seven."

"Your Honor," says Johannsen, "since we've brought the victim's computer down at the defense's request, I would ask if the witness could verify Mr. Garrison's schedule that day on his computer calendar."

The judge looks to Bennett.

"No objection," he says, "other than chain of custody. Provided Ms. Johannsen can tie that up with another witness. . . ."

"Thank you, Counsel," says the prosecutor. "We'll do that."

Nice to see my attorney being so accommodating. This is partly out of some kind of ex-prosecutor kinsmanship, I suppose, but more than anything Ben seems to know which fights to pick. It only helps the judge's estimation of him and, ultimately, me.

The prosecution has connected the computer to a projector screen, so that we can watch the workings of the computer like a filmstrip instead of huddling around a little monitor. The screen is already set up, and a clerk emerges from an adjoining room with the computer and hard drive resting on a stand with wheels. They take a moment to connect the whole thing and then we're looking at the monitor of Dale Garrison's computer on a projector screen. The background is a sky landscape, light blue with white puffy clouds. The various icons are on the left side of the screen. Dale had pretty much the same setup I do at the law firm.

Sheila Paul gets out of the witness chair at the prosecutor's urging and takes the computer mouse to direct matters. "Dale kept his calendar on the computer," she says. "Or actually, I kept his calendar on the computer. I'd print it out for him every day." The mouse moves to some icon and a new screen pops open, showing his computer calendar for the day.

Apparently, Dale had a court appearance scheduled for today. But Sheila Paul moves the mouse around at a faster clip than I ever have and goes to the date of Dale's death, August 18.

"This is the day," she says.

A giant version of a day's calendar is on the screen. It shows appointments on Friday, August 18, at nine, two, three, and with me at seven.

"Dale had a hearing before Judge Radke on a motion to quash arrest," says Sheila Paul. "That was at nine. Then he had a meeting with Jeff Caprice, one of the young lawyers down the hall. The 'OC' means 'office conference.' Then he had a conference call on another case at three." She waves a hand. "Then he had the meeting with Mr. Soliday at seven."

"Ms. Paul, did anyone come into the offices between three and the time you left?"

"No," the witness says firmly.

"And what time *did* you leave, Ms. Paul?"

"Pretty close to five. I usually leave between four-thirty and five. That day, it was closer to five."

"So—no one came into the offices between three and about five?"

"That's right."

"As far as you knew, Ms. Paul, was anyone else scheduled to come into the office later that day?"

"Besides Mr. Soliday, I don't know of anyone."

"And at the time you left, was it just you and Dale in the office?"

"Yes, that's right."

"No paralegals? No clerks? Nobody?"

"Nobody but Dale and me."

"All right," says Erica Johannsen. "Now, when you left, did you say good—" The prosecutor stops in her tracks. She was about to ask Sheila Paul whether she said goodbye to Dale before she left. Given the significance of their moment in hindsight, it's probably better to ask the question more delicately. "Ms. Paul," she starts again, "before you left, did you let Mr. Garrison know you were leaving?"

Regardless of the rephrasing of the question, Sheila Paul is now recalling her final conversation with her boss of over twenty years. Before the prosecutor has finished her question, the witness has retrieved some tissue from her purse. Her eyes glisten, though no tears have dropped as of yet. She freezes a moment, with a tissue balled in her fist, the fist against her mouth, before she releases with an exhale. "I told him I was leaving. I said have a nice weekend. He told me to have a good weekend, too. He made a remark about my husband, how I should make him fix the radiator this weekend. Dale was always poking fun like that."

"Can you describe his appearance?" asks Erica Johannsen. "His mood?"

"Same old Dale," she says. "Grumpy but sweet. He looked about the same as always."

"Okay." The prosecutor's voice is barely above a whisper. "Just a couple more questions, ma'am, and then my examination will be completed."

Dale Garrison's secretary waves the fistful of tissue in response.

The prosecutor is pacing. She waits a moment before continuing. "There's a front door to your office, is that correct?"

"Yes."

"Is there another door?"

"Yes." She blows her nose, a loud honk. "Excuse me. Yes. There's another door that leads into the hallway."

"Is that door locked or unlocked?"

"Unlocked from the inside," she answers. "Locked from the outside."

"You're sure it's locked from the outside?"

"I'm positive. It's an automatic lock. It's so the attorneys can take a shortcut to the hallway restrooms. You can't get in from the hallway without a key."

"All right, Ms. Paul. Thank you." The prosecutor sits, assuring herself that there's no way someone could have sneaked in surreptitiously, strangled Dale, and escaped.

"Counsel?" the judge says to Bennett.

Ben has already gotten to his feet. He walks back and forth slowly behind the defense table. No need to be too confrontational with this witness. "Dale was a good man," he says.

"He was a great man."

"Helped a lot of people."

"He sure did."

Bennett is expressing opinions here, something that is technically inappropriate but harmless. In fact, as I'm thinking about it, what's my attorney doing making the victim more sympathetic?

"And not just people who could pay," says Ben. "He did a lot of free work."

"He was very generous with his time."

"His door was always open."

The witness nods. "Yes."

"If someone needed a minute of his time, they'd get it."

"Always."

Bennett stuffs his hands in his pockets. Before we started the afternoon's proceedings, he emptied his pockets of change so that he wouldn't play with the coins while on his feet.

"And Ms. Paul, I realize you have no idea what happened at the law office after you left for the night, but isn't it possible that someone might have dropped by to see Dale? That could have happened, right?"

"Of course that could have happened."

"A lot of people came to Dale for advice."

"Sure."

"And if that happened, it wouldn't be unusual for Dale to invite that person in."

"No, I suppose not."

"In fact, Ms. Paul, based on the configuration of the office and where Dale's office was, it's possible that someone could have walked in without Dale knowing it, right?"

"Right."

"Because the front door to his offices—the main door—that was still unlocked when you left."

"Yes."

Ben nods. He rests his hands on the back of his chair. "Mr. Garrison was sick, wasn't he, Ms. Paul?"

"Yes."

"He suffered from lung cancer and lymphoma."

"That's right."

"When did he tell you about that?"

Sheila Paul's eyes move to the corner of the room. At first I think she's looking over there, but probably she's just trying to recall. "Maybe—six months ago."

Ben nods. "He'd been sick before that, though."

A smile plays on the witness's face. "That was *so* like Dale, to keep that private."

"Ms. Paul, do you know how long he had suffered from cancer?"

"I think it had been about four months before he told me."

"Dale didn't treat his cancer, did he? Didn't take chemotherapy, didn't take radiation?"

Ms. Paul's expression tells me that she struggled with Dale Garrison on this point. "He had seen both of his parents die from cancer," she says. "He said the treatment beat them up worse than the cancer. He didn't want to do it."

"Dale had lost weight, too, isn't that so?"

The witness is fixed on Bennett now. It's probably more appropriate to say she is looking through Ben. She has no agenda, doesn't appear to take issue with me, certainly wouldn't have a problem with a criminal defense attorney representing a client. "He lost weight over the last year, yes."

"Did Dale ever—" Ben inclines his head and pauses. "Hate to ask questions like this."

"Dale would tell you to go ahead," says Ms. Paul. She's really handling herself with dignity. I would find it moving were it not for the fact that she has been a good prosecution witness. The judge is going to have a hard time finding fault with her credibility. And that's a problem for me, because she has said that it was my idea to change the date of the meeting and that it's unlikely that anyone came into the offices between the time she left and I came in. These are not things we want the judge to believe.

"Did Dale ever talk about wanting to die?" Ben asks.

I turn to get a better look at my lawyer, a breach of courtroom decorum. I'm not supposed to let the judge see my emotions. But what a question. The thing is, Ben interviewed Ms. Paul and he wouldn't be asking the question unless—

"Sometimes he did," says Sheila Paul.

"He was afraid of a slow death." Ben says it quietly.

"Yes, he was." She chuckles, sort of a bitter laugh. "He said he knew he would have his ticket punched—that's the way he talked, if you knew him—but he wanted it to come fast."

"Did it ever occur to you that he might be suicidal?"

"Objection." Erica Johannsen belatedly stands, holds out a hand. "The witness is not qualified to render that opinion."

"I'm just asking for a lay opinion," says Ben. "The witness observed

Dale Garrison more than probably anyone else over the last year. Things he said, things he did, feelings he shared with the witness. That's all I want to know about."

The judge stares straight ahead a moment without movement, save for a quaint biting of her lower lip. "I will overrule the objection," she says.

Bennett nods at the witness. "Did you think he might be suicidal?"

"Not as phrased, counsel," the judge calls out.

"Thank you, Judge." Ben looks at the witness. "Ms. Paul, did Mr. Garrison ever give you the impression that he was depressed about his illness, that, in fact, he wanted to die very soon?"

Sheila Paul's eyes drop, hooded. It brings prominence to the flesh beneath her eyes. She swallows hard. When she speaks, it is in a haunting, even tone. "It was usually in the evenings," she starts. "When it got dark. It was something about darkness. He'd get very—I don't know, depressed. He hadn't gotten really sick yet. But he was starting to feel it a little. He didn't eat much. He lost weight. He was a little weak, I guess— he said he could feel it coming on a little, if that's possible. But he still felt good enough to keep going. He figured he had another six months or so. He used to say he was tired of hearing the ticking of the clock. He wanted it to come quick. Like lightning, he said."

Erica Johannsen is uneasy in her seat. This testimony, some of it, at least, is hearsay. She's probably done a calculation here—the judge already allowed the answer, so she probably wouldn't overturn herself. More to the point, the judge heard the witness's words even if she rules them inadmissible.

"Ms. Paul," says Ben, "do you leave room for the possibility that Dale Garrison hired someone to kill him?"

The prosecutor is no longer uneasy. "Your Honor," she cries, leaping to her feet.

The judge seems to disapprove of the question. She looks at Bennett like a mom looks at a child who did something bad. "The question calls for speculation," she says firmly. "The objection, such as it is, is sustained."

Bennett accepts the ruling without comment but moves on quickly. "To your knowledge, did Dale have financial problems?"

Now I'm the one who's uneasy. This would explain the blackmail note—that Dale needed a quarter of a million dollars. The better position for the defense is that Dale didn't need the money. He was a successful attorney. He had a client list that most lawyers would envy. Thus, the blackmail note doesn't make sense. What's Bennett doing?

"Not that I knew of," says the witness.

"You helped him with his checkbook, didn't you, Ms. Paul?"

She smiles meekly. "I paid his bills for him. Dale wasn't so good with that kind of stuff."

"So you knew his finances, at least in his checking account."

"Sure."

"Was he hurting for money?"

"No. Not at all. He had—something like twenty thousand dollars in his checking account. I always used to tell him to invest it, but by the end that became like a bad joke. You know, what was the point—" Her face turns sour.

"And you had knowledge of some investments, true?"

"Yeah. He had some mutual funds and stuff. I'd get his statements at the office and file them."

"Sure." Bennett smiles at her generosity. "Dale had over a hundred thousand dollars in investments, didn't he?"

The witness blinks and looks off. "I think it was close to a hundred and twenty thousand."

"He owned two houses. One here, one down in Florida."

"Right."

"And even at the end, Dale had plenty of clients coming through the door."

"Oh, yes." The witness is eager to talk up her boss. "He was shipping out clients to other lawyers and keeping a referral fee."

"Okay." Bennett paces now. "So he had some money on hand, and he had plenty of clients, and he wasn't spending any money on treating his cancer. True?"

"True."

"So, Ms. Paul, knowing Dale Garrison as well as you did, can you think of any reason why he would need two hundred and fifty thousand dollars?"

"No," says the witness, as the prosecutor jumps up.

"Objection—"

"That's what I told them—"

"Calls for speculation."

"—when they showed me that blackmail letter."

"Ms. Paul," says Judge Bridges, "I realize you were talking over each other, but when someone objects, I'd like you to wait until I rule before answering. Okay?"

"Sorry," says Sheila Paul. "When they showed me that note—"

"Ms. *Paul*," says the judge. "I haven't ruled yet."

The witness lowers her head, scolded.

The judge lightens her expression. "Actually, I think the question is proper. So now, Ms. Paul"—the judge allows a brief smile—"please finish what you were saying."

I smile as well. This is playing out pretty well.

Sheila Paul begins again. "When the prosecutors showed me that document—about Dale saying he needs all that money—it didn't make sense. What did he need money for?"

Bennett purses his lips. "Maybe so someone could help end his suffering?"

"Counsel." The judge doesn't need prompting from the prosecutor, who is on her feet but silent now. "Next question."

Bennett opens his hands. "Actually, I'm done, Your Honor. Thank you, Ms. Paul."

The judge looks at the prosecutor, who says she has no redirect.

The judge shuffles some papers and addresses the lawyers. "I have some matters I need to dispose of this afternoon," she says. She looks over what I assume is her calendar for tomorrow. "And I'm going to need part of tomorrow morning for some other matters," she says. Judges in the criminal courts have trouble setting aside too much time for a single trial. Criminal defendants have the right to a speedy trial, so judges have to fit in hearings wherever they can to move cases along. Because this is a bench trial—no jury—Judge Bridges can be more flexible with moving us around to accommodate her schedule. "Why don't we reconvene tomorrow morning at eleven?"

Both lawyers say eleven will be fine. Erica Johannsen tells the judge that she thinks the prosecution can conclude its case tomorrow.

We all stand as the judge leaves the bench. Day two of my trial is over. "No worse for the wear?" I whisper to Ben. All in all, we've made it through more than half of their proof without too much damage.

Bennett relaxes, truly relaxes for the first time today. He blows out a sigh as the crowd behind us shuffles out. I try to gauge his emotions—satisfied versus disappointed—but he's typically Bennett, unflappable. Erica Johannsen snaps her briefcase shut and leaves. Before long, Ben and I sit in the courtroom alone. There will be some press outside, but by court rule they can't accost us inside.

"They'll finish tomorrow, early afternoon," says Ben. "So we've got a long night ahead of us." Even Ben seems to acknowledge what I already believe—that the judge will not direct a verdict in our favor after the prosecution closes its case. Which means I will have to testify. We agree to meet back at the law firm for a working dinner and a night of preparation. I follow him to the door out of the courtroom. He will be my shield behind which I will penetrate the reporters. I put on my face for television—head up, calm and confident but not cocky—and lightly push Ben's back, signaling that I'm ready.

48

The first of three debates in the Trotter–Tully race is tonight. The League of Independent Voters is sponsoring and holding it in an auditorium in the city. William Gadsby, a local news anchor, is the moderator. He's walking around mumbling lines to himself on the stage, preparing his television voice. He offers a hand to me without comment, not acknowledging my current predicament, which is fine by me. I've spoken to Bill dozens of times over the years, even been on his program a few times. His best years are behind him, but he's a staple in city news.

Langdon Trotter and Grant Tully are in rooms behind the stage. They are rehearsing their lines with their aides and getting made up by the PR people.

It's Tuesday night. Ben and I have been working late hours and we need a break. Or at least I do, and Ben wanted to come with. The police still haven't put Lyle Cosgrove together with me, at least not as far as I know, but I'm waiting any moment for that bomb to drop.

I debated the idea of coming here but ultimately decided to attend. It will provide diversion. It will also be the decisive moment in this campaign. Lang Trotter has a solid double-digit lead in the polls. Grant Tully has to beat him tonight. This is not going to be Lincoln–Douglas by any means. But the voters have to see Grant as their governor. Form over substance, in my opinion, and given Grant's substance—I'm speaking of his position on a tax increase—I hope he's solid on the form.

I walk over to Langdon Trotter's side and knock on the door. The woman who answers is Maribelle Rodriguez, one of Trotter's press people. We've always gotten along all right. I've made it a point to get along with everyone in the capital.

"Jon, how *are* you?" Maribelle takes my hand with both of hers. She's wearing a perfume that reminds me of a former girlfriend, something with a strawberry scent. Maybe it's her shampoo, on second thought. Her hands sure are soft.

It's tough for me to answer her question, as we both understand.

"I've wanted to call, I really have meant to. I mean, this is awful. I mean—"

"I appreciate that, Mari."

"I mean, politics is politics, but all of us like you so much." She's still holding on to me with both hands, shaking. "I'm hoping for the best."

"That makes two of us," I say. Mari's laugh is overly accommodating. "I wonder if I might say hello to Lang."

"Well"—she looks over her shoulder—"maybe after the debate?"

A voice calls out from within the room. "Jon Soliday waits for no one." Lang Trotter. Mari lets me in and Attorney General Langdon Trotter stands. He looks like an actor on Broadway, a makeup bib hanging from his collar, a touch of rouge on his cheeks. His hair is stiffly combed and parted—too perfect, in my opinion. A half-dozen people, most of whom I recognize, recede into the background as Lang approaches. The room is big enough that we can get some distance, and Trotter finds that area and stops.

"Jon." Say what you will about him, Lang Trotter is charming, a focus in his address that leaves the recipient with the impression that nothing is more deserving of his attention at the moment. With me, at this moment, however, he seems uncomfortable.

"I always wish my opponent the best of luck," I say. Lang's line when I saw him at the diner.

He accepts the comment with a gracious laugh. "Jon." He turns sober, lets out a theatrical sigh. He's not looking at me. He waves absently. "You know I wouldn't do such a thing," he says to the floor. "What your lawyer's been saying. I would never instruct anyone to prosecute someone for political motive."

I would laugh under ordinary circumstances. Lang Trotter has prosecuted people for political gain his entire life. Every case is political, or potentially so. You never know when a simple domestic violence case turns into double murder and everyone looks back and wonders why the county attorney dropped the charges on an assault-and-battery when they could have put the shooter away. Everything is twenty-twenty hindsight.

"I appreciate the comment," I say. I'm staring at his face but he's avoiding eye contact.

Trotter places a hand on my shoulder and moves me toward the door. "I hope you win the case, Jonathan. I do."

I nod and extend a hand. We shake hands. I hold his grip a split-second longer than appropriate. This provokes the intended result. Lang Trotter looks at me.

"We might have a surprise or two," I say. I release his hand and wave to Maribelle on my way out. I find Bennett Carey over by Grant Tully's room and tell him I'll watch the debate at home.

49

"I want to begin by welcoming our audience at home and in this auditorium to the first of the three debates in the race for governor." Bill Gadsby, the moderator, is seated at a table with a single microphone. Each of the two candidates is introduced.

We negotiated for hours over the format. The Republicans—Trotter's people—wanted the men to stand side by side at podiums. They wanted that because Lang Trotter is a burly, six-foot-four man who towers over Grant, barely reaching six feet and rather slight. We have to overcome the presumption of inexperience that comes with a thirty-eight-year-old state senator with unfortunately boyish looks, and side by side the match-up is not flattering to us. For our part, we wanted cameras overhead as well as frontal, hoping to catch the small bald spot atop Trotter's head.

Trotter also pushed for spontaneous questions from the audience, as opposed to scripts. Trotter wanted this for two reasons. For one, Trotter figures he's better on his feet than Grant. Senator Tully has a reputation as a good behind-the-scenes politician, like his father, ideal for the position of Senate Majority Leader but not necessarily suited for firing off answers from the hip. The other reason Trotter wanted this was the hope that someone in the audience would ask Grant Tully about me, his top aide on trial for murder.

I happen to think that Grant would do just fine without a script, but we ultimately agreed on this format: the two men will sit on stools, facing the audience, microphone in hand; we don't know the precise questions, but the general subject matter has been provided us.

This is Grant's chance, right here tonight, to make up the double-digit gap in the polls. Frankly, I don't know why Trotter gave us these debates. He would take some flack from the papers but, in the end, I think he would have benefited from the lack of exposure afforded to Grant. If I were Trotter, I'd have put the kibosh on any joint public appearances.

"Bill, I'd like to thank you and the League of Independent Voters for giving me the chance to address the people of this great state." Langdon Trotter steps off the stool, holding the microphone like it's an extension of his hand. I am immediately worried. This guy just reeks of confidence and power, the perfect robust, silver-haired, baritone-voiced man to lead the state. "And Senator Tully, thank you as well for attending."

The cameras hit Grant now. He smiles graciously and raises a hand. It strikes me immediately that Trotter is the more telegenic candidate.

"I want to lead this state into the twenty-first century, and I want to tell you why." Trotter doesn't have to wear too much makeup because he has a nice tan. "This is a great state. I've lived here my whole life and I don't ever want to leave. But we have some work to do. People still don't feel safe in their streets, in their houses. People feel like the government takes too much of their money. People, small businesses, feel like the government gets its hands in their affairs too much. We aren't confident enough that our schools can prepare our children for adulthood. And there are too many threats out there to our children—tobacco for one, and obscene musical lyrics and violent video games and movies that shock good-minded people."

Pretty good start for a Republican seeking middle ground. He won't mention his opposition to gun control and abortion, two of the hot-button issues in our state. Because Trotter had no opposition in the primary, he did not have to veer far-right, which would have required him to go pro-gun and pro-life much more vehemently than he has. No, he's stuck to the easy stuff—lower taxes, more cops, anti-tobacco. That's how someone gets elected governor. If only someone could get that through to Grant Tully.

"He's good," Ben says. He joined me on the ride from the auditorium. We still have work to be done tonight.

"The Attorney General and I agree on the results we want to reach," says Grant Tully, standing in front of his stool, "but we disagree on how to accomplish them." The senator is in a blue shirt and red tie. The bangs of his hair are stiffly combed off his forehead, not his natural look but a more mature one under the circumstances. "I want safer streets but I believe we will accomplish that, not through expanding the death penalty but through gun control, taking guns out of the hands of gang members and kids. I want better schools but I don't want to do that by removing tenure for teachers or cutting state funding of schools that perform poorly. Schools that perform poorly are the ones that need our money the most. Teachers in those schools, with children who perform poorly on standardized tests because they don't have the support at home or because they couldn't afford to eat breakfast, are the teachers that need tenure the *most*. Mr. Trotter and I agree that we must fight to keep our children away from tobacco addiction, but we disagree on how to accomplish that. The Attorney General wants to take the money from the tobacco litigation settlement and hand it out as a tax refund. But *I* say, let's put our money where our mouth is. Let's take that tobacco money and use it like we should—by putting it into health care programs and preventive programs to keep children from ever *starting* with tobacco."

Not bad. I hope he hits gun control as hard as we've counseled him. That's the big divider in tonight's debate, at least the one that favors us. The big winner for Trotter is taxes. The Attorney General has promoted a cut in income taxes, which is rather laughable when you consider only about three percent of our income is taxed by the state. But the senator has opposed it and promoted the tax increase to change school funding in the state. Tonight is when he sells it to the citizens, or else.

The senator finishes his opening remarks. Bill Gadsby shuffles a paper. "The first question concerns taxes," he says.

"The first question concerns the position which is the least popular of Senator Tully's entire platform," I say to Ben.

"Starting with Attorney General Trotter, I'd like each of you to outline your plan for the state income tax."

"Thank you, Bill." Lang Trotter steps off his stool. Thank you is right. If I were Trotter I'd want to kiss the moderator right now. "We pay too many taxes in this state. It's that simple. The economy has slowed down and people are trying to find a little extra income to pay for school clothes for their kids, maybe stow a little away for retirement. I want to help you do that." Trotter nods, his eyes intent. "I'm not going to wow you with a fancy formula. Here's my tax plan, plain and simple. I want to give back five hundred dollars to every taxpayer. However much you pay, whoever you are, whatever age, race, gender. The average taxpayer in this state pays sixteen hundred dollars in state taxes. I will slice that by more than thirty percent."

That's pretty good. He's never said that before tonight. He's talked about lowering taxes in general but nothing that specific.

"That was great," Ben says.

"Yep."

"Senator Tully?"

Grant smiles in that relaxed way he has. "Well, I'm for lower taxes, too. I just want it to be fair. And when I say fair, I mean fair for our kids. I'm talking about schools. Education. Right now, the majority of our school funding comes from property taxes. Those are local taxes. So wealthy parts of this state have lots of money from property taxes, and not surprisingly, they have better schools. The poorer parts of this state don't have nearly as much revenue from property taxes, and they suffer financially. So when I talk about my tax plan, I'm talking about an over-haul of how we fund education. I want to fund education through in-come taxes, not property taxes. So when I propose a very modest increase in income taxes, I hope everyone understands that I would also *cut* prop-erty taxes. If you live in a wealthy part of the state, your income tax will go up, yes, but your property tax will go *down*. If you live in a poorer part of the state, your income tax will go up, but your *schools* will have more money. The Attorney General is a smart politician, and he thinks if he runs ads saying that I will raise income taxes, you will forget the other part of the story—a cut in your property tax."

Blah blah blah. I told him a hundred times, we *all* told him a hundred times not to take this position. He unveiled it a few weeks ago and it hasn't bought the senator a single point. You can talk all you want about property taxes, but in the end there's nothing but a lot of white noise, the only resonating sound bite being: *Senator Tully wants to raise income taxes, Attorney General Trotter wants to cut them.*

This is why I admire Grant. The guy says what he means. But couldn't he just propose this plan once he was in office, my suggestion? Does he have to tell five million viewers that he'll raise their income taxes? The truth is, I think his plan is solid. I think it's a great way to even out the educational imbalance, by raising the poor end without really hurting the wealthy end. But as far as a campaign slogan, it's right up there with "Let's drown all the elderly people."

"The next subject is crime," says the moderator. "Please explain your views on anticrime legislation and on capital punishment."

I close my eyes. This time, Grant goes first. Tougher laws for sex offenders and drug dealers. A quick mention of ending capital punishment but support of mandatory life sentences. More of a focus on rehabilitation. All of it can be trimmed down to: Grant Tully opposes the death penalty.

"Well, I'm *for* the death penalty," says Lang Trotter. "Because I believe it prevents crime. I prosecuted violent crime as the county attorney in Rankin County for sixteen years, and I know what it means to exact the ultimate punishment."

He's good. He's going to win. I wish someone would ask him the question, "Mr. Attorney General, isn't it true that your nominating papers are invalid? And that you are disqualified from running?" But the time to challenge his papers has run. Lang Trotter has no idea how close he came to having his gubernatorial dreams dashed on a technicality.

Or does he?

It comes first as a tickle in my brain, then a frantic mental exercise in sorting out the details. I leave my spot in the living room and head for the back door, to get some fresh air. The dogs follow me out into the small backyard and scatter. I pace back and forth as I work it out. The evening temperatures are low, but my blood is pumping furiously.

I leave the dogs outside and return triumphantly to the living room, where Bennett seems to have hardly noticed I left.

"I'm glad you're sitting down," I say.

Ben is focusing on the debate. "Where'd you go?"

"Forget the debate," I say. "Are you ready to hear your opening statement when the defense puts on its case?"

That gets his attention. "Sure."

"Let me tell you a story, my friend." I stand in front of the television and frame my hands. "I find a problem with Lang Trotter's nominating papers, right?"

"Right."

"I tell Dale."

"Right."

"But we decide it's best not to use the information to knock Trotter off the ballot. Makes us look mean, and the Republicans would replace him with a more moderate candidate."

"Yeah."

"So using the Ace publicly doesn't work. Then there's the notion of using it privately. Passing the word to Trotter confidentially and getting him to throw the election."

"Right."

"Dale knows I'm skittish about doing that. He knows I don't like it. And he knows Grant will probably, in the end, do what I tell him."

"Sure. Fine."

"So now we have the Ace out there, don't we? Dale knows that the Tully campaign will not use it. But it's still out there. Right?"

"Right."

"So *Dale* decides to use it."

Finally, new information. Bennett draws up. "Dale uses it? How?"

"Hang on a minute." I rush to the kitchen and retrieve the folder on my case. I remove the blackmail note and hand it to Ben.

I guess I'm the only one left who knows the secret that nobody knows. I think $250,000 should cover it. A month should be enough time. I wouldn't presume your income source, but I imagine if anyone could find a way to tap into the campaign fund without anyone noticing, you would. Or I suppose I could always just talk to the senator. Is that what you want? One month. Don't attempt to contact me about this. I will initiate all communications.

Ben reads it like it's the first time and not the hundredth.

"*Dale* sent that note to *Lang Trotter,*" I say, unable to contain my excitement. "He's saying to Trotter, give me a quarter mil, or I tell Senator Tully."

Bennett nods as he reads the note again. "Dale's acting like *he* discovered the Ace."

"Right! Like he's the only one who knows about it. And it will stay that way, if Trotter gives him the extortion money." I point to the letter. "The 'campaign fund' is *Trotter's* fund, not Grant's."

Bennett considers the theory, the voice of reason. "That works, Jon, to a point. I accept that this gives Trotter a motive to kill Garrison. I accept that Trotter would probably be willing to do it, too."

"Hell, yes."

"Okay, okay, but wait." Bennett is treading lightly here. My enthusiasm is plain enough. He wants the rain on my parade to fall in small droplets. "How do you explain that *you* received a copy of that blackmail letter? And how do you explain Lyle Cosgrove's involvement?"

"I explain it this way, Bennett Carey." I point to him. "Trotter was elected AG in '92."

"I think so, yeah," says Ben.

"And he served four terms as county prosecutor in Rankin County before that."

"Yup."

"That puts him as county attorney in 1976."

"Uh-huh."

"That also puts him as county attorney in 1979."

Ben turns and looks at me. The mention of that particular year sparks his attention. "Yeah, so?"

"These prosecutors," I say, "it's a little sewing circle with them, isn't it?"

Bennett shrugs. "I don't know. What's your point?"

"Maybe after what happened in 1979, word got around. Maybe the prosecutor in Summit County talked. I mean, Simon Tully's working behind the scenes to protect his son's best buddy? That must have been quite the tidbit."

"Wouldn't that have come up sooner, if the Summit County prosecutor talked?"

"Not necessarily, Ben. It's juvenile stuff, right? It's not like you can just leak it. A reporter couldn't print it."

Ben's mouth crinkles. "But the prosecutor in Summit County? He'd talk to Trotter?"

"Sure," I say, the excitement beginning to well. "The prosecutor out there now is golfing buddies with Jimmy Budzinski. Summit County's just over the state line. And Trotter's county, Rankin, is on the east side of the state, straight south of us. Not that far at all."

Ben frames his hands. "So you think Trotter found out about what happened back then—about you and Grant."

"Maybe, yeah."

"And he did what? He's blackmailing you?"

"No," I say. "No, no. He just kept the information stored away, for a time it might come in handy. He had his eyes on the AG's seat for a long time. He knew Simon Tully has plans for Grant—everyone knew that. He probably figured that someday his and Grant's political paths might cross. So he kept the information to himself back then. Waiting for the moment."

"And all these years," Ben says, "Grant Tully didn't mean squat to Trotter. He was over there in the senate. He wasn't a threat."

"But now, of course, he is."

"Wow." Ben looks around for a notepad. He likes to record his thoughts.

"Trotter was probably going to spring this a month or so before the election," I say. "Grant wouldn't have enough time for damage control." I raise a finger, a point of order. "But then the landscape changed. Now, Dale Garrison is blackmailing him about the Ace. Trotter needs to kill Dale. So he's a smart guy, he puts the whole thing together. He will send a copy of the blackmail note to me, then kill Garrison and frame me. And the story will be, Jon Soliday had a secret from 1979 that Dale Garrison was going to expose, so he killed him. He kills two birds with one stone, Ben. The Ace will disappear in a puff of smoke with Dale Garrison's death, and Grant's top guy gets indicted for murder."

"And Lyle Cosgrove?"

"Lyle Cosgrove—Trotter knows about him, too, Ben. He probably has the whole goddamn file from 1979, the prick." I snap my fingers. "Trotter's the prosecutor who put a 'hold' order on the file so it would stay around."

Ben, even in his role as devil's advocate, concedes the possibility.

"So he uses Cosgrove to kill Garrison," I continue, my voice trembling with excitement. "That's brilliant. He uses the guy from 1979 to do it. Then he kills Cosgrove afterward. That just makes me look worse. It's smart. Christ, it's damn smart."

"He's sure Cosgrove will do it?"

"Sure, he's sure. Langdon Trotter is the Attorney General. Lyle Cosgrove just spent a third of his life in prison. If Trotter says jump, Cosgrove's gonna say, 'How high?'"

Bennett snaps his fingers. "The document on Dale's computer. About the Ace. The one the prosecutors haven't breathed a word about?"

I raise a hand to my forehead. "I hadn't thought about that."

"But it all makes sense," says Ben, leaping to his feet. "Trotter thinks that Dale and only Dale knew about the Ace, right? That was the point of Dale's blackmail. Trotter thinks, he kills Dale, the Ace is gone, and everyone looks at you. Everyone thinks Dale blackmailed you about 1979."

"Right."

"But then the prosecutors find this memo on the computer. Elliot Raycroft, loyal servant that he is, shows it to Lang Trotter."

I point at Ben. "So now Trotter knows that *I* know about it, too, and the senator. The Ace didn't die with Dale Garrison."

"So." Ben sweeps a hand. "So the best thing that can happen for Trotter is for the thing to go away quickly. So he has Elliot Raycroft offer you a sweetheart of a plea deal. The best possible deal he could give you."

"And I reject it."

"And you reject it. So there's gonna be a trial, there's nothing Trotter can do about that. So he tells Raycroft not to mention anything about the blackmail letter. Suddenly, the prosecutors are withdrawing the letter as evidence."

"So that's why," I mumble.

"Yeah, that's why. And that's why Dan Morphew dropped off the case, I bet. He was protesting. The guy's a pretty straight shooter. He didn't like being told how to try his case. They bring in a new person, Erica Johannsen, and probably keep her in the dark about most of this."

"So now," I say, "they won't touch this blackmail issue. They want a straight story without a motive—I was the only one there, I lied to the security guard, who else could it be?"

"And Lyle Cosgrove?" Ben asks. I think he knows the answer, but he senses how much I'm enjoying unraveling the ball of string.

"Lyle Cosgrove emphasizes 1979," I say. "Now he's been murdered, and the prosecutors are going to start asking the right questions. They are going to put all three of us—Lyle, Dale, and me—together in 1979. They've got their story."

"So after all of that, if you try to implicate Lang Trotter," says Ben, "it's the act of a desperate man, who now has killed two people to bury an ugly secret."

"Trotter killed Dale and Cosgrove." I say the words to myself more than Ben.

Ben is pacing now. "I suspect we're going to be hearing a change of tune from the prosecutors in the next day or so. Suddenly, they are going to want to introduce the blackmail letter. And they're going to talk about

1979. Trotter puts you deeper in the soup, *and* he produces a sensational story about his opponent a month before the election."

I feel a weight lift, for some reason I can't explain. I always knew I was innocent of murdering Dale, it's not that. And it's more than the fact that we have solved the riddle. An emerging sense of salvation has gathered within me.

Ben is looking at me now. "Is that why you wanted to go to the auditorium tonight?"

I shrug. "I guess. I hadn't put it together yet, but something was gnawing at me. I wanted to see if he'd look me in the eye." I shake my head. "He wouldn't. He did his whole charming routine, but he wanted nothing to do with me."

"No wonder," says Ben, casting a glance at the television screen. "You know, we won't be able to prove it. We might get reasonable doubt but—"

"We'll prove it," I say as I watch Attorney General Langdon Trotter smile sincerely into the camera.

50

Erica Johannsen asks to be heard in chambers before the start of court this morning. The judge sits with us in her chambers and waits out the prosecutor.

"Judge, we'd like a continuance," says Johannsen.

"Why is that, Counsel?" The judge is looking for something in a drawer.

"Your Honor, we have just learned that a person who plays an important role in this case has been murdered. His name is Lyle Cosgrove."

"All right," says the judge. "Tell me about Lyle Cosgrove."

"Your Honor, Mr. Cosgrove was just found murdered. He was a client of Mr. Garrison's, recently released from prison. We believe he was on the other end of the cellular phone call to Mr. Soliday around the time of the murder."

"Why do you think that?"

"Because the person whose phone was stolen gave a description of the thief that matches Mr. Cosgrove."

"And you want time to investigate," says Judge Bridges.

"We do, Judge. We feel sure we will tie Mr. Cosgrove to Mr. Soliday. We haven't yet." She looks at Bennett and me. "The defense's speedy trial extends to ninety days. We have another almost fifty days before it expires. If we could have a week or two, that's all we need."

"Counsel?" The judge looks at Bennett.

"Smoke and mirrors," says Ben. "They've looked at Lyle Cosgrove since day one. He's a recently released ex-con. They investigated him immediately upon Mr. Garrison's death. Really, Judge, he's the first person any good investigator would look at. He pleaded ineffective assistance on appeal after his last conviction—he was complaining about Mr. Garrison. They looked at him and decided, for some reason, that he wasn't their man. And they interviewed that woman whose cell phone was stolen right away, weeks ago. They had the description of the person, who apparently resembles Mr. Cosgrove, back even before my client was arrested." Ben opens his hands. "There's nothing new here. If Cosgrove is a suspect, he already should have been. The fact that he is now dead doesn't change anything about his potential involvement in this case. It's a blatant attempt to get more time, because they know they can't beat reasonable doubt right now."

"All right, Counsel," says the judge. "Ms. Johannsen?"

"We want to investigate the possibility that Mr. Soliday murdered this man, Your Honor. That is certainly a new development."

"Not in *this* case, it isn't." The judge plants a finger on her desk. "You can prosecute Mr. Soliday for that offense down the road, if you can prove it. That doesn't change this person—Mr. Cosgrove—this doesn't change his involvement in Mr. Garrison's death. I agree with Mr. Carey. Either he's involved or he isn't. If he is, you've had ample opportunity to put that together." She shakes her head. "I'm not moving the trial date. We continue right now."

"Then we move to have bond revoked, Your Honor," says Johannsen.

The judge pivots forward. "Counsel, are you going to present me with more evidence than you already have, with regard to the defendant's involvement in the death of this witness?"

"This all just happened." Erica Johannsen opens her hands plaintively. "We are accusing the defendant of murder and we believe he may, possibly, have just committed a second murder. You have wide discretion in bond issues, Your Honor. All we're saying is—"

"I'm not revoking bond, Counsel." Her Honor shakes her head. "If you can give me evidence, I'll look at it. But this individual was not even someone you were going to call as a witness. Now you tell me he was material, and his death should be attributed to the defendant? No. You'll have to do better than that."

"I want to say something else, if I could, Judge." Ben sits forward. "Among other things here, you're the finder of fact. I think the prosecution is trying to taint your evaluation of this case. They're suggesting my client committed a murder for which he isn't even charged. For which he hasn't even been *questioned*. I would move for a mistrial but that's exactly what she wants."

"I understand that, Counsel."

"Yesterday, this Lyle Cosgrove didn't even warrant a mention on the witness list. Now he's critical? Of course he isn't, and Ms. Johannsen knows it. She just wanted another chance to call my client a murderer. I think we've been severely biased."

"Mr. Carey," the judge answers, "I can assure you that you have not been prejudiced. This will not factor into my consideration in any way. Now let's get out there."

I make a point of walking out with confidence, trying to remain oblivious to the fact that everyone in the judge's chambers probably believes I killed Lyle Cosgrove. The judge may have her doubts. The prosecutor doesn't. And Bennett, well, he would not bet the house on my innocence.

Oh, how close I came to doing it, the night that I followed him and waited to ambush him on the sidewalk. I stood within two or three feet of Lyle Cosgrove as he limped past me. I was filled with venom. I was bitter and furious and hateful, and along walked a man who was vulnerable to my wrath. I was ready to make him my scapegoat; his death would be the answer to a problem in the present, and resolution, if not absolution, for a problem in the past.

I was ready to kill Lyle Cosgrove with my bare hands, right there on the dark sidewalk. He approached me with the halt in his stride. He was whistling softly, no song that I knew, but something cheerful. I smelled tobacco on him. His face, cast in the faint illumination of the street and parking lot, seemed pale and meek. His beady eyes flickered in my direction as I stood at the gate of the parking lot. He nodded to me without alarm. I imagine he'd been scared of a lot more in prison than a medium-sized man leaving a parking lot. He resumed his whistling and I stood, frozen, as he slowly moved along.

I wiped my wet forehead and slowly exhaled. It was, in many ways, a completely unremarkable moment, two people simply noticing each other as they went on with their lives. But I learned something about myself, or maybe it's more appropriate to say I relearned something, in that span of five seconds. I thought I could kill another human being under certain circumstances, but I can't. I had the means and opportunity and I couldn't do it. It wasn't driven by rational thought; I wasn't thinking at all. I did not calculate the morals or the likelihood of being apprehended; I was freed of all such thought, acting purely on instinct—and my instinct kept my feet planted.

I enjoyed a brief moment of relief and celebration there by the sidewalk, unable to pinpoint the particular thing Cosgrove did, or emotion I felt, that prevented me from taking his life. My mind had been dark and cold only moments before; I was prepared to act without reason, and then suddenly I was unconsciously recognizing the humanity in this frail, flawed man.

The lawyers and I walk out of the judge's chambers and back into the courtroom. Ben and I look at each other but say nothing. This is precisely the kind of thing Ben predicted.

The judge settles in on the bench. "Call your next witness, Ms. Johannsen."

"The People call Brad Gillis."

Brad Gillis looks like a city cop, a real cowboy. I don't dislike the man. He was pretty straight-up with me, didn't condescend and didn't prejudge. I know before he opens his mouth he'll be a good witness for the prosecution.

But he doesn't have much to say today. Almost all the evidence against me consists of what happened before the cops showed up. There's not much dispute over the physical evidence, either. They found a few strands of my hair on Dale, but I was giving him mouth-to-mouth. They didn't find any traces of his skin under my fingernails but they also didn't arrest me for several days after his death, so I would have had time to remove any traces. In the end, there's no doubt that I was there, it's just a question of what I did.

"Placing the defendant at the scene obviously was not a priority," he explains. "Given that he was found there and admitted as much in an interview afterward."

"Nevertheless," says Erica Johannsen, "you investigated the crime scene."

"Yes, of course," says Gillis. "But when the call first came in, there wasn't any particular reason to believe that a murder had been committed. It was possible, but it was equally likely that an elderly man had simply died. We had to wait for the autopsy. So I spoke with the defendant a few minutes and let him go."

"Tell us what was said."

"The defendant claimed that he had left the building for a few minutes, but that he returned when he was phoned by the victim."

"Phoned by Mr. Garrison?"

"That's what he said. He said Mr. Garrison called the defendant."

"On the defendant's cell phone?"

"Yes."

"Did the defendant show you his cell phone?"

"Yes. I took down the phone number." The detective states my phone number. Bennett has already stipulated that this is my number, and that the phone records are accurate. The detective explains that he checked my cell phone records, that a call was made to me at 7:22 p.m. on August 18, 2000, from a phone owned by Joanne Souter.

"Did you check the phone records for Mr. Garrison's office, Detective?"

Johannsen hands the detective phone records from the law offices of Dale Garrison. We stipulated to their authenticity, too. No point in disputing things they can prove, anyway.

"So there were no phone calls made from any phone at the victim's law firm after seven p.m. that evening? August eighteenth?"

"Correct."

The prosecutor then confirms that Dale did not own a cell phone of his own.

"Let me ask you about Joanne Souter. Did you speak with her?"

"I did."

"What did you learn about her cellular telephone?"

"It had been stolen earlier that day, August eighteenth. Her purse had been stolen, and the phone was in it. It was stolen at a public library."

"All right. Now, did Ms. Souter provide any description of the person who stole her purse?"

"She did," says Gillis.

I look at Ben, who is making no attempt to object. We've stipulated to this testimony, and anyway, we agree that Lyle Cosgrove stole the phone.

"She stated that the perpetrator had long red hair in a ponytail, and wore a denim jacket."

"Let me show you a photograph, Detective." The prosecutor walks over and hands Bennett a photograph of Lyle Cosgrove from his criminal file. It's in color, showing red hair.

"Detective, was this photograph shown to Ms. Souter?"

Gillis nods, yes. "I took it out to her myself last night."

"What did she say when she saw it?"

"She said it could have been him."

Johannsen looks at Bennett. "Can we agree this is a photograph of Lyle Cosgrove?" She speaks with a hint of distaste. It's obvious now that we've known about Lyle Cosgrove for a while, and she does not like that fact.

"We'll stipulate." Sure we will.

"Thank you, Mr. Carey." She admits the photograph into evidence.

"All right. Let me take you back to the scene, Detective. You spoke with the defendant. Was anyone else present at that time?"

Gillis reviews his notes and rattles off the names of the security guards.

"Anyone else, though?" asks Johannsen. "Lawyers, paralegals, secretaries?"

"No laypersons," he answers. "Mr. Soliday was the only person in that office with the victim."

"Okay. Now, at some point, the county coroner ruled the death a murder, right? Asphyxiation by manual strangulation."

"That's correct. That's when I returned to Mr. Garrison's office."

"Why?"

"I needed to check the offices again. Look at possible entries and exits and the like."

"Tell us."

"There's only one entrance into the office. The front door. There's two exits. One is that same door, the other is a side door for people to go out to the hallway, usually to the bathroom. But it's not an entrance. Not without a key."

"Had the cleaning people been there?" she asks. "That night. The eighteenth. Before Mr. Garrison's death."

"No, they hadn't. We checked their records. In fact, they walked in while I was there that night."

"Did you interview the other people who worked in those offices?"

"I did. No one had been near the place at seven on Friday night."

"No one," says Johannsen, "other than the defendant."

"That's correct."

"Thank you, Detective." Erica Johannsen walks to the prosecution table, feeling pretty good about her presentation. I look at the judge, who makes eye contact with me and quickly breaks it. I suppose that's just judicial decorum, but I can't shake the feeling she's giving off. The look on her face, however momentary. She thinks I killed Dale. The feeling of dread is sudden and powerful, and as Bennett Carey rises for cross-examination, I look to him with a hope I've never felt, a vulnerability so suddenly clear, so palpable, that I begin to tremble.

51

"Detective Gillis," says Ben. "There are two exits from Mr. Garrison's suite of offices."

"Yes." Gillis crosses a leg but otherwise shows no change of attitude under cross-examination. By now, he's been in court enough. He can handle himself just fine.

"That side exit you mentioned—you don't need a key to leave the office from that exit, do you?"

"To leave? No. Just to come in from the hallway."

"So if someone were in the offices, they could leave whenever they wanted."

"That's correct."

"Did you dust that exit for fingerprints, Detective?"

"I—I did not do that initially, no."

"You weren't sure it was a homicide at all, when you first got there."

"That's right."

"And you're still not sure, are you?"

"I didn't say that, Counsel. I'm confident in the findings of the coroner."

"Okay," says Ben. "But the night of Mr. Garrison's death, you didn't dust the exits for prints."

"No. I didn't necessarily consider it a crime scene."

"Did you try to pull prints later?"

"The cleaning people had been through four or five times by the time we returned. There was no point."

"You didn't secure the office?"

Gillis smiles. "In hindsight, I wish I had. It wasn't a crime scene initially. A lot of people work there. I wasn't ready to tell those people not to come into the office when I didn't even know the autopsy findings. It was rather unusual."

"Understood." Ben doesn't gain anything here by beating up the witness. That's not the point. "So any prints that may have existed were probably wiped clean by the crew that services the building on a daily basis."

"Yes, sir."

Bennett stops, hands on his hips. For a moment I'm not sure whether he forgot his next line of questioning—he works without notes—but it turns out he was making a decision. He walks over to the defense table and opens a file resting on the corner.

"Detective, in the course of investigating the death of Mr. Garrison, you searched my client's office, didn't you?"

"Yes, I did."

"And you found a letter in his top drawer."

Erica Johannsen gets to her feet. "Your Honor, I was under the impression that if we were going to discuss the letter—"

"I'm not introducing it into evidence, Your Honor," Ben interrupts. "I just have some questions about it. At which point, I may have established the basis for admissibility. Which I can't do anyway, not during the prosecution's case-in-chief."

"It's also beyond the scope of direct," says Johannsen. The cross-examination is supposed to be limited to the topics discussed in the direct examination.

"I could always do this in the defense's case," Ben answers. "I could re-call the detective. But this is a bench trial, Your Honor. In the interests of judicial economy, I suggest we cover everything now."

The judge seems concerned. She raises a fist to her mouth and works her jaw. She really is a gorgeous woman, this woman who probably thinks I committed murder.

Ben takes advantage of the silence. "If the objection is relevance, Your Honor, I can assure you the relevance will be clear. The admissibility of this letter is not an issue."

"I guess I'm a little surprised that *you* want to discuss this letter," says the judge. "But that doesn't mean you can't. Proceed. Ms. Johannsen, you can treat your redirect as a cross-examination on this subject."

I look at Erica Johannsen, who, like any lawyer, doesn't enjoy losing an argument. She is attentive but she does not appear particularly distressed. I know that the county attorney has made the decision not to pursue the blackmail theory, and now I know why—because of the person it implicates, someone near and dear to the county attorney. And I know that Dan Morphew dropped off the case as lead prosecutor because he refused to go along with the restriction. But I wonder how much of this Erica Johannsen knows. Did she believe what she told the judge before the trial started—that they weren't going to introduce the blackmail note because they couldn't tie it into me—or was she fronting for the county attorney? Did they choose her because she's less experienced and wouldn't question the direction from overhead, wouldn't know what they were doing when they told her to ignore the blackmail? Or did they choose her because she's willing to go along with the dirty political side of this case?

Does she know what Bennett's about to do?

"Thanks, Judge." Bennett brings a copy of the blackmail letter to the detective, after handing copies to the prosecutor and judge. "I've marked this document Defense Exhibit number one for identification. Detective, is this a copy of the letter you found in Mr. Soliday's desk?"

"Yes, it is."

"Please read the contents into the record."

Detective Gillis slowly reads the words of the letter in open court, the first public display of the blackmail letter.

I guess I'm the only one left who knows the secret that nobody knows. I think $250,000 should cover it. A month should be enough time. I wouldn't presume your income source, but I imagine if anyone could find a way to tap into the campaign fund without anyone noticing, you would. Or I suppose I could always just talk to the senator. Is that what you want? One month. Don't attempt to contact me about this. I will initiate all communications.

An audible response from the gallery. This is juicy stuff, whether they understand the context or not. It's about to get juicier.

"The copy you found at my client's office," says Ben. "Is this the only copy?"

"I don't know."

"Who wrote this document?"

"If I were to bet—"

"Don't bet. Tell me whether you know for certain."

"For certain, no, I do not."

"Do you know who sent this letter?"

"I don't know."

"How did Mr. Soliday receive it?"

"I assume in the mail." The witness notes Ben's glare. "I can't say for certain."

"This letter isn't addressed to anyone, is it?"

"It doesn't say 'Dear Jon Soliday,' if that's what you mean."

"What I *mean* is that you don't know who this was written to."

"I guess I can't tell with absolute certainty, but I can certainly read between the lines."

"So," says Ben, "you don't know for certain who wrote this, who mailed it, how many copies exist, or who it was addressed to, isn't that correct, Detective?"

"There are only two people who have access to the senator's campaign fund," says Gillis. "So it's pretty clear it was written to the defendant."

"The *senator's* campaign fund," says Bennett. He walks still closer to the witness. "Does this letter say the *senator's* campaign fund? Or does it say the campaign fund?"

The judge looks down at her copy of the letter, slowly nodding.

The detective rereads it, too. "Obviously," he says in a quieter voice, "it only says the campaign fund."

"So this could be *any* campaign fund."

"Well—theoretically, I suppose."

"Theoretically?" Ben waves his arms and stares at the witness in wonderment. "Detective, are you aware that there are hundreds of races being voted on in the November 2000 general election? President, U.S. Senate, Congress, as well as dozens and dozens of state and local races?"

"Well, now hold on, Counselor." The detective holds out his hand. "We're talking about two hundred fifty thousand dollars in a campaign fund. That should rule out some of those campaigns. Let's also keep in mind the next sentence in the note: 'Or I suppose I could always just talk to the *senator.*' That tends to narrow the field, wouldn't you say?"

Ben nods. "Would it rule out the campaign fund of Attorney General Langdon Trotter?"

More stirring in the courtroom, enough to prompt the judge to call for order. Judge Bridges, an elected official herself, adjusts in her seat. Erica Johannsen starts to scribble on some paper—I still can't read how much she knows about the politics in her own office concerning this case.

Of all people, Detective Gillis seems the least affected by the mention of the Attorney General. "I guess it wouldn't, not completely."

"He's running for governor. I assume you know that, Detective?"

"Of course."

"And I assume you can tell the court how much money is in *his* campaign fund."

"That I cannot do."

"No?" Bennett slowly moves forward now, toward the witness. "Why, Detective, I'm sure when you were in the initial stages of your investigation, you wanted to keep an open mind about suspects. True?"

"That's true. Any *reasonable* suspects."

"Well, Detective, don't tell me that you just *leaped* to the conclusion that this unnamed campaign fund must automatically be Senator Grant Tully's. Tell me that you at least *checked* into Attorney General Trotter's fund."

The detective seems to be coloring slightly now, probably the most you'll get from him in terms of embarrassment. "Based on the fact that your client was in possession of the letter and has access to a campaign fund, *and* his boss goes by the title of senator—well, yes, I took a leap of logic."

"Who told you not to look at Langdon Trotter?" Ben asks. "Was it the county attorney, Elliot Raycroft, his political ally?"

"Objection—"

"That question is stricken," says the judge, but her words are not delivered harshly.

"Someone told you not to look at Langdon Trotter," says Ben.

"Not true," says the witness. "That's just not true. We focused on the person who made sense, and the campaign fund he had access to."

"That was quite an open mind you were keeping there, Detective."

"That comment is stricken, Mr. Carey. Please move on."

"You wanted to investigate Langdon Trotter, didn't you, Detective?"

"Well, Counselor, no, I—"

"Someone told you to stop, right, Detective?"

"No, Counselor." If anything, Detective Gillis seems amused by Bennett. His confidence makes the intended impression, I fear, raising his credibility with the judge and disarming us. "There's no conspiracy, I promise you. Your guy had the letter. Your guy works for the 'senator.' Your guy can access a large campaign fund. It's true, I can't tell you who sent the letter to him or if there's another copy, but that's just because your client wouldn't tell me."

This was to be the end of Ben's line of questioning. But this is a terrible way to finish. Ben senses this, too. He is pacing a moment, trying to come up with something off the cuff. Finally he returns to the defense table to confer with me. He's asking me if there's anything else I can think of, but what he's really doing is trying to buy time, put some space between a pretty good answer from Gillis. Finally, Ben looks up and says he's done.

The prosecutor stands again. "Detective Gillis, how much money is in the campaign fund of State Senator Grant Tully?"

"Millions," he answers. "I would have brought the precise number with me but I didn't realize we'd be discussing—"

"And this 'secret that nobody knows,' Detective. You see that in the letter?"

"I do."

"Did you ask the defendant what that secret might be?"

"I asked him that, yes."

"Did he tell you?"

"Objection!" Ben leaps to his feet. "The defendant has a Fifth Amendment right to silence that cannot be used against him."

"Sustained," says the judge, her eyebrows raised at the prosecutor.

"Did you ask *Senator Tully* if he knew of any secret?"

"I did."

"What did he say?"

Another hearsay objection Bennett Carey does not make.

"He said he didn't know of any secret," says Gillis.

"And that's pretty much the point of this letter, isn't it, Detective? It's a secret that the senator doesn't know, a threat to tell him?"

"That's—"

"Objection," says Ben. "That calls for speculation."

"I'll allow it," the judge says. "And I understand the point, Ms. Johannsen."

"Detective," the prosecutor continues, "did you ever find any amounts withdrawn from Senator Tully's campaign fund in the amount of two hundred fifty thousand dollars? Or any large amounts like that, paid to Dale Garrison or to cash?"

"No, I didn't," says Gillis. "Nor did I find that kind of money deposited in any account of Mr. Garrison's."

"No, you didn't. Instead you found Mr. Garrison dead, didn't you?"

"That's right. Beats the hell out of paying a quarter of a million bucks."

The judge looks at Bennett, who doesn't object to the commentary. That comment works for us, too, as long as it's Lang Trotter and not me who did the killing.

The prosecutor takes her seat. Bennett stands again. "Detective, did you ever ask Langdon Trotter what the 'secret that nobody knows' is?"

"I never spoke to him, no."

"You are still investigating this case, Detective, right?"

"I—. Well, technically, the file has not been closed."

"Are you going to talk to Langdon Trotter and ask him that question?"

The detective sighs audibly. "I couldn't answer that question at this point."

Bennett shakes his head and sits back down.

"Ms. Johannsen," says the judge, "is the case-in-chief completed?"

"The People rest, Your Honor."

"I'll hear Mr. Carey's motion tomorrow morning," says the judge, before adjourning for the day.

We all stand as the judge steps down from the bench. I grab Bennett's arm. "She practically invited you," I say, referring to the judge's mention of our motion for a directed verdict. That's the motion the defense makes at the close of the prosecution's case, arguing that the evidence is so lacking that the judge should acquit me without my putting on a defense. This is what I need, to win this case before there's any further mention of Lyle Cosgrove, any possible discovery of 1979.

Bennett is solemn, surprisingly so after a successful cross-examination. He doesn't respond until the shuffling and chatter in the courtroom reaches its peak. "It's standard," he says. "She knows I'll move, that's all." He leans into me. "We're not going to get the case tossed. Be ready for that. So I'll ask you again. You still want to testify?"

Bennett and I have batted the idea around plenty, debated it for hours. Despite all of our theories about Lang Trotter, we could put on no defense at all and argue that the evidence does not beat reasonable doubt.

But I have the urge of any innocent defendant. I want to say my piece. I want to deny this. Regardless of legal strategy, regardless of the discipline of the judge, there's something about *not* speaking up in your own defense that will raise eyebrows. I won't let this trial end with people thinking I was hiding.

"Yeah," I tell him. "I still want to testify."

Bennett turns to me, places a hand on my arm. "Grant Tully can fight his own battles, Jon. Do whatever you do for yourself."

Our new defense, implicating Lang Trotter, is not perfect. We won't be able to prove that Trotter made Cosgrove work for him. We won't be able to prove that Dale ever contacted Trotter about the Ace. There is probably a whole lot else we can't prove. Bennett correctly senses that one of the reasons I like the argument is that it attacks Grant's opponent, gives him a fighting chance in the election.

"I want to testify," I say again.

"You know we're going to talk about everything, then. Everything. It's the only way we can explain it."

"I know that." Ben and I have had this conversation numerous times, including last night and this morning. "Unless you think we win right now," I add. "I mean, now their case is done. We've heard everything. Do you think we can win, right now? Rest our case and roll the dice? Do we have reasonable doubt?"

Bennett Carey swallows hard. He breathes in and out, his eyes blinking rapidly, while he takes in the entire trial to date. "I don't think so," he says.

"I don't, either," I agree. "So let's put our game face on. We've got a long night."

"We tell everything," says Ben.

"Yeah," I say. "We tell everything. And I mean everything, Ben."

He doesn't catch my meaning.

"I'm not telling the story I told in 1979. I'm telling the truth as I remember it."

"Now, Jon—"

"I'm not seventeen anymore," I say. "And I'm not going to act like I am. I'm telling the truth tomorrow, Ben. And what happens, happens."

Bennett takes this pronouncement less as my lawyer and more as my friend. He purses his lips and nods in admiration. I don't need that. A grown man shouldn't be congratulated for telling the truth. It's well past time things were settled. It's time to do it right.

52

For the first time today, close to seven o'clock in the evening, I read the *Daily Watch*. The headline covers the debate last night between Trotter and Tully. The top line reads CANDIDATES SQUARE OFF, with pictures of each of the candidates in action. Then the story splits into two, covering each candidate's position separately. The story on Langdon Trotter is entitled A CONSERVATIVE VISION. The one on Grant Tully says TULLY DEFENDS PLAN FOR TAX HIKE. That tells me enough right there, before I go to the coverage inside, which includes an overnight tracking poll that now puts Grant Tully a firm twenty-one points behind the Attorney General. He lost four points in the debate. He got clobbered for telling the truth.

"If we can, we get the senator and you tomorrow, we get both of you on and off the same day." Ben has a mouthful of popcorn, sitting in his chair in the conference room at the law firm. "The judge gave us the whole day tomorrow. We throw everything at the prosecution in one day and give them little time to sort it out. Then maybe we'll rest and they're stuck."

"That seems unfair," I say. "To the prosecution. Not that I'm complaining."

"Oh, Erica'll complain like crazy. But we don't have to give her notice of this stuff. It's not like we're adding new witnesses or making an alibi.

That would require notice. Besides, they heard me today talk about Lang Trotter. They know we're pointing at him."

My mouth opens, a nervous yawn. I stretch my arms to shake the trembles. "I can't believe we're really going to do this," I say. "Grant's going to take a beating."

"I've gone over his testimony a few times," Ben answers. "He's ready. We've got it down pretty well. And *Lang Trotter's* going to take the beating," he adds. "If we do it right."

Ben's cell phone rings. "Hey, Cal," he says. He listens for a moment, his eyes widening, before he covers the mouthpiece. "They found ten thousand in cash in Lyle's safe-deposit box," he says. "He purchased the box a week before the murder."

"Trotter was paying him," I say. "He hid the money by putting it there instead of a checking account. We have to subpoena Trotter's bank records, his campaign money, everything."

Ben nods but he's still listening. "Okay. Okay. Keep trying. Hire anyone you need. As many people as you want. We need anything you have, and we need it yesterday." He covers the phone again, speaking to me: "No luck so far tying Trotter to any communication with Garrison." Then back into the phone: "Is that all, Cal? Okay, what's the best for last? You—you *did*—and?"

"Ten thousand tax-free is plenty for a career felon with a minimum-wage job at a pharmacy," I say to Ben, though his attention is on the information he's receiving over the phone.

"No," Ben says into the phone. "Cal, I have no—" Ben's face colors. He closes his eyes. His mouth parts. He makes a noise, something guttural. He looks like someone has pulled a pin and let out all his air.

"What?" I ask, pushing him lightly.

"Are you positive?" Ben asks. "A hundred percent positive?" Another pause. Ben doesn't say anything further. He simply folds his cellular phone and places it delicately on a stack of papers in front of him.

"Tell me," I implore. "Come on, Ben, what's the—"

"Rick," he says.

My heart skips a beat. "Cal found Rick?"

"So to speak." Ben places a hand on the table to steady himself.

"So to speak? What does that—" I watch Bennett bring his hands to his face. "He's dead, isn't he?"

Bennett's eyes creep over the hands covering his expression. He nods.

"Jesus Christ, this guy." I slap my hand on the table. "Trotter just erased the lot of them. This guy won't stop at anything. He—"

"Trotter didn't kill him." Bennett straightens again, looking me in the eye. "I did."

It takes a moment, a moment to ensure that I heard my friend correctly, another moment to recall the name of the person who broke into his house a week before Dale Garrison was murdered. "Brian O'Shea," I say. "Brian O'Shea is Rick—wait—" I drop my hands on the table. "Oh, for God's sake." I hold out my hand. "You get it, Ben? Brian O'Shea is Rick O'Shea. Ricochet."

"Brian 'Rick' O'Shea," says Ben.

"That's a nickname a bunch of dumb kids would come up with," I say. "Well, Brian or Rick or whoever—why was he breaking into *your* house, Ben?"

Bennett throws his hands up in exasperation.

"Trotter used O'Shea just like he used Cosgrove," I say. "He uses the guys from 1979 to do all the killing. So everything would point at me. And make the senator look bad." I point to Ben. "O'Shea was planning on killing you," I say.

"Maybe," says Ben. "Killing me or hurting me."

"Trotter was sending a message to Garrison about the blackmail," I say. "He picked someone close to Garrison, close to us. He was telling Garrison, this is how it's gonna be. Violence. Pain. Death. But then it got turned around. You killed O'Shea, not the other way around. So the message wasn't sent. So Trotter had to take out Garrison. It was the only way to ensure that the Ace would never be public."

"But why *me?*" he whispers.

"You make sense," I answer. "It can't be me, because he might need me later—I'm the guy he set up for Dale's murder. And you live alone. You're part of the legal team. Dale knows you. It makes sense, Ben."

Hard to read Ben's expression. He's doing some serious thinking, but I don't think he's trying to connect the dots on this case. I don't think he's listening to me at all. I think he's realizing, for the first time, that the man who broke into his house may really have been a killer. Ben's shooting was justified. Not just under the law, but in Ben's own mind now, too.

I'm glad for that, too, but I'm concerned with more immediate topics. "Ben, listen," I start. "I know the whole thing being dredged back up—that whole night of the break-in—can't be easy for you. But the truth is, I need you right now."

Bennett blinks out of his trance and looks at me, waving me off with a hand. "I'm fine." His face is crimson; his eyes are red, almost rabid. If anything, this probably makes him want to take down Lang Trotter even more.

"I need two things from you tomorrow," I add. "I need you to convince the judge of my innocence."

"What else could there be than that?"

"Make the senator come out okay," I answer. "He has enough trouble already."

53

On my way out of my office after meeting with Bennett, my cell phone rings. I don't answer in time but there's a voice-mail message. It's Tracy. She tells me she's been out with friends, tried me at home first, was just checking in, wondering how things are going. She says they're going to the bar at the Washburn, she understands if I'm not up for it—she's with a bunch of people, no doubt—but the offer stands.

Yeah. That would be a real hoot for her girlfriends. The arrival of a murder suspect to the party. We can discuss theories, evidentiary rulings, the impact on the governor's race. Maybe we can speculate on the details of spending the next forty years in prison.

The thought hits me that Tracy is falling into a pattern that started about two years ago, when our marriage was sliding downhill. Nominally inviting me to things she knows I'll decline. Not wanting me to come but understanding her obligation to ask.

But I don't think so. She came to town for me. But what's she supposed to do if I don't call her? Sit home at her friend Krista's place and hang her head? She should have some fun. She deserves it. It's about time.

I find myself avoiding the cabs that slow as they pass me. I'm heading east toward the lake. The walk is enjoyable. It's unusually mild for October, and even with the wind tunnels we're famous for, there is little more than a light breeze.

The Washburn Hotel is like a glorified train station. The place is magnificent, a forty-story palace along the lake. The interior always brings to mind an amusement park, too many things going on in one spot. There's a restaurant, a lounge, a slot room, a salon.

The lounge has a sizeable bar, with an interior garden area outside the bar with tables and chairs. The place is hopping, with a couple dozen people milling outside the bar in the garden area and a packed crowd inside.

I slow my walk and move to the doorway. The bouncer doesn't bother to card me. I stand practically next to him and look about the place. A once-over produces no sign of her, and I find relief in this fact. But then I see Tracy, sitting with three of her friends near a corner.

Not surprisingly, she looks terrific, dressed for a night on the town. Her friends Krista, Stephanie, and Katie are with her. They're all midthirties, all married. Stephanie has two little girls, Krista and her husband have been trying for a couple of years. I haven't spoken with any of them since the divorce. I don't think there's animosity there, just the lack of a common element since their friend, my bride, left town.

She's laughing, the way she always did, throwing her head back, a wide smile splashed across her face. A couple of men are trying to work their way into the group, presumably with Tracy in mind, but her body language suggests her indifference.

Tomorrow, everything will be different. A terrible secret will arise from my past, a secret that not even Tracy ever knew. I suppose there should be some significance in the fact I never told her—that I've always known I did something wrong, and that I never completely opened myself to my wife. Was that it? That I closed her out? Hid my emotions? It's not the first time I've wondered, but I always reach the same conclusion, that it's impossible to look back and identify the source. Because everything is intertwined with everything else.

There's no rewind button in life. Like anybody else, I'd do things differently, given the chance. The question is, what would I do differently? Everything seems important at the time. Everything's a priority. In hindsight, the details of legislation and meetings and backroom deals and elections merge together in a meaningless blur, leaving me only with the fact that my wife is gone.

This is too much. Overload. It's not so simple as the fact that I've got the trial, no time to mourn our past. No, the truth is I've made plenty of room for thoughts of Tracy all along, more so since she returned to town. And it's not the past I'm thinking of. It's our future. That's what scares me. Besides, the wind blows one way and I spend the rest of my life in jail. And I'm thinking about our future?

I nod to the bouncer, who's looking at a guy who never left the entranceway.

"Didn't find who you're looking for," he says to me.

I turn back to Tracy once more. She's listening to one of her friends tell a story, her hand rising to her face as she breaks up in laughter. She was always good at listening.

54

The first order of business today is the defense's motion for a directed verdict. Ben is asking the judge to find the evidence so insufficient that the trial is over. Judge Bridges lets Bennett Carey argue for over ten minutes about the deficiencies in the prosecution's case. She doesn't interrupt him, and she has a passable poker face, but it's not hard to see where she's going. Especially when she tells the prosecution not to argue in response.

"There is competent evidence of homicide," she begins. "Death by strangulation. There is, at this stage, unrefuted evidence that Mr. Soliday was the only person who possibly could have committed the strangulation. None of this is conclusive. I haven't heard any evidence from the defense. But the motion is denied. Mr. Carey, if you choose to offer a defense, you have the right to your opening statement."

My heart sinks, not from surprise at the ruling, but at the words delivered by the person who is the sole finder of fact in this case. Judge Bridges is my jury. She has found competent evidence of strangulation and she believes that I was the only person there. We will point all over the place at motive, but we will never be able to put Lyle Cosgrove or Langdon Trotter in that office with Dale Garrison and me. Not unless Cal Reedy finds something good.

"Thank you, Judge, I *would* like to make that opening statement." Bennett rises and buttons his coat. I want, more than anything, to close my eyes and shut out what's coming. But this is our offensive, and however uncomfortable it may be, I have to look Judge Nicole Bridges squarely in the eye.

"I'm going to tell you two stories," Ben starts. "They will appear to have nothing to do with each other. But the evidence will show that they do. They are quite related."

Ben positions himself in the center of the room. "Let me take you to the summer of 1979. Jon Soliday and his best friend, Grant Tully, are seventeen years old. High school grads. They take a drive to Summit County, across the state line. They were attending a party they'd heard about. They meet up with a gentleman there, someone neither Jon nor Grant had ever met before. That person's name was Lyle. We now know his full name is Lyle Cosgrove."

The judge cocks her head. A name she has just recently heard. A man who was murdered. I hear the noise of pen to paper, scribbling, from the prosecutor's table. I don't think Erica Johannsen knows this stuff. Maybe Lang Trotter decided not to funnel this stuff to the county attorney yet. Or maybe she's just surprised that we would bring this stuff up.

"Lyle had a girlfriend named Gina. Gina Mason. And there was another person there, too. That person went by the name of Rick. As a nickname, he used 'Ricochet.'" Ben shrugs. "So we have Jon Soliday, Grant Tully, Lyle, Rick, and Gina. And they did what kids who are in their late teens, maybe early twenties do. They partied. They had some beer. Some of them—not all of them—even used drugs."

Ben takes a step to the side. "The night is coming to an end, and people are set to go their different ways. The young woman, Gina, she left by herself. Rick drove Grant home. That left Lyle Cosgrove and Jon Soliday."

I hold my breath. I have just been connected to a man recently found murdered. The story has to start this way, chronologically at least, but the first impression on the judge can't be favorable.

"Lyle and Jon, it turns out, went to Gina's house. Jon Soliday was intoxicated. Quite intoxicated, more than he'd ever been. He had little experience with beer and none with drugs. So he didn't know much. But when Lyle Cosgrove pulled up in front of Gina's house and told Jon to go in, Jon did. He went in."

I feel a slow burn run through me. The press in the gallery is silent, but there is bombshell after bombshell spewing forth now. Grant Tully. Drugs. More evil to come. In politics, they say your career is never finished unless you're found with a live boy or a dead girl. Well, here's a dead girl.

"Jon was welcomed into the home by Gina. They were attracted to each other. And they did what some teenagers would do in such a situation. They were—intimate. They had sexual relations in her room."

This is golden stuff from a gossip's perspective. The scribblings of pen to paper—from behind me and from the prosecution—provide a background hum as my lawyer continues.

"As Jon was leaving the house, the man he came with—they were really just boys—Lyle Cosgrove was leaving his car and going to the house, telling Jon that it was time to go. Jon was leaving anyway. So he left with Lyle. Two days later, Jon Soliday is working a summer job when he's visited by sheriff's deputies. He learns for the first time that this young lady, Gina Mason, died that night. A death," he quickly adds, "that was later determined by the medical examiner to be an overdose."

A sufficient murmur arises behind me, sufficient that Judge Bridges bangs the gavel lightly for silence. Hearing this in public makes it all the more tangible. What a sordid affair, and what a tragic conclusion.

"There is an investigation," Ben continues. "The police and the prosecutors in Summit County investigate. They investigate the possibility of homicide, of rape. They speak to Lyle Cosgrove. They speak to Jon Soliday. They review the medical evidence. And they conclude that this young woman died by overdose. There was no murder. There was no rape. A very unfortunate situation but not a criminal one."

The understatement of the year, one that is certainly not lost on the judge. She casts a sour glance in my direction. My heart is pounding against my chest. This isn't working out so well. She's going to hate me before she hears anything that helps me.

"Lyle Cosgrove, by the way, retained an attorney during this investigation. The same attorney who would serve him in 1988, when he is charged with violent crimes. The same attorney who helped him get parole this year. An attorney named Dale Garrison."

For a moment, the judge is too taken aback to note the clamor in the courtroom. She looks at the prosecutor for some reason. I do, too. Erica Johannsen is waving to someone, a clerk or another assistant prosecutor, to come to her. She begins whispering feverishly. Finally, the judge calls the courtroom to order.

Ben pauses a moment, returns to the defense table, and takes a drink of water. He casts a look through me, wipes some sweat off his brow, and returns to the center of the room.

"The news isn't public because all of the boys are juveniles," he continues. "But among law enforcement, you better believe it's a juicy bit of gossip. The son of Senate Majority Leader Simon Tully, connected, however indirectly, to a scandal? It's at the top of any gossip list. Does the prosecuting attorney in Summit County mention it to some of his prosecutor buddies? You bet. Who was among the people who find out about it? The Rankin County Attorney at the time—Langdon Trotter."

I keep my breathing even. My eyes begin to well but I stay composed. The judge's face reads horror and intense curiosity. She is leaning forward with her hands propped under her chin. The press behind me must be in a feeding frenzy. Now we've thrown in Langdon Trotter as well. But we will never prove that Lang Trotter heard about the 1979 incident. We can suppose it, but it will never be a fact. And that's the lynchpin of our theory. If Lang Trotter didn't know about 1979, he wouldn't know to use Rick and Lyle, so it doesn't make sense that Trotter was behind these murders. Which points to me.

"Trotter can't do anything with the information," Ben continues. "It's a sealed juvenile case. But he stores the information away. He keeps track of the players—Lyle and Rick. He waits for the time that the information can prove useful." He opens his hands. "That's the first story. Now, the second."

Okay. At least we're on offense now. Steady as she goes.

"This year," says Ben. "The governor's race. Attorney General Langdon Trotter coasts to victory in the Republican primary. No one runs against him. No one looks at his nominating papers. But when Senator Grant Tully wins the Democratic primary, his attorney, Jonathan Soliday, *does* look at the papers. And what does he find? He finds a mistake. A major mistake. A fatal mistake. Langdon Trotter did not submit the original statement of candidacy with the board of elections. He submitted a photocopy."

Erica Johannsen probably doesn't even understand this. Judge Bridges does. She had to file one of those when she ran for judge. But she might not understand the legal point, the deficiency in the papers.

"The failure to file the original statement of candidacy renders the statement invalid," Ben says. "And without a statement of candidacy, there is no candidacy."

The judge nods.

"And this was not only the conclusion of Jon Soliday, who is probably the single foremost expert on election law in this state. It was also the conclusion of another lawyer whom Senator Tully consulted—"

The judge could probably say the name along with Bennett.

"Dale Garrison."

Ben comes over to the table and removes a copy of Dale's memo on the Ace. "Defense number two for identification," he says. "We will introduce a memorandum prepared by Dale Garrison on this very point. It's on Mr. Garrison's computer. The prosecution has had it in their possession all along, though it's notable that they've never mentioned it." He turns and looks squarely at Erica Johannsen. She had her head down writing something but looked up when Ben referred to her, and she appears unsure of any response.

"So, Senator Grant Tully has the information in hand. He knows he has the ability to knock his opponent off the ballot. So what does Grant Tully do with this information? He consults with Jon Soliday and they come to a conclusion. They decide to do nothing. Nothing. They decide it would be wrong to knock off a gubernatorial candidate on a technicality. They could have. Nothing could have stopped them. But they don't. And they tell Dale Garrison that. They tell him the information is going nowhere."

This is more than a stretch but it's relatively harmless.

"But the story doesn't end there, Your Honor. Because Dale Garrison still has the information. And what does he do?" Ben returns to the table and picks up the extortion letter. "He seeks out the Republican candidate for governor, Langdon Trotter. The man whose nominating petitions are insufficient." Bennett opens his hands. "He tells Langdon Trotter that he and he alone knows of this mistake. And for a nice quarter of a million dollars, the 'secret that nobody knows' will remain a secret. Or else he can always tell the senator—Senator Tully."

The judge has shuffled through her papers and is reading the blackmail note now.

"Dale Garrison was extorting the Attorney General. Give me two hundred and fifty thousand dollars or I'll tell Senator Tully about your defective statement of candidacy. But money never completely silences someone, does it? There could be more demands for money. The only way to really silence a blackmailer is to kill him."

The noise from behind is not murmuring so much as a collective gasp. The judge is frozen in attention. During this trial and beforehand, she had warned both sides about making explosive accusations. The fact that the judge is not stepping in means that things are making sense to her. Besides, if this is what we intend to prove, how can she keep us from arguing it?

"This is where the information from 1979 comes in handy," Ben says. "Lyle Cosgrove was recently released from prison. He's a violent career criminal. And he's penniless. He makes minimum wage at a pharmacy. Attorney General Trotter comes to him and offers him money to kill an elderly man who won't put up a fight. He takes it. He doesn't know why he's been picked. There are plenty of ex-cons who could have recommended him. All Lyle Cosgrove knows is that he's spent years and years in prison, he doesn't want to go back, and when the chief law enforcement officer of the state says to do something, he'll do it. Especially for ten thousand dollars."

The last comment catches the judge's attention most of all. The rest of this could appear to be speculative, but the mention of a concrete amount of money tells the judge we have evidence.

Bennett nods with satisfaction. "Langdon Trotter was very deliberate in picking Lyle Cosgrove as the killer. Because if the evidence ever pointed to Lyle Cosgrove, it would eventually point back to 1979, too, and embarrass his rival for the governor's seat." Bennett holds out two fingers. "Two birds with one stone. The blackmailer's out of the way and his election opponent gets smeared."

Bennett flaps his arms. "It was easy to set up. First, he makes a copy of the blackmail letter and he sends it to Jon. So it will be in Jon's possession beforehand. Then he begins his plan. The Attorney General is not without his resources. He finds out Dale Garrison is set to meet with Jon Soliday on a Thursday for lunch. The Attorney General has that appointment changed to Friday, August eighteenth, at seven in the evening. How does he do that? Simple. He calls Garrison's secretary, Sheila Paul, pretending to be from Jon's office, and reschedules. Then he calls Jon's secretary and pulls the same stunt. Neither Dale Garrison nor Jon Soliday changed the appointment. Each of them thinks the other one did."

The judge purses her lips. We might be gaining some ground here.

"On the day of Dale Garrison's death—Friday, August eighteenth—Lyle Cosgrove, at the direction of the Attorney General, steals a cellular telephone from a woman named Joanne Souter. He needs an untraceable phone. Cosgrove hides in Dale Garrison's office that night, some time after five and before seven. As Sheila Paul, Mr. Garrison's secretary, testified, someone could easily walk into that office without Dale Garrison knowing about it."

I look at the judge, the most important person in the courtroom. She is not pleased. I don't think it is from disbelief—I hope it isn't. This case is getting bigger and bigger. Both candidates for the state's highest office are implicated to some extent in this case; one of them is being accused of murder. That means more headlines. A spotlight. Nicole Bridges is a relatively new trial judge who, like almost every judge in the state, would like someday to occupy the court of appeals, maybe even get an appointment to the federal bench. This case can do nothing to assist her. If she does a perfect job on rulings and flawlessly conducts this trial, she will receive few accolades. On the other hand, if anything goes even slightly amiss, it could all fall on her. Particularly if there is the appearance that things are out of control. That's the worst thing that can be said about a judge. And here we are, throwing out inflammatory accusations that may not be proven. There's not a lot she can do. We are entitled to predict the evidence. But the more she hears, the uglier the downside for her.

Which leads me to another thought. If she acquits me, there will be no appellate review of this trial. She says "not guilty" and the proceedings stop right there. If she convicts me, the appeals court might criticize her, and there would be stories about that as well. Things will go easier for her with an acquittal. I wonder if that has entered her mind, as well.

"So Cosgrove hides in the office and he waits," Ben continues. "He waits for Jon Soliday to arrive and leave. Then he kills Dale Garrison. First things first. He strangles Dale Garrison. It couldn't have been very hard. He does what he's told by the Attorney General. Besides, Cosgrove always blamed Mr. Garrison for not providing an adequate defense when he was convicted in 1988. Sure, he's happy to do it."

Bennett wags a finger. "After the killing, which wouldn't have taken more than a few minutes, Cosgrove uses the phone he stole and calls Jon Soliday. Jon couldn't have gotten far. Couple blocks, at most. And he tells Jon to return to the office. Continue the discussion. Jon will tell you, when he testifies, that the reception was bad, cell phone to cell phone. He couldn't hear very well. So what does Jon know? He has no reason to be suspicious at this point. He thinks Dale Garrison has called him, so he goes back to the office."

Bennett strolls a moment. He likes to break up his oration.

"Lyle Cosgrove leaves the building before Jon comes back. And when Jon returns to the office, Dale is in the same place he was when Jon left. At his desk. Only this time, his head is on his desk. Now, what does Jon think, when he initially sees Mr. Garrison—in the first two, three seconds he sees Mr. Garrison? He thinks that a seventy-year-old man, frail from cancer, at past seven o'clock at the end of a long week, may have fallen asleep." Bennett shrugs. "That's what he thinks. But almost as soon as he has arrived, Mr. Hornowski, the security guard, comes down the hallway. And after they look at Mr. Garrison a moment—about ten seconds, Mr.

Hornowski said—they realize something might be amiss. Jon"—Bennett opens a hand toward me—"Jon attempts to resuscitate his colleague. He tries mouth-to-mouth, everything, to bring Dale Garrison back. He tried to save his life. He didn't kill him."

Bennett moves toward the judge. "But it sure looks bad, doesn't it? Being in the same office with the deceased? That's why Langdon Trotter set it up that way. And now he has his opponent's top aide on trial for murder. The Attorney General kills the blackmailer *and* assists his campaign effort, in one blow. Perfect. Or I should say, almost perfect. There is one person who can still spoil this plan. Lyle Cosgrove. Who now has conveniently turned up dead."

Bennett places his hands together, as if in prayer. The analogy may be apt. "Your Honor, Jon Soliday did not kill Dale Garrison."

Ben takes a seat and reaches for the water again. Erica Johannsen rises. "Your Honor—so much—Mr. Carey has thrown out so many allegations here. This is all new. I respectfully request a continuance."

From his chair, Ben says, "There's nothing here that requires notice to the other side, Your Honor. There's no alibi. There are no new witnesses. Langdon Trotter is on our list. And frankly, I find the whole notion of surprise a little disingenuous. They've had this memorandum about the Attorney General's nominating papers all along. If they chose not to investigate that, at best it is negligence. At worst, it's something else."

"Mr. Carey—" the judge starts.

"There's no surprise, Your Honor. Nothing unfair whatsoever. We're not required to disclose our theory of the case."

"We're going to recess for a half hour," the judge says. "At which time, Mr. Carey, you may call your first witness."

"Thank you, Your Honor."

"And Mr. Carey?" the judge adds. "Nothing you have said in your opening statement is evidence. I expect you to back up each statement with facts."

"Of course, Judge," Ben says. He looks at me, each of us wondering if we'll be able to accomplish that.

55

"The defense calls Senator Grant Tully."

I hear the faint repetition of the name from the back of the courtroom—the bailiff or some court officer, hollering out into the hallway. I turn back to look. The courtroom has about a dozen members of the press there.

Grant Tully has been inside this building for two hours. He didn't want to arrive to a flurry of reporters who had heard Bennett's opening statement. That's what they expected. Instead, he came into the building through the private judges' entrance with one of the jurists he helped put on the bench. Then he stayed in the office of the county recorder, a political patronage office, someone who's a good friend of the senator, on the eleventh floor.

Grant Tully looks like he always does—pretty much an ordinary person. He is handsome and youthful but, probably because of his age, he doesn't reek of power like some of the silver-haired old-schoolers. This is a good thing for me. He makes a good, subdued appearance. The judge gives Grant his due, making a point of saying "good afternoon" to the senator and wearing a respectful expression. This judge didn't get elected with Grant's help, but Grant Tully could still make plenty of trouble for her if he were so inclined. He could talk to the chief judge of the circuit courts, who assigns judges to courtrooms. Judge Bridges could find herself in night narcotics court if the right person wanted it that way.

Bennett takes the senator through some warm-ups—name, rank, and serial number. "I realize you're in the midst of a campaign," says Ben. "So why don't we just get right to it?"

Grant is wearing his public face. This is going to be painful but he'll handle it.

"June of 1979," says Bennett. "You and Jon Soliday are seventeen years old."

"That's correct."

"You and Jon went to a party."

"That's correct."

"You go to a town in Summit County, across the state line."

"That's correct."

"Did you meet some people at the party?"

"Yes. We met someone named Lyle, someone named Rick, and someone named Gina."

"Last names?" asks Ben.

"I didn't get their last names," he says.

"Is the 'Lyle' you mentioned someone named Lyle Cosgrove?"

"I don't know. It certainly could be."

Bennett will not elaborate on Rick—who we now know is Brian O'Shea, the man who broke into Ben's home. He didn't mention Rick's true identity in the opening statement, either. It's beyond what we need to show, and there are enough things already that we probably won't be able to establish.

"All right," says Ben. "Now, at the end of the night, Senator, did you leave that party?"

"Yes."

"With whom did you leave?"

"I left with Rick, I believe. It's been a long time." Grant was not too pleased to hear that Rick's name emerged in this case. But there was little that could be done.

"You left with Rick?" asks Ben. "Or Lyle?" He seems confused a moment. He's had to digest a lot of information about 1979 in a short time.

"I left with Rick," says Grant.

"You're sure about that? You remember leaving with Rick in your car?"

"I do remember that. As well as one can remember something like that so long ago."

"Okay." Ben delivers the next question quietly. "You'd been drinking."

"Yes, I had. I had drunk beer."

"But not Rick."

"No."

"So Rick drove you home."

"Right."

Voters are far beyond the shock value of a seventeen-year-old drinking some beers. It makes us look forthcoming without hurting Grant. There could be plenty else to damage him.

"What about the others?" Ben asks. "Gina and Lyle and Jon?"

"They left separately."

"Why didn't you leave with Jon?"

"It was my understanding that the young lady had asked Jon to her house."

"Gina Mason, you mean?"

"Gina, yes."

"Who told you that? That Gina wanted Jon to visit her at her house?"

"I don't know, Mr. Carey. One of the other boys. Lyle or Rick."

"And then what happened?"

Grant shrugs. "I went home."

"So, just to be clear here, Senator. You and Rick took your car. Jon and Lyle took Lyle's car. Gina had already gone home before you all."

"That's correct."

"But Gina had invited Jon to her house."

"Yes."

"All right. Now, did you come to learn that the young lady, Gina Mason, had died that night?"

"I did learn that. I was very sorry to hear that, obviously."

"Did you speak with the police about that incident?"

"I spoke with someone at the investigator's office. Yes."

"All right. Do you happen to know whether Mr. Cosgrove was questioned?"

"I understand that he was."

"Do you know whether Mr. Cosgrove had a lawyer?"

"Yes. Mr. Cosgrove—the Lyle I knew—had a lawyer. Dale Garrison."

"How did he come to retain Dale Garrison?"

"He asked me if I could recommend someone. I gave him Dale's name."

"Senator, what was your state of mind at this time? Did you have a belief as to Jon's guilt or innocence?"

Grant slices the air with a hand. "I wasn't there, so I didn't know. But I believed, number one, that Jon Soliday was my best friend and someone I trusted and respected. And someone who could never commit an act of violence like that. Never. And number two, I was aware that he was highly intoxicated. Even still, I didn't think he would do something like what they were investigating. I didn't. I still don't."

"Senator, you're aware of this supposed blackmail note."

"I am."

"Okay," says Ben. "Senator, let's get something out of the way. Let me show you this exhibit." Ben leaves the lectern and grabs the blackmail note, then hands the copies to the judge and the witness. "Please read this over to yourself."

Grant complies.

"Now, Senator—you're aware of this letter."

"Yes, vaguely."

"Let me ask you, sir. Is it possible that this blackmail pertains to what happened in 1979?" Ben takes a step. "I mean, is it possible that Dale Garrison was threatening Jon to tell you something about 1979 that you didn't already know? A secret?"

"Objection," says the prosecutor. "Speculative."

"Sustained."

"The letter mentions the 'senator,' Your Honor."

"That doesn't make your question any less speculative, Counsel," says Judge Bridges. "Move on."

Bennett is stuck a moment. He composes himself, reaching for an appropriate question.

"Senator, we know that Mr. Garrison was Lyle Cosgrove's lawyer back in 1979."

"Yes, we do."

"Okay. Is it possible, Senator, that Mr. Garrison was threatening to tell you that Jon was in fact guilty of a crime back in 1979?"

"Objection." Erica Johannsen is on her feet. "Calls for speculation."

"No, it does not," Ben answers quickly. "I think the senator's answer will show that."

"I'll strike the answer if it is speculative." The judge nods to Grant. "Senator."

Grant nods backs at the judge, then fixes on Bennett again. "There is nothing about 1979 that hasn't already been discussed by Jon, and Dale, and myself. All of us know that there is a minute possibility that something occurred there, between Jon and that young lady—given Jon's intoxication. A very minute possibility. But all of us believe that Jon did nothing wrong."

That conversation never occurred. Grant is covering for me.

"But, Senator," says Ben, "couldn't that be the point? You didn't think he was guilty of anything, but maybe Dale knew something different?"

"Dale knew very well that I had no interest in dredging up the past. I made it very clear to him and to Jon that what happened in the past should stay there. Dale knew very well that I wouldn't discuss the topic. Jon knew that, too. There was no threat."

That's not true, either, but it's not far off. And no one will contradict the testimony.

"Well, Senator, is it possible that Dale was simply threatening to expose the fact that you were involved, however tangentially? I mean, it's not the most pleasant topic in the world. And you *are* running for governor. Is it possible that Dale was going to spill the fact that there was an incident in the past in which a young woman died—maybe a rape/murder—and you and Jon Soliday were near it in some way? Just guilt by association?"

"No, it's not possible," Grant answers. "Dale is one of my closest friends. One of my father's, too. And more to the point, Mr. Carey, if Dale needed money, I would have given it to him. All he'd have to do is ask." Grant shakes his head, as if the notion is ridiculous. "Dale Garrison would never blackmail either Jon Soliday or me. It's preposterous."

"All right, Senator. Fast-forward. Let's talk about the governor's race. The primaries."

Grant covers the background, that he and Trotter won the nominations for the governor's race, that I looked at Trotter's papers and found a problem with them.

"As Jon explained it to me," says Grant, "it meant that Mr. Trotter's petitions were invalid. The statement of candidacy has to be 'signed,' and a photocopy of a signature is not a signature. It's no better than a blank piece of paper."

The judge's brow crinkles. She is thinking through the legal issue herself.

"Meaning the Attorney General could be knocked off the ballot if you challenged him?"

"Yes."

"Did you seek a second opinion on Jon's conclusion?"

"I probably wouldn't call it a second opinion. Jon knows this stuff better than anyone. I might call it another perspective."

"Whose perspective?"

"Dale Garrison's."

"Did Dale Garrison draft a memorandum on this topic?"

"Yes."

"Your Honor, I'll resort to Mr. Garrison's computer if counsel prefers." Ben is handling a copy of the memo on the Ace. "Defense number two for identification."

"That copy is fine," says Johannsen. Ben showed it to her during the recess. She matched it up with the one on the computer. Ben hands out copies to everyone.

"This is it," Grant says. "Dale agreed with Jon. The error on the statement of candidacy was fatal."

"How did this memorandum come to you?"

"Dale sent it over by messenger to our office. I think he sent it to Jon."

"When was that, Senator?"

"It was August fourth."

"And how do you remember that day?"

"Because when Dale sent the messenger package over with the memo, he also included a birthday card to me. In fact, Mr. Carey, I think you were the one who handed it to me. My birthday is August tenth. And I remember specifically thinking that Dale was six days early. It was just a thought that came through my mind that stands out."

I remember seeing the birthday card. Good. That ties the date down well. That is critical for us, because we need to push that date as far before Dale's death as possible. We need time for Dale to blackmail Trotter, then for Trotter to get hold of Lyle Cosgrove, then to send the blackmail letter to me, then to kill Dale. Dale sent the memo to us on August 4, and he died on August 18. Trotter had two weeks to plan this out.

"So, Senator." Ben locks his hands at his waist. "At that point, you had the option of filing a challenge to Mr. Trotter's papers."

"I did, yes."

"You could have knocked your opponent off the ballot."

"Yes, I could have."

"Did you file a challenge?"

"No, I didn't. That's not how I want to become governor. The voters deserve a choice."

"Was that communicated to Dale?"

"It was. I told him myself. And Jon told him, too. He knew we would not use it."

Not entirely true. Grant is hedging in my favor again.

"When was this, Senator? When did you tell Dale Garrison that you were not going to file an objection to Mr. Garrison's papers?"

"I don't recall the exact date," says the senator. "But again, it was before my birthday. Because I thanked him for the card, and I told him my birthday was still a few days away. We joked about it. We joked about not wanting the birthdays to come."

This conversation didn't happen, of course. We were still thinking about using the Ace. Grant isn't hedging here—he's out-and-out lying for me. In his mind, I'm sure, the ends justify the means—a rationale he's made before in my defense.

"So it was between August fourth and your birthday—August tenth—that you told Dale not to pursue this issue."

"That's correct."

"Were you emphatic on this point? Were you waffling?"

"I was quite emphatic. I told him we weren't going to challenge Lang Trotter's papers. End of discussion."

"Did Mr. Garrison object?"

"Quite the opposite," says Grant. "He told me I was doing the right thing."

"Object to the hearsay," says Erica Johannsen.

"It's not hearsay, Judge," Ben replies. "I'm just showing Dale Garrison's state of mind. Dale Garrison was glad that Senator Tully didn't want to use the information because it left Dale Garrison free to blackmail Attorney General Langdon Trotter."

"Overruled," says the judge. She looks at the prosecutor. "It's not hearsay."

Ben continues on. "Do you have any knowledge, Senator, as to whether Dale decided to use this knowledge—this knowledge about Mr. Trotter's nominating papers—in any other way?"

"No, I don't."

"Do you have any knowledge, for example, whether Dale Garrison used this information to extort the Attorney General?"

"No, I don't, Mr. Carey."

"Can you tell us with certainty that Dale Garrison, after your conversation, felt sure that *you* would never use this information yourself?"

"Objection," says Erica Johannsen. "The senator is being asked to speculate as to someone's state of mind."

"Sustained."

"Okay," says Ben. "Well, did you *tell* Mr. Garrison that you would never use it?"

"That *is* hearsay," says the prosecutor.

"If that's an objection, Ms. Johannsen, it is sustained."

Ben's hands move into his pockets. "Okay. I have nothing further."

The judge looks at the clock. It's a quarter to eleven. Too early for lunch. "Ms. Johannsen?"

"Thank you, Your Honor."

I lean into Ben. "We got everything we needed?"

Ben nods. Grant killed the notion that either of us would be blackmailed about the rape. He made it clear that Dale Garrison knew we wouldn't use the Ace, which left him free to blackmail Trotter.

The prosecutor rises slowly. I would have expected more anger. But my read on this woman is that she's not part of the dirty side of this case. I think Erica Johannsen is more interested in getting the right guy than in winning. I never thought I'd say that about a prosecutor. Maybe she's re-thinking this whole case.

"Senator Tully," she starts, "you have no idea whether Langdon Trotter has anything to do with this blackmail note, do you?"

"I've made that very point several times, Counsel."

"You can't rule out the possibility that this note was, in fact, written to the defendant."

"The point I've tried to make is that it just wouldn't make sense."

"But surely, Senator, you don't know what the 'secret that nobody knows' refers to, do you?"

"Not for sure."

"In fact, that's the point, isn't it? That you don't know. But the blackmailer was going to tell you."

"If you say so," says Grant. "That's not impossible."

"So this note could have been written by Dale Garrison to the defendant. Isn't that true?"

"Aside from the fact that there is no logic to it? Yes, it's possible."

"So it's possible that this 'secret' has nothing do with this statement of candidacy issue."

"As I've said."

The prosecutor examines her notes. "Senator, you can't specifically recall the date of August fourth as being the date that Mr. Garrison sent the document to the defendant by messenger, can you?"

"Counsel, I said that I *did* remember the date."

"Because of the relation to your birthday?"

"Right. I recall Mr. Carey handing me the letter, and we joked that Dale was early."

"Good," Ben mumbles.

The prosecutor deflates as she pores over the scribbles on her notepad. "And about this other thing, Senator. This thing about the murder in 1979."

"I believe it was determined to be an overdose, Counsel."

The prosecutor smiles with the clarification. "Are you telling this court that you no longer would care if you learned that Mr. Soliday had killed this young woman?"

"That is *not* what I said. What I said was, first of all, I didn't believe and I don't believe that he did such a thing. But in addition to that, I was not interested in something that happened over twenty years ago. I know Jon Soliday to be an honorable man. A decent man. A dear friend. If it so happened that something occurred that night, taking into account that Jon was quite young and more intoxicated than I'd ever see him, then I suppose I would forgive him. I might yell at him and lecture him. But I'd forgive him. But we're making a huge assumption when we say he might have done something wrong. The law enforcement authorities in Summit County concluded otherwise."

Erica Johanssen nods. "And you'd still make him your top lawyer? Even if he was a murderer?"

Grant considers the question, as well as the gallery filled with media. "Jon is my chief counsel. I had no intention of changing that."

"And if you were elected governor, were you planning to make the defendant the governor's chief counsel?"

"Yes. Of course."

"The defendant knew that?"

"Yes, I imagine Jon knew that."

"And if you were to learn that your lawyer had been part of a murder, you wouldn't rethink keeping him on."

A good question from the prosecutor. What can Grant say to this? "That—that is a question I haven't confronted," Grant answers.

"So it's possible, Senator, that if the defendant had committed murder in 1979, and you were told that by someone, you would fire the defendant."

Grant inhales. "I have told you that I would forgive him. Because he was intoxicated and because he was so young. But I absolutely do not believe he did anything wrong."

"Forgive him, yes. But allow him to assume one of the highest ranking positions in state government? Senator, are you telling this court that for absolutely certain, you would have kept a murderer as your chief lawyer?"

"I guess I can't answer that for certain."

"If you knew for a fact that he had committed a murder, at *any* time in his life, you would have fired him, wouldn't you?"

"Objection," Ben says. "Asked and answered."

"Proceed," says the judge. "Overruled."

"I would be quite concerned, I suppose," Grant concedes. What else can he say? He's testifying to the entire state right now. How can he guarantee that he would keep on an admitted killer?

"All right, Senator. So it *is* possible that the defendant might have lost his job if you learned such a thing. It's *possible*."

"I suppose it's possible."

"And if the information became public, it would make it hard for the defendant to find *any* work in state government, wouldn't it?"

"I don't know if that's true or not."

"You'd help him look for work, Senator? You'd help a murderer and rapist find another job, as long as it wasn't with you?"

"He's a friend," Grant says. "A friend who made one mistake when he was very vulnerable. He was young and confused and intoxicated. He didn't know—" The senator catches himself. The room is silent.

"Jesus Christ," Ben mumbles. I freeze in my chair. Grant is suddenly realizing what he just said. He didn't say it as a hypothetical. He said it as fact. I killed Gina Mason. What does he know that he never told me?

"What I mean to say," he continues.

"The defendant *did* commit that murder, didn't he?" the prosecutor asks. "You just said so."

"No," says Grant, leaning forward. "No. What I meant to say was, if I were to learn that this was the case, I would still consider Jon to be a friend."

"I don't care about what you were *going* to say, sir. Please answer my question. You are under oath. Do you have personal knowledge that the defendant committed that murder?"

Grant doesn't miss a beat. "No, I do not."

"Did anyone ever tell you that the defendant committed murder?"

Grant looks at me.

"Objection," Ben calls out. "Hearsay."

"It's not offered for the truth of the statement," says Erica Johannsen, moving toward the senator. "This is all about state of mind, Judge. That's the whole—"

The judge raises her hand. "The objection is overruled."

Erica Johannsen turns back to the senator with renewed vigor. "Please answer this question, keeping in mind that you're under oath. Senator Tully, did anyone ever tell you that Jon Soliday murdered that girl in 1979?"

Grant wets his lips. The moment of silence is deafening, surpassed only by the sudden drumming of my pulse.

"No," he says.

"Do you know for a fact that he *didn't* commit murder?"

"I suppose I don't."

"And if you were to learn that the defendant *did* commit murder, it's possible you might reconsider keeping him on your staff. It's possible you might fire him."

"I suppose that's possible."

"And Jon Soliday knew that, didn't he, Senator?"

"Objection," says Ben. "There's no foundation for that question."

Erica Johannsen takes her seat as the judge sustains the objection. "I'm done," she says.

"Mr. Carey?" asks the judge. "Any redirect?"

"A few questions," Ben says.

The judge looks at the clock. "More than five or ten minutes?"

"Probably."

"Let's take lunch, then. Come back in an hour."

56

Bennett and I confer very briefly with Grant in the courtroom as the press waits outside the door.

"I couldn't go all the way," says Grant. "I'm sorry, Jon."

"Of course you couldn't," I answer. "You can't admit that you'd keep a killer on staff."

"You did fine," says Ben. "I'll do a little redirect to soften it up."

"And hey." Grant flicks the back of his hand against my shirt. "Sorry about that slipup."

"No problem," I say, leaving unmentioned whether he was speaking the truth. There are only so many things I can confront right now.

We decide it's better not to be seen together. We'll meet back in court. Ben and I angle our way through a considerable amount of reporters. This has been a big day for them, what with Ben's opening statement and now Senator Tully's testimony. This will be national news tonight. A candidate for governor, accused of murder. The other candidate closely connected. We'll be the laughingstock of the country.

As for this election, it's clear now, after hearing the words. Grant Tully is finished. We will never be able to prove that Langdon Trotter is guilty of Dale's murder, not unless we can find a smoking gun. And Trotter is too smart for that. We might conjure up reasonable doubt, but Trotter will deny our claims as a desperate criminal throwing out whatever he can to beat the rap. At best, we will get a nice, quiet "Not guilty" from Judge Bridges, and Trotter will spin it however he wishes. Worst case, I spend the rest of my life in jail.

But either way, Grant Tully played a part, however tangentially, in something suspicious in 1979. He never talked about it, never told anyone. And it won't be hard to figure out that the Tullys did more than mention Dale Garrison to Lyle Cosgrove. They hired him and dispatched him to Summit County to clear things up for me. I know it now and I've known it all along. The governor's race is over. And Grant, realizing this as well, no doubt, actually apologized to *me* a moment ago.

And I don't even have time to feel bad about this.

Ben and I drive to the Maritime Club, the senator's club, where Grant has reserved a small parlor room for us for two weeks running. We haven't used it but we figured the time might come that we need the privacy, and after today's revelations, a private club is about the only place we could go.

Ben knew this would be the case today, so he packed sandwiches, turkey with mustard. We sit in leather high-backed chairs, ignoring the extravagant artwork and the vintage baby grand piano, looking like two people who have seen ghosts.

"What a crazy morning" I say as Ben unwraps the cellophane off the first sandwich. "Do you think she's buying it?"

"I think she finds it plausible," he answers. "All of it makes sense. Making sense is not the hard part. We have to make it more believable. We need facts. And we don't have them, not yet. But we need them fast."

Bennett issued the subpoenas only yesterday. We didn't want to tip off the prosecution as to our theory—pointing the finger at Lang Trotter—so we had to wait. We are chasing everything. Trotter's bank statements, personal ones, corporate ones, political ones. His phone records from his home, his work office, his campaign office, his cell phone—we need one phone call to or from Dale Garrison or Lyle Cosgrove or Brian "Rick" O'Shea. Ben even issued a subpoena to the computerized legal research company that everyone uses, to look at the searches that Langdon Trotter's attorneys might have conducted during the relevant time. We are hoping to find a search that includes the words "statement of candidacy" or "original" or "copy" or anything—anything that will prove that Lang Trotter was looking at the issue after Dale Garrison started his blackmail scheme. We are ignoring the fact that the attorney–client privilege might bar this information, hoping that the mere invocation of it by Lang Trotter might turn the judge our way a little. I see more clearly now why Bennett was content with a bench trial, where the trier of fact also hears contested evidentiary issues.

"Lang Trotter didn't become AG by being stupid," I say. "We're not going to come up with anything."

"Don't say that, Jon." He hands me a soggy sandwich. "And anyway, we just need reasonable doubt."

"She thinks I'm a killer." I start for the sandwich but can't muster the appetite. "She thinks I'm a killer, and the prosecutor made the point well—if Grant learned it, he'd have no choice but to can me."

"He wouldn't do that," Ben says.

"He probably wouldn't," I agree. "But he can't admit that in public." I shake my head. "I had motive and opportunity. The judge knows both of those things. She knows I was the only person in that office because of me—I told the cops that. And she knows about 1979 because *we* told her."

"They would have found out," Ben says. "It was only a matter of time. They already had connected you to Lyle in some way. It would be a matter of simple investigation before they found out about 1979. And they'd get the arrest notes. You *were* a suspect, Jon, even if you weren't arrested. We look better fronting the issue, looking like we have nothing to hide."

"We *don't* have anything to hide." I hurl the sandwich across the room. I bounce out of the chair. "Goddammit, we just ruined this election for Grant and probably gained nothing in the process. We can't pin anything on Trotter. This judge is ready to convict me."

Ben watches me a moment, a mouthful of food in his cheek.

I take a seat on the piano stool. "Sorry about the sandwich."

"I don't have much of an appetite, either." He places his food back in the wrapper. He rubs his hands together and then laces them between his knees. "Jon, you want me to do whatever it takes to win. I'm doing that. And I'll keep doing it. We're going to win."

"How the hell can you say that?" I exhale, air deflating from a balloon. The ceiling is an ornate pattern, an Italian design, I think. My question is rhetorical. There's little my lawyer can say to me right now.

"I'm leaving after this, Jon."

I look back at my lawyer. That one, I didn't expect.

"I'm quitting and getting out of town."

"When did you decide this?"

He shrugs. "I don't know. Something I've been thinking about."

"Where are you going? What are you going to do?"

"Don't know. Leaving the big city, though. Probably, I'll find a prosecutor's office somewhere. I don't know."

"I might need you."

"What—for an appeal? You aren't going to be convicted, Jon. We're going to win."

"Then why leave? If you're going to win, you'll be a celebrity."

"My name'll be mud. I'm taking down Lang Trotter, or at least trying. Who's going to want me?"

"That's naïve. Every criminal defense firm in the city, for starters. By tonight, you'll have CNN and the *Times* and the *Wall Street Journal* covering this thing. You'll be a star."

"Not my style." Bennett smiles softly. "It was probably a weird time to tell you. But I wanted you to know. I also want you to know that I believe you're innocent and I believe you didn't kill Gina Mason. I do believe that."

"Well—thanks."

"And I promise you, we're going to beat this."

I move from the piano and sit on the couch next to my lawyer. "Well, before we say our goodbyes, maybe we could work on my examination. I'm up next, I believe."

Bennett nods and removes some papers from his bag. "The first thing I'm going to ask you is whether you killed Dale Garrison. What's the answer?"

"No, I did not kill Dale Garrison," I say. "And then I turn to the judge and say the same thing. And then I say, 'Judge, I swear to God that I didn't.'"

Bennett smiles. That last part was my idea. He didn't like it so much at first, but his first rule is that it has to be natural, so he went along with it.

"We're ready, Jon," he says. "We've gone over it a hundred times."

"Okay," I say. "You're right."

Bennett stares into space. "You know something, Jon? You're probably the best friend I've ever had." He looks at me. "I imagine that surprises you. It surprises *me*. I didn't even think I'd like you at first."

I look at Ben a moment. This is an odd time for him to say such a thing, but the high tension of this trial has brought out more than one unexpected emotion in me. And I do appreciate the sentiment, even though at the moment I need a lawyer more than a friend.

I check my watch, the evil hands of the clock that are quickly approaching the close of our one-hour recess. Only fifteen minutes from now, it will be time to go to court and convince Judge Nicole Bridges of my innocence.

57

Bennett is poring over his notes as Grant Tully resumes his position on the witness stand. The judge reminds him that he is still under oath.

"Ready?" I say to Ben.

He looks at me. He is not smiling, no attempt at reassurance. He looks haunted, his face drawn and solemn, his eyes red and watery. He leaves his folder open and rises again, to face Senator Tully.

"Senator, this morning, Ms. Johannsen asked you if you knew for a fact you received the memorandum from Dale Garrison on August fourth—the memo about Mr. Trotter's petitions."

"Yes."

"And you said that you did recall specifically receiving the memo on the fourth."

"Yes."

"You recall that because of the birthday card that Dale Garrison also sent you."

"Yes, that's correct. Because it was early. It was the first card I received."

"And you recall my handing that birthday card to you."

"Yes, you did. I imagine that was because you and Jon had opened the package from Dale and found that card."

"Right," says Ben. "And I believe I accidentally opened that card, before realizing it was for you."

"I think that's right," says the senator. "Most of my mail is opened for me before I see it. Although usually it's my secretary, not my lawyer, who does it. It's not in your job description."

A light chuckle from the audience. The senator seems more composed now. I can't imagine he can be looking so good, after the revelations of today's trial. I figure he spent the entire lunch hour on the phone with Don Grier, his press guy, working on a spin.

Ben doesn't even smile. "Senator, do you recall this morning that Ms. Johannsen asked you if you knew for a fact that Langdon Trotter sent this blackmail note to Jon?"

"I recall that, yes."

"And you said you couldn't know for a fact."

"That's right."

Ben approaches Grant and hands him a copy of the note. "And I believe it was you who made the point that we don't know who this note even references."

"I believe that's correct."

Ben stares at his copy of the letter. I remove one from Ben's notes and do the same.

I guess I'm the only one left who knows the secret that nobody knows. I think $250,000 should cover it. A month should be enough time. I wouldn't presume your income source, but I imagine if anyone could find a way to tap into the campaign fund without anyone noticing, you would. Or I suppose I could always just talk to the senator. Is that what you want? One month. Don't attempt to contact me about this. I will initiate all communications.

"In fact," Ben says, "this notes references the 'senator.' It doesn't say 'Grant Tully,' does it?"

"No, it does not." Grant puts down the letter and looks at Bennett.

"How many senators currently serve in this state?"

"Thirty-eight."

"This note could have referred to any one of those senators."

"Of course."

Bennett leaves the defense table and paces behind the lectern. "In fact," he continues, "this note could even refer to *retired* senators, right?"

"I suppose it could."

"Retired senators often go by the title 'senator' afterward, don't they?"

Grant Tully pauses a moment. His eyes move to me, then back to Ben. "Yes."

"There are lots of retired senators, aren't there?"

"Yes, there are."

"This note could have been referring to any one of them, as well."

"I suppose."

My eyes move to the documents by Bennett's side of the desk. Since he removed the copy of the blackmail letter, the document on top of his stack is the memorandum that Cal Reedy prepared for us, summarizing Lyle Cosgrove's history.

No juvenile history obtained. Driver's license revoked on 12/18/78, following DUI convictions on 2/24/78, 8/29/78, and third arrest on 11/04/78. Pleaded no contest to final charge. Agreed to surrender license for five years.

Arrested for sexual assault on 6/19/81. Pleaded guilty to simple assault. Served fifteen months in medium-security prison.

Arrested on 4/15/88 for armed robbery. Convicted on 8/28/88. Served twelve years, paroled on 7/22/00.

Bennett has placed a circle around one sentence in the first paragraph: *Agreed to surrender license for five years.*

My head whips up at Bennett Carey.

"In fact, Senator, your father is a retired senator, isn't he?"

"Excuse me, Your Honor." I'm on my feet. "Could I have a word with my attorney?"

"Of course."

Bennett looks at me curiously but eventually comes to my side.

"What the hell are you doing?" I whisper. "Sit down."

"I'm making the point that this note could have referred to—"

"I *know* your point, Ben. Everyone knows your point. Stop it. Sit down."

"*You* sit, Jon," he replies. "Trust your lawyer." He walks away from me again, over toward the jury box. He casts a look back at me, the guy standing without purpose in the middle of the courtroom. I finally take my seat.

"Senator?" Ben asks.

"Yes, Mr. Carey, my father is a former senator."

"And he goes by 'senator,' doesn't he?"

"He does, yes."

"So, I mean"—Bennett expels a laugh—"this note could have referred to your father."

The senator smiles, but not for the purpose of being pleasant. "I suppose in theory, yes."

"I mean, maybe this note refers to a secret *you* were keeping from *him*."

"I don't have any secrets from my father," says Grant.

"Oh, sure. But the point is, this note could have been written to you, right, Senator? Threatening to expose a secret that you wouldn't want your *father* to know?"

I jump to my feet again. "Your Honor, I want to terminate this examination. We're done. I don't authorize my attorney to continue."

The judge's eyebrows lift. She looks between my lawyer and me. "Mr. Carey?"

"I'm not done, Your Honor."

"Maybe you and your client would like to confer."

"Fine." Ben shrugs and makes his way back to me. I draw him closer and whisper in his ear. "What in the *fuck* are you doing?"

"I'm defending my client."

"You already did that, Ben. Sit down."

"You wanted me to do everything I can," he whispers harshly. "That's what I'm—"

"Not this," I say.

"And why not, Jon? What are you afraid of?"

I shake his arm. "Sit *down.*"

He draws into me, so close he's almost kissing my ear. "If you can look me in the eye and tell me it's never crossed your mind—if you can look me in the eye and swear to God and say that—I'll sit down." He pulls away from me and stares at me.

I am speechless. My heart is pounding furiously, the white noise echoing through my head, the sound of my pulse banging through my body. Noise from every part of my being, except for my mouth. It's as if I've never seen the man standing two feet from me. His look is beyond intense, closer to a bitterness. He is silent but his chest is heaving. A trickle of sweat zigzags from his hairline.

"That's what I thought," he says.

"Are we ready, Counsel?" the judge asks.

Ben doesn't address the court. He says it to me. "I think we are, Judge."

I sit back down, more a response to my wobbly knees than in compliance.

My lawyer strolls across the courtroom, his hands behind his back. "Senator, I think we left off with the notion that this blackmail note could have been threatening *you,* threatening to tell your *father*—the 'senator'—about a secret. Right?"

"That is where you left off, Mr. Carey. I assume you were offering the example out of pure speculation. Because it's certainly not true." The senator's face has reddened, but he is more angry than worried, from my take. He turns to me but I look away a moment, then return my stare to him. We lock eyes as the next question comes.

"You have access to your campaign money, don't you, Senator?"

"Not directly, no, I do not."

"But you tell your people when and where to spend, don't you?"

"I certainly have a say, of course."

"Well, then, let's talk about your father, the 'senator.' As far as you understood it, what was your father's understanding of the alleged rape and murder in 1979?"

"His understanding? I don't catch your meaning."

"Did your father think Jon had committed rape and murder?"

"I'd imagine he did not. But you'd have to ask him."

"Well, as far as you knew, what was your father's understanding of *your* involvement?"

The senator draws back. He takes a moment to be sure he heard the question correctly. "*My* involvement?"

"That's what I asked you."

"I didn't *have* any involvement. I went home."

"And that's what you told your father, wasn't it?"

"Well—of course it is." Grant looks at me.

"So your father thought you had nothing to do with what happened to that young woman."

"I *didn't* have anything to do with that woman's death."

"And that's what your father thought."

"Objection." Erica Johannsen gets to her feet. This is not the first objection she could have made. She's a little off guard herself. "Objection. Calls for speculation."

"Sustained."

"Senator?" Ben asks. "Didn't you tell your father that you had nothing to do with that girl's death?"

That question has already been asked. Bennett is not his normal polished self. He's not himself at all. There is an animation to him, an emotion I've never seen in my lawyer.

"Of course I told my father I had nothing to do with the woman dying," says Grant. "I just said that."

"But Dale Garrison"—Bennett wags a finger, his voice rising—"Dale knew differently, didn't he?"

"I have no idea what you mean, Bennett."

"Take you back to 1979, Senator." Ben approaches Grant. "Who'd you leave the party with?"

"I left with—with Rick."

"You did?" Bennett makes a point of looking confused. It's an act, courtroom theater. "Rick took you home?"

"Right."

"And Lyle drove Jon home in his car, later?"

"I can't say for sure what happened with them."

"But that was the story, right, Senator? The party line? Jon went with Lyle Cosgrove, you and Rick left together?"

The prosecutor makes some objection. The judge sustains. I find myself furiously rubbing my forehead, staring into the table only inches from my face.

"Are you sure, Senator? You're sure Rick drove you home?"

"Yes, I am."

"That's a good forty-five minute ride, isn't it?" Ben waves a hand. "You had to get on the interstate, right?"

"That would be the case, yes." Grant has reddened. He didn't expect this from Bennett, but now he sees where it's going.

"It was *your* car you took," says Ben. "You drove to that party in Summit County in your car, right? You and Jon?"

Grant adjusts in his seat. "Yes."

"So if Rick drove you home in *your* car, how'd he get home? He hitched a ride back to Summit County?"

Grant opens his hands. He answers weakly. "That much, I cannot tell you."

"And Senator," Ben says. He moves across the courtroom and stops. "What would you say if I were to tell you that Lyle Cosgrove didn't *own* a car back then?"

My eyes involuntarily move to the memo on Lyle Cosgrove again.

Agreed to surrender license for five years.

"Objection," says the prosecutor. "Assuming facts not in evidence. Calling for speculation."

"Sustained," the judge replies, with little conviction.

"Weren't you aware, Senator, that Lyle Cosgrove had his driver's license revoked in 1978? A five-year revocation?"

"No, in fact I was not aware of that, Mr. Carey."

"So how did Jon get home that night, Senator? In fact, how did Jon get to Gina's house?"

"Objection."

"Sustained," the judge answers quickly.

Bennett's hands rise and drop to his sides. He stares into his witness, who is making every effort to compose himself. He's waiting a moment for the drama, for the unexpected question. I could ask the question myself.

"The truth is," Ben begins, "that you went to Gina's house that night, too. Isn't that the case?"

"What?" Grant rises from his chair as he answers. He turns to the judge. "Your Honor, this is unfair. This was not my under—" He shakes his head and settles back into his seat.

This was not his understanding of how this examination would proceed, he was going to say. It was not his understanding that a friendly lawyer, one of his employees, would be turning things around on him. But Grant surely understands that this is no basis for refusing to answer. And the moment he pleads the Fifth, you've got your headline tomorrow. He's trapped in that seat. And I suddenly find myself unwilling to come to his defense.

"No, that most certainly is *not* true, that I went to her house." Grant casts a look in my direction. I have no idea of the expression I return. I have no idea of anything anymore.

"*Rick* drove Jon, right? And you and Lyle followed? Isn't that how it went?"

"No, Mr. Carey."

Bennett moves toward the witness. "You and Rick were inside Gina Mason's room, too, weren't you?"

"No, sir. That is completely false. This is"—he looks up at the judge—"this is preposterous."

"Oh, you let Jon have his privacy, first. One of you went to get him and found him in Gina's room passed out. Right? And one of you pulled him out through the window, right?"

"I don't know what you're saying. I went *home*." Grant slams a fist on the railing.

"Then," Ben continues, turning toward the gallery now, "once Jon was done, it was someone else's turn." He turns back to Grant. "Who went next, Senator? You? Rick?"

"I don't have to listen to this. I don't have to take this."

"Listen, Senator, if you have something to hide—" Bennett turns to the judge. "I suppose, Your Honor, we should make Senator Tully aware of his right against self-incrimination." Then back to Grant: "You wanna take five, Senator?"

"I'm not taking the Fifth," Grant says. "I have nothing to hide."

"So, what, Rick went next?" Ben asks. "And in the course of things, it got a little rough, right? And Gina died."

Grant collects himself a moment. He's working out his options and reaching the same conclusion I did—he has nowhere to run. "I don't know anything about that."

"But Jon"—he wags a finger in my direction—"Jon was passed out in the car. He barely made it out of Gina's window."

"Again, counselor, I don't know anything—"

"So Jon became the patsy." Bennett moves away from Grant, again addressing the entire courtroom. "The son of a senator can't be involved in something like this. So you had Lyle stand up and say he was there with Jon."

"No."

"You and Rick had sex with Gina, so you two had to be left out of it. Lyle, there was no evidence implicating him, so you put him with Jon."

"No. No."

"How'd that work?" Ben asks. "Did you pay Lyle? Did Rick offer him free cocaine the rest of his life?"

"Objection. Your Honor, ob—"

"Sustained."

Bennett is quieted only momentarily. "You made the plan that night," he says. "There you are, Lyle and Rick and you, with Jon asleep in the car, and one dead girl. You tell Lyle to say he was there outside—just there, didn't do anything—and the story will be that Grant Tully and his pal Rick went home. Just went home."

"Not a shred of that is true." The senator's eyes dart in my direction but don't hold.

"In fact, the police never even *heard* about Rick, did they?"

"I have no idea."

"You made sure they didn't, right, Senator? Because Rick meant cocaine, and you couldn't be anywhere *near* cocaine. And then you pulled all the political strings you could. You had the coroner make an inconclusive finding. You had the prosecutor take a pass on the case. You set up your best friend to take the fall but then made sure he'd walk." Bennett points a finger at me. "You made him believe that he had done something wrong. Your best friend."

Grant swallows hard. The prosecutor rises and objects to the compound question, to the fact that Bennett Carey is making speeches. The judge sustains. A quiet falls over the courtroom.

It is Grant who speaks next, clearing his throat first. "Are you suggesting that your client perjured himself at that trial—at that hearing they held? Did Jon not testify that he went to that woman's home, that he kissed her goodbye, that he got in Lyle's car and left? And that I was nowhere to be seen?"

"I am suggesting that my client didn't remember *anything* that night other than going into Gina's room and having sex with her. I am suggesting that the rest was spoon-fed to him by you and the people working for you."

"Objection."

"Sustained."

Bennett nods. "You dispatched Dale Garrison back in 1979 to keep Lyle Cosgrove on the same page with you. Keeping you and Rick out of it, and clearing Jon."

"No, sir."

"And *that's* the 'secret that nobody knows,' isn't it, Senator? Dale Garrison knew it. Lyle told him the truth, under the veil of attorney–client privilege. Dale knew that Lyle's story to the prosecution was hogwash. He knew you were involved in Gina's death."

"No, Mr. Carey. Absolutely not."

"Dale Garrison was threatening to tell the truth to your dad—the 'senator,' isn't that the case, Senator Tully?"

"This is completely wrong." Grant is shaking his head, almost absently, punchdrunk from the accusations.

"You had Lyle Cosgrove do the dirty work, didn't you?"

"I don't even know him."

"You guys went back, didn't you, Senator? You two used to party together back in 1979."

"I didn't know Lyle after that time."

"But you kept tabs on him, didn't you? You knew he was out of prison. You hired him to kill Dale Garrison, the man who was blackmailing you."

"No. No." Grant looks up at the bench. "I—Judge, I don't even know how to respond to this."

"Or maybe you did. Maybe you wanted to set up Jon for the murder."

"That's completely, utterly wrong, Bennett."

Bennett waits a moment, standing near the jury railing. "Dale Garrison sent that blackmail note in the birthday card that accompanied the legal opinion, didn't he? In that same messenger envelope."

"I've never seen a blackmail note."

"But you got the birthday card, right? I'm the one who handed it to you."

"I remember Dale sent a birthday card. I freely testified to that."

Grant freely testified to that because it locked down the date that Dale wrote the memo on the Ace. It gave a loose time frame for when Dale Garrison would have the opportunity to blackmail Lang Trotter. Bennett impressed on the senator the need to be forceful on this date.

Grant Tully has been ambushed.

"Sure," says Bennett. "And the birthday card was opened already, as you said. I opened it without knowing, because it was part of the same package the memo came in, then I realized it was a birthday card for you and I gave it to you."

Grant shakes his head. He must be getting dizzy by now. That would make two of us.

"And you wondered, didn't you, whether I opened the card and read the note that went along with it?"

"There never was a note. I don't remember any of that."

"That made me a threat, too," says Ben. "So you sent your other buddy from 1979—Brian O'Shea—to kill *me*."

"*What?*"

"You remember my house was broken into, don't you?"

"I remember that."

"And the person who broke in was named Brian O'Shea."

"Okay. I've heard that—"

"Brian O'Shea," Ben repeats. "Rick. 'Rick' O'Shea. His nickname."

"I don't know what you're talking about."

"You don't remember Rick, Senator? Your drug dealer from 1979?"

"That's outrageous, Counsel. This is slander. None of this is true." His last comment is delivered to the media in the gallery.

"You thought I might be aware of the blackmail note, right? You couldn't have me out there as a loose end, could you, Senator?"

"This is—" Grant lifts off his seat. "This is preposterous and you know it. You're just making this up."

"You got people you could count on to do the work," says Ben. "People who proved their worth, when they covered for you in 1979. Lyle Cosgrove kills Garrison, O'Shea is supposed to kill me. And just to keep things covered up, you frame your top aide, Jonathan Soliday, a man who has served you faithfully, so if anything comes back to you, he'll protect you."

"I didn't do that." Grant is looking at me, not Bennett. "I wouldn't."

"You raped Gina Mason," says Ben. "You killed her."

"No."

"No?" Ben mimics. "She wanted to be gang-raped by three guys and choked to death?"

"I had nothing to do with it."

"That's what your father believed, right? That's what Jon Soliday believed, all these years. And you had to preserve that belief."

"My father believed it because it was true."

"You know that Lyle Cosgrove is dead, don't you, Senator?"

The change of topics brings a small comfort, but only a small one. "I've heard that."

"Have you also 'heard,' Senator, that the police discovered a sealed envelope containing a woman's underpants?"

"I—no, I hadn't." The senator scratches his face.

"Wanna bet whose undies they are?"

"Ob—objection." Erica Johannsen slowly rises. She's been as blown away as anybody by this. She has allowed improper question after improper question, getting caught up herself in the snowball.

"Think there's still some DNA on those panties, Senator?"

"That's enough, Mr. Carey," says the judge. "I am sustaining that objection."

Bennett stares at the senator for a long minute. He's attempting to make eye contact with Grant, who is not looking in his direction.

"I'm done with this witness," he announces.

Bennett Carey stands in the courtroom as we adjourn, his chest heaving. The senator is calling out denials, angrily denouncing the ambush. The judge decides to recess for the day.

Slowly, my attorney returns to the defense table. He delicately places the blackmail letter on the stack of papers before him and speaks to me as I stare at the table.

"*Now* we're done," he says.

58

Calamity around us. The prosecutor wheels and waves her assistants forward. Grant Tully, finally finished decrying these "ludicrous" suggestions to a court reporter who has ceased typing, to a judge who has left the bench, marches off the witness stand without looking in my direction and plows into a herd of feasting reporters. The bailiff hobbles over to the crowd, vainly trying to enforce the rule of no reporters' questions in the courtroom. The press is hurling bombs at the senator, even some at me. Others in the crowd, not part of the media, are talking among themselves about the spectacle.

It's all over in less than fifteen minutes. This is probably because the senator has made it through the mass, and it is clear that neither Bennett nor I will be talking, so the reporters see little point in lingering in the courtroom. It's like one of those old movies, all the reporters rushing to the pay phones to break the story, only now they're using cell phones or sending e-mails.

I look at Bennett. It's coming in waves now, the realization, the clearing of the picture, so obvious in hindsight and so overwhelming that I struggle to keep my breath.

"I guess it's something I wouldn't confront," I say.

"There was no point in bringing it up," Ben says. "You never would have allowed me to go after him."

"Nice work," I say. "You put all that together from that license revocation."

Bennett gathers his papers. "I knew you wouldn't have been a part of that girl's death," he says. "And I knew Tully was capable. You always had a blind spot for the guy."

I nod. "Sure, that works. All of it worked, in the end. It made for a nice, tidy story."

Bennett is dropping stacks of paper on the desk to even out the sheets. "I suppose, yeah."

A hopeful reporter sticks his head into my view but I shake my head without comment, and he disappears.

"Nice work," I repeat. "We have reasonable doubt." I offer a hand. "Have a nice trip, wherever you're going."

Bennett, in the midst of stuffing a folder into his briefcase, stops. His eyes rise to mine.

I let my unshaken hand drop to the table. "I assume that goodbye before court this afternoon was effective immediately."

"Huh?" Bennett Carey draws up. He measures me a moment, his eyes clear and intense. He is suddenly aware of the room. Try as he might, he can't contain the sense of urgency in his eyes as they dart about. His finger waves a small circle. He grimaces in confusion. "Jon, we still have a day or two—"

"Go," I say.

His expression hardens, his eyes search my face with a boy's curiosity.

"I'm not going to be convicted," I say. "We both know that. These guys are going to find that file from 1979 in the matter of a day, at most. They'll figure it all out."

Bennett nods slowly, looking confused.

"*All* of it, Ben."

My lawyer swallows hard. He doesn't seem to understand my point.

"The way it ends up," I continue, "everyone got their due. Garrison's dead. Lyle and Rick are dead. Grant Tully's ambitions are trashed. And I—well"—I shrug—"I pissed my pants a few times." I raise a hand. "Deservedly so, to some extent. I did something awful, too, even if I didn't kill her. It's always haunted me, Ben. But I let it go for a while. I never will again. I'll never forget the things I've done."

Ben says nothing to this, but simply stares at the judge's empty bench.

"It's important to me that you know that, Bennett."

My lawyer turns to me with these words. There is a sheen to his eyes, the first sign of vulnerability he has ever shown me. His lips part but he doesn't vocalize a response, simply nods curtly. I do not, I could not expect more from him.

"So get out of here," I say. "Before they figure out who Gina Mason's brother is."

William Bennett Carey considers my warning a moment, though he doesn't seem especially worried. He reaches into the inner pocket of his suit coat and removes a small audiotape, which he places before me on the table.

"That makes sense," I say. "You better hurry now."

Bennett's expression turns mild, even placid. He rises from his chair and straightens himself. Again, he starts to speak but cannot find the words. But I can read them on his face. Nothing is going to bring her back or erase the pain, but at least there is some rough sense of satisfaction. He starts to offer a hand but recognizes the impropriety. Instead he gives me a long look—harder and more worldly, but in many ways no different than the one he gave me twenty years ago—before grabbing his briefcase and silently leaving the courtroom.

NOVEMBER
2000

59

Judge Nicole Bridges brings the parties into chambers. I walk in with my new lawyer, Paul Riley, one of the elite defense attorneys in the city. Erica Johannsen, the prosecutor, comes in by herself.

The judge is without her robe, wearing a burgundy blouse. Her hair is braided. Her hands are together on her desk. "I wanted to do this informally, first," she says. "Consider it a proffer. Nothing admissible. You know the drill."

"Sure, Judge," says Paul Riley. His salt-and-pepper hair is finely combed as always. His tie cost more than my suit.

"The state is stipulating to a dismissal with prejudice," says Johannsen.

The judge nods. "So tell me. You first, Ms. Johannsen."

"Your Honor, you remember hearing at the end of the trial about the murder in 1979."

The judge laughs, and in response all of us at least smile. "Yes, I think I remember that, Counsel."

The prosecutor works her hands. "We now know that Mr. Soliday's attorney, William Bennett Carey, grew up with the woman who was the victim, Gina Mason. After Mr. Carey's parents were killed in a car accident when he was two years old, Mr. Carey went to live with his aunt, Gina Mason's mother. Gina was his cousin."

"He changed his name?" the judge asks.

"No, actually he didn't," says Johannsen, indicating her surprise. "He just went by his middle name when he became a lawyer. His last name was always Carey. He was never formally adopted. When the murder was investigated, he was mentioned in the report only as Billy Mason. It was an assumption. Gina had always called him her brother. He called Gina his sister. They both called Mrs. Mason 'Mom.' There was never any reason for the police to assume otherwise, I suppose. Why would they?"

"Okay. Go on."

"We believe that Mr. Carey set up a plan to, essentially, pay back the people who were part of the crime. Brian O'Shea was the first victim. We have learned that Mr. Carey contacted O'Shea and hired him to break into a house. He didn't specify whose house it was, or if he did, he lied. But of course, it was Mr. Carey's house."

The judge's solemn expression breaks. For a moment I think she's going to smile. Bennett was quite the cunning devil. "Mr. Carey hired someone to break into his own home."

"Yes, Your Honor. We have learned from a friend of Mr. O'Shea that Mr. Carey paid O'Shea five thousand dollars to break into the home and to steal something valuable from the bedroom. He described some heirloom, an ancient timepiece. That's what O'Shea was going for when he went into the bedroom."

"I take it," the judge says, "that O'Shea did not expect anyone to be home?"

"That's correct, Your Honor. Mr. Carey surprised the intruder."

"And looked reasonable in doing so." The judge nods along. "No one's going to tell a person he can't shoot at a home intruder in his bedroom."

"His plan was to kill O'Shea in the bedroom," I add. The prosecutor looks at me, but we're informal here, so I don't apologize for the interruption. "That looks the least suspicious. When the guy survived and ran down the stairs, Bennett had to follow him down. He couldn't let the guy leave alive."

That must have been the strangest five minutes of Brian O'Shea's life. He breaks into a house and finds the guy who hired him, pointing a gun at him. That's why the detective kept asking Ben if he heard any shouting. The neighbors must have heard it. O'Shea was probably yelling at Ben, *What in the hell are you doing, shooting at me?*

"Okay, fine." The judge opens her hands. "But why didn't he just kill this O'Shea the same way he killed Mr. Garrison and this other person—Cosgrove?"

The prosecutor looks at me. I let her field this one. "We have spoken to people close to Mr. O'Shea," she says. "O'Shea was told that he was working for someone very powerful, an old friend of his."

"Senator Tully," says the judge.

"That's what Ben wanted us to think," I say. "It turns out, Ben got away with the crime. It was an open-and-shut self-defense. But if he hadn't, there would have been an investigation. And sooner or later—probably sooner—the police would have talked to his friends and gotten a bead on Senator Tully."

"We *did* have a different theory," says Johannsen. "The police were under the impression that Brian O'Shea tried to harm Mr. Carey because Mr. Carey had prosecuted O'Shea's brother, when Mr. Carey was a county prosecutor here. Sean O'Shea was convicted of possession with intent to distribute heroin. He had argued that Mr. Carey and others had framed him. Planted the evidence. His final appeal had just been denied, before Brian O'Shea broke into Mr. Carey's home."

"So you thought it was an act of vengeance, the break-in." The judge inhales deeply. She is quite impressed by all of this. And she's seen a lot, no doubt, some pretty horrific things and some brilliant stuff as well. "And is your office considering the possibility, now that we know what we know, that maybe Mr. Carey *did* plant that evidence?"

"We've been looking into it," she says. "We don't think it was a frame-up. There would be too much to plant. There were all kinds of indicia of possession with intent—scales, pagers, blades, baggies. The police had been looking at Sean O'Shea for months. He was a real dealer."

"So it was just coincidence?"

"Well, I'm sure that Mr. Carey was more than happy to be part of the team going after Brian O'Shea's brother. But I don't think he framed him.

Judge, I understand the concern, but I checked over this file personally. I talked to everyone, including Mr. O'Shea's defense counsel. I want to make sure as much as you do."

That I can believe. I think this lady's all right. Erica Johannsen wasn't a part of the seedy side of this prosecution. She didn't know that the blackmail note could turn against Lang Trotter. She didn't know about Trotter's problem with the statement of candidacy. After the former prosecutor on the case, Dan Morphew, dropped out, she was thrown in with little preparation and handed her instructions.

"Bennett wouldn't have framed O'Shea's brother," I add. "That's not him. He limited his payback to the people who deserved it."

The judge shakes her head and tells the prosecutor to continue.

"Once O'Shea was killed, next on the list was Cosgrove's lawyer, Mr. Garrison," says Erica Johannsen. "And he set up Mr. Soliday in the process."

The judge holds up a finger. "I understand that, but how—who called Mr. Soliday here back into his offices?"

"Bennett did," I answer. I remove the tape which Bennett gave me before leaving me that day in court. "You have a Dictaphone, Judge?"

"Sure."

"Play this, if you would."

The judge inserts the tape.

"We have a transcript of the tape as well," says Johannsen. She hands a copy to the judge. "Some of the words were cut off. We did the best we could."

The judge activates the recorder and sets it, speaker up, on the desk. She reads along with the noise.

"Dale Garrison."
[Static for 4 seconds]
"Run up for a minute?"
[Static for 5 seconds]
"Let's talk about it."
[END OF TRANSCRIPT]

The judge looks up at me. "I take it this was the conversation on the cellular phone that sent you back to Mr. Garrison's office."

"Right," I say.

"This call was recorded? I only heard one voice."

"That's Dale's voice," I say. "Tape-recorded. I don't know how Ben got that tape but it wouldn't have been hard. It was probably cut from several conversations." I smile weakly. "I was talking to a tape recorder, Judge."

"Mr. Carey called you?"

"Yes. He was hiding in Garrison's offices. When I left, he went into Dale's office and strangled him, then called me. He put the tape recorder up to the phone. From my cell phone, it just sounded like a bad connection. And Bennett gave himself some time. I was about two blocks away."

The judge's eyebrows rise. She closes her eyes a moment.

"It wouldn't have taken long. Dale was ill. He was old. And you've seen Mr. Carey. He's built like a commando. He did it quick. Then he went back out the side entrance."

"Well, this seems incredibly risky," the judge says. "And not entirely plausible."

"Well, Judge, as Bennett said while he was defending me"—I almost smile at the irony—"that was the point. To make it implausible. My story sounded far-fetched. I looked guilty."

"I understand that, Mr. Soliday. What I meant was, it was risky to assume you wouldn't catch him."

I nod. "Agreed. But I think Bennett was ready for that contingency." The judge looks at me. Her lips part as she catches my meaning. I feel a shudder as I say the words. "Yeah, he would have killed me, too. Two dead lawyers, connected to Senator Grant Tully, the only ones who knew a dark secret about his past. It would have been easy to point the finger at Grant Tully."

"Oh," she says.

I start again. "That's not what Bennett wanted to do. He didn't want to kill me. He wanted me on the hook. Then he wanted all of the evidence to point to Grant Tully. He wanted to see what I would do—if I would go after the man I've called my best friend."

"I see."

"All these years since his sister's—well, I guess his *cousin's* death, Bennett thought I was covering for Grant Tully's participation. He thought I confessed to being the only person in Gina's house out of some loyalty to Grant. Maybe I was expecting him to carry me on his coattails through his career. But the truth was, I *believed* I was the only person. I didn't remember anything. And Grant knew that. So he got all of these people to agree that I was the only one there, and everyone fell in line."

"So at some point," the judge says, "Mr. Carey learned that you were—duped, so to speak."

"Right," I say. The moment at my house, when I spewed forth the revelations about 1979 to my lawyer, crystallizes now. How upset Bennett became, causing him to leave in a trance—not because of a possible rape or murder, not because of drugs, not because of perjury. He became upset when he realized that I didn't remember anything after leaving Gina's house. He made me swear it to him, over and over. That's when he figured that I was just a pawn, a patsy, set up by Grant and the others.

"That," I continue, "and the fact that he liked me, are the reasons I'm alive today." I watch the expressions on the judge and prosecutor. "But all these years, Bennett thought I was part of a deal, showing loyalty to Grant. So he put me in the soup on Garrison's murder, let the evidence line up against the senator, and watched to see what I would do. He gave me another chance to implicate Grant Tully."

"Mr. Carey stole the cell phone?"

The prosecutor nods. "We think so. Put on a red wig and wear a denim jacket and you fit Lyle Cosgrove."

"And he sent all of the rest of this woman's purse back to her," I add. "That's what I mean—he didn't want to hurt anyone else. He was probably sorry as hell he had to steal her phone. I'll bet you anything that when he returned the rest of her purse, he threw some extra cash in there, too, to cover the cost of the phone."

"That's quite a set of priorities," says the judge. The same reaction I had. She places her hands on the table. "Okay. So now Mr. Carey is in control. He's murdered Dale Garrison and he's representing the accused. Then, I take it, he killed Lyle Cosgrove."

"Yes," both Erica Johannsen and I answer. "And," I add, "he placed that bag with Gina's underwear in Lyle's apartment."

What I do not mention is my break-in of Lyle's home, where I found the incriminating letter from Garrison to Lyle, begging Lyle not to dredge up the past. That letter, of course, was written by Bennett and sneaked into Lyle's apartment for me to find—after Ben conveniently planted in my head a good way to break into Lyle's place. Tell them you're from the Department of Corrections, he had told me, and they'll hand you the key.

"So he was turning up the heat," the judge says. "Sprinkling new evidence into the story."

"Right," I say.

"Still," says the judge, "very risky. Once Lyle Cosgrove is in play, anyone could discover the case in 1979. And they'd start looking at witnesses from back then, and it wouldn't be long before they discovered that the boy was Bennett Carey. Especially when he hadn't bothered to conceal his name."

We all nod in silence for a moment.

"It *was* risky," I agree. "But Bennett's overriding goal was to have the truth come out about 1979. His secondary goal was to inflict punishment. He killed the two guys and their defense attorney, he ruined Senator Tully's chances at being governor, and"—I pause a moment—"he sure made me sweat." I open my hand to the room. "What has to be understood, I think, is that Bennett Carey was not concerned with the details. He didn't care how it came out. A lot of things could have gone one way or the other. Maybe even Bennett himself would have been caught. But all of that was secondary to the truth coming out, however it came out."

"We would have found that information about 1979 in probably another day or so," says Erica Johannsen. "We had just learned about Lyle Cosgrove's death. You recall I wanted the continuance."

Nice jab. She's lost but she'll go down swinging.

"It probably would've taken more than a day to find Bennett's connection to it," I say to the prosecutor. "And even if you discovered it and caught Bennett, I don't think he would have cared. He had gotten what he wanted."

"Speaking of," says the judge. "Any idea where Mr. Carey is?"

"No," says the prosecutor. "He walked out of court that day and no one ever saw him again. We found a car he had rented at an oasis near the northern border. We aren't aware of any plane trips he's taken, but the truth is, he got a head start on us."

When Bennett walked out on me in court, I could have chased him. I could have called out to the judge and found a bailiff or police officer to restrain him. But I didn't. And when the judge questioned me the next morning as to the whereabouts of my lawyer, I dummied up. I said I had no idea. Eventually, the judge was forced to recess for the day, with promises of a contempt citation for Bennett Carey.

I waited until the next morning to inform Erica Johannsen. I told her I believed that Bennett was related to Gina Mason and that he might be on the lam.

I gave Bennett that head start, in other words.

We spoke with the judge and she agreed to put things over for another day. A day was all it took for Johannsen to get confirmation of Bennett's identity and, combined with the fact that Bennett appeared to have fled the jurisdiction, there was ample reason to suspect that the county attorney was prosecuting the wrong guy. The trial was held over pending an investigation. It took the prosecutors a good three weeks to fill in all the pieces. A couple of days ago, Erica Johannsen called me with the news that they were dropping the charges.

"Okay." Judge Bridges looks at Erica Johannsen. "I take it this extortion letter was phony."

"Yes," she answers. "We believe Mr. Carey mailed it to Mr. Soliday."

"And Bennett changed the appointment with Dale from Thursday to Friday night, too," I say.

"All right," says Judge Bridges. "All right. And you're sure of all of this."

"We're satisfied," says Johannsen. "We know Mr. Carey was Gina's cousin—or brother, in their minds. We believe he walked in on the rape, which turned to murder."

"Assuming it was a rape and a murder," Paul Riley says. "The evidence is inconclusive."

"Inconclusive." The prosecutor rolls her eyes. Paul's just being my lawyer, but regardless, he isn't wrong about this. I tend to believe that something bad happened in that room with Lyle, Rick, Grant, and Gina. But three of those four are dead, and Grant will never come off his denial, no matter what, because he's a public figure and he can't. That's the irony of Ben's actions. The whole point was to bring out the truth but the only truth is, we will never know. We will have nothing but the perspective of an eight-year-old boy who probably couldn't comprehend *what* he was seeing. And even if we could ask Lyle or Rick what they truly believe, I'm not sure they would see it the same way Gina did. Each of them—the boys and Gina—was so intoxicated that the line might be blurry even to a dispassionate observer. I think what Ben believes is probably true but I don't know.

I draw a finger along my chest. "When Bennett—or Billy—was a child after his sister—or cousin—" I sigh. "You know what I mean. When he was a kid back then, he cut himself with a kitchen knife. On his arms and chest. I saw one of those scars when I went to Ben's house after he shot O'Shea. In fact, he told me the scar was twenty years old."

"All told," says the prosecutor, "we're confident of reasonable doubt. We don't believe Mr. Soliday is guilty of any crime here."

These words should mean more than they do.

"Very well," says the judge. "Mr. Soliday—"

"I lied," I say.

"I'm sorry?"

"I lied under oath in 1979. I had no memory of much of what I said. I committed perjury."

"Well." The judge stares at me, then at the other lawyers. "I suppose I don't know quite what to say about that." She looks at the prosecutor.

"It's not in our jurisdiction," says Johannsen, "but I would assume that the statute of limitations has expired."

"It has," says Paul. He didn't want me to say a thing about this.

"I guess that's something you're going to have to deal with," the judge says to me. "I hope it's something that never leaves you."

It won't. That much, I can promise. I get up, along with the other lawyers, ready to march into the courtroom and make the necessary stipulations before the county attorney officially exonerates me.

60

Tracy walks into the diner with a hanging bag over her shoulder and a suitcase in her hand. When she finds me in a booth, she greets me with a kiss on the cheek. This is the most overt affection she's shown me, and this time it was on her own initiative. We take our seats in the booth but don't bother with the menus.

Tracy went back to work two weeks ago, after everything exploded at my trial and it was pretty obvious I was in the clear. We said a very quick goodbye then because, from what I could tell, she'd hit her limit with her bosses back east. She'd taken a good three weeks off, after she'd just been promoted. I insisted she leave. She said she'd be stopping over in the city on the way to Atlanta in a couple of weeks, and we'd have a proper good-bye then.

"You look good," she tells me.

"Definitely better than the last time you saw me." I smile into the table, but it's time I looked up. "Listen, Tracy. Thank you."

"For what?" She fingers the glass of water before her. "For coming to town?"

"For *staying* in town. Taking almost a month out of your life. Even though I barely had time to say boo to you." I sigh. "Thanks for stand-ing by me."

I see that I've offended her. "What did you expect, Jon?"

"It's exactly what I expected. I still appreciate it."

She waves me off. The waitress takes drink orders. We hold off on lunch.

Tracy has something to say. In some ways she's a stranger now, in some ways she'll never be. We dabble in small talk but I don't help her out too much. She struggles a moment, as it's clear to both of us she needs to get something out.

"I changed," she says. "You didn't."

That could be read more ways than one. The blame could be on either party. But she's not putting it on me. She's saying, I was the real article from day one, she knew going in.

"You grew," I say. "No crime in that. I was supposed to grow with you."

She appreciates the comment. But she's not content.

"I made you feel like the second fiddle," I continue. "That's never the way I saw it. I never knew. I think you tried to tell me, in many ways."

Tracy looks into my eyes. We never seriously discussed the cause of our breakup. By the time it was over, it was so obvious that we just had to broach the topic and it was done. That's my fault. Like I told her, the signs were there. I didn't want to see them.

"I married a guy in politics," she says. "I knew you'd be downstate half the year. I knew you wouldn't leave Grant. I knew how much you loved it."

I reach for her. "You had every right to ask for more. Things aren't carved in stone, Trace. Relationships evolve. You just happened to marry a Neanderthal." I smile at her. "You weren't wrong here."

Her eyes narrow. Tracy can be emotional but she won't be here. She's a strong woman, and anyway, the well of tears from our divorce is long dried up.

"Do you think we made a mistake?" she whispers.

I force myself to maintain eye contact, to show resolve. Mistake is the wrong word. It's frozen in time, back almost a year ago. The relevant question is, what do we do now?

But I know my Tracy. She's always had a gift with words, and she's the bravest person I know. She's worded the question to give me maximum room, even opened the door to what she believes I may say. She wants the truth from me. She wants to know how I feel.

I know how she feels. I've known it from the moment we made the decision to split, the expression on her face. She's not sorry about the divorce. She just wants to know that I'm okay with it, too.

Come back to me, Tracy Soliday. Let me show you how important you are to me. Give me the chance to make up for all that time. Let me run my fingers through your hair and hold you and caress you and dote on you and make you giggle. Let's have children and grow old together. Let's hold hands on the beach and cuddle each other to sleep.

"I will always love you, Tracy." I grip her hand, which she returns. This is, in many ways, one of the most brutally honest moments of our relationship, and in many ways one of the phoniest. "Go on with your life. Just keep me posted once in a while. Be *happy*."

She breathes in. This is relief. It's what she wanted to know from day one, what she wanted to ask me, but couldn't, when she first came to town. She got the answer she wanted.

"I love you, too," she says.

"I know." I nod outside. "Go catch your plane."

She doesn't smile. She leaves the booth, luggage in tow. She looks at me one last time. And when Tracy Stearns walks out of the diner, she doesn't look back.

61

―――――――――――

"With sixty-four percent of the precincts in, Newscenter Four is prepared to project a winner in the race for governor. . . ."

This election day has been a lonely one. As the chief Democratic lawyer in the state, I am typically fielding phone calls and putting out fires from the moment the polls open at six in the morning. A voting machine is broken. An election judge isn't letting our poll watcher into the polling place. A cop is pulling up our signs. Republicans are handing out palm cards or leaflets within one hundred feet of the polls. There's a line of voters out the door at such-and-such precinct, and we need a court order to keep the polls open there.

This year, nothing. I don't know who is handling such things for Grant Tully or the myriad of candidates for the state house or senate. I just know that it isn't me.

Anyway, this election, at least at the top end of the ticket, has lacked suspense. It's not nine-thirty and they're already calling the gubernatorial election. A landslide. It was a foregone conclusion. He probably wouldn't have won anyway, but the sordid details of an encounter with a defenseless girl in 1979 and the prosecution of his top aide for murder—to say nothing of the allegations of his own involvement in that murder—doomed State Senator Grant Tully.

Give or take depending on how the final votes tally, Grant will receive just over thirty percent of the vote. The independent candidate, Oliver Jenson, who has benefited remarkably from a trial that potentially implicated both major-party candidates for governor, will get close to twenty percent. And Attorney General Langdon Trotter should clear fifty percent.

Senator Grant Tully will be recorded as receiving the smallest percentage of the governor's vote for a major-party candidate since the Reconstruction era. To state the obvious, he will never receive his party's nomination again.

Grant was depending on the Democratic turnout in the city and the downstate union vote. On paper at least, he had all the right endorsements, but I understand there was whispering. Grant was damaged goods. The pre-election work lacked its typical urgency, particularly what you would expect on behalf of the man who controls the state senate.

Grant should be lucky he's not prosecuted for the rape and murder of Gina Mason. But there's really no proof. Lyle Cosgrove and Brian O'Shea are dead. Gina Mason is dead. Her brother/cousin Bennett is nowhere to be found. The underwear found in Lyle's apartment, placed there by Bennett, does not contain any DNA. Bennett was bluffing.

Because Grant ran for governor in midterm, he doesn't have to seek re-election for his senate seat for another two years. Two years is a lifetime in politics. Besides, with the organization he has in place, he could win re-election with his eyes closed. If that's what he wants.

My pugs, Jake and Maggie, have had a good couple of weeks with me home. Maggie has her smashed face right in mine now, trying to wake me up to get me to let her out. Jake is about ready to jump off the couch. "Okay," I tell them, the only word they needed to hear. I look at my watch. It's close to midnight now. Election reports are still coming in on the tube. Used to be, this was one of the most electrifying nights of my life. Now, I couldn't even stay awake.

When I'm returning from letting the dogs out, my doorbell rings. I can see through the picture window. I certainly recognize the car.

I open the door to Grant Tully. We haven't spoken since that day at trial. He didn't call me, I didn't call him. I didn't shit on him to the press, either. I just clammed up.

"Have a minute for an old friend?" he asks. He looks better than I would expect. At least now, it's over, I guess. All of it.

"Sure," I say. "If I see one, I'll let him know." But I open the door.

Grant walks in but doesn't take a seat. We stand near each other in the threshold.

He frames his hands. "I let you take the fall," he says. "Yes. I'm sorry."

I wasn't sure I'd ever hear those words from Grant. "You could have told me."

"Not then, Jon. The son of a senator? It wouldn't matter if I was guilty or innocent."

"You let me think awful things about myself. If it hadn't been for Bennett, I always would have thought that way. I would've gone through life wondering whether I'm a killer."

"I know the feeling," he says.

"What does that mean, Grant? Tell me the truth."

His eyes break from mine. "I'm not sure, is the truth." Grant's tie is pulled down, his collar open. He is defeated, in more ways than one. He looks at me again. "I remember being there. I don't remember if—" He throws his hands up. "I don't know. All I can say is, at the time, it was like—like a big party or something. Christ, she certainly didn't seem like the kind of girl who'd mind."

My stare freezes him. "Why don't we strike that last comment from the record, Senator?"

"It's Grant," he corrects. "It always has been. Come back to work, Jon."

I don't answer.

Grant invites himself to the couch and gathers himself a moment. "I swear, Jon—I don't recall anyone doing anything like—like—"

"Like strangling her?"

"God." He sighs, shows some hint of remorse but quickly leaps to his own defense. "Look, keep in mind the circumstances. None of us was even close to being sober."

I don't respond. I will wait him out.

"It wasn't me, Jon. I never touched her. I believe it was Rick. They were going at it on the floor. It's not like I was watching." Grant loses himself in the memory. All of a sudden, he's not speaking to me but simply reciting the events. "Yeah, it seemed kind of rough. Maybe she didn't want him on top of her. And then, all of a sudden someone was saying, 'Oh, shit.' Gina, she was—" Grant turns his head sharply, closes his eyes.

"She was vomiting."

Grant nods. "I don't know. Maybe Rick had his hand on her throat. In hindsight—yeah. She got sick, started choking. . . ."

"And you all got the hell out of there."

Grant nods. He gets off the couch and walks in a small circle.

"With me asleep in the back of the car."

An audible sigh from Grant, his back turned to me. Slowly, he turns back around, looking me in the eye.

"I swear, I didn't lay a hand on that woman. I was just left to clean up the mess. I'd go down with those guys, and it would be a big scandal for my father. You can imagine."

"Sure I can," I answer. "So you just put it on me."

"I knew I could keep you in the clear." After a lengthy moment without comment from me, he continues in a more pleading tone. "Look, I fucked up, okay? I'm sorry."

That's supposed to be enough for me, I suppose. A state senator doesn't take to groveling easily. The fact that he's making the effort is supposed to be all I need

I will say this much. He did post bond for me when I was arrested. He did keep me on his staff, and unabashedly so. He was willing to risk votes to stand by my side. He didn't recognize the name "Brian O'Shea" any more than I did. He didn't know what Bennett was up to. Helping me wasn't selfish of him. He was doing it as a friend.

But I'm still feeling a little mean and angry. I don't know where my future lies, or Grant's. All I know is that it won't be decided tonight.

I step to the side, clearing a path from the senator to the door. Grant catches the point.

"Maybe I wanted you to look up to me," he says. "I was the guy who came through for you. Saved you. Yes, I admit it. I liked that. Okay?"

I open my hand to the door.

"Take a swing at me or something," he says.

This is really bothering him. He needs my forgiveness. He can find other lawyers. Anyone can learn the election laws. But he's feeling a real loss here. He just suffered the greatest political defeat of his life and he's worrying about our friendship.

"Go home," I say. "I have to get my dogs." I nod to him, the first softening in my armor.

"I'll talk to you later?" he asks.

"We'll see," I say, walking away from him.

62

The demons always come at night. This is when I hear Gina screaming, even when I never heard it to begin with. This is when the echoes of fear rise within my chest, creating such a deafening crescendo of panic that for a moment, I forget where I am.

But all is quiet in the cemetery where Gina Mason lies forever. It's a nice enough place but not well-kept. It's the kind of place where someone with no money buries her daughter.

Gina Mason. 1960–1979. A beautiful soul.

She was nineteen when she died. That's all I knew. I didn't know anything else about her, all of the things that made her human. I saw sex and lust. Maybe I saw promise, too, in both of us.

I reach down to the tombstone for no particular reason, run my fingers over the words her family left the world to know about her. My hand grazes down to the grass, and my finger catches on a thorn. A single rose has been placed on the grave. Freshly picked.

Probably placed there today.

That's not smart. The police may think Bennett drove north when they found that abandoned rental car, but that won't stop the local cops, maybe even the FBI, from making the occasional pass by the cemetery. They find any hint that Bennett stopped by for a visit, they'll be crawling all over the region. His aunt, the one who raised him, died from liver failure four years back, one of many details of Ben's life that came out after this whole charade. Ben is the only remaining family for Gina. He might as well have left a business card on her grave.

I pause a moment as a shiver courses through me. If there is nothing else to learn from everything that happened, I should know not to underestimate Bennett Carey. And as I think about it, it seems obvious. Of course. There is a part of him, at least, that wants to get caught, that always did. After his successful escape, the story is left hanging, not fully explained. The public, the carnivorous media, is left with Grant Tully's denials, with my new lawyer's assertion that the evidence is "inconclusive." With Bennett in custody, the press will hang breathlessly on his every word, his entire account of what happened. And in truth, there is little downside. He's not concerned with his own fate. Bennett was given a life sentence at age eight, and he will serve it faithfully, even now.

I fish through my jacket pocket and find an empty envelope and a pen. I scribble my message to Ben and place it next to the rose, with a small rock on it to hold it in place. Two simple words that Gina would utter, I'm quite sure, if she could. But as I head back to my car, navigating through the enveloping darkness and misplaced shadows, I realize that Ben will never follow my advice, and that if I were honest with myself, I would admit that I have never done so, either. Maybe it's time now, for both of us.

Move on.

DAVID ELLIS

ACKNOWLEDGMENTS

My time working as an attorney for the Speaker of the Illinois House of Representatives was helpful in providing me with background and context for this novel. From that background, I have created anecdotes and stories that are entirely of my own imagination. This is a work of fiction. Nothing in this novel actually happened.

There are many people to thank for their direct or indirect participation in the drafting of this novel. Mike Kasper, a friend and sometimes mentor, looked over a draft of this novel and provided excellent feedback. Ed Nystrom, my future father-in-law, read the first draft and provided outstanding insight that changed the novel. Jim Jann once again provided criticism that gave a depth and perspective to the novel that was lacking.

Dr. Ronald K. Wright, an internationally renowned forensic pathologist, provided creative and insightful information for the scientific aspects of the crimes that take place in this novel. Thank you for your time and your enthusiasm.

Many of the usual suspects looked over early drafts and provided critical commentary and encouragement: Dan and Kristin Collins, Jim and Jill Kopecky, and Jim Minton. Thanks to each of you for the impact you made on this book. My mother, Judy Ellis, and my sister, Jennifer Taylor, once again played the roles of critical readers and loving, supportive family members.

Thank you to my law partners, Lisa Starcevich, David Williams,

Doug Bax, and Dan Collins, for your support and enthusiasm for my "other job."

The lawyers and friends on the eleventh floor of 111 West Washington could not realize how much they have influenced me and this novel. Thank you in particular to William Harte, a legendary Chicago lawyer, for everything you have taught me about the practice of law in Chicago.

Thanks again to my agent, Jeff Gerecke, for keeping a steady hand. Thanks to my editor, David Highfill, for your excellent critique and for your friendship.

As always, the final word goes to my future bride, Susan, for the beauty that you bring to my life. None of this would mean a thing without you.